Whisper to My Heart

JoAnn Durgin

Author's Note
~~♥~~

Dear Readers,

Our family recently visited The Ark Encounter in Williamstown, Kentucky, the life-sized reconstruction of Noah's Ark based on the dimensions given in the Bible. The enormity of it was astounding, and the experience was fascinating. Why did God direct Noah to build the Ark? The world was increasingly evil. Man's depravity had reached a level that was so sin-stained there was nothing within him that was *not* evil. Those living upon the Earth were wicked *beyond* the hope of changing.

Like in Noah's time, our world is increasingly sinful, but God promised He'd never again flood the Earth. The responsibility of believers is not to condemn or ridicule others, but to walk among those in the world and be *set apart* as shining examples of the love, grace, mercy, and *hope* to be found in a personal relationship with Jesus Christ.

In *Whisper to My Heart*, I present the idea of purity of the heart, mind, body, and soul. In a world darkened by sin, I want to celebrate faith, family, community, and love. At its core, this is a contemporary Christian romance based on solid biblical principles. It's a story of how each one of us can impact the lives of others in ways we might not ever imagine.

I challenge you to pray about the realities in *your* life but also to dream of the possibilities. How can you impact someone's life today for Christ? We never know how a smile, a kind word, or an act of kindness—no matter how large or small—could change someone's life for the better.

We need not walk in fear, my friends. Walk with the Father and be a shining light.

Until His Nets Are Full,

JoAnn
Matthew 5:16

Theme Scripture Verses
~~♥~~

1 Samuel 16:7
But the LORD said to Samuel, "Do not look at his appearance or at the height of his stature, because I have rejected him; for God sees not as man sees, for man looks at the outward appearance, but the LORD looks at the heart."

Isaiah 40:31
Yet those who wait for the LORD will gain new strength;
They will mount up with wings like eagles,
They will run and not get tired,
They will walk and not become weary.

Isaiah 45:2
I will go before you and make the rough places smooth; I will shatter the doors of bronze and cut through their iron bars.

Psalm 37:4
Delight yourself in the LORD; And He will give you the desires of your heart.

Psalm 51:10
Create in me a clean heart, O God, and renew a steadfast spirit within me.

Matthew 19:26
And looking at them Jesus said to them, "With people this is impossible, but with God all things are possible."

Mark 10:6-9
[6]But from the beginning of creation, God made them male and female. [7]For this reason a man shall leave his father and mother, [8]and the two shall become one flesh; so they are no longer two, but one flesh. [9]What therefore God has joined together, let no man separate."

2 Corinthians 5:17
Therefore if anyone is in Christ, he is a new creature; the old things passed away; behold, new things have come.

Galatians 5:1
It was for freedom that Christ set us free; therefore keep standing firm and do not be subject again to a yoke of slavery.

Ephesians 2:10
For we are His workmanship, created in Christ Jesus for good works, which God prepared beforehand so that we would walk in them.

I John 1:9
If we confess our sins, He is faithful and righteous to forgive us our sins and to cleanse us from all unrighteousness.

I John 3:9
No one who is born of God practices sin, because His seed abides in him; and he cannot sin, because he is born of God.

I John 4:4
You are from God, little children, and have overcome them; because greater is He who is in you than he who is in the world.

I John 5:14
This is the confidence which we have before Him, that, if we ask anything according to His will, He hears us.

Chapter 1

Anna cringed, waiting for the inevitable crash. The accident couldn't have been prevented. Not really. She'd tripped over a child's forgotten toy, sending that stack of slippery plates flying. Slapping her hands over her face, she waited for the impending wrath of Roz the Terminator.

Her first mistake? Rinsing her hands and then forgetting to dry them before bussing tables. Who knew there'd be so many details to remember? She'd thought this job would be easy. How could people *do* this for a living? After only three days on the job, she should turn in her apron and acknowledge the truth—she was a terrible waitress.

Wait a second. No crash. Only the sound of clattering, not *shattering,* plates. And people were…clapping?

"Go, Weston! You are the man!"

Splaying her fingers wide, Anna dared to peek. One of the construction guys who'd been sitting in the back corner booth—Weston, apparently—crouched in front of her. He attempted to stabilize the stack of wobbly plates in his hands while his comrades whistled, stomped, whooped, and hollered. Appearing unsteady, his forehead creased with a deep frown.

Anna wanted to tell his cronies to pipe down their rowdiness in case it made Weston nervous, but they probably wouldn't listen. She glanced at the floor. Surely she'd missed one of the plates falling in the midst of all the loud cheering? Nope, no shards lay scattered across the hard floor. How had he managed to corral them without any casualties?

"Let me help you." Anna started forward but then hesitated. On second thought, that wasn't the best idea considering she seemed especially clumsy tonight. Who knew what chaos she might create? They'd probably both end up on the floor. That'd be interesting but solve nothing.

"No problem. I've got them." Weston's focus didn't waver, and he'd captured the attention of everyone in the diner. A slow grin spread across his face as he cautiously rose to a standing position— six feet or thereabouts of controlled muscle in a white but dirt-covered T-shirt and worn jeans. His light brown beard was neatly trimmed and curls peeked out from the bottom of his backwards Atlanta Braves cap. Cute guy.

Anna clapped with the others as Weston moved to the front of the diner and carefully deposited the plates on the counter. The other waitress, Candee, scooted beside her and leaned close. "Let him be your hero for the day." She patted Anna's arm. "Every gal needs one of those. And every man wants to *be* one."

"I'll keep that in mind." Walking over to the counter, Anna gave him a weary smile. "Thank you for saving my job. At least for now."

They were only plates. She shouldn't even care. But for some inexplicable reason, she did.

"Welcome. You looked like you could use some help. Glad I came in, well…handy." Weston shot a disparaging glance at his clothing. "As you can see, nothing's going to make me dirtier than I already am." He lifted his baseball cap and scratched the side of his head. "Okay, that didn't come out right."

Maybe not, but she liked the way he'd said it in his charming southern drawl.

Baby blue eyes, offset by tanned skin, settled on her. "I'm Weston Galloway. And you are?"

She appreciated how his gaze didn't dip south of her name tag. In spite of how he was dressed, and the somewhat rough-cut company he kept, Weston seemed like a gentleman.

"I'm Anna. Anna Redmond. It's nice to meet you." Was it wise to give him her last name? At least she'd only given him the shortened version of her first name. The odds were against Weston recognizing her name or knowing who she was.

"You, too." He started to wipe his hands on the front of his T-shirt. "I'd shake your hand, but it's better if I keep my hands to myself." His cheeks flushed, and dimples peeked out beneath his beard. "Sorry. I'm saying all the wrong things tonight." Laughing under his breath, he raised both hands. "I promise you, I'm not weird or anything."

An embarrassed Weston was even cuter. If only he knew what a refreshing change he was compared to most men.

"Hang on a second. Don't move." She hurried behind the counter.

"Yes, ma'am."

After lightly rinsing a paper towel in the sink, Anna squeezed out the excess water and then handed it to him. "Here you go."

"Thanks." Weston wiped his hands and glanced at her feet. "Is your ankle okay?"

"What? Oh, yes. It's fine."

"Good." He tossed the used paper towel in the trash can beside the register. "Before the excitement, I was headed over here to ask for our check."

"Sure. I'll have Candee bring it over to your table in just a minute." Should she offer to comp their check? Probably not. Guys could be weird about a woman paying for things, and it might come across as odd. Besides, a woman working in a small-town diner wouldn't be able to afford it, so it wouldn't be a normal thing to do.

Normal. Above all, that's what she wanted, what she needed. She hadn't lived a normal life in so long, she wasn't sure she remembered how. But she could try.

As Weston returned to his table, Anna sensed Roz watching from her post at the register. Didn't her boss know she was promoting good customer relations? Weston *had* saved those plates, after all.

Anna walked over to where Candee worked on refilling the napkin holders at the front counter. "My hero is asking for the check. Do you mind if I take it to him?"

"Course not. I insist on it." Candee pulled the order pad from her apron pocket. "I'll bet he cleans up real handsome, and Weston seems a whole lot nicer than those other Neanderthals he's with. If I weren't twenty—okay, thirty—pounds overweight and happily married with four kids, I'd give you a run for your money." Tearing off the check, Candee handed it to her with a smile.

"Thanks." The group of six men crowded into the corner booth slowed their conversation as Anna approached their table. Except for Weston, the rest eyed her up and down. Ugh.

Focus on Weston. Ignore the others.

The blond man sitting next to Weston gave her a lazy grin and winked. "What time do you get off work tonight"—his gaze moved south, making her bristle—"Anna?"

3

Without hesitation, she handed the check to him and then turned to Weston while the others chuckled. "Weston, can I get you a slice of homemade pie on the house? To say thank you?"

The same man elbowed him. "I wouldn't turn down anything she's offering, Wes."

"Be respectful, Neil." Weston nodded to her. "Toss in a cup of coffee, and I'll come over to the front counter once I ditch these guys." He grunted. "It won't be long."

As she pivoted to leave, one of the guys said, "Better not tell that girl to toss something or she just might *do* it." Closing her eyes, Anna kept walking, leaving their snickers and muffled comments behind. Why did so many men act like that? Was it some kind of ingrained *I'm God's gift to women* male cockiness?

Roz counted receipts at the register. She was always doing that, but as the owner and manager, the diner was her livelihood. Without looking up, she jerked her head in Anna's direction. "Come over here, girl."

Anna did as she asked, wondering what she'd done wrong now. It would be nice if her boss dropped the derogatory way she called her *girl*.

"I hope you're plannin' on payin' for that man's pie and coffee," Roz muttered under her breath with a sidelong glance. "I'm not in the habit of givin' out freebies to customers."

"Of course, I'll pay. He did me a favor. It's the least I can do." Anna couldn't complain about Roz's grumpiness considering she'd dropped, spilled, and broken a few cups, plates, glasses, and bowls since she'd started her training. She'd also mixed up a few orders and written a couple down wrong. If she were the boss, she'd have fired *herself* on the first day.

Digging into the pocket of her apron, Anna pulled out a ten dollar bill and handed it to her boss. "This should cover it."

Roz took the money and deposited it in the register before running a hand over the top of her graying hair. "Don't go thinkin' you can flirt on my time, girl. I've got my eye on you. I don't like my waitresses givin' away anything else for free, either. Don't want *that* kind of reputation even if it brings in more business." She sniffed. "If you know what I mean."

"Good gracious, the *straw dispenser* knows what you mean, Roz. Leave Anna alone." Candee sidled beside Anna and lowered her voice. "The last girl who worked here…well, let's just say she had a habit of gettin' too friendly with some of our male customers."

"She was a good waitress. Didn't drop or spill anything." Roz cleared her throat. "Shame she left her morals at the door. If she had any to begin with. That's the problem with you young people today."

Determined not to let the insult bother her, Anna straightened her shoulders and assumed her best imitation of a Cockney accent. "I'm a good girl, I am!"

Roz and Candee stared at her as though she'd lost every ounce of sense in her brain. Maybe she had. She'd never been on her feet for so many hours at a time, or worked so hard physically, as in the past three days. Even her muscles were complaining and screaming for relief. What she wouldn't give for a good massage.

"What?" she said. "You've never seen Audrey Hepburn as Eliza Doolittle?"

More stares from the two women.

"The movie *My Fair Lady*?" Who wasn't familiar with that classic movie? "The famous songs 'I Could Have Danced All Night' and 'The Rain in Spain'?"

"I've heard of it," Roz said. "Don't reckon I've ever seen it, though. Seemed too highfalutin to me."

Candee snapped her fingers. "By George, I think she's got it! Is that the movie you're talkin' about, Anna? The one where the guy's a snooty professor who looks too old for her and he teaches her to speak all fancy? Oh, and then she starts wearin' beautiful dresses and carries a little umbrella at a racetrack?" She frowned. "Somethin' like that."

Anna smiled. "Yes, that's the one. It's based on George Bernard Shaw's play, *Pygmalion*…" She needed to be careful so she didn't come across as high and mighty or a know-it-all snob. "I hope you can see it sometime. It's a good movie."

With a harrumph, Roz grabbed the dirty aprons and dish towels from beneath the counter. Pushing the swinging door, she disappeared into the kitchen.

Candee patted her arm. "Don't let Roz's sourpuss attitude bother you, sweetie. She's just jealous 'cause that good lookin' man has his eye on you. And you're a lot smarter than the both of us put together."

"I'm sure that's not true," Anna protested. "Has Roz ever been married?"

"Once. She was married for seven years, no kids, and got divorced about fifteen years ago. Says she's sworn off men forever. Hasn't stopped her from readin' them trashy romance novels, though. She can deny it all she wants, but I've seen 'em stickin' out of her purse."

Roz's story struck Anna as somewhat sad. She might be lonely, especially if she didn't have much family around. Or *any* family. With her large frame—not overweight, but big-boned—and rather forbidding demeanor, customers sometimes called her The Warden.

"I like the name Weston," Candee said. "Sounds like a good cowboy name. A *hero* name, all strong and manly. Rugged. Suits him well, don't you think?"

Anna grinned. "I think maybe *you're* the one who reads romance novels."

"Bite your tongue," Candee said. "Why read those when I've got a fine man waitin' for me at home every night?"

Yes, she did—Jesse, a wheelchair-bound war veteran, an amputee as the result of an IED explosion in Afghanistan. Candee had introduced him to Anna when he'd stopped by the diner earlier in the day.

A customer raised his hand to signal her. After refilling his glass with sweet tea, Anna eyed the selection of homemade pies. "What do you think, Candee? I offered Weston a piece of pie. Do you think he'd like banana cream? Apple? Lemon meringue? That's what we have left."

"He seems like an all-American apple pie kind of guy to me." Her grin was sly. "My guess is Weston might be comin' into the diner more often now that he's met our newest waitress."

After Anna flicked the dish towel at her, Candee did a little sashay.

"None of that foolishness," a gruff female voice said from behind them.

Anna tried not to roll her eyes. If anyone *did* have eyes in the back of her head, it was Roz. Or else she had a ridiculously accurate sense of timing.

Needing to keep busy, Anna switched out the old carafe and filter basket and pushed the button to start a new pot. Weston deserved a mug of fresh coffee to go with his pie.

Gingerly lifting the glass lid of the pie keeper, she set it on the counter and then cut a generous slice of the apple pie. From the corner of her eye, she noticed when the guys from Weston's table congregated around the register. A couple of them glanced her way and mumbled things under their breath, making Anna uncomfortable and grateful she couldn't hear their words.

Shaking his head, Weston shoved Neil out the door in a playful manner before crossing the diner and sliding onto a seat at the front counter.

Anna placed a mug beside him and poured his coffee. "Would you like creamer?"

"Two, please. Listen, I'm sorry about those guys, Anna. I work with them, but they're not good friends. My boss handpicked the crew from all over the area. I've worked a few jobs with Neil before, but I only met the other guys last week. We're working a two-month construction job here in town, and for better or worse, I'm sharing a place with Neil and three others for the duration."

"I understand. No harm done." She pulled two creamers from the container beneath the counter and then grabbed the basket with sweeteners, putting them beside his coffee. "Be right back."

Darting into the kitchen, she returned less than a minute later with his apple pie à la mode. She lowered it to the counter with a flourish, ignoring Roz's scowl.

Weston's eyes widened. "Wow. This is great. Want to share it with me?"

"I wish I could, but *no eating on the job* is one of Roz's hard and fast rules."

He waggled his brows. "Rules can be broken."

Warmth slid up her neck. "Um…"

He slapped his head with the heel of one hand. "Sorry. I don't know what's wrong with me tonight. You must think I'm worse than Neil." He met her gaze. "Seriously. *Not* weird. Promise."

Anna grinned. "No worries. I believe you."

He closed his eyes and bowed his head. A guy who prayed for dessert? He'd done it so naturally, as though it was second nature. Weston was obviously a *good* guy. He'd also prayed for his meal with his coworkers gathered around him. Some had bowed their heads, some not.

Given the same situation, she'd normally close her eyes for a few seconds and say a quick, silent prayer. Not that she was ashamed to be known as a Christian. Not at all, but Weston's boldness was inspiring. Rare was the man who *lived* his faith in public if he wasn't a pastor.

Stepping farther down the counter, Anna pulled a handful of wrapped plastic straws from a box. She darted several glances his way while refilling the dispensers spaced across the counter.

Finished with his prayer, Weston dug into the pie with enthusiasm. "This is really good," he said a few seconds later. "I'll have to come here more often." The corners of his mouth lifted. "For some pie."

Oh, my.

This man might be dangerous…for her heart.

Chapter 2

"I take it this is your first time here at The Darling Diner?" Anna shook her head. "You know, no matter how I say it, the name still sounds ridiculous."

"I don't know. I think it fits. We are in *Darling*, Georgia, after all." Weston's chuckle held an appealing hint of huskiness. "And yeah, it's my first time here. I usually hang my safety helmet at a house on the outskirts of Atlanta, but depending on the project, it's nice to get out of the city. How about you?"

"I don't have a safety helmet to hang anywhere."

"Very funny, Miss Evasive." He had a point. If only her manager could see her now. On second thought, it was best she couldn't. Felicia would hyperventilate.

After twisting off the top of a salt shaker, Anna refilled it. What did it hurt to share a little conversation? Roz had conveniently moved elsewhere in the diner and was nowhere to be seen.

"I'm just passing through town," she said. "Earning my keep and then moving on."

Now he'll think you're a drifter. She didn't like telling lies, and that's what it felt like. Not the kind of lie to smooth over someone's hurt feelings but more the kind to hide the truth. Weston was a great guy, and she liked him more than she should, but she'd only just met him.

She didn't know him well enough to know if she could trust him with the truth.

You don't have time *to get to know him.*

Anna continued with her busy work, this time checking the pepper shakers along the front counter and refilling several of them.

Weston surveyed her through narrowed eyes as he sipped his steaming coffee. "You don't seem the *passing through town* type." When she frowned, he added, "I didn't mean that as a bad thing. And you're obviously not a troublemaker. How long have you worked here?"

"Since Monday. I don't know about the troublemaker part, but I appreciate the vote of confidence. Depends on who you talk to, I guess. I'm sure it's obvious I'm still in training here."

"I also detect an accent, but I can't place it. If you say something else, I might be able to figure it out." After Weston took another drink of his coffee, Anna retrieved the coffee carafe and refilled his mug.

"Something else." Lame answer, but it was all she could come up with at the moment. Because of all the traveling she'd done, she'd lost most of her native accent although she'd never had a strong one.

Catching Roz's frown, Anna grabbed a damp cloth and began to wipe down the counter.

"Okay, you stumped me," Weston said. "Where are you from originally?"

"Guess." She also hated being elusive. Perhaps conversation wasn't the best idea, after all. She pushed her glasses higher on her nose. They hadn't deterred Weston like they did most men. Then again, he was quickly proving he wasn't anything like *most* men.

Weston stopped chewing. "Fine. I get it, Anna. Classic avoidance. If you don't want to tell me, I can live with it. Just trying to make a little friendly conversation." The ice cream had melted, and he leaned over his plate for the next bite.

She wanted to tell him not to take it personally but instead handed him a spoon and kept quiet. Taking it from her with a nod, he avoided her gaze. Great. Now she'd put him off with her standoffish attitude. Problem was, she couldn't blame him.

At the risk of her plate rescuer thinking she was giving him the brush-off, Anna wanted to live the simple life for the time being. Do her job and then go home. Think about nothing more taxing than keeping orders straight and not breaking or spilling anything. Surely that wasn't too much to ask. Easy enough, right?

For now, she had no valid reason to linger behind the counter talking with Weston. Roz had sent the teenage busboy home early since it'd been slow most of the evening. Of course, no sooner had Lance clocked out than it got crazy busy. Law of averages, perhaps. At least Roz had pitched in to help take and serve orders, but she'd stopped on occasion, leaning heavily against the front counter to massage one hand over her lower back.

Time to get back to work. Several tables needed to be cleaned and cleared. Anna headed into the kitchen and retrieved one of the gray plastic bins stacked in a corner.

"How's it going, pretty lady?" Using the high-powered sprayer, Mike the dishwasher eyed her while Hector the fry cook gave her a polite nod from the grill. Francie, the self-proclaimed head "chef" worked on preparations for tomorrow's fare. As usual, Francie ignored her, a good thing since she currently wielded a sharp knife and chopped vegetables with an almost scary vengeance.

At Mike's question, Anna paused beside the swinging door. "I almost had a casualty with a stack of plates, but thank goodness a vigilant customer saved the day."

Mike shook his head amidst the steam bath at the stainless steel sink. "You're doing fine. It'll get easier."

"I hope you're right." She wasn't sure she'd ever get used to everything she had to remember on this job much less *do*. Being a waitress meant she had to be organized and multitask, skills she'd never needed to call upon much before. They'd never been a part of her everyday life.

Mike shot her a wink and swiped one hand over his heated face. "Never met a babe who looks like you and uses hoity-toity words like *vigilant*."

"Mind your manners." Hector leveled his gaze on Mike. "Anna's a lady. Smart, too."

That was her cue to leave. With a grateful smile for Hector, Anna returned to the dining room. Mike was harmless, and she appreciated Hector's chivalry. At the last minute, she remembered to wipe her hands on her apron before she began to clear the tables.

Busy with her work, she pretended not to notice when Weston glanced her way, and he'd done it more than once. He was engaged in conversation with an older man sitting farther down the counter. She'd seen the man in the diner once before. He'd been quiet and stuck to himself, so everyone had left him alone. Not so this time.

The two men laughed, and Anna smiled as she carefully stacked dishes in the plastic bin.

"Miss?" A man who looked to be in his mid-thirties beckoned from a side table. "Can we get our check?"

"Oh, sure." Pulling out her order pad, Anna located the check. She wouldn't bother asking if they wanted dessert. The way these two had mooned over each other while sharing a burger and cheese fries, they had another after-dinner delight in mind. At least they wore wedding rings. Any further speculation was none of her business, or *beeswax*, as Candee would say.

"I like how you do things the old-fashioned way here," the woman said. "It's very quaint. We always stop in at the diner on our way through this part of Georgia. We have family an hour down the road." She squeezed her husband's hand. "Brent's parents started the tradition by bringing him to The Darling Diner when he was a teenager."

"Except for some updates, this place hasn't changed much." Brent chuckled. "Neither has Roz. Still crusty as ever, I see."

"I'm glad you could stop in again." Anna hesitated as she handed the man their check. "I deducted a few dollars for dry cleaning because of the ketchup I squirted on your shirt. I'm so sorry."

She couldn't look at him as she made her apology. And why had she said come and see *us* when she'd probably be long gone the next time they stopped in Darling?

"You didn't need to do that," he said. "It was an accident and could have happened to anyone."

The guy's wife wore a mystified expression. She must not have encountered many food servers who freely admitted their mistakes or offered to make amends. Come to think of it, neither had she.

"Thanks again, and be safe in your travels." Hopefully Candee would cash them out and not Roz. As Anna moved to another table, she breathed a sigh of relief when she spied Candee walking toward the register.

"Would you like more coffee?" she asked an older woman who'd come in for supper every night. As Anna refilled her mug, the customer proudly showed off photos of her newest grandbaby, a plump, smiling cherub named Nevaeh.

"That's heaven spelled backwards, you know." The woman shook her head. "The things they come up with nowadays."

Life in a small town was different but refreshing. People in cities talked to each other, but most had to warm up to a person first. Get to know someone before they shared their lives.

Without being asked, total strangers in the diner would launch into stories that sometimes revealed personal details better left unspoken. She hadn't needed to hear about Aunt Norma's botched hysterectomy or how Grandpa Roy's big left toe had to be amputated before it fell off due to gangrene. Even now, Anna shuddered at the thought.

A rambunctious group of a dozen teenage boys and girls occupied two rectangular tables they'd pushed together in the middle of the diner. Being the second week in July, the local 4-H Fair was in full swing. A couple of the girls had plopped oversized teddy bears on nearby chairs, most likely won at the arcade shooting gallery.

One of the boys moved his arm around the pretty blonde sitting next to him. Then, turning her chin toward him, he kissed her with reckless abandon. Neither one of them looked old enough to be out of the house on their own, much less locking lips. Why, they weren't even coming up for air! From the looks of things, more than their lips were locking.

Anna swallowed her surprise at their amorous, and very public, behavior. Why wasn't Roz all over *that* situation?

"They start out young in this town." Candee came alongside her.

"Am I that obvious?" Anna carefully set a glass in the plastic bin and kept her gaze trained on her task.

"Just a little, but it doesn't matter. Those kids are oblivious to anyone or anythin' around them. Sometimes I wonder if I was *ever* that young. That's the kind of thing you expect to see at the drive-in, not here in the middle of the diner. It's true what they say, I suppose. The older you get, the younger they seem. How old are you, honey?"

"Twenty-six." Twenty-seven next month. Candee couldn't be that much older, but she'd married Jesse at eighteen and they had four children ranging in age from twelve to three.

The other woman waved her hand. "Still a baby. Old enough to do what you want and not feel guilty about it. Within reason, that is. My mama would have tanned my hide good at that age if she caught me doin'"—she nodded to the kids—"*that*. Mark my words, if their hands start roamin', and especially if any clothin' comes off, guaranteed Roz or I will step in. Until then, we're expected to turn our heads and pretend we don't notice."

Anna frowned. "Why wait until then?" Those girls weren't wearing much as it was.

"Business has been a little slow lately, and Roz doesn't want to make people mad. She figures their antics are harmless. Kids just bein' kids, that kind of thing. She says it's our job to feed them, not police them."

Candee darted another glance at the teenage lovebirds. "If only Pastor Anderson would come in about now. That man always has his Bible in one hand and the word of the Lord on his tongue. That'd separate those two right quick."

Anna moved to the next table. "I take it you know most of these kids?" What a silly question. Everyone in Darling seemed to know one another. Half of them must be part of the same extended family tree.

"Yep, I sure do." Candee helped to clear more nearby tables by loading dirty dishes into the plastic bin. "I've known the smoochers—Janelle and Ronnie—from the time they were babies in diapers. I can name every one of those kids sittin' around those tables. Tell you who they're related to and best friends with. They're all local, and most of their families have been comin' into the diner for years. Matter of fact, I can tell you the exact day some of those kiddos were conceived."

Okay, then. Case in point that too much information wasn't always a good thing.

A quick frown creased Candee's brow. "I might need to have a chat with Janelle's mama, though. She won't want to be raisin' another grandchild."

As Candee worked beside her, Anna thought more about the townspeople she'd met in Darling. Overall, they were endearing. Good-hearted, church-going, Bible-believing, salt-of-the-earth people. Americana. Didn't get much better, really. They gave their honest opinion, asked or not. They didn't mince words, didn't dole out false flattery, didn't expect anything.

More importantly, they wouldn't try to gain anything by being friendly with *her*.

They didn't know who she was, where she came from, what she did for a living...well, other than attempting to be a waitress.

She'd deflected the few inquiries from friendly townsfolk by turning the conversation around and asking *them* questions. People in general preferred talking about themselves, and that wasn't limited to small-town Georgia.

A sudden, unexpected sadness coursed through Anna, bringing with it the same melancholy she'd experienced in recent days. Being on the road a large percentage of the year didn't allow time for personal interactions and certainly not enough time to maintain an ongoing *romantic* relationship.

Most girls her age could claim at least one serious dating relationship in their past or present.

Not Annalise Redmond.

Deep in her heart, in a place she'd never allowed anyone else to glimpse, Anna was the tiniest bit envious of that teenage girl. *Janelle and Ronnie.* Their names even sounded good together. Sure, those kids were only babies—and not that she didn't want to jump between them and warn them to be careful—but in a small town like this, these two might be married in a few short years and start having babies of their own. Be grandparents by the time they were in their late thirties or early forties, about the same age as Brent and his wife. That boggled Anna's mind.

From what Candee told her, few citizens of Darling ever left home to go to the big city, another state, or to find work elsewhere. "We call it deeply rooted in Darling," she'd said.

After high school, most found work at one of the manufacturing or industrial plants somewhere between Darling and Atlanta. Others worked with parents or relatives in family stores with the goal of assuming ownership one day.

A notable exception to the rule was the girl who'd started a highly successful Internet baby clothing business.

"She changed her name from Sally to somethin' European and thought she could do better sellin' her stuff from her glitzy new place up there in Atlanta. Just cost her more money to *make* money," Candee had observed. "Now, you tell me, what good financial sense does *that* make? Just lookin' at fancier walls. That's all it is."

Just lookin' at fancier walls. An apt description for her own life. Traveling the globe from city to city had been Anna's world for so long she couldn't imagine another way of life. On the flip side, she was growing tired of it. Although she loved what she did, she should consider cutting back and focusing on her personal life for a few years.

If she didn't, she'd wake up one morning in a hotel room at forty, an old maid who'd barely been kissed. Especially not with the kind of *passion* Ronnie had for Janelle.

And *that* would be truly tragic.

Anna longed to meet a man who loved God, a praying man, and a man who wanted children and wasn't afraid to admit it. A man who'd love her for the person she was on the inside as much as the outside, and who'd appreciate her talent without taking advantage of it. A man content in his own skin and confident in his relationship with Jesus.

In order to fulfill those dreams, she wanted a relationship with a real flesh-and-blood man. Ideally, she'd one day conceive a child the old-fashioned way, not from some nameless sperm donor as her manager had suggested. "That way, you can be a mother and continue to tour without the complication of a man."

Anna had laughed off the suggestion, but the comment settled in deep and disgruntled her. What a world. She'd hold out for what she wanted. That wasn't too much to ask. Was it? From the time she was fifteen, she'd trusted her career to the Lord. Now she needed to trust Him to guide her personal life. Not always easy, but she normally didn't even have *time* to ponder such things.

Her gaze strayed once more to Weston. Did he normally work this late in the summer? Once this project was over, where was he headed?

To learn the answers, she'd need to engage him in more conversation. The idea was appealing, but should she encourage a friendship with Weston—or anyone else, for that matter, male *or* female—when she'd be leaving town in a few short weeks?

Her mind said no.

But her *heart* told her something entirely different.

Chapter 3

The older guy down the counter grabbed his check and patted Weston on the shoulder as he passed behind him. "Hope to see you around town, youngster."

"Thanks, Jerry. Same here. Nice chatting with you."

After Jerry departed, Weston darted frequent glances at Anna beneath veiled lids. Kind of hard to do without turning sideways on the counter seat. He didn't bother masking his fascination although he tried not to be rude as she cleared the tables. He might make her self-conscious. Being stared at by some guy she didn't know probably made Anna uncomfortable.

Above all, he didn't want to risk her thinking he was leering or disrespecting her. Guys like his roommate must hit on her all the time, but she hadn't seemed flustered when she'd put Neil in his place by handing him their check.

That'd shown spunk. He admired spunk.

Try as she might, Anna couldn't disguise her femininity in spite of that shapeless black uniform and the ugliest shoes he'd ever seen, practical or not. Her red glasses must be nothing more than readers considering they were sitting halfway down her nose. Small waist, long legs, gentle curves, and pretty but tired brown eyes. Not a *weary with life* tired, but a genuinely *exhausted* tired. He could identify.

Anna's long, dark hair was pulled back in a loose braid, the bottom portion covered with a hairnet. When she turned under the lights a certain way, he caught a glimpse of red highlights. She wore no polish on her short nails, and other than faint color on her lips, she looked makeup-free. That alone was a nice change from most girls he knew. Her skin was a light golden color that looked natural instead of one of those fake, orange-y, sprayed-on tans.

He'd been more surprised than anyone when he'd caught those rogue plates after they'd flown out of Anna's hands. How one hadn't shattered on the floor was another small miracle. At least she hadn't twisted her ankle when she'd tripped over that little girl's toy. She definitely wasn't the type of woman he'd expect to find working in a small-town Georgia diner.

She'd never waitressed before, that much was obvious. After she almost tipped over a glass, she was adorably clumsy as she righted it and blew out a sigh of relief. Nerves could do that to a person. What he found most intriguing was how she appeared to be a walking contradiction. When she wasn't being uncoordinated, Anna seemed almost…graceful.

"Everything okay here, sweetie? Need anything?" The blonde waitress whose nametag read CANDEE stopped beside him on her way into the kitchen.

Anna's phone number? "I'm fine. Pie's great."

"Glad to hear it. Thanks for helpin' Anna out earlier. You let me know if you need anything else."

Weston nodded. "Will do. Thanks."

The way Anna had acted aloof and danced around his questions made him even more curious. At first, he thought she simply wasn't interested. She could have a boyfriend or just gotten out of a relationship. Maybe she had issues with men or could be running away from someone or a bad situation.

Lord, I hope she's not in some kind of trouble.

He'd noticed the way she'd interacted with Candee and the customers, male and female. There was a certain reserved quality about Anna, and she was friendly while still maintaining a safe distance. He didn't get the impression she purposely tried to be mysterious or wanted to give him the cold shoulder. Neither did she strike him as the type of girl to play games.

Unless he was way off the mark, something more than basic physical attraction had sparked between them, although that element was undeniable on his part. The smile Anna flashed in unexpected moments tugged on him somewhere inside. She had the kind of smile a guy could come home to the rest of his life.

Yeah, I must be more tired than I thought.

If he hadn't noticed how Anna bowed her head and closed her eyes a couple of times, as though saying a quick prayer, he'd let it go. He only hoped she prayed to the same God he did. These days, he couldn't always know for certain, even in church. What a sad commentary.

Weston focused on finishing his pie. That'd been a nice gesture on Anna's part. While he could appreciate Anna's beauty, he wasn't looking for a relationship, at least not while he was in Darling. He'd recently gotten out of one tricky relationship. More like he'd been kicked to the curb.

He hadn't dated in a couple of months, not since Madison dumped him for the new guy in their singles class. Some financial investment hotshot—Tate something or other—who claimed he could make them all some serious cash. In his sleek designer suits and new silver Mercedes, the money whiz obviously had the wrong idea about church, but Tate had done him a favor and spared him trouble down the line.

If Maddie wanted a guy for his slick image and material wealth, then her priorities weren't in line with his. He'd apparently been misguided in thinking the elementary school teacher would place a higher value on solid character and a strong work ethic than looks or money. For a halfway smart guy, he'd made some dumb dating choices.

At one point, Weston almost darted off his perch to rescue the loaded bin of dirty dishes as Anna carried it toward the kitchen. "I've got it," she insisted. Her pointed glance told him he'd done his good deed for the evening, so he remained seated. She was out to prove herself. But to whom? And why?

You want more.

That might be true, but no matter what *he* wanted, he wouldn't be in Darling long. Didn't change the fact he'd like to get know Anna better. Call it intuition, but something about her clued him in that she might need a friend.

Candee cleared dishes farther down the counter. Beckoning to her, Weston lowered his voice. "Can I get another piece of pie to go? I'd like to take a slice for a friend. Room temperature, no ice cream."

"Well, isn't that nice? Sure thing, sugar. I'll get it for you right now." She turned to go.

"Hang on a sec, Candee." Weston pulled a twenty from his wallet and handed it to her. "Keep the change." He hadn't planned on giving her that much, but a little nudge told him it was the right thing to do. He'd learned to follow those nudges.

Candee's eyes rounded. "This is amazing. Ask and ye shall receive." She moved one hand over her heart, taking a moment to compose herself. "We've had some car repairs lately, so I'm a little short on lunch money for our kids—my husband, Jesse, and I have four—the rest of the week."

She glanced up at him with bright eyes. "Thank you. If it weren't inappropriate, I'd give you a big ole hug."

Weston was touched by her gratitude, pleased he could fulfill a need. He loved how God worked. He'd been on the receiving end of random acts of kindness a few times himself.

"Hold onto your kids or your husband extra tight when you get home tonight."

"I'll do that." Candee sniffled. "Let me go get that piece of pie."

"No rush." Weston pushed aside his plate and downed the rest of his coffee.

Within a couple of minutes, Candee returned with the boxed dessert inside a plastic bag. "Here you go." She tied the ends of the bag together. "I threw in a couple of plastic forks, a knife, and some napkins for you."

"I appreciate it. Enjoy the rest of your evening." He tugged a few singles from the pocket of his jeans and tucked them under his empty pie plate. Not that she'd expect a tip, but he hoped it'd make Anna smile and brighten her evening.

Waving to catch her attention, he called to her over the laughter from the group of teens as they ambled toward the register. "Thanks for the pie and coffee. They were fantastic."

"You're welcome." Anna stopped straightening the condiments on a nearby table. "Do most people call you Wes or Weston?"

"Both, but since you're the one asking, it's Weston."

The diner grew suddenly quiet as the teenagers departed. Anna stepped closer to where he stood beside the register.

Dipping her head, she fidgeted and avoided his gaze. "I hope you'll come in again, Weston. In case I need your help...rescuing salt and pepper shakers. Or so you can try to figure out my accent." She lifted her chin. "Something."

He couldn't stop his grin. "Why, Anna, are you asking me to join you on a *diner* date?"

"Maybe. I don't know." She appeared genuinely confused. What a puzzle she was, self-confident one minute and seemingly shy the next. He'd always enjoyed the challenge of a puzzle—trying to figure out the way the pieces fit into the whole and the satisfaction in solving them.

"Good night. I'm sure I'll see you again soon." Weston headed for the door.

Ask her.

He turned back. "Can I maybe walk you to your car when you get off? It's dark out tonight." What a brilliant statement.

Candee laughed. "Well, that *was* the forecast. If you two aren't like a couple of shy kiddos skirtin' around each other. You head on home with your handsome escort, Anna. We're almost done here, and I can close up."

"But Roz—"

"Is already gone for the night," Candee said. "She left ten minutes ago and put me in charge. Hector and Mike will help. We'll be fine. Now get on out of here, sweetie. Y'all have fun gettin' better acquainted. I'll see you tomorrow afternoon. You're on at two, right?"

"Last I checked, but I'll look again before I leave." Anna nodded to Weston. "Give me just a minute."

"I'll be here." Weston's brows lifted when she took his tip money and quickly stuffed it into the jar for a local charity. Interesting. His gaze fell to those orthopedic shoes. Bright white and brand-spanking new. She wore small, emerald-colored stud earrings, and a matching necklace around her neck partially hidden by her uniform. Although he wasn't sure why, he suspected those earrings and necklace were the real deal.

This girl wasn't hard up for money. She had class, but what was the other word? *Refinement.* Yes, that was it. He almost snapped his fingers. The biggest mystery? Why a woman like Anna would *choose* to live in a little town like Darling and waitress in a diner.

She'd more or less invited him to come back to the diner. Then accepted his suggestion to walk her to her car although they were both bone-tired. Maybe if they talked for a few minutes, she'd open up and tell him more.

Just be a friend, Galloway. That's all.

Removing her apron as she walked, Anna headed for the swinging door. As she disappeared from view, Weston overheard the sounds of a high-powered sprayer and animated conversation from the guys in the kitchen.

Weston's curiosity got the better of him. He stepped closer to where Candee swept the floor. "So, what's the story with Anna?"

Candee continued to sweep. "All I know is, she came in here last Saturday askin' for a job. She'd never waitressed anywhere before and had no references. Not a one. But she wasn't desperate, and she already had a place to live. Those things are always a plus, so Roz was feelin' charitable and decided to take a chance. Anna's an extra hard worker, always shows up on time, has a good attitude, and the customers seem to like her."

She darted a glance at him. "I can tell you're in that last category."

"Yeah, you could say that." What woman Anna's age didn't have any job references?

"Of course, she's only been here a few days, but from what I know, true character shows itself early and holds true." Pausing in her work, Candee swept aside a loose blonde curl with the back of her hand. "There's a gentleness about that gal, a sweetness you don't see much anymore even though I suspect she's hidin' some secrets. Know what I mean?"

"I think I do." He ran a hand over his beard.

"I'm not talkin' about *bad* secrets, mind you, although I suppose you never really know about a person. Bless her heart, I just pray that girl's okay and not runnin' from any kind of trouble."

"I share that prayer." Weston pulled chairs away from the table so she could sweep beneath it. Then he grabbed the nearby dustpan and crouched low to hold it in place for her.

"Thanks again. You sure are handy to have around," Candee said as she finished sweeping.

He turned as he heard the sounds of laughter and Anna emerged from the kitchen. With a lightweight sweater draped over her arm, she couldn't be from anywhere near this part of Georgia or she'd know this time of night still boasted high temperatures.

The hairnet was gone, and her hair was a mass of tangled dark waves, no doubt from being cooped up in that hairnet for hours. It reached almost to her waist, longer than he'd expected.

Weston set the dustpan aside and rose to his feet. "Ready to go?"

"I sure am. Thanks again, Candee."

The other waitress smiled at them both. "You bet. Weston, I hope we'll be seein' you in here again. Don't be a stranger."

He doubted anyone was a stranger to Candee. "I'll be around."

Chapter 4

The night was hot, humid, and sticky as Weston exited the diner behind Anna. Standing beside her, he felt like a disgusting, stinky mess and hoped he didn't reek.

"Sorry I'm such a grunge. I'll stay at least three feet away."

"Don't worry about it." She waved her hand with a small smile. "It's evidence of hard work. Nothing a hot shower won't cure."

He couldn't resist teasing her. "Are you saying I stink?"

"No, it's just that you. . ." When he grinned and she could tell he was teasing, her lips twisted. "Since I started working in the diner, I smell like grease and disinfectant spray. I don't think Macy's will be clamoring for the formula."

That made him laugh. Yeah, this girl shopped at the department stores, not the big chain superstores. "I like your style, Anna. Is your car parked nearby?"

"I'm renting a house five blocks east from here on Magnolia Avenue, and I walked to work. I know you're tired, too. If you can't take the time, I understand—"

"No, that's not it. I want to see you home. I thought your feet might hurt, and you'd want a lift. My truck's parked a block from here. I can run and get it, and then come back to get you."

"I'm okay, thanks. Let's walk." She hesitated. "Except that means you'll need to come back to get your truck."

"Not a problem." Anna hadn't told him to get lost, and she didn't seem adverse to conversation. Weston fell into place beside her, the bag with the pie dangling from one hand. He'd give it to her at the house.

"I know my shoes are hideous, but they save my feet. For that reason alone, they'll always hold a special place in my heart." Pulling a hair elastic off her wrist, Anna quickly scooped her hair back into a high ponytail.

Weston chuckled. "I don't know about a special place in my heart, but I'm kind of partial to my steel toe boots."

"Your group came in awfully late tonight," she said after they'd walked a half-block. "Do you always work such long hours?"

"Only if we have delays. We were behind today because some of the building materials were delivered late. Couldn't be helped, though. There was flash flooding in Kentucky and Tennessee, and some of the roads were blocked. The driver was detoured."

"That's too bad. One of the customers said there'd been heavy rains. What are you building?"

"A bank. It's two blocks straight up from here on Magnolia."

She nodded. "I know exactly where it is. I pass by the construction site on my way to work."

Anna had walked by the site and none of the guys had whistled or made a comment? That surprised him—in a good way—but the crew was one of the best he'd seen in terms of dedicated workers. His employer was known for stellar standards, professionally speaking.

"We did what advance work we could while we waited, and the truck finally came in about three this afternoon. Our foreman called the boss, and the crew agreed to work late tonight. This project is different in that we only work daytime hours on staggered shifts. We're also closer to a residential zone which means different regulations than when we're building in downtown Atlanta."

"That must be frustrating with the building materials being delayed. Kind of like you're a chef who doesn't have all the ingredients for the main course," Anna said. "Then once you finally gather everything together, you can't wait to start."

She shook her head and laughed under her breath. "I know that sounded random, but it's late, so don't hold anything I say against me."

"It makes sense, but I've never thought of it that way. *If* that scenario happens, though, you'd risk botching the final product because then you're rushed and impatient. At least if you mess up in the kitchen, you only end up with a bad taste in your mouth. That's not an option in construction." He sighed. "The not botching up part, not the—"

"I know what you meant." They walked in companionable silence a few hundred feet. "I'm sure you're very good at your job," she said. "I'm trying, but I'm not a very good waitress."

"I'm sure you're good at a lot of things. I get the feeling waitressing isn't in your blood, not your passion. That makes a big difference."

"I look at working in the diner as a learning opportunity."

"Yeah, right. That's a line if ever I've heard one." When he noticed her shoulders stiffen, Weston figured he should change the subject. "You're serious, aren't you?" He might want to lighten up on the teasing.

"I know it's obvious I've never waitressed before. If nothing else, it gives me a greater appreciation for those who work in the food industry. Does that answer suit you better?"

"Much better. What were you like as a kid?" Surely that'd be a safe subject.

"Curious, quiet, a bookworm." Anna hadn't hesitated to answer.

"What did you like most about reading?"

That question brought back her pretty smile. "I liked reading different types of books, but I loved how *Alice in Wonderland* and the Narnia series carried me away to magical places. They unleashed my imagination and gave me wings to soar. Not that I wanted to escape my reality, but I always loved the idea that anything was possible. Reaching for the stars, that kind of thing."

"That sounds lyrical and kind of poetic." Tilting his head, Weston cocked a brow. "Are you a famous author hiding out in Darling? Doing research for your next bestselling novel?"

"Hardly. My imagination's not that creative."

"Well, even though you're a reader, I'd say you don't really need…" Weston gestured to the red glasses.

Appearing self-conscious, Anna whisked them from the end of her nose and tucked them in the front pocket of her uniform. "How about you? Tell me what you were like as a kid."

"I wasn't much of a reader, I can tell you that much." He shoved his free hand into the pocket of his jeans. If he hadn't, he'd be tempted to grab *her* hand.

"I made decent grades," he said. "History, phys ed, lunch, and geography were my favorite things, but I was bored with the rest. Both in and outside of school, I was your standard daredevil—stubborn and bull-headed, way too smart-mouthed and defiant for my own good. I gave my parents grief for a few years. I don't know if it's a good or bad thing that I'm an only child."

"Sounds like you would have made a good firefighter or police officer."

"Funny you should say that. I *was* a firefighter." He wouldn't have brought it up, but Anna's observation caught him off guard. Stunned him, actually. To say something like that, she must be speaking from personal experience or have firsthand knowledge.

Anna slowed her steps and glanced over at him. "You were? I mean…"

"In Atlanta for five years. Then I lost one of my best friends, and that changed everything. David had a wife and three kids. I *hated* what his death did to their family. I still pour everything into my work, and there's always the chance I'll take a wrong step or something could go wrong, but at least I don't have to worry about a buddy being carried out of a burning building in a body bag."

He heard her quiet gasp and realized Anna was no longer beside him. Massaging his forehead, Weston slowly walked back to where she'd stopped a few hundred paces behind. "Wow. I'm really sorry, Anna. I'm not thinking straight tonight. Here I barely know you, and I shouldn't have run off my mouth like that."

"No, it's okay," she assured him. "I'm glad you shared those things with me. I'm not used to people being so honest, especially with someone they've just met."

Anna looked up at him, her eyes shining. "Don't misunderstand. That's a *good* thing. I can't imagine going through something like that, Weston. I hope you were able to lean on your faith to help you through the grief of losing your friend."

He squinted into the distance. Buzzing insects flittered about the overhead street lamps, the only sounds to break the quiet of the night. A trickle of sweat ran down his neck and a few other places, unwelcome reminders of the almost stifling humidity.

"God had to do a lot of work in me before I finally came around. He's always working on me, but I was angry at Him, angry at the world, angry at the guy who fell asleep smoking in his bed and killed his wife, angry at the fact that I couldn't save that poor woman or my buddy. I saved the guy's life, though."

Swallowing his lingering bitterness, Weston shrugged. "I guess there's something to be said for that, right?"

She nodded. "Yes, of course. You were doing your job, and your anger is understandable. You needed time to work through it. I've always believed that if something like that happens—when one person survives and another doesn't—it means that God has more work to do in that person's life."

Anna's compassion was obvious. He liked that she thought about God. In his home church, he'd met few girls willing to discuss the things of the Lord outside of the singles class or the worship service. Talking was good, but *walking* in faith was the truer testament of a life lived *for* Christ. He wasn't perfect, by any means, but leaving his faith and Christian testimony behind in the church parking lot every Sunday wasn't his style.

"I'll admit I don't always understand God's ways," he said. "I've learned that's not my job. I just need to trust Him and know He's got it all under control."

"Sometimes that's the hardest thing to do, isn't it?"

"Yes." His gaze locked with hers as understanding passed between them.

"Before David was killed, the chief warned me against bringing my 'religion' onto the job. I went ahead and prayed with the families of victims, anyway, and counseled them as best I could. Sharing with them brought the family members comfort, and it seemed to make their pain a little more bearable. The chief usually looked the other way. In situations like that, people often cling to Jesus when they never would otherwise."

Blowing out a deep sigh, he glanced into the distance. "The thing is, if I hadn't shared my faith, I'd always regret it. My conscience wouldn't have let me go. It's like the words were burning inside of me—pun intended, I guess—and I had to let them out or I'd…I don't know, combust or something."

Weston removed his cap and ran one hand through his damp hair. "You must think I'm crazy, going on like that. Now I just sound corny."

"I don't think that at all." Anna's voice was quiet. "I think you're incredibly brave, and your faithfulness and obedience are admirable. Too many people are intimidated by what the world thinks. So, they don't take a strong stand and say nothing. The world isn't changed by the people who stand on the sidelines."

"Who said that? Someone famous?"

Her lips curved. "That was an Anna Redmond original. Too corny?"

"I don't think that at all." They shared a smile. What was happening here?

I really like this girl, that's what's happening.

Weston snapped to attention. "When you work with life or death, sometimes faith is all you've got. I feel for the doctors and nurses who deal with it constantly. How can you put blinders on your heart and emotions? I couldn't, and I can't imagine being that strong."

Anna nodded. "I can't imagine working around it all the time if you *don't* have faith."

"I was put on suspension after I'd worked too many hours straight and then jumped on the truck for another call," he told her. "Tired or not, what was I supposed to do? Stand by and watch as the truck pulls out, wave them off, and holler, 'Bye! Good luck! Hope no one dies today!'"

Weston replaced his cap, this time in the forward-facing position. "On a residential call, I stumbled and almost dropped a hose on another firefighter from a second level window. Filled with water, that length of hose weighs about six hundred pounds. Then David was killed a month after that, and that was the end of my career as a firefighter."

Drawing in a sharp breath, he let it out slowly. Why had he spilled his innermost thoughts to a woman he'd just met? He'd confessed things to Anna he'd never told *anyone*. Maybe he felt more free to share with her because they were both only in Darling temporarily and then they'd go their separate ways.

No, that wasn't it. He liked talking with her, felt comfortable with her. She wasn't the type of woman where he had to work at keeping the conversation going. Anna seemed to care about him without expecting more than friendship, and that made her different from the majority of women he met.

That was the irony that might gnaw at him from the inside out. Anna was exactly the type of woman he'd prayed to meet. The kind of woman he wanted to date. God didn't bring opportunities into his life only to cruelly snatch them away, so he'd keep an open mind.

"Do you miss being a firefighter?"

"I miss the camaraderie with the guys. We were a special team. Not to sound morbid, but it's like part of me died and was buried beside David. I also learned I can't live in fear if I want every day to *mean* something."

Anna's steps slowed and then she stopped walking altogether. "My uncle was a firefighter. When I was little, I called him a soldier. In many ways, I think public servants *are* soldiers on the home front, watching over us and keeping us safe. There aren't enough words to adequately say thank you."

Something in her voice clued Weston in that something bad might have happened to her uncle. He hated to ask but had to know. "Is he…?" He faltered, unable to continue.

Anna's gaze dropped. "Uncle Stewart was a heavy smoker, but he also took too much solace in the bottle. He died of acute alcoholism when I was fourteen."

Reaching for her hand, Weston wrapped it in his. "Unfortunately, those are side effects of the job stress. I was a social drinker and packed away beers with the guys after-hours, but I haven't touched a drink in a few years."

"Do you like working construction now?"

She would ask *that* question. As if realizing their hands were still joined, Anna gently withdrew from his grasp as they continued to walk.

"Depends on what day you ask," he said. "I like the physicality of what I do and the work is challenging. But in other ways, I'm spinning my wheels. The best way to explain it is that I'm content, but I don't expect to be doing this forever. When I was little, all I ever wanted was to grow up and be a firefighter. It wasn't so much the element of danger that attracted me as the idea of helping people who can't help themselves."

"I'm sure you help more people than you realize. No matter what you do for a living," Anna said. "Walking a waitress home from a diner, for instance." She pointed out a two-story white house up ahead on the right. "That's the house I'm renting."

"That's an American Foursquare." Grateful to lighten the mood, he studied the house as best he could in the dim lighting.

"I know nothing about architecture. Have you ever built a house?"

"No, I only work commercial construction. I've picked up things here and there." He shot her a grin. "I've been known to read a few books about architecture, believe it or not. The American Foursquare was a popular style in the late nineteenth century until about 1930. It's very popular here in Georgia. It represents solidity and strength and was created to counteract the ornate Victorian homes."

Standing on the sidewalk beside Anna, Weston pointed to the house. A light fixture mounted on the front porch afforded him a better view. "The hallmarks of the style are the simple, boxy design, hip roof, dormer in the center, and the front porch."

"What's a hip roof? Snooty and popular? Looks down on every other roof?" Anna shook her head. "Sorry. I also get punchy when I'm tired."

He chuckled. "I'll walk you to the door." Weston stayed beside her as they headed up the front walkway lined with small, low-to-the-ground, blooming flowers. "A hip roof means the sides slope down to the walls without gables or vertical sides. I'm guessing the inside of the house has a quartered floor plan, simple and straightforward."

"Quartered?" Anna's tone revealed her weariness. She wouldn't remember any of these details come morning. His fault for trying to impress her.

"Two rooms deep by two rooms wide on both stories," he said. "This type of house was very efficient and economical to build."

She glanced up at the house. "Practical, in other words."

"Right, but I like to believe they hold their own unique charm." Weston motioned for her to start up the front steps. "After you. I promise not to bore you with any more architecture talk."

"I'm not bored. Thanks again for walking with me," Anna said as they reached the porch. "It's been a long time since anyone's done that."

He quirked his brows, finding that difficult to believe. "I'm sure you have guys falling all over themselves to walk you home."

"I meant not many people take leisurely strolls together anymore. It's...refreshing."

Weston smiled as he spotted a double swing in the shadows of the front porch. "My grandfather on my mom's side courted my grandmother on a porch swing like this."

Crossing the porch, he clasped the metal chain and gave it a slight push. "As the story goes, Grandpa Keller kissed his sweetheart for the first time sitting side-by-side in one. Then six months later, he asked her to marry him in that same swing."

"That's sweet and romantic," Anna said. "It's wonderful to hear family stories passed down through generations. Testaments of love and commitment. Those stories show the *heart* of a family, don't you think?"

"Agreed. I also think past generations were more romantic as a general rule." Where had *that* come from? He'd never thought about it before, but it was true. The word "romantic" wasn't a word he'd used much and yet, an hour after meeting Anna, there it was.

"I'm sure a lot of it has to do with today's more impatient lifestyle." Walking to the front door, Anna dug her keys from her purse. "Getting to know each other and sharing thoughts and exchanging ideas has become a forgotten tradition."

"It doesn't have to be forgotten."

Her eyes searched his, beautiful and questioning. Neither one of them moved or spoke for a long moment. That same feeling as before, shared understanding perhaps—real and solid—passed between them. He hoped he could give her a reason to stay.

"Look, Anna, I know we only met tonight, and this might sound kind of forward, and maybe kinda crazy, but being with you tonight has been better than the best date of my life."

Weston resisted the strong urge to touch his lips to hers. If nothing else, to thank Anna for giving him renewed hope he might eventually find a woman to share his life. He'd all but given up lately.

She gave him another small smile. "I enjoyed it, too. Be careful working in the hot sun tomorrow."

Great, Galloway. Now you've done it. With his hasty words, he'd probably scared her off. When he showed up at the diner again, she'd avoid him and duck into the kitchen. What was wrong with him? He shouldn't expect anything from her. Not one single thing.

"I'm, uh, used to it," he managed. "Thanks for your concern. Oh, I almost forgot. This is for you." He handed her the bag with the slice of pie.

Thanks for your concern? What a goober.

"What's this?" Anna took the bag from him with a curious expression.

"My way of sharing the pie, I guess. I asked Candee for an extra slice. To go with a late dinner. Midnight snack. Or breakfast tomorrow. Whenever you want." He should give up trying to make conversation, say good night, and beat a hasty retreat.

"Thank you, Weston. That's very thoughtful."

"You're welcome." He ran one hand over his jaw. His beard had now entered the prickly zone. Reason enough not to kiss her. If he did, he wouldn't aim for her soft cheek when Anna's lips looked way too tempting. Then for sure she'd want nothing to do with him.

How could he think about kissing her when they'd only met an hour ago? On "real" dates, he always waited until at least the third one to think about kissing a girl, and then only if she gave him a clue that she was ready, willing, and able.

"Good night, Anna." They stared at one another for a few seconds before he finally broke the silence. Now he was acting like a smitten teenager on his first date. "Just so you know, I'm going to stand here until you're inside safe and sound. Not that you can't take care of yourself since you're a big girl…"

He groaned and squeezed his eyes shut for a second. "I hope you know I didn't mean you're actually—"

"I know what you meant." She dipped her chin, but he caught her smile. "Good night."

Anna headed inside the house and quietly closed the front door. As if she knew he still waited, she turned the lock.

Feeling like a kid, Weston bounded down the front steps and headed back up the street. Fireflies flitted nearby, flickering pinpoints of light in the dark sky, reminding him of when he was little and chased them around the backyard. Such freedom he'd felt back then. Kids had no concept of how easy life is when you're young and carefree, when everything in the world is simple and uncomplicated.

If such a thing were possible, his heart felt lighter, his spirits higher. Energized and hopeful with a newfound optimism he wasn't about to waste. Some moments in life were meant to be just that— one moment in time. But sometimes that moment held the potential to change *everything*. If tonight was all he was meant to share with Anna, he'd always be grateful for the opportunity.

And then move forward.

But an inner nudge told him there'd be more moments like tonight. Or maybe it was his wishful thinking. The best thing he could do was pray.

That was *always* the answer.

He didn't know where Anna was from or what her life had been like before coming to Darling. He didn't know much about her at all, yet he'd pretty much spilled his life story to her. She might think twice about associating with him, be a bit wary of him even, but he was willing to take the chance.

Anna was worth it.

If only she stays.

Chapter 5

Anna tossed her sweater, purse, and the bag with the pie on a chair. Darting a glance at the front window, she hesitated only a moment before moving closer. She couldn't resist. Lifting a corner of the curtain, she peeked.

"He's already gone."

Anna screamed and shivers ran through her. For the second time that evening, she clamped her hands over her mouth. Turning slowly, she narrowed her eyes as she made out the familiar figure in the dim light. Then she lowered her hands and crossed her arms over her middle.

"Charley! You almost scared the life out of me. Couldn't you have warned me you were coming? Or at least turned on a light?"

"Sorry, sis. You know I like the element of surprise. If I'd turned on a light, you'd have called the police. You're also way too predictable in leaving the extra key in an obvious *hiding* place. It's like, somewhere in your subconscious, you know I'm going to show up."

"Surprise is one thing but a premature heart attack is another." Anna switched on a table lamp.

With her petite stature, hazel eyes, and long straight blonde hair—currently streaked with lavender—Charley looked nothing like Anna although they shared the same father. A mostly absentee father for Anna after he'd divorced her mother when she was three but their father all the same.

"Get over here and give me a hug." When Charley moved closer, Anna wrapped her in her arms and held on tight. She could never stay mad at this girl for long. Other than her father and a few scattered relatives she'd never known, Charley *was* her family.

Stepping back, her sister's gaze traveled over her. "Looks like that Caribbean sun did you some good." She tweaked Anna's cheek, bringing attention to her bright purple fingernails. "You've finally got some healthy color in those pale cheeks. About time. I take it you enjoyed your jaunt to St. John?"

"I did, and it was gloriously private except for a few tourists. Just the way I like it."

Loud pounding on the front door startled them both. Anna frowned. "Now see what you've done? My neighbors probably think I've been murdered. Or else they're wondering what riffraff has moved in on their respectable street."

"Or maybe the hot guy's back." A slow grin spread over Charley's face, and she lifted her slender shoulders. "I saw him through the window before you came inside."

"Anna?"

Weston. Thankfully, he'd downgraded the pounding to hard, insistent knocks.

"Are you okay?" he called from behind the front door. "I heard a woman scream. Please come to the door so I can see you."

"Congrats, Annalise. You've already found yourself a real live hero. Nice work."

"Let me handle this."

Inhaling a quick breath, Anna swung open the front door but couldn't quite muster a smile. "Everything's fine, Weston. I'm sorry I alarmed you."

He seemed slightly out of breath, no doubt from sprinting back to the house. Stepping to the side, he glanced over her shoulder. "I know it's none of my business, but I had to come and check things out. Make sure you're all right. A woman doesn't normally scream without a good reason. Did you see a mouse or something?"

Anna narrowed her eyes. "Mice don't scare me."

"Well, *I'm* not fond of them, so you never know."

Moving across the room, Charley held out her hand. "It's all my fault. I showed up in town to surprise my sister, and it worked *too* well, I'm afraid. Very nice to meet you, Weston. I'm Charley Parker."

Weston glanced at Anna as he shook Charley's hand. "You, too. Wait a minute. You mean like the jazz great Charlie Parker?"

"Uh, yeah. I get that a lot. I can't play a horn to save my life, but I fell in love with and married a guy with the last name Parker. My first name's actually Charlotte, but I've been called Charley since I was a kid. Just like my older sister here—"

"Needs to let Weston get home now. I'm sure he's exhausted." Anna couldn't have her spouting too much information and needed to send Weston on his way.

"It won't happen again, Officer Weston." Charley gave him a small salute.

"I'm glad you're all right. You ladies enjoy the rest of your evening." Weston headed for the door.

"I appreciate your diligence," Anna said.

"Make sure and lock the door behind me."

Anna started forward. "I'm sure you'll wait until you hear the lock turn."

He opened the door with an irresistible grin. "You know it."

After closing and locking the door again, Anna arched her brows as she faced Charley. "I honestly don't know what to say except *that* was embarrassing." Her exhaustion threatened to overtake her, but first she needed to talk with Charley and find out why she was here.

"No reason for embarrassment. If Weston cared enough to come charging back here to your rescue, he's not going anywhere soon. That's actually very sweet when you think about it, especially from a guy you just met."

Charley's comment snapped Anna from her musing. "That's not what I meant. Weston used to be a firefighter in Atlanta. It must be ingrained in him to check out a potentially dangerous situation."

"That's all good and well, but the man obviously likes you, Anna. Great looking, buff with muscles that won't quit, *and* an honest-to-goodness hero with a sexy southern drawl. Can't ask for more than that. The key words being *used to be* a firefighter. What's he do now?"

"Construction." Weston *was* very attractive. That was a given. His charm was only enhanced by his gentlemanly ways and tendency to say the wrong thing. The guy was a deep thinker, and he seemed to revere God and respect womankind. What she *didn't* need was her sister pointing out his appealing qualities. Any potential relationship with the man was doomed before it could even begin.

"Good for him! Nothing wrong with honest labor."

Anna kneaded her knuckles in circles on her forehead, finding Charley's statement highly ironic considering her sister hadn't worked anything more than part-time jobs her entire life.

"I didn't say there was anything wrong with it. If you want the truth, Weston's the nicest man I've met in a long time."

"Well, you should know considering you swim in a tank full of sharks in fancy suits most of the time. Yet somehow you always manage to evade them. A very good thing, by the way."

Charley dropped onto the sofa. "So, while you're regrouping, your manager called and left a message on your machine. Morticia Addams wants to know how you're making out. Ironic choice of words, don't you think?"

Grabbing a throw pillow, Charley looked up at Anna with her big eyes. "So, tell me more about Weston the Construction Guy. Cool name, by the way, and he's ever so dreamy with those gorgeous light blue eyes and great chiseled...everything. Doesn't he just make you tingle?"

Seemed her sister wasn't going to let up on the topic of Weston anytime soon. "You're a married woman, Charley. Stop noticing his...everything, chiseled or not. I didn't 'make out' with him nor do I expect to. And, for the record, the word *tingled* is not in my vocabulary. Banish it from your mind."

Anna dropped onto the sofa beside her. Might as well tell her more now so they could move on. "Weston was at the diner and rescued some plates that I dropped. Then he offered to walk me home because I was an accident waiting to happen, and he wanted to make sure I didn't hurt myself or anyone else. We were just talking, and we're both only in town temporarily, so don't make anything of it. And it's Felicia, not Morticia. You know that."

To be fair, her longtime manager *did* wear her dark hair straight and parted down the middle, so Charley's nickname was understandable.

Charley laughed. "Don't get so defensive. I'm only having fun and teasing you. Do you have a spare bed I can curl up in tonight?"

"Of course. Always. Just promise next time you'll give me fair warning." Anna leaned forward to unlace her shoes. "I'm tired all the way down to my *bones*. I've never felt this exhausted in all my life. People don't give waitresses enough credit. It's very hard work. I'm sure servers and salespeople keep podiatrists in business." At least her customers had been kind and understanding for the most part, not surly and rude, after her mishaps.

"Uh huh." Charley angled her head toward Anna's shoes and wolf whistled. "Nice—"

"Don't say it." Anna raised one hand. "These shoes have been a godsend this week, and I can't have you maligning them."

"That's all good and well, but someone needs to come up with designer orthopedic shoes."

"Here's a thought—that can be *your* calling in life. Buy a sketch pad and get to work." Anna stuck out her right foot. "But first, make yourself useful and help me pry these things off my feet before they're permanently attached."

"Sure." Charley slid off the sofa and fell to her knees. "You didn't answer my question on the phone the other day. Explain why you're working as a waitress in a no-name town in Georgia, seventy miles southwest of Atlanta."

That comment gave Anna pause. "Charley, how did you get here? To Darling?"

"A taxi from the airport. How else?"

"All the way from *Atlanta*?" Anna slapped a hand on her forehead. "Why would you do that? You should have called me." When Charley didn't answer, she continued. "Just because you have money doesn't mean you should squander it."

After tugging off Anna's right shoe and then the left, her sister plopped beside her on the sofa. "Don't change the subject. I know you wanted to escape for a while. Flying to a Caribbean island makes perfect sense, but don't you think this little adventure is taking it a bit too far?"

"The short answer why I did it? Because I *can*."

Charley scoffed. "That's a horrible reason! You could at least give me some made up but more plausible excuse like *I've lost my mind* or *I'm running away from my life*."

"I agree, but it's all I can give you at the moment. My brain is too tired to think about it." Anna yawned and didn't bother covering her mouth.

"I promise to give you fair warning about my next visit if you promise not to do anything crazy at that diner," Charley said. "Seriously, Anna. You've got to protect those valuable hands at all costs. I know they're insured, but it won't do you any good if you get injured and can't play. Nothing's worth the risk."

"I'm being careful, Charley. It's not like I'm going to volunteer to clean the meat cleaver or handle the knives. Chef Francie does that well enough on her own. She's got the whole samurai warrior slice and dice thing down pat." To punctuate her statement, Anna moved her hand up and down in the air, mimicking a chopping motion. "I needed a break, and the southern states have always appealed to me. The people are *real* here, you know?"

Charley's mouth gaped. "People are the same everywhere, but yeah, I think I get it. Plus, in a small town like this, they don't know you, so hopefully they won't try to hit you up for favors. You can be free to be yourself or whatever."

"That's what I'm trying to find out. Who I *am*. Felicia wasn't thrilled with my taking a break, but she learned to live with it once I proved I was serious by renting a car and driving down here by myself. I think the biggest shock was that I actually *did* it."

Anna shifted her position to face her sister. "Besides, like you said about construction, waitressing is good honest labor. Gives me a new perspective. These people work hard and deserve our respect."

"Sure they do, but you have to know everyone's wondering what's going on with you. You have to admit this is out of character. There are rumors flying and, I have to say, the speculation is a little crazy."

"Why do people care? I'm not that important, and it's not like I've been gone for a year." Why wasn't Felicia handling the rumors? Her manager was paid handsomely to handle her career, including damage control.

"You're more important than you think," Charley said. "At least listen to the theories. They're pretty interesting, and you'll probably get a kick out of them."

With a light moan, Anna plopped back against the sofa cushions. "If you must."

"First, there are the stories that you've been kidnapped, and it's being kept secret from the press because a ransom is involved. Or you've suffered a nervous breakdown and are holed up at some high-priced, mental health facility. Then there's the one that you're a raging drug addict or alcoholic and you're going through withdrawal at an exclusive rehab center on the West Coast. But my personal favorite? You eloped and are shacked up with your new husband somewhere along the breathtaking Amalfi Coast."

"That last one sounds good." Anna laughed. "It's the least offensive, anyway. Not to mention ludicrous since I haven't dated in…well, a while. You mean there's not a rumor floating around that I'm sitting in a jail for some unknown offense?"

That made Charley laugh. "No, although I'm surprised no one's come up with that one yet. No worries. Anyone who knows you understands it's all stupid gossip. They won't believe any of it. You're like the poster girl for clean-living concert pianists."

"The *truth* would shock them most of all, you realize. I can see the headlines now." Anna danced her fingers in the air as though writing an invisible headline. "Concert Pianist Slings Hash in The Darling Diner."

Charley sputtered. "That's seriously what it's called? And you actually work there—as in pouring coffee and serving food? Will wonders never cease." She shook her head in amazement. "You're right. The press would have an absolute field day. Do the people you work with know who you are?"

"No, and if I can help it, they'll never find out. On both counts. And as Weston pointed out, we *are* in Darling, Georgia," Anna said. "I'm not giving anyone my real first name, so it should be fine. It's not like I'm well-known outside of my narrow world. My work is better known more than my face, and that suits me perfectly fine. Like you said, it allows me freedom to come and go as I like. So, in a way, I have the best of both worlds."

Anna yawned again and stretched her arms over her head. "If I sit on this sofa much longer, I'll fall asleep. Come into the kitchen and we can talk some more. Are you hungry?" When Charley shrugged, she persisted. "When's the last time you ate? The truth, Charley."

"I don't know. Yesterday sometime. When's the last time *you* ate?"

"I ate a sandwich on the run earlier in the day." Anna checked her watch. "Huh. That was more than seven hours ago. Time for me to eat, too." Even if she wasn't hungry, she'd eat again to keep Charley company and make sure *she* ate something. "I can offer you a ham and turkey sandwich." She glanced at the bag from the diner on the chair. "And warm, delicious apple pie. How does that sound?"

"Like a little bit of heaven."

Anna offered her hand and tugged Charley off the sofa. Grabbing the bag with the pie, she led the way into the kitchen. She switched on the light, illuminating the sizable kitchen with its granite countertops, brick walls, wood flooring, ultramodern stainless steel fixtures, and up-to-date appliances. A dream kitchen if she wanted to try her hand at cooking.

"Wow. Nice place you've got here." Charley surveyed the room with an approving nod. "Who could have guessed an older home like this would be so well-equipped and modern? Are you planning to buy it so you can rent it out after you leave?"

"For now the plan is to rent. My Realtor found this house fully furnished, and it's one of the reasons I'm here in Darling." Anna gazed around the kitchen with appreciation. "It *is* great, isn't it? I *could* buy it and then rent it later."

"Sometimes I come up with something inspired." Charley's gaze settled on her. "You're honestly not worried about any of the rumors and innuendo, are you? I don't understand how you can disregard what other people say, but I'm glad you can, Anna. Shows backbone and confidence."

Charley scrambled onto a barstool beside the kitchen island and kicked her aqua heels to the floor. Those shoes had to be at least five inches high. Boosting her height was one thing, but those babies looked dangerous.

"I'm not worried," Anna said. "I'm sure Felicia's on top of the rumors. She'll have the publicity company issue a statement if she feels it's necessary. Besides that, God will take care of me, and I take comfort in His promises, not the idiocy of men."

Charley stared at her and then slowly clapped. "Congratulations. That's quite the holier-than-thou speech, big sister."

"Sorry. I didn't mean to sound…like that. But I meant what I said." Anna rolled her eyes. That line would give Weston a run for his money. His verbal *faux pas* came across as endearing, but she just sounded ridiculous. And yes, a little too holier than thou.

"I suppose this fabulous rental home is as good a reason as any to come to Darling, Georgia." Charley had affected an exaggerated southern accent with that last statement. "Pull out a road map, close your eyes, and point your finger. 'Oh, look! I think I'll go live *there* tomorrow.'"

Typical Charley. She always changed the subject whenever God entered the discussion. One of these days, Anna prayed her sister would understand how faith could give her a center for her scattered life. Charley's husband, Nick, had no interest in organized forms of religion. As a result, Anna's invitations to join her at church had always gone by the wayside.

"Not funny," Anna said. "If you want a place to lay your pretty blonde…and lavender…head tonight, curtail the sarcasm. What I do is my own business. I don't owe anyone any explanations. Not even you. I'm not in the mood."

"Sorry. Really. But, on the other hand, *that's* the spirit! I'm grateful you're not on the lam, or in a medical facility, or a drug rehab…although you're right that the secretly married idea *was* promising. You've worked hard since you were a teenager, Anna. You deserve a break so stay gone however long you want. It's no one else's business. It's not like you skipped out on concert dates. You don't owe anyone a blessed thing."

"Are you trying to convince me or you?"

Charley smirked. "All I'm trying to say is that if you want to hole up in this town and play waitress with a hot ex-firefighter turned construction worker, then that's exactly what you do. That's the trouble with today's world. Everyone wants in everybody else's business. There's no respect."

Anna had to agree with the no respect part, but it struck her as odd to hear those words from her spoiled sister who'd rarely wanted for anything. She was the baby, her dad's pampered princess, but her comment gave Anna hope that Charley's head wasn't completely filled with worldly values.

Now, time for *the talk*.

"Charley, why aren't you home with Nick?" Nick Parker, a trust fund baby belonging to one of Manhattan's richest families, and a rising star in the hip, young art world. They lived in a penthouse overlooking Central Park West he'd inherited from his grandparents although he seemed more the West Village upscale bohemian hippie type. All at the ripe old age of twenty-six.

Anna admired Nick's sculptures—he *did* have talent—but his paintings resembled what a four-year-old child might make by randomly throwing colorful splotches of paint on a canvas. Amazing what some people considered valuable.

Charley pouted. "Nicky made me mad. I needed to get away and think over some things."

"Honey, Nick's…eccentric and moody. I almost think that's inherent in an artist's personality. It says so on his website, and he wears those qualities like a badge of honor." She refused to call her brother-in-law Nicky. Coming from her, it somehow sounded too personal.

"True, but *you're* creative, and you don't act like that."

"Nick and I have completely different personalities and temperaments."

"Okay, you've got me there. Anna, I think Nicky might be cheating on me." At least Charley didn't wail or shake her hands. She seemed reasonably calm considering the loaded statement she'd just made.

"Cheating in the traditional sense?"

"Well, duh. What other kind of cheating *is* there?" Charley crossed her arms over her middle. In her designer jeans and expensive blouse, she sounded more like a petulant teenager than a twenty-five-year-old married woman.

"Do you have proof?" Anna's gaze fell on the insanely large, blinding diamond ring on Charley's finger. "Not that I'm asking for specifics." Anything but that.

"Sort of. Maybe. I don't know."

Charley had the unfortunate tendency to jump to conclusions. In five years of married life, she'd run off three times when she'd had a spat with Nick. With her limitless financial resources, Charley had hunted her down and flown to join her. Anna had been shocked when she'd discovered her in a Brussels, Belgium, hotel suite three years ago. The year after that, it'd been in a concert hall in Dallas. Last year, she'd found Charley in her dressing room in Nashville.

Anna sat on the barstool beside Charley. The food could wait a few more minutes. "Spill it."

For the next five minutes, Anna listened to *My Life According to Charley* until she finished her spiel. "So, you don't know who this woman was that Nick was meeting with?"

"No, but he had his shirt off and was running around barefoot. And he looked guilty when he saw that I was home. I didn't like it. We had words, and I can admit it wasn't my finest hour."

"But he was in the living room," Anna said, measuring her words carefully. "I'm sure there's an explanation. Nick likes getting tattoos, right?"

"Yeah. I kind of like them, too, and at least he doesn't have too many. Yet, anyway."

"Is it feasible that's why Nick had his shirt off? For a client of Nick's magnitude, I can't imagine he'd set foot in a tattoo parlor. The artist would most likely come to him, right?"

"I don't know." Charley lifted her head to the ceiling and closed her eyes.

"If *he* thinks you don't like them for some reason, that might explain why he felt guilty."

"Okay, here's the thing." Charley's eyes flew open. "The girl was way too pretty, too blonde, too tall, too *everything*. I'm talking lingerie model gorgeous. What kind of tattoo artist looks like *that*? My husband is a great looking guy. Women are after him all the time. It's shameless the way they throw themselves on him. At him. Over him."

"I get the basic idea." Anna didn't share that opinion of Nick, but the skinny, high-strung artsy type appealed to a certain type of woman. He did have his wacky charm. He'd always treated Charley well and genuinely seemed to love her, and that's what mattered most.

No, the *most* important thing was that Nick understood Anna would kill him—or have him killed—if he mistreated her little sister.

"Was Rosamond in the house when this woman was there?"

"I'm not sure. Probably." Charley's brow furrowed as if she hadn't thought of that angle.

"Charley, please listen to me." Anna grabbed her hand and made sure she'd captured her eye contact. "You can't run away without giving him a chance to explain. I'm not defending Nick, and I'm not blaming you. All I'm saying is that for a relationship to truly *be* a marriage, you need to stop running and face the man. He's your *husband*. Have an honest conversation."

Charley's gaze bore into hers. "Be a grown-up, you mean."

"Well, yes, in so many words. Honey, believe me, I understand. You have a life most people can only dream of, but you know firsthand it's not all champagne and roses. It also doesn't mean you should go running off whenever something happens just because you *can*."

Her sister wiped away a tear. "Tell me about it. Sometimes I think it'd be easier if Nicky worked some normal nine-to-five job, and I worked at…oh, I don't know, Gap or something."

"Why is that?" Anna tried not to smile as Charley wiped away more tears. "Here." She handed her a paper napkin.

"Thanks." Charley daintily dabbed beneath her eyes. "This will be a test of my new mascara. As much as it costs, it'd better not run."

Anna handed over another napkin and waited. She knew it wouldn't take long.

"Sometimes I think it'd be easier if we had a tiny apartment. A cute little love nest or whatever it's called. We wouldn't have so much room to run away and hide from each other, and we'd bump into each other because of how small it is. But mainly because we'd *want* to…bump into each other." Charley laughed through more tears. "Did that make any sense?"

"Yes, it did." Anna squeezed Charley's hand. "I think the question is why you'd want to hide from each other in the first place."

"Not for anything bad," Charley said. "You know how passionate things are between Nicky and me. That's never been a problem."

Anna cleared her throat. "Well, that's a given."

"Hide isn't the right word. More like we need our space. Because things are always so intense between us, we need some breathing room every now and then."

"We all need that. It's perfectly normal," Anna assured her. "I pray for you and Nick every day. You're at the top of my prayer list along with Dad and Kaye."

"You really pray for us? I know I make fun a lot, but that's really nice." Charley's eyes brimmed with moisture. "What kinds of things do you pray? I mean, if that's not too personal, and you can share it with me. I don't want to get you in trouble with God or anything."

Anna smiled. "You won't get me in trouble with God. That's not how He works. I pray that you and Nick will enjoy a strong and healthy marriage. That you'll grow more in love every day, and that you'll keep discovering new things to appreciate about each other. And that you'll be able to push aside all the little things that annoy you about him so that you can have more confidence in yourself and not be insecure in his love."

Squaring her slender shoulders, Charley gave her an emphatic nod. "You're right. Nicky's a good husband, but I know he worries about whether his latest painting or sculpture is any good, and whether or not anyone will want to buy it. Or if his parents put someone up to buying it. I guess those are the kinds of things we *should* talk about together, right?"

"Yes. It'll draw you closer together," Anna said. "Your husband should also be your *friend*. For what it's worth, I'm glad you came to see me. It's good to know you value my opinion." Not many people asked for her input, and it was gratifying to know someone cared.

"Always, although I know I don't always act grateful."

"You're okay." Anna gave her another quick hug. After retrieving two plates from the overhead cabinets, she set them on the counter.

Charley sniffled, but she'd visibly brightened. "This is nice. There's only so much fancy food a person can eat. Rosamond fixes awesome meals, but every now and then I want to beg Nicky to take me out for a juicy cheeseburger and cheese fries."

"Do you?" If only most people should have such problems. Although spoiled, Charley was an innocent in so many ways that Anna couldn't fault her.

Charley stared blankly at her. "Huh? Do I what?"

"Do you tell Nick what you want? Share with him and tell him what's on your mind? In your heart?"

"No, Miss Psychologist. I'm sure you're talking about more than cheeseburgers. I figured he wouldn't listen, so why bother?"

"You never know. Nick might feel the same way you do. Like I said before, communication is the key. Tell you what. Come and see me at work tomorrow afternoon. I'll have Hector fix you a Darling Deluxe Cheeseburger. Guaranteed, you'll be a huge fan."

"I'll think about it." Charley sounded skeptical.

"I can't ask for more." Anna opened the refrigerator and pulled out the ingredients for their sandwiches. "After we're done eating, I'm going upstairs to make the bed in the spare bedroom. Can you guess what I'm going to ask *you* to do while I'm doing that?"

"Call my husband?"

"Yes. Once you talk to him, you'll sleep better tonight."

"Okay, but if Nicky doesn't answer, I can't make any promises."

"Fair enough." Anna put their plates of food on the island a few minutes later and sat opposite Charley. "Do you mind if I ask the blessing?

Not that she was asking permission to pray, but Charley usually protested the mere suggestion. This way, her sister held the power to say no. Whether reverse psychology or a wise decision, Anna hoped it would work.

Charley shrugged. "No, I don't mind. It's your house. Rental home. Whatever."

Anna hid her smile, pleased her tactic worked.

That was a promising sign. A very *good* one.

Chapter 6

Weston frowned as the front door slammed.

Neil Carter strolled into the apartment kitchen a few seconds later. The guy looked ragged and still wore yesterday's work clothes. Heavy stubble covered his normally clean-shaven face. He was a good looking guy, a few years younger, but his hard partying ways would catch up with him one day if he didn't change his lifestyle.

"Morning." Weston continued adding raisins and almonds to his oatmeal.

"Hey. What's for breakfast?" Neil ran a hand through his messy blond hair and yawned. When he stretched his arms over his head, Weston caught sight of a colorful tattoo above the waistband of his low-slung jeans. Looked like some kind of winged dragon in flight.

"Oatmeal." Weston stirred the contents in his bowl. "Want some?"

Neil shook his head. "Nah. Hate that stuff. What else did you get at the grocery?"

"There's cereal in the cabinet and bread for toast. Eggs, milk, and juice is in the fridge. Peaches, bananas, apples are in the bag here on the counter. Help yourself. I'm going to make a pot of coffee."

"Good deal." Neil opened the cabinet and grabbed a box of cereal. "This works for me. Thanks for not getting all healthy stuff that tastes like cardboard. Kind of like how all work and no play makes us dull boys, you know?"

Interesting analogy. Weston handed him a bowl. "Sometimes the bad helps me appreciate the good even more."

"Whatever." Tearing into the box of cereal, Neil poured out a good amount. "What time did you get in last night?" He glanced over at him. Weston had on his boxers with no shirt, the same as he always wore to bed. Besides that, he despised air conditioning and had opened his window last night.

"Whoa, buddy. You got a woman here now? That brunette from the diner? Man, even in that uniform, she was—"

"I don't bring women home. That's not my style." Weston pushed the START button on the coffeemaker.

Neil shrugged. "Suit yourself. Some of the guys went to a local dive bar after we left the diner. Met up with a group of girls, and I ended up with this chick named…." He shook his head. "Can't remember her name. It'll come to me. We had ourselves a real sweet time. Who knew a town like this would have such hot women?"

His roommate followed up with an explicit detail Weston wished he'd never heard. He didn't know what to say, how to respond, but he didn't care to hear about Neil's nocturnal adventures.

"I think it'd be a good idea to set some house rules while we're rooming here together."

"Rules?" Neil cursed under his breath. "You gonna be like our den mother? That's no fun. I'm cool with the old rubber band on the doorknob trick if one of us has a woman in our room." He pulled out the milk and poured it over his cereal.

"More like your conscience. We're here to work, Neil. Not carouse and bring women home. Tonight the four of us are sitting down and discussing this."

Neil yawned. "Did Tom and Brandon make it home?"

"I don't know. I haven't seen them. Were they with you at the bar?" Weston hated to ask the question, afraid he already knew the answer.

"Yeah. I think Brandon came back, but Tom went home with the gal he met."

Wonderful. All the more reason to set ground rules. After saying a quick prayer for his breakfast, Weston moved over to the table with his bowl of oatmeal.

Neil grabbed a spoon from the drawer and joined him. "Seems to me if it's three against one, you're outnumbered in the morality department, bud."

"That's fine. I'll tell the company I need to be put up somewhere else. What should I tell them when they ask why?" The company wouldn't move him to a separate place, and they both knew it. The other construction crew members also shared apartments in the building, but Weston would come across as a whiny kid if he requested a switch. He'd need to stay put, deal with his circumstances, and pray he could be a good influence.

Neil slurped his cereal. "What's your problem, Wes? We work hard and deserve to have a little fun."

"I'm not denying that." Weston spooned the now overly thick oatmeal into his mouth. "I just know it's possible to have a lot of fun with a woman with*out* sex."

"Wait a second." Neil's eyes widened. "You're not. . ."

"Not what?" Weston growled. It'd been a bad idea to ask *that* question. "Getting to know a woman is a great thing, Neil. God intended sex for marriage, not casual encounters. I'd appreciate it if you didn't elaborate on your…experiences. And please keep your language clean."

Neil laughed. "Relax, man. I saw the way you looked at that waitress last night. She digs you, too. I could tell."

"Her name is Anna. I'd appreciate it if you'd treat her with more respect next time you're in the diner." Yeah, he wasn't a morning person as much as he tried to be, as much as he *should* be, especially considering he worked construction. At least he'd gotten some decent sleep. Sitting across the table from a guy like Neil first thing in the morning apparently brought out his less than admirable qualities.

"Someone's a grouch in the morning. Already protective of her, are you? Define respect."

"I'm sure I don't need to spell it out," Weston said. "But so we're clear—no double entendres, innuendo, lewd staring, that kind of thing."

Neil scoffed. "What planet did you come from? Chicks like it when guys look at them. Makes them feel desirable or whatever. That girl I was with last night? She's got a body that won't quit. If a girl's got it, why shouldn't she flaunt it? I don't know where she works, but she could be the headliner in a strip club if she wanted. I appreciate the way she looks, and she seems to like me. Why bother playing stupid games?"

"Keep in mind a woman who dresses like that wants the attention of *any* man, not just you," Weston said. "Chances are, she *gets* that attention from more than one guy." He couldn't fathom that mentality. Neither was he in the mood to couch his comments in softer, more palatable, or politically correct terms.

Neil wagged his head. "Man, you sound like a preacher. Fine. You respect Waitress Anna and be all proper with her. I'll be the one with a satisfied smile on my face every morning."

"At least I remember her name." Okay, that was a low blow. *Jesus, help me hold my temper around these guys since I have to live with them for now.*

Surprised Neil didn't slam him for that one, Weston knew he needed to keep talking. "I walked Anna home last night. We got to know each other. She's a terrific girl. There's a lot of value in good, old-fashioned conversation." He spooned another bite of oatmeal into his mouth.

"Did you kiss her or is she all prudish and hands-off? Hard to tell with a woman like that. She seemed to have some fire in her. That can be a good thing, you know."

"I didn't kiss her, but yeah, I wanted to." Might as well be honest. "If I *do* kiss her, it'll be better because we waited and didn't jump into anything physical too soon."

"Okay, what's *too soon* by your definition?"

Good question. "During a twenty-minute walk last night, I got to know her better than most girls. Maybe because it wasn't a date, we bypassed all that usual *getting to know you* talk. I don't know, I guess it was more real and personal. Deep, even."

Neil wagged his head. "You are so full of it. I bypass that stuff, too. What's the point? Tell me you at least held the girl's hand." The guy was having fun with him now.

Weston blew out a sigh and sat back in his chair. That last statement had royally backfired. "Anna seems to *get* me, and she appreciates where I'm coming from. More than the last girl I dated back home, that's for sure." He shouldn't diss Madison, but he was still a little sore about that whole situation. He wasn't used to getting dumped, and his ego had been bruised. God was working on him, but he still had a long way to go.

"You date a lot?" Neil slurped more cereal. This guy could stand to learn some table manners.

"Not really," Weston said. "I did when I was younger. I don't date for sport, and I haven't found many women who *do* get me."

"Probably because you've got antiquated standards. See, that's the difference between you and me." Neil rested one elbow on the table and waved his spoon in the air. "I'm guessing you want the whole relationship thing. The mystery and thrill of the hunt. That's not what I'm after. Have fun and make no commitments is my motto. Cuts out a lot of—"

"Answer something for me, Neil. Are you happy?"

Neil studied him for a few seconds as he continued eating. "Do you have parents who actually love each other or something?"

That question took Weston by surprise. "I do, actually. They're great. Celebrated their twenty-fifth wedding anniversary a couple of months ago."

"I'm guessing y'all had a big bash, huh? Invited all the friends and family? Had cake and ice cream, punch, all that stuff." If Weston didn't know better, he'd think Neil sounded almost wistful. His tone wasn't mocking.

The rich aroma of freshly brewed coffee permeated the kitchen. "The ladies at the church planned a surprise party. We managed to pull it off, and a good time was had by all." Rising from his chair, Weston retrieved two cups from an overhead cabinet. After pouring a cup of black coffee for Neil, he placed it on the table. "Cream?"

"Nah, thanks. I take it unpolluted." Neil cradled the ceramic cup. "My old man left my mom when I was six, and I never saw him again. Not once. I don't know if he's alive or dead and buried somewhere. My mom's been married three more times that I know of. She jokes about how she trades in husbands more often than cars. Real funny, huh? The second husband after my dad knocked me around a few times. After he broke a few ribs, I left when I was sixteen and lived with friends for a while. I moved out for good at eighteen, and I've been on my own ever since."

Sixteen? Compassion surged through Weston. At that age, he was discovering girls, avoiding homework, spending time with his buddies, and rebuilding the engine on his first truck.

"I'm sorry, Neil. That's tough. Are you in contact with your mom?"

Neil took a quick sip of his coffee and shrugged. "Sometimes. Mainly holidays."

"Did you finish school?"

"Yeah. Barely, but I made it."

"Good for you."

"Is it? You think so?" Anger sparked in Neil's light gray-blue eyes. "All I'm qualified to do is construction."

"Nothing wrong with construction. Pays decent. Keeps us in shape. You're very good at what you do or you wouldn't have been chosen for this crew."

Neil laughed under his breath. "Chosen? Right. Like we're so special. We're just the ones stupid enough to volunteer."

"That's not true."

Neil stopped eating. "What are you talking about?"

"Brad Colson handpicked us. They set it up so it *looked* like we volunteered, but they specifically asked you to sign up, didn't they?"

"Now that you mention it, yeah, they did." Neil seemed surprised but pleased.

"Colson was born in Darling. His family moved to Atlanta when he was eight. So, this project is special to him for sentimental reasons. He wanted to hire reliable workers to guarantee there'd be no screw-ups or issues."

"What about the materials coming in late? That wasn't a good sign." Blowing on his coffee, Neil's eyes narrowed to slits as he took a tentative sip.

"The delay was beyond anyone's control. Colson knew we'd stay and get it done, and we did."

"You make a good point, but it's not like we're going to be young forever. I don't want to be doing construction when I'm fifty. At least my friend last night appreciated that I keep in shape. Liked my stamina. That woman gave me a workout."

Neil ran his hand over his face and yawned. "You make a decent cup of coffee, man. Much obliged." He lifted out of the chair.

"Welcome. I'd appreciate it if you'd put your empty dishes and cups in the sink when you're done and run water over them." He'd ignore the other comments. Neil didn't know any different. He'd pray for him and try to set a good example. Although crass in certain ways, Neil had demonstrated a modicum of southern manners when it came to a basic *please* and *thank you.*

"Another house rule? Okay, Mom. That one I can handle." Chuckling, Neil did as he asked. "So, what time is this powwow tonight?"

"Whenever we're all here. After last night, I'm hoping we'll all be in residence." He appreciated Neil's question since Tom and Brandon generally followed his lead. If Neil came, they probably would, too.

Neil paused in the doorway. "Don't count on it, although I'm pretty wiped after last night."

Weston frowned. "Not to lecture you, but we work with heavy equipment and can't afford to be tired on the job or we'll get sloppy. That puts all of us in potential danger."

"Don't you think I know that? Look, Wes. We might as well get one thing straight from the start."

"Sure." Weston spooned a last bite of oatmeal into his mouth. "What's that?"

The other man's gaze bore into him. "You're not the boss, and you're not my mother, father, brother, keeper, or whatever. You can express your opinion, but if I bring a girl back here and that bothers you, then you're welcome to find other accommodations for the night. Got it?"

"I heard you. Doesn't mean I have to like it. That's another reason for this meeting tonight. Like it or not, Neil, I'm going to pray for you."

Neil slapped his hand hard against the doorjamb. "And there we go. Man, I *knew* you were a holy roller with all your God talk. Just lay off my case, man. Don't preach to me, and we'll get along fine."

"I didn't say I'd preach." Weston forced calm into his voice. "I said I'd pray."

"Same thing, dude." Neil grumbled under his breath as he made his way down the small, narrow hallway leading to the bedrooms. The walls shook when a door slammed seconds later.

Weston had learned a long time ago to plant seeds where and when the opportunity presented itself. Then he'd pray for God to take over and do the rest. Was that a cop-out? Probably. In the face of Neil's opposition, he'd need to keep trying to plant those seeds however and whenever he could.

Lord, grant me patience. Help me not to be a taskmaster. If he were like-minded with Neil, he could admit he'd resent some guy calling the shots and bossing him around. It was supposed to be *they'll know I'm a Christian by my love*, not acting like a holy roller and leveling criticism and edicts. Finding a balance and that elusive happy medium was definitely a challenge.

He'd observed things Neil had said or done for guys on construction crews, both here and back in Atlanta. The guy wasn't all bad.

Now it was time to get ready for work. As he lathered up in the shower, the lyrics of the first verse of "Take My Life and Let It Be" ran through Weston's mind. He'd sung the hymn as a kid and memorized it as a member of the church worship team in the past year. It amazed him how the words of hymns written that long ago could be so relevant today. Important for *his* life.

Take my life and let it be
Consecrated, Lord, to Thee.
Take my moments and my days,
Let them flow in endless praise.

Stepping out of the shower, Weston toweled off. After wrapping the towel around his waist, he wiped the steam from the mirror. While he trimmed his beard, his mind wandered to a certain waitress at The Darling Diner. He usually took a sandwich and fruit for lunch and energy bars and snacks for the short breaks. Eating out on a regular basis was a luxury he couldn't justify. Not until this job, anyway. He might need to rethink.

You want to see Anna.

"Tell me something I don't know," he murmured.

Finished with his grooming, Weston turned off the bathroom light and headed down the hall.

A brand new day. He looked forward to the possibilities.

Chapter 7

The sound of brakes in the driveway brought a wide smile to Anna's lips. Tossing her book aside—she'd read the same page at least five times in the past ten minutes—she jumped off the couch and hurried to the front window. She almost clapped like a little girl when she spied the delivery truck with the name of a piano company emblazoned on the side. Inside, she was jumping up and down with excitement.

This was so much *better* than Christmas.

Anna opened the door to the driver as he approached the porch. "Good morning!"

The middle-aged man smiled. "Morning to you, too, Miss. I have a sweet baby grand piano on my truck shipped from Atlanta for"—he dipped his head and checked a clipboard—"A. Redmond. Might that be you?"

"Yes, that might be me. I've been waiting for you."

He laughed. "I don't hear that line from a pretty woman near enough. Looks like we've got the right place. Where are we gonna put it, Miss Redmond?"

Anna pointed to the far corner of the living room. "I'd like it positioned in that cleared space facing the seating area." Earlier that morning, she'd moved a few smaller pieces of furniture to accommodate the white baby grand.

The man surveyed the doorway. "Looks wide enough. Some of these older homes don't have an entrance with the width we need. It forces us to be mighty creative."

"That's one of the main reasons I ordered a baby grand."

His brows quirked and then he winked. "Yeah? Is that a fact? Then I'd say you know your stuff, little lady."

"You could say that." These southern gentleman and their flirtatious ways might take some getting used to, not that she was complaining. She'd had the Realtor check the dimensions of the entrances in the event she decided to stick around town for the entire six weeks. After last night, that seemed a given. She wouldn't dwell on the reasons why. Her piano was here!

"Good enough," the man said. "Give us a few minutes, and we'll get it moved inside."

"Thank you, and please take all the time you need." Not that she was trying to tell the man how to do his job, but she understood full well that, while heavy, a piano was an exceedingly delicate instrument.

While she waited, Anna grabbed her cell phone and located the number for the piano tuner who lived a few towns away. She could thank Felicia for that information. Her hands shook with nervous excitement. Within a few minutes, she'd set up the appointment for early the following morning. After signing the delivery order a short time later, Anna sat on the bench.

"Hello there, my friend. It's been too long."

She lovingly fingered the keys, lightly, almost reverently. She'd wait to play—*really* play—until after the tuner could check it over thoroughly.

Charley was still sleeping, and she didn't want to disturb her. Anna had peeked in on her sister on her way downstairs for breakfast a couple of hours ago. Based on the rumpled condition of the bedsheets, her sister must have tossed and turned throughout the night. Whether or not she'd talked to Nick was anyone's guess, but if she had, it must not have gone well.

After taking the time to warm up her fingers, wrists, and shoulders, Anna began to quietly play her warm-up exercises. The keys beneath her fingers felt *right*.

Back where she belonged.

Home.

Although she'd needed a respite from touring, the lure of the keys, the pure *joy* she found in playing, remained as strong as ever. This was her therapy, her passion, her livelihood, her *life*, for the past decade. She hadn't gone this long without playing. The lack of practice wouldn't do any lasting harm, but she'd missed playing the same as she'd miss a best friend.

If you had *a best friend.*

After her mom died, Charley had been her closest friend in the world. Like she'd told Charley, Anna also lived the kind of life most people could only dream of—trips all over the world, glamorous gowns, and all the money she could ever want. Until the past year or so, it'd been more than enough.

Was it wrong to want a change? To wish for something different? She'd disappoint a few people if she left the concert circuit, but it wasn't as though they depended on her for their sole income. Maybe she could cut back on the touring. That could be a workable alternative.

"Concert pianists never go out of style," Felicia had told her recently. "As long as you perform well—which you always do—you'll continue to be in high demand with orchestras all over the world as well as for your solo concerts."

"That's all good and well, Felicia, but *this* time? I play only for Annalise." She continued to play, pushing thoughts of everything else from her mind.

Lost in the moment, Anna closed her eyes, swaying slightly on the piano bench as her fingers flew over the keys. This was also how she worshipped, the way she gave Him praise, offering the Lord her best. In the last few years, the private times when she played *only* for the Savior had grown increasingly precious for her heart.

The Lord. He's *your best friend, Anna.* Why hadn't she understood that before now? God was with her when she performed in a concert hall filled with people. In essence, that's why she played—for an audience of One. *He* sat on the bench beside her each and every time she played the piano. The Lord had blessed her with what talent she possessed, and Anna fully intended to use it for His glory.

The sweet awakening filled her soul and brought a smile to her lips. She should wait until tomorrow, but now that she'd started playing, there was no way she could stop. The piano seemed well-tuned or she would have quit immediately instead of risking harm to the beautiful instrument. She transitioned from an easy piece to a more sophisticated composition, effortlessly fingering the keys, pleased she didn't falter. Time and place faded into the background.

"The piano is your drug of choice, isn't it?"

She started and her eyes fluttered open. How long had she been playing? She'd lost all track of time. Lifting her fingers from the keys, Anna breathed out slowly before turning around.

Charley sat cross-legged on the sofa in tiny sleep shorts and a skimpy tank top. Her morning hair was unkempt and hung halfway in her face. In spite of it, her sister's natural beauty shone through in her clear skin, bright eyes, and smile. Considering the way she was *under*dressed, it was a good thing Charley hadn't wandered into the living room while the men were delivering the piano.

"Good morning." Anna gave her a bright smile. "That's an interesting way to put it, but you're right. Do you want some breakfast?" She wouldn't ask whether Charley had talked with Nick. If she wanted to bring it up, she would.

"In a few minutes." Charley yawned. "I must have been more tired than I thought last night. How did I miss the piano?"

"It was delivered this morning. I hope I didn't wake you. I was going to wait for the tuner to come tomorrow, but then I sat down and started to play, and couldn't help myself."

"Understandable. You must have been going through withdrawal." Charley settled back against the sofa cushions. "Don't let me interrupt. I enjoy hearing you play, and I'm glad you're getting your fix. Please proceed." She moved her hands as though she were the conductor of an orchestra.

She wouldn't question the drug references. That wasn't something Charley had ever struggled with, thank goodness. Needing no further encouragement, Anna resumed playing through her familiar routine.

When she finished, she twisted around on the bench. "That was cathartic. I soooo needed it."

"That's your Tausig ritual, isn't it?"

"Yes. I'm impressed you remember. Carl Tausig started out young, like I did. He was born in Poland in the 1840s, and his dad was a pianist and composer who introduced him to Franz Liszt when he was fourteen. He became a favorite student of Liszt and traveled with him."

Anna stretched and flexed her fingers. "Can you imagine taking piano lessons and studying counterpoint, composition, and orchestration from one of the greats like Liszt?"

"I'm thinking I'm doing well to know Tausig's name. Tell me more."

"You'd probably find it boring, but thanks for listening." Anna started to rise from the piano bench.

"I wouldn't ask if I wasn't interested," Charley protested. "Besides, it means a lot to you, so that makes it important. Sit back down and give me my morning history lesson. I could use some more culture in my life."

"You're married to an artist."

Charley inspected a fingernail. "Different kind of culture. Trust me."

"All right, but cut me off when you've heard enough." Anna lowered back onto the bench. "When he was sixteen, Carl became a friend and follower of Richard Wagner. Ditto Johannes Brahms."

"I'm guessing those were some pretty awesome friends, huh?"

"I'd say so. Liszt, Wagner, and Brahms were a dream trio, the best of their time. Tausig's concerts in Germany and Vienna weren't well-received artistically and failed financially. He stayed out of public view for a few years and married a fellow pianist named Seraphine."

"Ser-a-phine," Charley repeated, drawing it out. "What a beautiful name. It sounds elegant and European. If you ever get married and have a little girl, you should consider naming her that."

Moving on. "Tausig toured in Europe, but the strain of traveling weakened his health. He died from typhoid when he was twenty-nine."

"Well, that's tragic." Charley frowned. "I didn't expect your little history lesson to end like *that*."

"Yes, but think about what a legacy he left! Tausig was considered to be one of Liszt's most talented students. He carried pure virtuosity to heights equaled only by Liszt. Because he died so young, you have to wonder how magnificent Tausig *could* have been if only he'd lived longer."

"Correction. Piano virtuosos like *you* wonder. The rest of us commoners? Not so much."

"That's only a few years older than I am now," Anna mused. "Do you ever wonder where you'll be and what you'll be doing in the future? What kind of legacy you'll leave?"

"Not really," Charley said. "Are you saying you're not happy being Annalise Redmond anymore?"

"No, I'm saying that being away from the tour has given me time to think about my life. I'd still like to tour, but not at the same pace. I've been toying with the idea of staying in one place more. Maybe open a music school and teach students whether or not they can afford it. Sharing what I've learned is something I'd like to do.

I've earned more money than I'll ever need in a lifetime, and I'd like to give back. Invest in the future. That kind of thing."

"I think you could do it," Charley said. "You have the patience of a saint with kids, I know that much. At least the times I've seen you interact with them." Tilting her head, she gave Anna a knowing grin. "You should find a nice guy, settle down, and give birth to a few little piano virtuosos of your own. Now *there's* an idea!"

Without answering, Anna turned on the bench and studied the piano keys.

"What are you thinking about now?" Charley said when the silence grew long. "You're not mad at me for that suggestion, are you?"

"No. I'm thinking about Tausig. When he played, he'd sit motionless at the keyboard."

"Okay, that's random. Why are you thinking about that now?"

"I've been thinking about technique. It's not really something that can be taught because it's individualized for each student. For example, Liszt used flamboyant gestures but Tausig hated what he called 'the spectacle of it all.' His fingers worked miracles on the keyboard without mistakes, and I've heard the only sign of tension or stress was a slight tightening in one corner of his mouth. I can't fathom how anyone could be so expressionless while playing the piano."

"Like this?" Charley twisted her mouth in a comical way and pretended to play a keyboard.

"Maybe," Anna said, laughing. "In some countries, students go through practice drills for five *years* before they're ever allowed to play, believe it or not. I would *hate* that. One of the major problems with that method is that students learn to play accurately and quickly, but they lack any feeling and emotion. If there's no emotion in the musician, it's flat and boring, and no reason for the listener to be invested."

"I see what you mean. For the record, Anna, I've never seen you make flamboyant gestures *or* twist your mouth weird. You're like a totally normal concert pianist, but you know what I love most?"

Anna's brows lifted. This should be enlightening. "What's that?"

"When you get going and you're really into your music, it's like you can *see* the joy you feel in playing. First, you get this little smile that tugs on the corners of your mouth." Charley demonstrated again. "Then as you keep playing, the full smile emerges and you become absolutely…radiant."

"I do?"

"You do." Charley smiled. "It's a beautiful thing to see. I think that's one reason you're so popular. Your fans love to watch your facial expressions on the big screen. Hey, maybe that's why Tausig's concerts failed. He was b-o-r-i-n-g," she said. "At least he found Seraphine."

"You might be onto something there," Anna said. "Thanks for sharing your perspective. I had no idea, and I do have a few quirks no one ever sees, you know. I've just learned to mask them well."

"Like what?" Charley propped her feet on the sofa and clasped her hands around her knees. "This should be fun. Do tell."

"The first one's not a quirk but more of a tradition. I whisper a quiet prayer and ask the Lord to help me give the best concert I can. I pray that if someone in the audience is hurting or in need of prayer, they'll be enveloped in His peace. Then, toward the end of my solo concerts, I play a hymn. I have a rotation of a few favorites, but I think that tradition is as much for me as for the audience."

"I find it admirable that you follow your convictions, and it's cool that Felicia and the tour people let you do it," Charley observed. "Now, I want to hear more about your quirks."

Anna laughed. "If this ever gets out, I will hunt *you* down. Remember the quilt Grandma Redmond made for me when I was a baby?"

"Well, sure, if you're talking about that ancient tattered quilt you keep tucked in the corner of your lingerie drawer."

"How do you know about *that*?"

"I'll never tell. Sisters know stuff, okay? Go on."

Anna couldn't believe she was admitting such a thing. And not that she had anything to hide in terms of lingerie, but still. . . "I have a little square from that quilt that I always carry onstage with me."

"You mean like a good luck charm?"

"Sort of, but I don't call it that. More like a reminder of Grandma's faith in me. Having it with me gives me comfort and helps calm my nerves."

"Where do you carry it? Do you stuff it down in your bra?"

Charley's question made her smile. "It's small, so I curl it in my hand when I walk onstage, and then I put it out of sight on the far side of the piano. *I* know it's there but no one else can see it."

"You're not channeling Grandma or something with that quilt piece, are you?"

Where had *that* come from? Anna prayed Charley wasn't getting into anything New Age.

"Not at all. Grandma was such an encourager for me early on, and I'm pretty sure she helped Mom financially while I was at Juilliard." Anna ran one hand over her hair and glanced out the front window. "Having part of that quilt with me helps me feel like Grandma's there with me. Mom, too, in a way."

Charley chewed on a fingernail and studied her. "I'm not sure if that's incredibly sweet or just really weird." Her smile faded. "I didn't know you still got nervous before a performance. Every time I've seen you in concert, you're in total control. They call you unflappable, you know."

She *didn't* know that. "Once I start playing, by the end of the first piece, my confidence kicks in, and it's me and the piano. Like two old friends getting together."

"That's a great analogy. At least you have a set program to follow. With painting, it's a matter of Nicky giving his imagination wings to fly and take him wherever." Charley waved one hand in the air like a bird.

"I love to do that, too, only not during a concert. My sponsors wouldn't appreciate it."

Charley appeared thoughtful. "Have you done any more composing lately?"

"A little. I might work on some pieces while I'm here in Georgia." Slapping her hands on her knees, Anna rose from the bench. "Right now, I need some coffee. How about you? Care to join me? I can whip up an omelet for you."

"I never turn down coffee, and I appreciate your efforts to make sure I eat." Charley's eyes were moist when they met hers. "What time do you have to work at the diner today?" She half-laughed and crossed her eyes. "I can't believe that sentence just came out of my mouth."

"Two o'clock." Anna's gaze traveled to the front window. Streams of sunlight filtered through the sheer curtains, bathing her in the warmth and optimism of a new day.

Might be another good day to walk to work. Right past the new bank building.

Chapter 8

Closing the front door of the first floor apartment, Weston headed out into the sunshine. In the city, he opted to walk to work if he could, depending on the location and what gear he needed.

An image of Roswell, a homeless man he'd passed every morning on the last construction project, popped into his mind. Roswell, named for the Georgian city, was in his mid-fifties and Weston often found him camped out on a downtown corner. He'd adopted the routine of dropping off a breakfast sandwich and bottled juice for Roswell most mornings.

In the last week before he'd come to Darling, Roswell hadn't been in his usual spot. Made Weston worry about the guy, but he'd learned to accept the transient nature of the homeless. They all had a story to tell, a life worth respecting. No one purposely *chose* to live in those circumstances.

Lord, bless Roswell. Keep him in your care today and always.

A boy about nine or ten zoomed by on a bike. Weston jumped after the youngster almost clipped him.

"Hey, be careful!" Weston shook his head. The bike wobbled back and forth before the kid wiped out, flying onto the grass. His bike fell to the sidewalk, undamaged at first glance.

At least he hadn't flipped over the handlebars like Weston had done when he was eight and broke his right hand. That'd been the first of many broken bones in the past twenty years. Hopefully, there'd be no more. The older he got, the longer it took for his body to heal.

"Owza yowza!" The boy pulled himself up to a sitting position on the grass.

"Whoa there, buddy. You okay?" Weston hurried to him and set his gear on the ground. He glanced at the child's right knee. "Looks like you've got yourself a nasty scrape there."

"Yeah. Don't tell my mama, okay?" Rocking back and forth, the curly-haired blond boy clutched his skinned knee. If he were in the city, this kid would probably have said something more profane. Not that kids in small towns didn't know those words, but they weren't as prone to using them. The old *wash out the mouth with soap* routine had worked the first time Weston's mother heard *him* say a curse word. He'd been thirteen at the time. Cured him real fast.

"Not a problem. I don't know your mama."

"Everybody knows her. Candee at the diner?"

Weston grinned. "Then you'd be right. I met your mama last night. I have a first aid kit in my backpack. I'll clean up that scrape and put some antibiotic cream on it. I have Band-Aids made just for knees, too. Is that okay with you?"

"I guess so." This was Candee's boy, so he should be safe treating him. Since he no longer wore a firefighter uniform, he needed to be careful in offering his services. People were way too sue happy these days.

Weston crouched on the sidewalk beside him. Unzipping his backpack, he pulled out the first aid kit and fished out what he needed.

"I'm Weston. What's your name?" he said, partially to distract the boy.

"Connor."

"How old are you Connor?" Using his teeth, Weston ripped open the packet with the antiseptic wipe and gingerly began to clean the kid's knee. Thankfully, it only bled a little and was merely a surface wound, not as bad as it initially appeared.

"Ten." Connor flinched slightly as he watched Weston's ministrations. "You look like you know what you're doin'."

"Yeah, well, I've treated a lot of scrapes."

"Are you a doctor?" Connor squirmed a bit.

"Nope. Sit still a minute more for me so I can finish cleaning your knee. Your mama mentioned there are four kids in your family."

"I've got one brother, Alex, and two sisters. I'm the second oldest. My brother calls me a runt."

"Nothing wrong with being a runt. Builds character and makes you stronger." Weston finished cleaning the wound and then applied the antibiotic cream. "There you go. Let me put that Band-Aid on and then you're all set. What are your sisters' names?"

"Taylor's a snit and thinks she can boss me around even though she's only seven. Peyton's my baby sister. She's three and a pistol.

That's what Mama calls her. Now, *she's* kind of cute, but Peytie plays with my action figures instead of playing with her dolls and girl stuff." Connor wagged his head. "It's enough to drive a man crazy."

Weston chuckled. "Sounds like a fun family. You seemed a little unsteady on your bike there, Connor. Have you tested the pressure in those tires lately?"

Connor's face scrunched. "I don't know what that means."

"You should check how much air is in the tires on your bike. That could be the reason you wiped out."

"Nah. My daddy checks those things. I wiped out 'cause I wasn't payin' attention."

"Well, I can respect an honest man who admits his faults. That's an admirable trait."

"You talk kinda funny with the things you say, Mr. Weston. My daddy does, too, sometimes."

"I know God gave you a terrific mother. I hope I'll get to meet your dad while I'm here in town." Weston angled his head to the construction site within view. "I'm working with the crew that's building the new bank."

"Yeah? Cool. How many stories is it gonna be?"

"Two."

Connor frowned. "I was kinda hopin' for more. We need a skyscraper. Like four stories."

Weston restrained his grin. "You know, it's fun to go into the city to see those tall buildings, and some of them have more than thirty floors. But I think Darling is special the way it is. Think about it. If you had a thirty-story building here in town, it'd look kind of weird. Don't you think?"

The kid shrugged. "Maybe. Have you built any skyscrapers?"

"I have, as a matter of fact. In downtown Atlanta."

"Wow, that's awesome. Must feel good, huh? I mean, you can show people a building and say, 'I made that.'"

"I had a lot of help, but you're right. It's a feeling of accomplishment. That building will be there a whole lot longer than I am."

"Why? You dyin'?"

Weston rose to a standing position. "Not anytime soon, I hope. It's all about leaving a legacy." He hadn't looked at working construction from that perspective before. Not that he was glad

Connor wiped out on his bike, but the fresh outlook was a good one. Helped him go to work with renewed purpose. He offered his hand to the boy.

On his feet again, Connor swung his knee back and forth, testing it. "Is it hard to learn how to build things, Mr. Weston?"

"Not really, especially if you enjoy it. Do you like puzzles? Like to make things with your hands?"

Connor nodded. "Yes, sir. And I'm good at math."

"Good. Those are important skills since you need to know how to measure things or the building might turn out lopsided." He used his hands to demonstrate, making Connor laugh.

"What else?"

"Well, you should be strong and coordinated. Eat well and exercise. Keep yourself in good physical shape. Being willing to listen and follow rules is another one."

"Watch where I'm going so I don't fall off my bike, right? And learn how to check the pressure in the tires."

"Right." Cute kid. "Accurate vision is also important, so get your eyes tested regularly. If your dad or someone you know uses tools, maybe they can show you how. Don't ever use power tools without a grown-up around, though. Another thing—construction sites always need skilled laborers, too."

"Like what?"

"Concrete finishers, carpenters, plumbers, electricians, welders, machine operators, millwrights, and HVAC technicians, to name a few. The possibilities are endless, kiddo. You want to know one of the best things of all?"

"What's that?"

"There'll always be a need for people who can build skyscrapers. And banks in small towns. All kinds of buildings. If that's what you want to do, ask God to help you, and He will."

"Sounds good. I'd better get moving or Mama's gonna be mad." Connor retrieved his bike and swung one leg over the seat. "Thanks, Mr. Weston. See ya around."

"Glad I could help. Be safe, Connor."

"Yep!" He waved over one shoulder as he took off on his bike. He liked the way Connor called him Mr. Weston. Southern manners that showed respect. Candee and Jesse were teaching him well.

Stuffing the first aid kit into his backpack, Weston slung it over his shoulder and started off again. His five-minute walk had taken fifteen minutes. Good thing he'd started out early. The project foreman, Travis Phelps, expected him to be on time or he'd face suspension. He needed this job and couldn't afford to lose it. Neither could he bypass a kid who needed help.

The children he'd lost on his watch during his firefighting days had been the hardest losses. Kids—the youngest and totally defenseless victims—he'd pulled out of burning cars or houses, some alive, some not. Why should innocent kids pay the ultimate cost? They rested in the arms of Jesus eternally, and it was that assurance that gave him comfort.

Then there'd been the two poor teenage boys he'd hauled out of the car submerged in a creek swollen by raging floodwaters…too late. Their blood alcohol levels were off the charts. They'd known better and paid for their stupidity with their lives. One mistake. That's all it took. He could only pray they'd known Jesus. Remembering that incident always socked him hard in the gut, twisting his insides every time.

The sun was already blinding. He wished he'd been scheduled to start earlier in the morning when it was still a decent temperature. He pushed his bangs off his forehead and squinted in the sunlight. A haircut seemed in order and some sunglasses would be good since he'd left his back home.

A few minutes later, as he shrugged into his safety vest, and then put on his protective helmet, Weston cast a glance at the sidewalk. Anna's shift was scheduled to begin at two o'clock. He'd try to watch for her.

Positioning the safety glasses, he called out greetings to the other members of the crew and headed to the south wall. Time to work.

Chapter 9

Charley followed Anna into the kitchen. "That's a secretive grin you're wearing this morning. It reminds me of the Mona Lisa. Nicky says da Vinci's paintings reflect his subject's inner turmoil. If you ask me, Mona definitely had a man on her mind. It's in her eyes and the set of her mouth."

"I'll take your word for it."

"You're thinking about your handsome new friend, aren't you?"

"Charley, why does everything with you always have to be about a man?"

"It doesn't." She winked. "Only most of the time."

Anna pulled out the drawer with coffee selections for the Keurig. "I can offer you Frosted Oatmeal Cookie, Cinnamon Churro, Bananas Foster Flambé, or Salted Caramel. What sounds good?"

"The caramel one," Charley said. "They all sound rich, but that sounds like the lesser evil."

"I'll make us a full pot."

"Sounds good. Anna, how long has it been since you've been on a real date? I'm not talking about meeting up with a guy for coffee or lunch. I'm talking about a full-blown date where you dress in a sexy dress and stilettos. Show a little skin. The guy picks you up and takes you to dinner at an elegant restaurant and then dancing. Later that night, on your doorstep, he softly brushes his lips over that sensual, erogenous zone just below your earlobe and whispers something romantic in your ear. . ."

"I get the idea." Had her sister been reading romance novels, too? Sounded like she could *write* one. The kitchen felt a little warm.

"And then he pulls you close and kisses you like he means it."

"Like he *means* it?" Maybe she shouldn't ask. Her gaze skimmed the kitchen counter. What could she use to fan herself?

"Yes, like he's ravenous for you and, if he can stop kissing you long enough, he's going to scoop you into his arms in the manner of Rhett Butler and carry you—"

"Into the sunset?"

Charley grinned. "Fine. Here's the PG-rated version just for you, Anna. The man gives you the kind of kiss that clues you in that he's going to call you again, and when he does, you'd better pick up your phone." She lifted her slender shoulders. "Sisters look out for each other. You make sure I eat, so I need to see that you date at least once a decade."

"Like it's the same thing. *Not.*" Opening the refrigerator door, Anna pulled out the milk and set it on the counter. "Okay. If you must know, it was June 28th."

"That's not so bad."

"Three years ago."

Charley's eyes widened. "No way! Three *years?* I knew it'd been a while, but I was really hoping you'd had a secret rendezvous somewhere in the past year. Not even a romp on the beach with a cute cabana boy in St. John? Talk about tragic. Anna, you are seriously man-deprived. More than I thought."

"Look, I know it's sad that I know the exact date of my last evening out with a man, and it was nothing like that romantic fantasy you just described."

A *vast* understatement.

She'd gone to dinner with a well-known, handsome, slightly older maestro of an international orchestra. It'd been a lovely evening until he'd taken her back to his country manor and pounced on her like a predator. She'd managed to knee him strategically and escaped, clothes torn, no shoes, running down a gravel road. . . The whole experience had been surreal, like something in a movie.

The ugly aftermath involved attorneys and a confidentiality agreement Felicia convinced her to sign where Anna agreed to never make the incident public. She couldn't breathe a word to anyone, not even a pet, if she'd had one. She still had the occasional nightmare over signing that agreement. She'd been sworn to silence, and that episode was the one thing she'd never told anyone, not even Charley.

Dating pretty much lost its appeal after that.

"Think about it," Anna said. "When do I have time to meet a man much less go on a *real* date? And not that I'd ever indulge in reckless behavior with a man. It's a crazy world out there and there are…diseases and stuff."

She knew she'd been hanging around Charley when she ended a sentence with *and stuff.*

"I'm not buying that reasoning," Charley said. "You play multiple dates, no pun intended, in the same city. Long enough to develop a connection with a man and go out with him. If things seem promising, you have the means to fly and join him during your free weekends. Pardon the cliché, but where there's a will, there's a way. Besides, a woman needs a man in order to—"

"To feel desirable? To feel worthy? I'm not buying into *that* reasoning. That's so bogus, Charley. I have a great career, a terrific place in New York to lay my head at night—*alone*—and people who manage my tours, publicity, and finances. All I have to do is show up for concerts, do something I love, wear beautiful gowns, and get paid an insane amount of money to do it."

"I was going to say you need a good man who makes you laugh and puts a sparkle in your eye because you like being around him and he's your friend," Charley said. "In spite of everything, Nicky's my *friend.* As far as your career, you've come by that honestly because you're *that* good, Anna. Don't ever underestimate your talent."

"I thank God every day for the privilege of doing what I love, and I'm thankful others appreciate it. If I played only for my own enjoyment, or for charity galas, I'd still love it."

Anna darted a glance at her sister. "I think *you've* got love and romance on the brain because you miss Nick."

"Of course, I do." Charley avoided her gaze. "But girl talk with you is something else I miss. You've been touring so much, and then when you have a break and I thought we could catch up, what did you do at the first opportunity? You took off on me!"

"I didn't come here to get away from you, so please don't take it personally." After starting the Keurig, Anna pulled out a bag of cinnamon raisin bread. "Want a couple of slices with low fat cream cheese?"

"Good to know you've got something low fat. Got any bagels?"

"Why, yes, I do. Imagine that, especially since I didn't know you were coming."

"It's like you knew. Or wait, maybe *God* told you?" Charley caught the bag of bagels Anna tossed at her. "Silverware's in this drawer, right?" She pulled open the correct drawer. "Bingo! On the first try. Wow, I am good."

"You must have been paying more attention than I thought last night. The way I see it, what talent I have is on loan from God." She placed the raisin bread in the toaster.

"There you go again. Why is it always *God this* and *God that* with you these days?"

"Because sometimes I feel He's all I have. But that's more than enough. I mean *He's* enough." Anna forced down the sudden lump in her throat. "He has to be."

"Now you sound like a nun. That's kind of scary." Charley dropped the separated halves of her bagel in the microwave. "Just tell me this, Anna. Do you want to get married? Like ever?"

"Of course, I do. But it has to be the right man." She'd add *of God's time and choosing* but didn't want to risk Charley accusing her of forcing more God talk down her throat twice in one conversation.

"And when will *that* be, big sister?" Leaning against the counter, Charley crossed her arms. "When you're old and your reproductive organs are dried up like prunes? By that time, they might be more like raisins."

"You're one to talk about reproducing," Anna said. "When are you and Nick going to give me some kiddos to spoil? Aunt Annalise has a lot of love to give, and I'll give them indulgent gifts bordering on the obscenely expensive. That'd be another enticement for me to stop touring so much. I'd be a great babysitter and hands-on wiper of spit, snot, and…you know."

The microwave dinged, and Anna handed Charley a plate for her bagel. The sweet, tempting aroma of cinnamon filled the kitchen, mingling with the scent of the rich coffee.

"Here's the thing, sis." Charley sat on a barstool at the island and pried open the container of cream cheese. "Nicky's dad's side of the family has some strange genetic abnormality."

After peeling back the cellophane wrapping, she licked her fingers. "Nicky got tested last week. Until we get the results, we don't want to get pregnant. That wouldn't be wise."

"I'm sorry, sweetie. I had no idea." Anna plopped her toasted raisin bread on a plate and set it on the island. After pouring two mugs of coffee, she sat opposite Charley.

"On the other hand, I'm happy to know you'd like to start a family. I'm sure you have a top doctor in New York, right?"

Charley nodded, her eyes brimming with tears.

Anna reached for her hand. "I didn't mean to make you cry, honey. I'm sorry."

"You didn't. It's just that I'm worried about the results of the test. Nicky didn't want me to tell anyone, not even you, but he should have known better. You're my best friend, and it feels really *good* to finally share this with someone. It's some weird chromosome or gene with a name so long I can't even remember it, much less pronounce it."

Charley wiped away her tears with the back of her hand. "You can't know how much I *hate* it that some abnormality or whatever is making the decision for us as to when to have a child, or whether or not we *can*. How is that fair? Could you ask God for me?"

"No, it's not fair, but life isn't always fair." Anna was secretly pleased Charley was the one to bring up God this time. "You learn to meet the challenges head-on and go from there. God's *got* this, Charley. He always does, and all He asks is that you trust Him."

"That might work for you, but this is me." Charley poked a finger on her chest. "You've got more confidence than I do. You're always so together and sure of yourself. What if that test reveals something really bad?"

Anna's heart jumped when Charley's lower lip trembled. Professionally, she was confident, yes. Her personal life wasn't nearly as settled as her sister seemed to believe.

"Then you adopt or explore other options so you can make an informed decision. Couples deal with infertility and childbearing issues every day. I learned a long time ago you can't worry about things that haven't happened yet or may *never* happen. If you do, you'll live in fear and tear yourself up with the stress. When do you expect the results from the test?"

"Next week sometime."

"Charley, I might seem like I have it all together professionally, but I barely *have* a personal life. I have fears, doubts, and insecurities. Everyone does because *no* one has all the answers. So, we do the best we can to get through each day and hope we're making some kind of difference. That our life *matters*."

Charley wiped away more tears. "Your life matters to me."

Anna squeezed her hand. "I love you, too. Tell you what. I'm going to pray for you now."

"Again? Right this second?" Charley sniffled. Her big hazel eyes tugged on Anna's heart.

"Why not? You wanted me to ask God about it, and prayer's the best way to counteract worry."

"I guess that'd be okay." Charley bowed her head and Anna did the same.

A very good start to the day.

Another breakthrough, really.

Chapter 10

"Annalise, love!"

Anna jerked her head toward the diner entrance. "Nick," she breathed.

Feet planted apart, arms spread wide, her brother-in-law wore his customary, lopsided, goofy grin. Hopefully, not many noticed his use of her legal first name, but the chances of Nick *not* drawing attention were slim. And what was with the British accent? The man had been born in Manhattan with the proverbial silver spoon in his mouth. He was nothing if not dramatic. Considering the man was insanely wealthy, he'd always been friendly and surprisingly unpretentious.

She should have known he'd make an appearance. Nick had a difficult time coping whenever Charley was away from home and reminded Anna of a faithful puppy dog. Since he'd met her, Nick had never been far from her sister's side.

She's only been gone one night, Nick. Another part of her turned to mush to think he'd come to claim his wife. That kind of loyalty was inspiring. Not too shabby in the romance department, either. Score one for Nick.

While she was relieved to see him, Anna also dreaded his presence in town. Charley could be high maintenance on her own. Combined with Nick, they'd be a handful if they stayed in her house for more than a day. Would Nick sweep his wife into his arms and spirit her back to New York? A girl could hope.

Sprinting across the diner, Nick gathered her close in an enthusiastic hug. He whirled her around and lifted her off the floor. "How are you, lovely?" He lowered her to the floor. After planting a noisy kiss on her cheek, he eyed her up and down.

"What's with this ugly as sin frock you're wearing? In whose world is this fashionable?" When he touched her apron and then her hairnet, she swatted his hand. At the same time, she tried not to laugh. Like with Charley, Anna couldn't stay mad at Nick. He could be annoyingly buoyant, but that wasn't such a bad quality.

"I'm working here." She kept her voice low, hoping he'd take the hint and follow suit. "I could ask the same thing about what you're wearing." Nick's tight black jeans, white T-shirt, and black leather jacket were so…well, she supposed his clothing might be hip in *his* world. Nick's medium length dark hair had too much product, and his artfully arranged bangs hung low on his forehead. No doubt he thought it gave him an edgy, brooding look.

Hooking her arm through Nick's, Anna guided him to the front counter, ignoring the stares of others around them. "Have a seat, please. What's with the accent?"

"You know me, love. Trying it out for a spell." He straddled a counter seat. "Is it working on you?" His gaze fell on her nametag— "Anna." Good grief. He'd pronounced it *Awna*. Silly man.

"No, but it's not supposed to work on *me*. Have you ever stopped to think that people from Britain might be offended?"

"On the contrary, love. Coming from me, it's the highest form of compliment."

Charley loved an authentic Brit accent. Could that be what prompted Nick's latest assumed affectation? If so, it was rather sweet in a very strange way.

"Are you hungry, Nick? Thirsty?"

"What's the best thing you can offer?" Nick gave her his trademark cheeky grin. "On the menu, that is?"

Anna shook her head. "Don't be fresh. Practice your flirting skills on Charley. And best or most expensive? There's a difference."

Nick clutched his T-shirt, bunching it in his hand. "You wound me. Is that a slam on my artistic ability?"

"Not at all. Now you're acting paranoid. I'm only talking about food."

"Speaking of which, what *is* that smell?" Nick's nose wrinkled as he sniffed. "It's not altogether bad, but it's…intriguing."

"That would be the phenomenon known as fried food. Welcome to Georgia." Anna had noticed the same thing when she'd started working in the diner. In no time flat, she'd grown accustomed to it and appreciated the oddly comforting combination of fried food, sizzling beef, and baked goods, all of which teased her senses and tempted her taste buds.

Her brother-in-law's raspy chuckle was genuine. "My stomach rumbled, so it can't be all bad now, can it? All righty then. Let me take a quick gander at the offerings."

Stretching across the counter, Nick grabbed a laminated menu and opened it. "Isn't this quaint?" He fingered the cleft in his chin as he scrutinized it.

Anna mock gasped. "Nick Parker, are you wearing eyeliner?" She slid one hand to her hip. "Don't tell me you had a permanent eyeliner procedure done." He wore small silver studs in both ears. "What's next? Lipstick?"

"No worries, love. Nothing like that. Just trying it out. Too much? Too feminine?"

"Well, it's. . .not masculine. You're a married man. An artist and sculptor, not a rock star like. . .Mick Jagger. Is *that* why you're speaking like a Brit?"

"No reason I can't look like one, eh? Relax. I'm just having a little fun." Nick laughed and shrugged out of his black leather jacket to reveal a tight muscle shirt—not a T-shirt, after all—stretched across his chest, as well as a new cross tattoo on his upper left arm. Considering his church embargo, Nick's cross had nothing to do with Jesus.

After draping his jacket over the back of the seat, he flexed his left bicep. "What do you think? I've had a weight room added to the penthouse. Been lifting nearly a month." He eyed his arm and flexed once more. "I think it's coming along nicely. Charley seems to like it."

"That's what's most important. Good for you." She had to ask. "Nick, why do you have a cross tattoo?"

He glanced at the tattoo. "Why? Don't you like it?"

"I didn't say I didn't like it. I'm just curious."

"I like them is the short answer, love. I suppose you're going to tell me how sporting ink is somehow irreverent or sacrilegious?"

"Not if it's for the right reasons. Since when have I ever beat you over the head with my faith?" Anna lifted her eyes to the ceiling and silently counted when he seemed to be contemplating his answer. Served her right for asking.

"Go ahead, love. I can tell you're dying to share."

Catching Roz's glance, Anna moved behind the counter. "That's the point. *Dying*. The cross has great spiritual significance. For

Christians, it represents Jesus's death on a cross. He didn't *stay* on the cross, Nick. He *rose* from the dead, and it's through His sacrifice that we can have a personal relationship with Him and the assurance we'll spend our eternity in heaven."

"Bravo, my dear sister-in-law." Nick quietly clapped. "You've done your good deed for the day in trying to convert me with your ten-second *find Jesus before you die* speech." Averting his eyes, Nick stared at the menu again. "How about something to drink?"

Anna forced down her overzealousness and gave him a smile. "Sure. What can I get you?"

He beat a rhythm on the counter with both hands. "High-end hydration sounds good. I'll take the fanciest bottled water in the house." His eyes widened. "You *do* have bottled water, do you not?"

The man should be an actor.

"Of course, we do." After reaching into the small refrigerator beneath the counter, she set a cold bottle of water on the counter. "Here you go. Drink up in good health and continued prosperity."

He eyed the bottle. "Good enough, thanks. Speaking of keeping Charlotte in the manner to which she's become accustomed, where might I find my wife?" Although his tone sounded flippant, the dark-eyed gaze Nick leveled on her was intense.

Crossing her arms on the counter, Anna leaned close, fully aware Roz watched. "I was wondering how long it'd take you to ask. She's at the house, but I expect her to show up here any time. I invited her to come in for one of our cheeseburgers. They're fantastic." She checked her watch. Four thirty. "Now it'll be more like an early dinner."

Nick's brows rose. "A cheeseburger? Is that a fact? She didn't balk at the idea of eating beef? That's a shocker. Seems Charlotte has forgotten she's supposed to be vegan this month. Or is it vegetarian?" He waved his hand in a dismissive manner. "I can't keep up with her. We have a revolving door until she finds the one she likes. One month it's vegan, the next it's a microbiotic diet, the next a ketogenic green protein diet. I believe it's lacto-ovo-vegetarian next month. Not sure I have that one right. It's a rather complicated and confusing word to remember."

"The life you two do lead. I wasn't aware she was following any diets. I have to ask, what does lacto-ovo-vegetarian mean?"

"I believe the mantra for a person of that persuasion is that if you have to *kill* an animal to get food, then you don't eat it." He raised both hands. "Simple enough, right?"

"As long as it's not dangerous." Nick knew as well as she did that Charley had suffered from an eating disorder in her early teenage years. "Would you like to try a cheeseburger or are you observing no-meat rules? The diner's also known for its southern fried chicken and biscuits."

"I'm sure. When in the South and all that. If it's allowed, I'll stay 'parkered' here and await Charlotte's arrival. We'll order something together and share our food. Don't worry, love. I'll tip you extremely well."

"You'd better." Ah, Nick, and his silly *parkered* joke as a play on his last name.

"You actually have a home here? Is this little Georgia town going to become your personal retreat?"

"Long story, but I needed a break. The house is a furnished rental with the new addition of a baby grand delivered this morning."

"I'm proud of you, love. Take a breather from the touring. Doesn't explain"—he waved a hand down the length of her—"*this*, but I see you're embracing the concept of variety being the spice of life. That can only be a good thing."

"You should know. I figured it was time to experience *real* life for a change."

"Perhaps your knight in a shiny red truck will come along and whisk you into your happily ever after. Not that you need a man, but it'd put a sparkle in those lovely brown orbs of yours."

Orbs? Anna rolled her eyes. "No wonder you and my sister get along so well."

Twisting on the counter seat, Nick surveyed the diner. "This place could use an update, but it's not bad. It has a certain primitive charm." Twisting the cap off his water bottle, he took a long draw and smiled with satisfaction. "Splendid. Perfectly chilled."

One of her customers signaled to her. "I'll be right back. Try to be good." Anna prayed Roz hadn't heard Nick's use of the word *primitive.*

"Go right ahead. I'll be sitting here observing the mind-boggling sight of the world-renowned Annalise—"

"Shh," she hissed. Not that it really mattered, but why complicate things?

A few minutes later, Anna headed out of the kitchen with the food for Table 7 occupied by a young couple and their three lively kids—identical twin girls in high chairs who made a sport of flinging their pacifiers to the floor, and a boy about five who ran his toy fire truck back and forth on the tabletop and made alternating *vroom vroom* and screeching noises.

As a safety precaution, Anna glanced at the floor around their table. No random toys had fallen to the floor. Whew. The way looked clear, always a good thing.

"Here we go." She rested the tray on the side of the table and carefully handed the plates to the mom and dad.

"Karli, stop that!" Anna glanced down to see one of the dark-haired twins smearing her hand—she didn't want to speculate with *what*—on the side of her uniform skirt.

"I'm sorry, Anna."

"No problem, Jill," she assured the harried looking mother. "I'm sure I'll become a laundry expert in no time flat." No kidding. She'd not only learned how to separate loads and treat stains, but she'd used an iron for the first time. Hated ironing, but at least now she knew how to *do* it.

After taking care of several more customers, Anna made her way back to Nick. Charley still hadn't made an appearance, not that she was surprised since her sister was almost always late.

"What?" she said when Nick stared at her with obvious amusement.

"You're quite good at this. I am impressed."

Anna smiled. "Stick around. I'm bound to mess up or spill something any moment now. Did you talk to Charley today?"

"I tried." Nick's shoulders slumped a notch as a deep frown creased his brow. "She's currently *not taking calls*. I suspect your sister adopted that unfortunate phrase from me. When we spoke last night, Charlotte genuinely seemed to miss me."

Nick's eyes met hers. "I miss her."

"I know you do, Nick. I'm sure she'll be around soon. I take it she doesn't know you were planning on coming to Georgia?"

Of course, Charley wouldn't know. Like his wife, Nick preferred the element of surprise. These two did what they wanted and operated on whims. If they ever *did* have a child, that would change their lifestyle, but wasn't that the case for most couples?

"No, she's not aware." Nick pocketed his cell phone.

"How did you even know to come to Darling, Georgia?"

"Charlotte made sure to leave a few clues. She knows I pay attention and would figure it out. Plus her phone location told me." He released a sigh. "So, tell me, did she happen to share what grievous sin I've apparently committed this time?"

Anna collected a few dishes in the sink to carry into the kitchen. "Honestly, Nick, I believe it's only a minor disconnect, but it's not my place to say. This is something Charley should discuss with you privately. I encouraged her to communicate and share her feelings instead of running away. That's not healthy for your marriage."

"I owe you a debt of gratitude. You are a wise woman, Annali—"

"Anna?"

"That's my boss," she said in a low voice. "Pretend to study the menu or something."

"Will do, love. My, that one looks rather scary, doesn't she? Reminds me of a bouncer at our favorite club in SoHo. Wouldn't want to come across her in a dark alley." Opening the menu, Nick hid behind it.

"She's all bark. I can handle her."

"This I'd like to see."

"Stay," Anna commanded when he started to rise from the counter seat with a wicked grin.

Anna followed Roz into the kitchen, wishing she felt as confident as she sounded.

Chapter 11

The older woman crossed her arms. Odd how Roz's biceps were noticeably larger than Nick's. "I should have fired you for any number of things since you first walked into my diner."

Anna lifted her chin. "I'm sorry I haven't been the best waitress, Roz, but I *am* trying my best." What sin had she committed now? The worst that could happen was that she'd be fired. It shouldn't matter if she lost this job, but somehow she *did* care.

"Is your name really Anna?"

"What?" She shook her head. "Yes, it's Anna."

"Then why did that strange skinny foreign man say it was Annali—something? And he called you renowned. I'm not as smart as you. What's that mean? Are you wanted by the law?"

"It means she's famous."

Both women turned as Mike crossed the room, his eyes trained on Anna. "I knew you didn't belong here. You've got too much class, and you're way too pretty. I bet you're an actress, aren't you? One of them reality stars or an undercover reporter?"

Stunned, Anna stared at him a second before she burst into laughter. "I assure you I'm not an actress. Not that I've ever tried acting." Well, that wasn't the entire truth. In a way, wasn't she acting now, playing a role, pretending to be someone she wasn't?

"I *am* a performer, but I'm not an actor. Trust me."

"Then who are you and what are you doin' here, girl?"

Anna glanced at red-haired Chef Francie. The woman had barely spoken two words to her since she'd been hired, but she'd dropped her work—no doubt hacking away at something with a machete—to join their little kitchen huddle.

Inhaling a quick breath, Anna knew she had to come clean. "I'm a concert pianist currently on hiatus."

Roz's frown deepened. "And what's *that* mean?" When Anna didn't immediately answer, her boss and Francie both looked at Mike.

"It means she's taking a vacation." That came from Hector as he flipped a burger on the grill. He glanced up at her. "I'm sure it's well-deserved." The sizzling beef permeated the air, making Anna's stomach growl as the gazes of the others ping-ponged between one another and then back to her.

"I've been touring constantly for almost ten years. I needed a break." That probably sounded whiny but she honestly didn't care.

Mike whistled under his breath. Hector shot her a look filled with empathy. Francie shook her head. Where was Candee when she could use a little extra moral support?

The lines of Roz's face softened. "We all need those, honey."

Honey? *Roz* called her honey? Anna thought she might faint. "The guy at the counter is my brother-in-law, Nick Parker. He's an artist in New York, married to my younger sister, Charlotte, who showed up on my doorstep last night. So, there you have it. That's pretty much the short version of my life. Now, may I please get back to my customers?"

"In a minute." Roz touched her arm with enough pressure to prevent Anna from making her escape. "What's your real full name?"

"Annalise Cecile Redmond is my legal name."

"I'll add lyin' to your growin' list of offenses."

Anna twisted her lips. "You're right although I'd prefer to call it the sin of omission for not giving you my full first name and not listing my true occupation. I hope you can understand why I didn't. Everything else is true. So, am I fired?"

"Not yet, but that still doesn't explain why you're in Darling and workin' in my diner."

Not yet? Part of her knew she should quit and save Roz the trouble somewhere down the line. Why put herself through the aggravation, the aching feet, the stressed muscles? But no, she didn't want to give this woman the satisfaction.

I am not *a quitter.* Anna clenched and unclenched her left fist behind her where no one could see. Except for dear Hector, she felt like the subject of an inquisition with three pairs of eyes currently boring into her.

"The truth? I'm not sure I *can* explain it, except that I wanted to get completely away from everyone and everything." Anna's eyes filled with tears, and she blinked hard. She would *not* cry. "For once in my life, I wanted to see what it was like to live a normal life. To *be* normal."

Anna jumped when Francie stretched an arm around her. She slowly breathed out a sigh of relief, lifting a silent prayer of thanks the woman didn't have a knife in her hand.

"Did you go to that world famous school in New York?" Mike watched her intently. "The one that sounds like Julie…something?"

"The Juilliard School. Yes, I did." Then Mom died a few years after she'd finished her studies, leaving her bereft and alone in a strange city. Not that a person could ever expect to be struck down in their late thirties by a brain aneurysm. That's when Felicia assumed guardianship, and Anna had lived in her manager's Manhattan home until she moved into her own apartment at eighteen.

"Juilliard's a school for the best of the best," Mike informed the others. "They only take like the top people who audition. Seems our Anna here's got some real talent."

Anna stifled her smile at the dishwasher's reference to *our* Anna. Mike's words provided a sense of belonging she hadn't experienced in a long time, if ever. That one word made this experience—*all* of it—worth the trip to Georgia.

"Were you one of those child progenies or whatever?" That question came from Francie.

"Prodigy." Mike seemed to have all the answers today.

"Some called me that, yes." Anna couldn't deny the truth. She'd been labeled with that term since she was six and laid her hands on piano keys for the first time.

"Are you from New York?" Francie said.

"I was born in Philadelphia, but I've lived in New York for a long time."

"Well, I reckon I don't know what to say." Roz appeared uncustomarily flustered. "I've got a famous person in my diner, spillin' coffee, squirtin' people with ketchup, trippin' on stuff, and breakin' my dishes. Don't that beat all?"

"I'll be happy to pay you back with interest several times over—"

"Girl, you've already done that. This sure explains some things. I still don't understand why you're here, but you stay as long as you want or until I fire you. Bring in your famous friends."

"You sure you're not hidin' out from a boyfriend?" Francie acted as though she hoped to feast on a tidbit of juicy gossip.

"No boyfriend, so I'm not hiding out from one. I'm sorry to disappoint you."

"That Weston guy has his eye on you," Roz said. "I saw the sparks flyin' between you last night. Don't bother pretendin' they didn't. I thought you two were gonna burn down my diner." How ironic coming from her boss who'd warned her against flirting.

Mike made a sizzling noise which Anna conveniently ignored. Hector flipped another burger. Oh, the irony.

"Weston is a wonderful man, but I have a three-month concert tour starting in six weeks. I haven't met a man yet who's willing to wait, especially since I'm on the road so much. With no end in sight."

Why had she felt the need to say *that*?

"You should cut back on all that travelin' and settle down," Francie said. "You're not gettin' any younger." Interesting coming from a woman who—if rumor held true—had served time and been married four times and counting. If she *had* served time, Anna didn't want to know the charge.

She tried to hide her irritation. Francie knew nothing of her life. None of these people did. So much for trying to keep a secret. Her "little adventure" as Charley called it might be over before it'd begun.

Roz parked both hands on her hips. "Now you're givin' me notice, are you?"

Anna met the other woman's gaze. "When you put it that way, I guess I am. In a few weeks, I need to get back to my life. For now, I'd like to stay and work here if that's okay with you."

"You know it's all right with us." Hector shot a look at Roz. "Isn't that right, boss?"

Roz huffed. "As long as we're straight. I don't give special treatment to progenies. You still get paid the same wages as before. Understood?"

"Of course," Anna said. "I don't want or expect any special treatment during the next five weeks that I'm here." At least she hadn't called her *girl*.

"Right. You want to be *normal*," Mike said. "So, is this some big secret or can we tell people?"

"I'd hoped to keep it to myself, but with Charley and Nick showing up in town, I guess it was a pipe dream to believe I could work here for long without anyone finding out. It doesn't mean anything has to change. Please don't make a big deal of it, blab to the paper, or hang a sign out front. It's not like I'm a household name or that anyone would be impressed."

Anna took a moment to breathe. "Look, I'm just a girl who can play the piano pretty well. It's not like I can fry burgers like Hector or wash dishes like Mike, or…chop things like Francie. Or run the diner like you, Roz. You run a tight ship and keep us all in line."

"Good save," Mike said under the guise of a cough.

The swinging door closed behind Candee. "The natives are startin' to get restless out there. I just made acquaintance with Mr. Nick Parker from Manhattan." Coming over to Anna, Candee wrapped her arms around her. "I knew you didn't belong here, sweetie. You're different in all the *best* ways."

She'd kill Nick later. On second thought, he might have done her a big favor.

"We're glad to have you as long as you can stay." Candee released her. "Does Weston know who you are?" She rolled her eyes. "You know what I mean."

"I'll tell Weston when the time is right. I only met him last night. Nothing can happen between us long-term, so I'd appreciate it if you good people would stop matchmaking."

Candee shook her head, her expression skeptical. "Honey, we've got plenty of time to spare in this town. A lot can happen in a few weeks. You never can predict when true love will strike. Besides, you might want to tell *Weston* that."

"What do you mean?" *True love?*

"That handsome man's standin' at the front counter now, lookin' all sweet, and he's waitin' for you. He came in to order some food to go and asked for you special."

Mike snorted. "Did you tell him Anna's not on the menu?"

Roz shot him a glare. "None of that talk in my kitchen, mister."

"You might want to get out there before Nick gets ahold of him," Candee advised. "That man's a real character. He's fun, though."

Oh, no. Anna wanted to groan, but there wasn't time. She turned to leave.

"Wait up, girl. Your orders for Table 10 are almost ready. Wait for 'em before you go chargin' out of here." Roz's tone was *take no prisoners* firm.

Wonderful. She'd have to wait and hope Nick behaved himself with Weston.

She sighed. Fat chance of that happening.

Chapter 12

"Hey, mate."

Weston glanced over at the man who'd greeted him from a nearby counter seat. Looked about his age, maybe a few years younger. The way he was dressed, he must be an actor in a local play. Not to mention that pitiful accent was as fake as his Aunt Barb's fur coat. Was it supposed to be British or Australian? A tattoo of a cross decorated his left bicep. Now *that* looked real.

"Good afternoon." Weston nodded politely.

"Are you perchance waiting for the fetching Anna?" The guy gave Weston a thinly disguised once-over. He couldn't tell whether or not he passed inspection, not that he cared.

Leaning his left hip against the counter, Weston faced the guy. *Perchance?* "Yes, as a matter of fact."

"Me, too." The guy rapped the counter with his curled fist and pretended to study the menu. "She's quite the looker, eh?"

Weston had no desire to engage in a discussion about Anna's attributes, physical or otherwise, but she'd obviously gained another admirer. Why should he be surprised? He hadn't a clue what type of man Anna liked, but he sure hoped it wasn't *this* guy. The other side of the coin was that he had absolutely no claim on her.

Anna rushed into the dining room carrying a large round tray laden with food orders. "Oh! Hi, Weston." She stopped abruptly, sending the dishes in a precarious slide across the tray.

Reaching for the edge, he steadied the tray with both hands. Small blessing there were no glasses sitting on that tray or they'd be currently airborne.

"Thanks for being my hero. Again." She was slightly out of breath. "It's nice to see you."

"You, too." With her flushed cheeks and bright brown eyes, Anna did indeed appear fetching. Not that he'd ever *thought* that word much less used it in his lifetime.

The British wannabe dude snickered. What was his problem?

"Candee said you wanted to place an order. Don't go anywhere. I'll be right back."

"Take your time." Weston stared straight ahead as he waited, hoping to avoid more conversation. Seconds later, he heard a low chuckle from the man to his right.

"Something amusing?" Why did this guy irritate him?

"You've got the girl flustered, but it's all good, mate."

Weston ignored the comment, and Anna returned within the minute.

"All right now. What can I get for you today?" She pulled her order pad and a pencil from her apron pocket.

"I need five of the biggest, juicy cheeseburgers you've got. Normally, we don't eat like that at the site, but our section crew did some great work today, and the boss suggested it. He might regret it later, but it'll be on *his* conscience."

"Then you need the Double Darling. Two patties of prime beef—a quarter pound each—fully dressed, and two slices of American cheese. Is that okay?"

"Sounds like the perfect overindulgence to me. If the guys don't like something, they can pick or scrape it off."

Anna scribbled away. "Would you like fries?"

"Sure. Why not? Do you have an extra large order?"

"We have the Super Duper Darling Deluxe Fries. An order will easily serve four people with normal appetites." She'd managed that mouthful without cracking a smile.

The other man coughed into his fist. Anna ignored him. Smart woman.

"Comes with containers of ranch and cheese sauces on the side. For dipping."

"Outstanding. I'll take two orders of the Super Duper fries," he told her. "That should be enough food to fill their stomachs and hold off the coroner so we can finish for the day."

Anna's lips twisted as she jotted another note. "Got it. How about something to drink? A few gallons of sweet tea?"

"No, thanks. We have water at the site."

"Dessert?"

"That'll do, darlin'." As expected, the endearment brought a lovely flush to her cheeks.

"I'll, um, just go and turn your order in now. Give me—I mean us—ten minutes or so. Would you like something to drink while you wait? On the house."

Weston grinned. The other guy would love what he was about to say. For some unknown reason, he wanted to get under his skin. "No, thanks, but you should probably stop offering me things on the house. People might get the wrong idea."

Uh oh. Based on the way Anna's eyes widened, he'd stuck his size twelve construction boot in his big mouth again. Without another word, she darted back into the kitchen. Weston mentally kicked himself. Would he never learn?

"Smooth, *Hero*. What'd you do to earn that title? I'd venture to say it wasn't for your articulation skills."

Ignore the dig.

Weston slid onto a counter seat closest to the kitchen. "I rescued some plates she dropped." This stranger didn't need an explanation of how he'd also walked Anna home and then hightailed it back to the house when he heard her scream. None of his business.

"Is that a fact? Our Anna does like a good hero."

Our Anna? Was this guy baiting him? Goading him? "I think most women like a hero."

"I'm sure you're right, mate." The other man swiveled on his seat, facing the dining room, and leaned his elbows back on the counter.

Needing something to do while he waited for his order, Weston pulled out his cell phone and checked his messages. Madison called? That was a surprise, not necessarily a good one. Biggest issue with Maddie was her jealous streak. During the six months they'd dated, if he'd dared to look sideways at another woman—even a sixty-year-old woman in the church—she'd grab hold of his arm as if laying claim to her personal property.

Then she'd dumped *him* for Tate the Financial Whiz. A man could only take so much, one reason Weston had been glad to escape Atlanta. Breathe some fresh, clean, unpolluted air for a change. Be free, if only for a couple of months, from pretentiousness and people trying to be someone they weren't instead of looking to be the person God *wanted* them to be.

He should have known dating a girl from his singles class was a mistake if it didn't turn out well. Still, it was one of the few places to meet single women where he might stand a chance of finding a praying woman who wanted children. Not that he'd ever admitted that out loud to anyone. Not even his folks. Only the Almighty had been privy to all his secrets until he'd blurted out a few to Anna.

Time to listen to the message on the slim chance it had to do with important news of someone at the church. He clicked on the voice mail.

"Hi, Weston. I hope you're doing well, and I'm wondering how you're doing on your new project in that little hick town."

Leaning one elbow on the counter, he tried to ignore the honeyed tone of Madison's voice as she insulted Darling, a town he doubted she'd heard of until recently. A vision of the pretty blonde popped into his mind, but he consciously pushed it down and hoped it'd stay there. He was done with that relationship.

His gaze sought out Anna as he listened. She laughed at something one of her customers said. She didn't seem the type to send flying projectiles his way. Then again, neither had Maddie when he'd first met her. Even since last night, Anna appeared more at ease and less nervous. He'd thought she was pretty before, but Weston's pulse jumped as he watched her now.

Man, she was gorgeous.

"They're taking sign-ups for the mission trip to Haiti next spring, and I wondered if you're planning on going," Madison drawled in his ear. She was really working the sultry southern act. Weston closed his eyes as he listened, forcing himself to concentrate. The woman knew how to turn on the charm, and he needed to put up his guard.

"The deposit's due about the same time you come back home, so I thought I'd let you know. I can put your name on the list if you're interested. The core group from our singles class is planning on it, including me. I think it'll be fun."

A mission trip *could* be fun, but that wasn't the reason to go. Madison was aware he planned on returning to Atlanta most weekends, so he'd have plenty of time to sign up. So, why *had* she called? *Wait a second.* What about Mr. Smooth? He almost deleted the message but then realized there was more.

The odd guy jumped off his seat and headed toward Anna. Lightly touching her arm as she moved between tables, he leaned close and said something in a low tone. Suppressing the urge to growl, Weston turned back around.

"I also wanted to say…I miss you, Weston. Tate and I split up last week, and I realized how wrong I was to let you go. I hope you can find it in your heart to forgive me. I'd love to give dating another try if you're willing. Just think about it, please? We can talk if you want. You know the number. In the meantime, please take care of yourself, and I hope you'll get to come home for a weekend soon. It'd be great to see you."

Weston clicked off his phone and pocketed it. If Madison had called a couple of days ago, he might have considered calling her back and going home to Atlanta for the weekend like he'd originally planned. He'd call her back, but he'd give her time to cool her jets first. He knew from experience that if he returned the call too soon, Maddie would misinterpret it as wanting to resume their relationship.

So, she'd already broken up with Tate. That hadn't lasted long, not that he was surprised. As far as the mission trip, he hadn't decided yet. He'd been on a few mission trips, but the last couple of years, he'd preferred homegrown missions. Like his homeless friend, Roswell, there were a lot of hurting people everywhere, including on the streets of Atlanta. He couldn't help or save them all, but he could try, one soul at a time.

For now, the best course of action would be to send Madison a short email. He'd take care of that tonight. Put her off with the *wait and see* excuse for now. Besides, it was the truth.

"Bad news, mate?" The other guy bounded back to the counter and straddled the seat.

Weston bit his tongue not to snap and tell him to stop calling him *mate*. In his own way, he was being friendly. He clearly felt the urge to chat. "Not exactly."

The guy took a long draw from his water bottle and emptied it. "Women are mysterious creatures, are they not?"

"How'd you know it has anything to do with a woman?" Way to *not* encourage conversation.

"A man doesn't get that *here we go again* look on his face if he's listening to another bloke on the other end of the phone."

Anna came back into the dining room. "I need to check on my other customers, but I'll be back in just a minute."

"I know you're busy," Weston said. "No problem."

The other guy scoffed as if offended. "*I'm* your customer, Anna. You didn't check on me."

"When your wife arrives, I'll be happy to take your order. Do you want another bottle of water?"

"No thanks, love. I'll wait."

Wife? Weston didn't like how familiar he acted with Anna, especially if he was married. He darted a glance at his left hand adorned with a plain platinum wedding band. Where'd he get off openly disrespecting his wife? He needed to say something.

"A word of advice? You might want to cut the flirting. That's inappropriate, man." He'd almost said *tone down*, but he was glad he'd called him out for behavior unbecoming a married man.

He could hear Neil's voice in his head asking him who'd made him the marriage police.

Go away, Neil. Case in point of a soul that needed saving, but not right this second.

"No worries, mate. I know Anna well. She's used to me."

That comment didn't sit any better with him. "I'm not your *mate*, and if you're trying to throw bait my way, it won't work. I'm not biting."

The man surprised him by laughing as if he'd said the funniest thing he'd heard in a long time. "Relax, man. Trust me, I'm no threat for her affections. I'm Anna's brother-in-law."

Relief mixed with irritation flooded through him. "That must mean you're Charley's husband?"

"That's right." He extended his right hand. "Nick Parker. Honored to make your acquaintance."

"Weston Galloway. You, too." When he shook the other man's hand, some of the tension evaporated. "I'm from Atlanta and working a construction project here in town."

"Good for you. I take it you've met Charlotte?"

Weston nodded. "I walked Anna home last night, and Charley was at the house."

"No wonder you're Anna's hero. You rescue plates, protect her honor, and walk her home. I meant no offense, mate. Really."

"None taken, but neither are you British." Weston met the other guy's dark eyes. "You might rethink the accent. It's not doing you any favors." The black stuff around his eyes, his clothing, and the earrings were interesting. "Are you in a rock band?"

Nick's smile faded. "I'm an artist, actually. I've come to collect my wife, you see. Charley has a habit of running away from home on occasion. True to form, she came in search of her beloved sister. Who knew the trail this time would lead to Darling, Georgia?" The way he'd said it made Darling sound like a hole-in-the-wall town.

The trail this time? That was the more intriguing statement.

"You might like it here if you'd stick around," Weston said. "Sorry I came down hard on you, man."

"No worries. I was having a little fun with you, and it backfired." His smile returned. "Say, you don't happen to drive a truck, do you?"

"I do. Why?"

"Just curious." A wide grin stretched across Nick's face. "A *red* truck?"

Weston nodded, but there was no sense dwelling on this guy's unpredictable questions. "How long have you and Charley been married?"

"Six years come mid-November." Nick's uncluttered accent sounded like New York or New Jersey. Upper crust. This artist wasn't starving.

Anna came back to the counter and glanced between them. "Everything okay?"

"Peachy," Nick said. "I'm getting acquainted with your new friend, Weston."

Wanting to reassure her, Weston smiled. "Have you had a good day so far?"

"I'd say so. I broke one plate and deducted money from a check for spilling coffee on a customer. Mixed up one small order, and Roz has scolded me three times. That's a personal record low for one shift. Score!"

"Excellent." Laughing, Weston raised his hand in the air, and Anna high-fived him.

"My goal is to work an entire shift without any spills or accidents." He had to grin at her optimism and pride in her accomplishments. The woman was irresistible.

"Goals are good. Say, Anna, do you have to work this Saturday?"

Nick swiveled to face them, appearing smug. "Do I hear an invitation for a date?"

"Read your menu, Nick." Anna did a double take. "Thank you for dropping that ridiculous accent."

Nick jerked his thumb at Weston. "Your hero already told me to lose it."

"We'll talk tomorrow when we don't have an audience," Weston said to Anna in a lowered tone. He hadn't thought through what he wanted to ask her although Nick was correct. A date was definitely in his mind.

"Sounds good. Your cheeseburgers and fries will be ready in a few minutes. I have more customers coming in, but we'll get them boxed and bagged as soon as the order's up."

"Thanks. I can pay the check whenever you want."

Anna called over one shoulder. "Tell Candee what you ordered, and she'll cash you out."

As if on cue, Candee emerged from the kitchen seconds later and gave him a smile as she headed to the main dining room.

"Hey Candee, I met your son, Connor, this morning."

She backed up to stand beside him. "He wasn't shootin' his BB gun at the building you're workin' on was he?" The waitress's customary smile morphed into a frown.

"No, nothing like that, but he's sporting a Band-Aid on his knee courtesy of a wipeout on his bike. He flew past me when I was walking to work."

Candee's expression relaxed somewhat. "I keep tellin' that boy to watch where he's goin'. Connor's a dreamer. Nothin' wrong with it in some cases, and my Jesse's the same way. It's just that reality has a way of smackin' 'em both in the face sometimes if they're not payin' attention."

"We had a discussion about the bank we're building. Connor seemed disappointed it wouldn't be a skyscraper."

"Yeah, well. Like I said, he's a dreamer. He loves to design buildings on the computer. His teachers tell us Connor has a real good eye for depth perception, things like that."

Weston smiled. "I happen to believe dreams can be a good thing."

"If you don't have a dream, how can you make it come true, right?"

"Your son gave me renewed appreciation for what I do. He's a good kid. Listen, I need to pay my bill. Anna said you could cash me out."

"Sure thing, sugar. Anna told me what you ordered. I need to check on a table real quick, but if you don't mind waitin' over by the register, I'll join you in a jiffy."

After taking care of the check a few minutes later, Weston returned to the front counter as Nick abruptly jumped off his seat. The guy must have ADHD. He couldn't sit still for two minutes. When the noise level in the diner grew suddenly quiet, Weston turned to see what was happening.

Charley stood just inside the diner's front door, staring at Nick. Although Weston figured she had to be in her early twenties, she barely looked older than a teenager in her skinny jeans, T-shirt, and long, straight blonde hair streaked with light purple.

"Nicky." She hesitated, clearly torn between bolting or running to her husband.

"Charlotte." Nick quickly moved in her direction and opened his arms.

Whether or not they consciously sought attention, this couple had *presence*. Weston found it impossible to turn away as he watched this offbeat but oddly sweet couple, as drawn to the scene as everyone else, including Anna, who stood beside a far table.

Never taking her eyes off her husband, Charley darted through the diner, dodging customers to reach Nick. Meeting her halfway, Nick cupped her face between his hands and whispered to her. Then he enfolded her in a tight embrace and buried his face in her hair.

Weston averted his gaze as the couple locked lips. Passionately, but that wasn't exactly a shocker. A number of customers clapped while others chuckled quietly. Roz stood near the register wearing an expression of annoyance. Beside her, Candee had one hand over her chest and tears shimmered in her eyes. Love was in the air at The Darling Diner.

"Was that for real or are you two actors?" one guy hollered across the diner.

Ignoring the question, Nick only had eyes for Charley. Clasping his hands together behind his wife's neck, he rested his forehead on hers.

Everyone returned to their conversations, and Anna headed his way. He touched her arm as she passed him on her way to the kitchen. "Glad to see they're back together. I imagine that's the best show these people have seen in a while."

"That's the thing, Weston. It's *not* a show with them." When she brushed a tear from her cheek, he reached for a napkin and gently pushed it into her hand.

"Thanks." She dabbed at her eyes before balling the napkin and stuffing it in her apron pocket. "I know Charley and Nick can be quirky and immature, but I've seen them together for years. Their love is the real deal." Shifting from one foot to the other, Anna worried her lower lip. "They're unconventional, but that's what makes them so…"

"Fascinating? I didn't mean to imply their feelings aren't genuine. And I hate it if what I said made you cry." Tears from a woman always got to him, especially if *he* was the cause.

"I know, and you didn't." She swallowed. "I'll go check on your food. It should be ready now."

Weston watched her go, wondering why he always seemed to say the wrong thing around Anna. He didn't sound like an idiot with most people, and it's not like she made him nervous. Or maybe she did on some subconscious level he hadn't yet tapped into.

He moved his gaze back to Nick and Charley. Still standing in the middle of the diner, Charley ducked her head and blushed at something Nick whispered as he tucked a long strand of hair behind her ear.

Weston turned aside, feeling like an interloper. Public spectacle or not, this should be a private moment between them and not for public consumption.

Whispering to the other's heart.

Hmm. He'd never wanted to whisper sweet nothings to Madison. She wasn't the type. But with Anna? Yeah, he could imagine it.

He rolled the idea around in his mind. He couldn't seem to converse with Anna without saying the wrong thing. "Whisper to my heart," he murmured. The more he thought about it, the more appealing it sounded. He'd been short on inspiration lately, but this idea might work to jumpstart his creativity.

He'd write a song for her on his guitar. And hope he'd have the opportunity to sing it for her.

Chapter 13

Anna leisurely strolled toward downtown Darling. A clear night, the humidity was lower although the temperature was still high. Breathing in deeply, she enjoyed the sweet fragrance of blooming flowers and air so fresh it seemed almost intoxicating. The sound of chirping crickets, a rarity in the city, made her smile. Air conditioning units hummed and the sounds of a television reached her from the home of owners brave enough to leave their windows open.

She couldn't remember the last time she'd taken a walk like this where she didn't have to be somewhere by a certain time or for a specific reason.

Her cell phone buzzed in her pocket. So much for a peaceful, uninterrupted walk. She should have left her phone back at the house. Tempted not to answer it, Anna peeked at the display.

Felicia. She clicked on the phone against her better judgment. "Good evening."

"Are you bored with life in that little southern town yet?"

Felicia never failed to get straight to the point. She'd always appreciated her efficiency in business matters but tonight her manager's bluntness elicited a quick frown.

"Hello to you, too. No, I'm not bored. For one thing, people here appreciate the value of small talk."

Felicia laughed quietly. "Touché, but small talk doesn't pay the bills. I'm sure you could light a match in the center of town and it'd draw a crowd." She'd known her manager was a snob, but Anna bristled at the woman's obvious disdain for Darling and its citizens. Refuting her assumptions would get her nowhere, so she wouldn't try.

"At least personal interaction helps to forge relationships."

"Have you met a man?"

Her breath caught. "What makes you say that?"

"Dear heart, I've known you since you were a child and lived with you for ten years. You've never cared about *forging* anything, including friendships, unless it furthers your career. The word *forge* also implies a fraudulent practice. Remember that."

"It's only a word. Forget I said it." Irritation laced Anna's words, but she couldn't help it.

"Then tell me when you started caring about getting to know others."

Anna's spirits plummeted. *Was* she the type of person Felicia implied? No, that wasn't what she was about at all. As usual, her manager was trying to manipulate her, and she hadn't even bothered to be subtle about it. Felicia continued to treat her like the impressionable, naïve, teenager she'd once been. *She* was the one who cared about her career at the expense of Anna's personal life. As long as Anna showed up for her concert appearances, looked the part, and performed well, those were Felicia's primary concerns.

"Felicia, you know better than anyone how much I love what I do, but I'm beginning to see that touring shouldn't be my whole world. That's not healthy. I need close friends and a social life. When my career is over, what will it matter if I have no one to share my life with?"

"Where's this coming from, Anna? Your career will never be over unless *you* choose to end it. You have the kind of life most young classical musicians can only dream of, and it's not like you don't have social events."

"Galas, charity events, and fundraising dinners don't count," Anna said.

"Your drive to succeed has helped you reach an elite status very few ever achieve."

"I understand that, and I'm grateful. The way I see it, it's not so much a drive to succeed as fulfilling God's plan for my life. As for the rest, it's only lookin' at fancier walls."

"Don't tell me you just used the word *lookin'*?"

Anna almost laughed when she heard the horror in Felicia's tone. "I guess I did. Don't worry. It was a direct quote."

"If you start speaking like an uneducated backwater hick, I may have to come down there to Georgia myself and haul you back home. Then hire Manhattan's version of Professor Henry Higgins to undo the damage."

"Don't bother." Anna rolled her eyes at her manager's exaggerated dramatics. "I'm staying put in Darling for now."

"As far as *God's plan*, did you ever stop to think why He gave you such talent in the first place? To *use* and share it with the world, Anna. Anyway, I called because I thought you might like to know your tour dates have sold out."

"All of them? That's surprising but great to hear." Her last tour had been successful but by no means a sell-out.

"Every single one. Advance ticket sales have been brisk. We sold out in the first hour in Chicago, two hours in Los Angeles, as well as Dallas, Houston, and New Orleans. Congratulations. I'm pleased."

"Thanks for letting me know. I appreciate the call."

"Promise me you won't indulge in too much fried food. You're not used to it, and I understand it can become addictive rather quickly."

Felicia's warning effectively stole Anna's smile. She'd never been overweight and could generally eat whatever she wanted without negative consequences.

"And stay away from the rich, thick gravy. They like to pour sauces over everything in the South, and it'll stick to your thighs and settle on your waist and hips. I can't have my star client gaining weight and getting thicker in the middle. If you do, you won't fit in your performance gowns, and the benches will protest."

Ah yes, Felicia's dreaded piano *bench test*. "If one of the benches creaks, it's only because a leg is loose and needs to be checked, not because I've gained weight."

"I'm only suggesting you keep your priorities in mind. Like it or not, your image is a large part of your persona. Your gowns for the upcoming tour were designed and made to your exact proportions and measurements, and if you stay in that town and cut it close to the start of the tour, there won't be time to make any alterations."

Anna suppressed a groan. She didn't need the unwelcome reminder. What did it matter what she looked like? Her talent should be what sold tickets, not her appearance. Unfortunately, the world didn't operate that way.

"No worries. I'm eating well and getting exercise." She had the aching feet and sore back to prove the latter.

As Anna neared the square in the middle of town, she spied the silhouette of a man backlit by the street lights. He stood on the sidewalk a block away, facing her.

Weston. Her traitorous heart flipped. In his khaki cargo shorts, a dark T-shirt with a slogan splayed across the front, and boat shoes with no socks, he looked casual and comfortable.

Who was she kidding? Weston looked *gooood.*

Lifting one hand in a friendly wave, he walked in her direction. Slow, sure of himself, hands in his pockets.

"Felicia, I'll talk with you later." Without waiting for her response, Anna clicked off the phone and returned it to the pocket of her shorts.

"Evening, Miss Redmond."

"Hi." She ran her hands up and down her arms although she wasn't cold. In the light from the streetlamp, she could make out a cross and Scripture verse splayed across Weston's broad chest. She'd been trying to ignore the bulk in his upper arms and the taut muscles on his forearms since she'd first met him. The man was impossible to dismiss.

"Lovely night, isn't it?"

"Yes, if you don't mind ninety degrees at nine o'clock. I'm glad to see you survived the Double Darling."

He chuckled. "What brings you out tonight?"

How to couch it in politically correct terms? "Charley and Nick are at the house getting…reacquainted." A flush of warmth spread through her cheeks, making her thankful for the dim lighting.

"They're quite the pair. Where did they meet?"

At one of my concerts in New York.

"At a concert in New York seven years ago," she said. "What brings you out tonight?"

"There's some *acquainting* going on at my place, too. Unfortunately, not of the married variety. What a world we live in, huh? Free will, free love. Do what you want, whenever you want, with whomever you want, whatever feels good."

Weston sifted one hand through his hair. "There I go again with my verbal diarrhea. Sorry."

"Don't apologize, Weston. For what it's worth, I'm glad you're different. It's good to know you hold to higher standards. Nice to know there are men who respect a woman and hold traditional values."

"I tried to hold my version of a town meeting earlier tonight, tried to discuss some guidelines. I haven't had many roommates and have my own house in Atlanta. I'd never be a good politician since I failed at rallying the troops. They're going to do what they want no matter what I say or do."

Weston glanced away as though gathering his thoughts before settling his gaze on her once more. "Being completely honest here? If I didn't have Christ in my life, I might act the same way they do. Why obey a moral code if you're not accountable to anyone?"

"That's true, but even if you weren't a Christian, I don't think you'd be casual about it," Anna said. "At the very least, I think you'd be a one-woman man." She couldn't believe she'd said such a thing. Maybe the blunt honesty of the townspeople was rubbing off on her.

He seemed intrigued. "What makes you say that?"

"From everything I know about you, you seem like one of the really good guys."

"I'm glad you think so. How about you?"

"What about me?" Anna grinned. "Are you saying you're *not* one of the good guys?"

"I don't act like they do. If that makes me a good guy, then yes, I qualify. Hypothetically speaking, would you be a one-man woman? Hang on. Did I say that right?"

"You did, but I haven't dated enough to know." What a conversation, but she'd started it. This man was fun, and the Lord knew she could use more fun in her life. That irritating conversation with Felicia a few minutes ago only reinforced that opinion.

"Yeah, right. I don't believe that for one minute."

"What, do you want proof? Ask Charley." She must sound like a social reject to outgoing and personable Weston. Charley's one-time nickname for her—the "dating virgin"—still stuck in the back of Anna's mind. She hadn't felt as though she'd missed out on that much.

"To clarify, you mean you haven't dated enough *lately*, right?"

Should she admit she could count the number of dates she'd had in her life on *one* hand? No, that would only make her sound pathetic. *And* a social reject.

Weston dipped his head in an effort to catch her attention. "Hey, it's okay if you'd rather not answer. I believe you, but what I can't understand is how a guy could be around you and not want more."

Because I travel all the time. Because I'm never in one place long enough for a relationship.

The primary reason? She'd met very few *Christian* men, especially in her world. That's why the man beside her now was in a class all his own. At least Weston had spared her from having to explain.

"That's flattering, but you don't know me," she said. "Maybe I'm mental."

"Then that only means you're normal since most people are at least a little bit crazy." Leaning behind her, Weston rested a light hand on the small of her back.

"What are you doing? Should I revise my opinion? Maybe *you're* mental."

"You have incredibly great posture. It's one of the first things I noticed about you in the diner. You don't walk or move the way most women do."

She lifted her brows. "Thank you, I think?" Her spine wasn't rigid, by any means, but she'd fine-tuned her own unique "special posture"—the term used by her mentors and teachers at Juilliard—to achieve that harmonious balance between musician and instrument. If she tried to explain that concept to Weston, he'd probably think she *was* mental.

"I assure you, it's a compliment," he said. "Take me, for instance. My posture's okay, but keep in mind that I move around all day and stoop a lot. That's tough on the old knees. And I'm definitely mental sometimes. Try working in the heat all day, day after day, hours on end. That'll do it to anyone. Guaranteed some of my brain cells are fried."

Anna cringed. "What a lovely image."

He snapped his fingers. "You're a runaway ballerina. Fess up."

"Right. If I were, I'd be walking like this." Anna pushed the heels of her feet together and waddled forward in her flats like she'd seen future prima ballerinas do at Juilliard.

Weston's warm laughter filled the night. "Who knew the serious waitress at The Darling Diner could be so fun?"

When he ran a hand over his beard, Anna glimpsed those attractive dimples. She liked that his beard was light enough that she could still see them. Almost like he was trying to decide whether or not to grow a full beard.

"Weston, why do you hide your dimples behind a beard?"

He grinned as though pleased she'd noticed. "I look ten years younger without it. They called me Baby Face Galloway when I was in high school. The dimples were the bane of my existence."

"I imagine the girls didn't complain."

His brows lifted. "What do you know? The waitress is also a pretty serious flirt."

Busted. Anna sucked in her jaws not to laugh.

"I wanted to be taken seriously, so I've worn a beard since I was nineteen. With the work I do, it's nice not to have to shave all the time. Plus, it keeps my face warm in the winter."

She shook her head. "Why do men always use that excuse?"

"Hey, it's not a line. It's truth. You think I'm too lazy to shave, is that it?"

"You said it, not me." She laughed. "What are we even talking about here?"

"I'm not sure." He laughed with her. "But I'll have you know trimming a beard can be as tedious as shaving, sometimes more. In some ways, it's harder to make it look this good." He stroked his fingers over it again in the way men who wore facial hair seemed to do.

An irrational urge to touch his beard seized her. Would it feel bristly or soft to the touch? Would it stab her if she kissed him?

And that matters why?

Tilting his head, Weston surveyed her. "You're not going to tell me, are you?"

"Excuse me?" She practically choked out the question and hoped he couldn't read her thoughts.

"About the mysterious Anna Redmond. Instead of standing in the middle of the sidewalk, why don't we walk together? I noticed an ice cream shop on a side street that's still open. It's a couple of blocks from here. Feel like some dessert?"

"That sounds like the best idea I've heard all day. Lead the way." When he offered, Anna hooked her arm with his. *Take that, Felicia.* A little ice cream wouldn't make her flunk that ridiculous bench test.

She was surprised one of her coworkers at the diner hadn't said something to Weston about her earlier in the day. After Mike's question, she half-expected he'd hang a sign outside that read FAMOUS PERSON WORKS HERE with one of those hands that had a finger pointing to The Darling Diner.

"You must be exhausting." Anna laughed again when she realized what she'd said. "Exhaust*ed*. Freudian slip?"

He laughed. "Cute, but yeah, I'm tired. I have to say, though, that spending time with you is reviving me pretty fast." They shared a smile as he pulled open the door.

"Thank you, kind sir." Anna ducked beneath his arm and walked into the air-conditioned shop. The cool temperature was inviting and a scoop of ice cream sounded tempting.

"Evenin' folks." An older man in an old-fashioned uniform, with Paulson's Ice Cream Shop embroidered on his shirt and stamped vertically on his suspenders, welcomed them with a broad smile. "Y'all new to town?"

"Yep," Weston said, shaking the man's hand. "I'm Weston Galloway, and this is Anna Redmond."

"Pleased to meet you both. I'm Lew Paulson, owner of the shop. We're closin' up soon, but you're welcome to stay as long as you'd like. Well, as long as you don't have laptops and plan on campin' out. This isn't one of them fancy coffee shops. What can I get for you tonight?"

Anna surveyed the offerings. "They all look great. I can't decide between blueberry cheesecake or butter rum."

"Tell you what." The man took two wooden tasters and presented her with a sample of each. "Here you go. See what you think." He angled his head to Weston. "How about you, young man?"

"What can you show me in caramel?"

Funny man. Anna laughed under her breath as she enjoyed the samples.

"You're in luck. My wife made a fresh batch of caramel praline earlier today. Got the recipe from a friend down in New Orleans, and it's a new Darling favorite. Want to try a sample?"

"No need. Sounds great. I'll take a waffle cone with two scoops, please."

"Comin' right up." The man turned back to Anna. "What's the verdict, young lady?"

Anna finished the second sample and licked her lips. "They're both delicious, but butter rum wins out. I'll take one scoop in a cup, please."

"I vote we stay inside," Weston said as they waited. "The ice cream will melt too fast outside. I'll tell Lew to give us the ten-minute warning if he needs to kick us out."

"Sounds good. I'll go find us a table." When she started to pull her wallet from her pocket, he put a gentle hand on her arm.

"I've got it, Anna. My treat."

Weston's smile, combined with the kindness in his eyes, disarmed her. Tiny little lines around the corners of his eyes only added to his charm. For a man who worked outside in the elements, his skin was naturally smooth and tan. The absence of his baseball cap revealed a head full of thick, straight, light brown hair—except for the appealing curls on his neck.

Anna found a corner table and observed as Weston interacted with the older man. Women must constantly try to get his attention. Whether or not he paid them any mind was none of her business. *None.* Still, she could wonder. No harm in that.

She glanced around the quaint little shop. The only other customers were a middle-aged couple who gave her polite nods. Powerless to resist the urge to look at him again, Anna studied Weston's profile. He wasn't classically handsome, but she'd never been attracted to that type, anyway. Men who fit that description seemed too perfect and self-aware. Pretty boys, many of them, pampered and self-indulgent. She'd met enough guys like that on her tours to make her wonder if Felicia steered some of them her way as a *temporary distraction.*

Weston was more the ruggedly attractive type. He made her laugh. He was self-effacing, giving, and honest. He exuded raw masculinity—like Candee had observed—and sported a great…*everything*, as Charley had said. Funny how the married women were the ones pointing out this man's fine…ness. She wasn't blind, but she couldn't *do* anything about the attraction, so what would be the point? She needed to squelch those feelings. Immediately.

And that's why you're here with Weston now. It's not like she'd planned to run into him during her walk. She hadn't even planned to take a walk until circumstances back at the house warranted it.

Was it possible it was a *God* thing? Most of her life, others had told her where to go, what to do. The one thing she controlled was *how* she did it.

Charley would be so proud of her right now. Ice cream and shared conversation with a handsome man on a hot summer night sounded like the perfect remedy for her recent feelings of loneliness. Looking at it that way, spending time with Weston could be considered therapeutic.

Delusion was the first step to madness, right?

Anna drummed her fingers on the tabletop. "Squelching it down. Just being a friend," she mumbled under her breath. She was on the downhill slide into thirty. Time to finally start *living*.

In the back of her mind, Anna sensed she was about to embark on the ride of her life.

Chapter 14

Weston set her cup of butter rum on the table and swung into the chair next to her instead of across the table. "You have interesting taste in ice cream." He mock shuddered.

"I was pleasantly surprised by the flavor. You have to give me credit for trying something different."

"Oh, I'm not denying that. If I were you, I'd be more wary of the aftertaste, though. Something wrong with peach? You're in Georgia, after all."

"I'm well aware. Another night."

He grinned. "Sounds good to me."

She'd invite him to sample her ice cream before they left the shop. Weston struck her as the kind of man who'd welcome the challenge. He was definitely a *man's man*, and as such, also different from the majority of men she'd known the last decade. Men with more artistic leanings, many of whom suffered massive egos.

And so the comparisons continued.

Weston settled in the chair. Did he want to pray for his dessert like he'd done at the diner?

"Should we pray?" She felt awkward asking.

"Do you mind? Some girls think it's strange to pray over dessert."

"Not at all. I mean, I don't mind. I think it's refreshing. Can we ever pray enough?" She wanted to kick herself under the table.

"With me, it's about more than the food," he said. "It's the situation, circumstances, or the person I'm with at the time. I've learned to follow those inner nudges."

"Then by all means." When Weston bowed his head, Anna followed suit. She almost jumped when he rested his hand over hers. Goodness. He'd think she didn't like being touched.

Focus. The man is about to pray.

"Lord, we thank you for this time together. I'd ask that Anna and I can be good influences on our coworkers, families, roommates, new friends, and anyone else we meet while we're here in Darling. I pray that others will see *you* reflected in our actions and our words, and that we might be a shining light to the world of your grace, mercy, and love. We ask these things in the name of your Son, Jesus. Amen."

"Amen," Anna echoed, feeling humbled. "Do you know how wonderful it is to be able to pray with a man who understands how *important* prayer is?"

"It's the same for me in the reverse. I mean, the opportunity to pray with a woman who gets it. Gets *me*." His laughter escaped. "There I go again. I really have a knack for saying the wrong thing around you, don't I? Wait, don't answer that."

"Only adds to your charm." She dipped her spoon in her ice cream. Like most homemade varieties, it was firm and needed time to soften up a bit. Somewhere in that thought was an interesting analogy.

"If you think *this* is charming, I wonder what you'd think if I laid it on really thick?"

"Just eat your ice cream, Weston."

"This is great. Real homemade stuff. Made with family pride and love. Nothing like it." Laughing, he took a bite. The man couldn't be quiet if he tried.

"I was thinking the same thing." She smiled as she took another bite of her ice cream.

He glanced around the store. "I love family-owned establishments like this and The Darling Diner. They make a town special. Gives a person a sense of belonging, and the people become your friends the minute you meet them. A lot of them, anyway. Don't you think?"

"I agree. My customers at the diner tell me their life stories and show me photos of their families. Sometimes I learn more than I need to know. They freely offer all kinds of information or advice without a second thought. I've never met people so open and honest."

"The mystery surrounding you thickens." After taking another bite of his ice cream and licking around the top of the waffle cone, Weston tilted his head and studied her. "Do they ask you questions about *your* life or do they only talk about themselves?"

She'd ignore his hints about her life for now. "Sometimes they ask me about my life, but I think they're more interested in having someone else listen."

"But they don't come across as selfishly motivated."

"Not at all. Why do you say that?"

Weston leaned close, making her heart skip a few beats. "Do you think maybe some of them are lonely?"

"Could be, now that you mention it. There's one lady, a widow, who's come into the diner every night this week. Della always sits at the same table, and come to think of it, she's ordered the same thing every night—a turkey melt and broccoli cheddar soup. Although I'm not sure how or why that matters."

"She might feel a little lost," he said. "Della's routine might give her a sense of normalcy. Familiarity is comforting to people who've suffered loss. Do you know how long it's been since her husband died?"

"Sometime in the last year or two, I think. Her favorite topic is her newest grandbaby, Nevaeh."

"One of the guys on our crew has a little girl named Nevaeh."

"Heaven spelled backwards." They said it simultaneously and shared a smile.

"I think she might be Roz's friend," Anna observed. "From what Candee told me, Roz has been divorced a long time and doesn't have any kids. Roz stops and talks with her for a few minutes every night. My boss doesn't do that with most of the customers other than to ask if they have everything they need and if they're enjoying their meal."

Anna took another bite, pleased the ice cream was beginning to soften.

"I'm thinking *you* could use a friend."

The ice cream slid down her throat as Weston watched her with clear compassion.

She gulped. "What, um, makes you say that?"

"It's in your eyes. I don't want to overstep any bounds, but I see sadness there. Whether it's because of loss or something else, I have no idea. I realize it's none of my business, but I'd like to be your friend, Anna, if you'll allow me the honor."

Tears stung her eyes. "I'd really like that." Very few people had ever wanted to be her friend or tried to get to know her. Apparently, she hadn't been worth the investment of time or energy.

Yet this man called it an *honor*. Such precious words.

"Good. Now that we have that settled, eat up, my sweet. You're a dainty eater, aren't you?" Once again, he'd spared her from having to say more. But *my sweet?* She never knew what Weston would say, but he managed to keep the conversation lively.

"Thank you for not saying that with a bad British accent."

"Banish the thought," he said in a poorer imitation than Nick's, making her grin as Anna carved out another bite of ice cream.

"I stand corrected. Is my dainty eating a problem for you?" Anna purposely took her time spooning the ice cream and then brought the next bite ever so slowly toward her mouth.

Weston grabbed the plastic spoon from her grasp and licked it clean.

"You ice cream stealer!" Anna protested. "Now that you've had your way with my ice cream, you tell me. *Is* there an aftertaste?"

"Only the bitterness of my guilt in stealing from you." He laid the spoon on the table. "Sorry for my impulsive behavior. It won't happen again. I'll go get you another spoon."

"Impulsiveness can be fun. I'll assume you don't have any bad germs and take my chances."

Weston put his hand over the spoon when she tried to grab it. "Germs are germs. You don't know me well enough to share…" His lips upturned. "I'm going to stop before I say something we'll both regret. Be right back." Lifting out of the chair, he walked over to the counter.

Anna glanced around the shop. Mr. Paulson had disappeared into the back and the other couple had left. "I have another question," she said when Weston returned.

He handed her the replacement spoon and dug his spoon inside his waffle cone. "Ask away."

"Why is it people in Georgia drop their *ings* a lot, but when they pronounce Darling, why, there's the *ing*! For instance, Candee can be *sayin'* something, but then she'll holler to a new customer, 'Welcome to the Darl*ing* Diner!'"

The corners of Weston's mouth curved again. He seemed to find amusement in her question. "I'm a native Georgian, and I don't drop my *ings*. I'm a born-and-raised city boy, though. Okay, my turn. Different but still sort of related, I guess."

Anna grinned. "Go for it although you didn't answer my question."

"Oh, right. I think it's kind of like a colloquial or regional thing. Let me give you an example. My parents went on a trip to Germany a few years ago. They said people in one German town sometimes can't understand the citizens in another town that's only five miles down the road. Same language but different pronunciations or dialect or whatever."

"Interesting observation," she said, licking her spoon. "What's your question?"

"Have you noticed how singers from other countries lose their accents when they sing?"

Anna shook her head. "That's not the same thing at all. Certain words give them away."

"Yeah? Like what?"

Anna searched her mind for an example after she spooned another bite into her mouth. "Can't is one," she said. "Sounds like *cawn't*. Ask becomes *awsk*. And the word *girl* comes out more like *gull*. You know it does," she insisted when Weston chuckled. "Listen to Rod Stewart, Phil Collins, or Sting, and you'll see what I mean." She snapped her fingers. "Davy Jones!"

"O—kay. Who's Davy Jones?"

"Seriously, Weston? Davy's only the cutest Monkee ever."

"Monkey? Like the primate?" Weston finished his cone and wiped his mouth.

She burst out laughing. "You're hopeless. The Monkees were a singing group from the late sixties, and they had a TV show. Davy sang this sweet song once where he thanked his girl for making his morning brighter, the music softer, basically for making the world better. He made Marcia Brady a very happy girl. He was one of my first crushes, and the way he sang *gull* was adorable."

"Not sure I get the music softer thing, but *Brady Bunch*, right?" Weston's blue eyes lit and those appealing crinkles surfaced around his eyes. "I've seen some of the old reruns. Marcia Marcia Marcia was one *groovy* chick. I'm learning all kinds of fun things about you tonight. I'm glad we have this unexpected opportunity to spend some time together tonight." He grinned. "You've gotta love alliteration.

Try saying that one—*time together tonight*—three times in quick succession."

"I'll let you do that. So, what kinds of things have you learned?" Call her a flirt, but she wanted to hear his answer.

"Well, you're adventurous as evidenced by your daring choice of ice cream flavor. For the record, there wasn't an aftertaste. Butter rum is decent, but it's not something I'd purposely order."

When she rolled her eyes, his grin grew wider. "That diner uniform doesn't do you justice. You look terrific tonight in spite of the high humidity. Better than any supermodel."

Her cheeks warmed, and Anna lowered her gaze. *Supermodel?* Her white shorts were a decent length, nothing too short or revealing. Her father was tall, and her mother had been, as well, so she'd been blessed with long legs. She wore very little makeup, and she'd thrown on a plain pink cotton top, and swept her hair into a ponytail. Nothing memorable.

"Thank you." Coming from most men, Weston's compliment would have come across as self-serving.

"Anna, I'm sure it's no secret I think you're the prettiest girl I've met—"

"In Darling, Georgia?" Her question slipped out more from nerves than anything else.

Weston's gaze softened and settled in close proximity to her heart. "The prettiest girl I'll ever meet the rest of my life."

Oh, my. If Charley were here, she'd positively swoon.

What could she possibly say to that? Her cheeks must match the color of the retro Coca-Cola sign on the wall. When a giggle slipped out unaware, Anna's eyes widened. "That wasn't a giggle."

"Yes, it was definitely a giggle," he said. "It was adorable."

"I don't think anyone's called me adorable since I was six."

"How do you feel about sexy?"

Her pulse raced. "Adorable it is. None of that talk, please. I hardly know you."

"I'm trying to remedy that with the best of intentions. Never let it be said that Weston Galloway's not a gentleman." Rising from his chair, he gathered their trash and tossed it in the nearest trash receptacle. "Thanks, Mr. Paulson!"

"Welcome, Weston. Bye, Anna!" the man called from the back room. "Sorry. I'd come out, but my hands are in dishwater."

Anna grinned. "No problem. Bye! The butter rum was fantastic."

"Glad you liked it. Come and see us again soon."

"Will do." Weston held the door and escorted her outside. Thankfully, the temperature had dropped and a welcoming light breeze ruffled through the trees.

Ten minutes later, they sat side-by-side on the front step. The house was dark and quiet, and they continued to talk, lingering, enjoying one another's company and delaying the eventual good night. Anna couldn't remember the last time she had such a wonderful time. Talking about nothing with Weston was better than discussing anything with most people.

He nudged her arm. "I'm surprised you haven't asked me about my shirt."

"That's because it was too dim to read it outside and your arms covered it up when we were inside the ice cream shop. Or else you moved around too much. Well, that, and I'm pretty sure you'd have accused me of being a pervert if I kept staring at your chest."

He didn't laugh as Anna expected. "It's a shirt for Purity Promise, a volunteer ministry I began with a group of people from my church based on Psalm 51, verse 10. 'Create in me a clean heart, O God, and renew a steadfast spirit within me.' The basic concept is to apply that Scripture verse to our moral as well as our spiritual lives. The idea of cleansing and renewing our minds, our hearts, and our bodies, from the inside out."

"Sounds wonderful. Is it a ministry for both men and women?"

"Yep. Sure is. We have married couples who counsel other marrieds and engaged couples and same-sex counseling for singles—never married, widowed, divorced. We've assembled a solid team of pastors and youth pastors from the Atlanta area to help us out, too. We're trying to reach out across the state. We provide counseling services whenever and wherever they're needed, depending on the circumstances."

"I imagine there are a lot of hurting people who can benefit from those services."

Weston nodded. "It's been very successful in the few years since we started it. The aim is to give people hope that no matter what they've done in the past, or where they've been, there's no sin—sexual, moral, or otherwise—that can't be forgiven by the Lord.

A lot of men and women, including Christians, think God can't forgive certain things. Like there's a list of sins with degrees of severity and levels of punishment."

"That's a little...unbelievable," she said.

"I know, but like a lot of things, there's a lot of misinformation and misunderstanding out there. Our goal is to try and educate by applying Scripture. We tell them about Christ, first and foremost, if they haven't trusted Him as Savior. And if they're a believer, we want them to understand that God forgives all if they repent, confess, and in faith, ask Him for forgiveness."

Weston blew out a sigh and stretched out his legs on the steps below where they sat.

"For whatever reason—pride, stubbornness, lack of faith, whatever—there are some who can't believe that anyone, including God, can be *that* merciful and forgiving. They believe they'll lose their salvation if they indulge in sinful behavior. We counsel them that sin is sin, and no matter *what* it is, they all grieve the Lord. We try to give them the steps to resolve their guilt and get right with God."

"I imagine some see a believer's eternal security in Christ as free license to go ahead and sin," Anna said. "The idea that we can't lose our salvation, so go ahead and do whatever you want."

"That's true, unfortunately. We use a number of verses to counteract that philosophy. One of the theme verses is Second Corinthians 5:17 about being a new creature in Christ. The verse I personally use the most is First John 3:9. 'No one who is born of God practices sin, because His seed abides in him; and he cannot sin, because he is born of God.' That verse reinforces the truth that God is actively involved in refining us as believers and is changing us from the inside out."

"I love that, Weston. It's a powerful message. Thank you for telling me. See, I knew you were helping people, and that was before I heard about Purity Promise. It must be a challenge for you with your roommates here in Darling."

"It is, but I know God's put me there for a reason. I'm trying to be a good example and not come across as judgmental, but it's a fine line. Speaking of which, I should be getting back now."

He started to lift from the step but paused when Anna rested her hand on his forearm.

"Before you go, you know earlier when you said you thought I could use a friend? You were right. You also mentioned loss." Sadness clogged Anna's throat. "My mom died of a brain aneurysm when I was seventeen. Her name was Maura, and she was my best friend. I miss her every day, especially when I hear or see something I wish I could share with her. Sometimes I can't believe Mom's been gone for almost ten years." Her voice grew quiet. "It doesn't seem possible."

Weston laced his fingers with hers. "I'm sorry, Anna. I'm glad you had such a great relationship with your mom. When I was seventeen, I thought my folks hated me. To be honest, I wasn't too fond of them, either. They watched my comings and goings like a hawk and, in my cocky, adolescent mind, they had zero sense of humor."

"Maybe they wanted to try and stop you from making the same mistakes *they* did at the same age."

"I think my parents were trying to save me from myself, and they were right," he said. "Remember, I was pretty ornery. I wasn't a candidate for juvenile hall, but I had my moments. I wouldn't say I became friends with my folks until a few years ago. We have a very honest and solid relationship now." Leaning close, he squeezed her hand. "But I can't imagine losing them at *any* age."

She should tell Weston more about her life and circumstances so he'd better understand. The competition had been fierce at Juilliard, and she'd been younger than many of the other students. Although her instructors worked her hard, they'd *believed* in her while her peers eyed her warily with a pervasive *you're too young to be here* or *you can't be as talented as I am* attitude. Her mother had been her ally, her rock, her confidante.

But she couldn't tell Weston now. Not tonight.

Anna forced a small smile. "If it's not too personal, how old are you?"

"Nothing's too personal between friends." He nudged her arm and smiled. "I'm like the proverbial open book. I'm twenty-eight. I'll be twenty-nine in November. Your turn."

"I'm twenty-six, and my birthday's late next month." Why she'd told him that, she had no idea.

Offering his hand, Weston pulled her up beside him. "Tell you what. If we're both still here in Darling on your birthday, I'm taking you out for a great dinner. And *not* at The Darling Diner, no matter how hard you beg."

She clapped her hands. "A place with a tablecloth and candles?"

He laughed. "I'm sure that could be arranged. Maybe even soft music and real silver."

"I had fun tonight, Weston. Best time I've ever had getting kicked out of my own temporary home."

"I had fun, too."

Anna's breath caught when he reached around her. "My posture's still good, thanks."

"That's not what I'm doing." He gently tugged on her ponytail.

"Is that how a Purity Promise member says good night?"

Weston's gaze met hers. "Not exactly." His fingers slipped through the length of her ponytail before he released it, his expression one of wonder. "Good night, Anna. I'll see you again soon."

"Good night. Thanks for the ice cream and the wonderful conversation."

"Anytime." He kissed her cheek with a sweetness that brought tears to her eyes. "Thank you for making the evening brighter."

She bit her lower lip, momentarily unable to speak.

When he made no move to leave, Anna turned to go. Once inside the house, she made sure to turn the lock.

Moving to the window, Anna watched as he descended the front stairs. When he reached the sidewalk, Weston turned back toward the house and raised his hand.

The prettiest girl I'll ever meet the rest of my life.

No matter where the Lord led, no matter where her life's adventures found her, she'd forever remember this night and Weston's romantic sentiment.

After returning his wave, Anna moved one hand over her heart. "Weston Galloway, you make it awfully hard for a girl not to fall for you."

Chapter 15

Weston knocked on the bathroom door. "Come on, man. Sometime tonight!"

"Hold your horses! I'm coming out now."

Whoa. That voice didn't belong to Neil, Tom, or Brandon. Undeniably female.

The door flew open. A tall, slender but curvy brunette glared at him through eyes clouded with lack of sleep or alcohol, perhaps both. Judging by the faint red hue of her irises, she was intoxicated, although her words hadn't been slurred. Her long hair was disheveled, her lipstick smudged on full lips. She wore a wrinkled light blue T-shirt he'd seen on Neil earlier in the week that barely covered her from the plunging V on her chest to its über short length.

Lord, keep my eyes averted. He had no interest in a woman like this, but he was still a man, and not completely immune to the lure of a half-clothed female. Not to mention the lingering mental images.

Lord, keep my thoughts pure. Especially after telling Anna about his ministry, he figured the enemy would love nothing more than to grab hold of him and drag him down into the pit of sin.

Stand firm, stand strong.

Swaying a bit, the woman placed one well-manicured hand on the doorjamb. Her gaze raked him up and down, and a slow, provocative smile spread across her face. "Well, hello there, handsome." The woman's accent was southern, more Alabama than Georgia. Too bad her attractiveness was overshadowed by her brazen personality and overt sexuality.

"Hi. I need to get in the bathroom if you don't mind."

"Do you want to come and join our little party?" Unsteady, she swayed again in his direction but caught herself at the last second.

"No, thanks. I just need to use the bathroom." They had four small, separate bedrooms but only one bathroom. Go figure. The place was furnished to provide the basic necessities—beds, dressers, a desk in the living room, and kitchenware—clearly a place better suited for men. Utilitarian. The way things were going, their cramped living quarters weren't any better than a frat house for guys pushing thirty.

"Maybe I won't let you." She planted one hand on his chest and leaned close. "Nice abs you've got. What else you got to offer under here?" She bunched his T-shirt in one hand and lifted, stopping only when he stepped out of reach. This woman was too stinking drunk to focus on what his shirt said. If she even noticed it, the meaning behind Purity Promise would be lost on her or else it'd be a blatant mockery.

"Nothing for you." Weston's jaw tightened and he restrained himself from manhandling her. "I'd appreciate it if you'd move out of the way now so I can get into the bathroom. *Please.*" He should have turned and run from the start, but he'd thank the Lord later he hadn't yet stripped off his clothes.

"Make me." Her eyes challenged him, and she licked her lips.

"I take it your Neil's...friend?" He bit his tongue. *Lord, keep me polite.*

"That's right. I'm Darcy. And *you* are Mr. Sexy Gorgeous. Where've you been hiding yourself in this sleepy little town?" She traced a slow finger down his jaw and then squeezed his right bicep before he stepped away again. "We could have some fun, you and me. Neil wouldn't mind."

"Darcy, I'm going to get Neil now so he can escort you back...home." His fault for not jerking away from her sooner.

She shook her head and ran one hand through her dark hair. "Nope. Not going home. Neil and I are having a sleepover. Although I doubt we'll get much...sleep." She giggled and then a loud burp escaped. This entire scenario disgusted him. He could only pray she wouldn't get sick, although if she did, it might sober her up a bit.

He should have stayed in Atlanta and never signed on for this job, but the money was too good to ignore. Working this project would give him a good amount to stash away for the future. His house needed some repairs. So, for now, he needed to suck it up and get along with his roommates as best he could for the duration. Fun times.

Lord, help us all.

Darcy wasn't budging. She put her arms behind her and leaned against the wall. This woman knew all the moves to accentuate her body and try to entice a guy. He might as well flee and go outside to do his business under the cover of darkness. Be done with it.

Neil stumbled down the hallway wearing only cotton sleep pants that rode low on his hips, the drawstring hanging loose, the winged dragon tattoo nearly on full display. "Hey, Wes. What's going on, man?" Unlike Darcy, his roommate appeared more tired than drunk.

"Your friend and I are getting better acquainted." Darcy lost her balance again and stumbled forward, leaving Weston no choice but to catch her. Being careful to put his hands on her shoulders, he firmly pushed Darcy upright. He leaned her against the wall, making sure she was halfway steady before releasing his hold and stepping aside. If she fell again, Neil could take over.

This was another reminder why he'd stopped going to bars with the guys from the fire station. Some women couldn't resist any man in uniform. For some, a wedding band was an even bigger challenge to conquer. Weston didn't want to be a party to any of the games people played, then *or* now.

Neil stared at him, open-mouthed. "You hittin' on my girl, Righteous Man?"

He was done playing nice. "Give me a break, Neil. Look at her. Darcy's so wasted she can't stand up on her own." He addressed her again. "I'd appreciate it if you'd move out of the way now so I can go in…" With an exasperated grunt, Weston pointed to the bathroom.

"Darcy, move out of the way, baby."

At least Neil knew his overnight guest's name. That was progress. He assumed Darcy was the woman from before.

Darcy winked. "Very nice to make your acquaintance, Wes."

The muscles in his jaw clenched. "Good night." Maybe he'd been rude, but at the moment, he couldn't care less. He doubted she took offense or would even remember this conversation come morning.

"Nighty night." Darcy made a point to brush against him with full intent and purpose. Caught him completely unaware. Neil didn't pick up on what she'd done or Weston would most likely get blamed for coming on to the woman.

Going into the bathroom, Weston locked the door, something he rarely did. He didn't put anything past Darcy and didn't want to leave the door open, in more ways than one, for her to cause more trouble.

In his bedroom a few minutes later, Weston stepped out of his shorts and tugged the T-shirt over his head. After tossing them on the end of the bed, he crawled under the sheet and lightweight blanket. One of the guys had cranked up the air conditioning, and it was colder than he liked.

Darcy was a temptress who tried too hard.

Anna was tempting without trying.

Darcy was a seductress who used her body to lure a man. Anna was the essence of femininity, purity, sweetness mixed with beauty of soul and body, intelligent, a godly woman.

Hearing sounds coming from Neil's room, Weston turned over and buried his head beneath the pillow. Better to stifle his groan. Anything to tune out what was happening in the next room. He figured the Lord was trying to teach him something. Was he being tested?

Greater is He who is in you than he who is in the world.

Prayer would be good here. So, he prayed—out loud—for Neil. For Darcy. For Tom and Brandon. And then for Anna, Charley, and Nick. Candee, Roz, and the staff at the diner. Prayed for his parents. Prayed for the City of Atlanta, the State of Georgia, the country and the world. Prayed for Roswell, prayed for his boss, the construction crew in Darling, and anyone else in the free world and beyond its borders who needed prayer.

When he finished, Weston wondered if Anna was still awake. He hoped she was fast asleep and getting good rest. It was true, what he'd told her. Spending time with her was better than any date he'd ever had. Their time together tonight only reinforced that opinion.

He still knew so little about her. But what he knew, he liked. Very much. With each conversation, and each moment spent in her presence, he learned a little more about the puzzle that was Anna Redmond, and peeled away another layer.

"Lord," he whispered. "Thank you for unexpected opportunities and bringing Anna into my life. No matter your reason or purpose, help me to be her friend." He yawned. "In the name of your Son, I pray these things. Amen."

He lifted his head from the pillow and listened. Nothing but blessed silence.

Thank you, Jesus.

Weston checked the alarm, rolled onto his back, and willed sleep to come quickly.

Chapter 16

The next morning, in spite of a stormy forecast, Weston decided to walk to the construction site. He'd detour a few blocks so he'd pass Anna's rental home. Nothing like being obvious, not that he hadn't already crossed that threshold.

Lightning streaked across the sky and thunder rumbled in the distance as ominous, dark clouds rolled overhead. He'd never minded the rain and loved a soaking downpour. At the worksite, he normally didn't even bother putting on rain gear. A little rain never hurt until it caused flooding, and sometimes it did. Hopefully, not today.

He'd stayed in his room until he knew Darcy had left with Neil. Tried to study his Bible but ended up thinking about Anna. Tom and Brandon were working the earlier shift, giving him time to himself in the apartment, a precious commodity. Especially after recent events, he was grateful for the gift of silence.

Weston's steps slowed as he approached Anna's house.

He'd never camped out on a girl's front steps or porch, including when he'd fallen in puppy love with his first serious girlfriend, Laura Martin, when he was seventeen. The same age as Anna when she'd lost her mother. She'd mentioned her mother being her best friend, and she seemed tight with Charley. Did she have many girlfriends? What were her hobbies? Did she attend church regularly?

The unanswered questions were beginning to niggle at him. He wanted to know this woman. The sad fact was that if Anna left town today, because of privacy laws—a *good* thing—he'd have a hard time getting information out of anyone at The Darling Diner or from the real estate management company who'd rented the house to her.

Patience, Galloway. All in good time.

Spying rose bushes on the side of the house next door, he hesitated. Did he dare pick one? He hoped it wasn't illegal to pick a bloom from a flowering rosebush in Darling. No time like the present to find out. If it was, hopefully the local law enforcement officer wasn't around.

Heading up the front walkway, Weston knocked on the screen door. The home's occupants might not be up and moving around yet since it was still fairly early for some people—not yet nine o'clock. After waiting a minute, he turned to leave as a deep rumble of thunder sounded.

"What can I do for you, young man?" An older man peered up at him through the screen. A woman, presumably his wife, stood behind him. "If you've got something to sell, we don't want it. We've got everything we could ever want and then some."

"That's great to hear, sir. I'm not selling anything. My name's Weston Galloway. I was, uh, wondering if maybe you'd let me buy some of your roses?"

"Young man, you help yourself to a nice bouquet. Whatever you want." That response came from the woman, and he could vaguely make out her bright smile behind the screen.

"I think one or two will be enough, ma'am. It's the thought that counts, right?" Above all, Weston didn't want to overwhelm Anna.

"Let me guess," the man said. "They're for that pretty lady who moved in the house next door? I knew it wouldn't be long before the lineup of young men started."

"Raymond, that's none of our business." The woman spoke up again. "If they *are* for her, you tell her we've certainly enjoyed her music."

"Her music?"

"Piano. Classical stuff," the man said. "She had the side window in the living room open earlier this morning. The way the playing stops and then starts up again with the same thing makes us think someone's playing the piano."

The woman spoke up. "We saw a truck from a store in Atlanta pull into her driveway yesterday morning and deliver a baby piano."

"Baby *grand*, Lois," Raymond corrected.

"Whatever, Smarty Pants."

Weston restrained his smile. He loved older couples like these two. "I don't know about the music, but your roses sure are beautiful. I appreciate your generosity."

Lois pushed past Raymond and stepped onto the porch. "Excuse me still being in my housecoat, but come with me. That way if any busybodies are watching, they won't accuse you of stealing my roses." She started down the front steps with Weston right behind her.

"Good luck, Weston!" Raymond called from inside the house.

He waved to the older man and followed Lois around the side of the house. Sharp blades of dry grass brushed against the lower legs of his jeans, tall enough to reach the top of his boots. The yard was scattered with weeds, and the bushes and hedges along the side of the house and those lining the driveway separating their house from Anna's, could use some tending and trimming.

"Gonna be another hot day." Lois shaded her eyes with one hand and glanced up at the sky. "Looks like we're going to get rain, but it'll only make it steamier. July in Georgia, right?" She lowered her gaze to meet his. "Are you one of the men working on the new savings and loan?"

"I am. Our crew's from Atlanta."

"Well, isn't that nice? How about I send some lemonade, sweet tea, or water down to you later on this afternoon? I'm sure you must get awful hot working outside all day."

"Yes, ma'am, but I wouldn't want you to go to the trouble—"

"Oh, it's no trouble. Raymond has a wagon he can pull. It'll get him out of the house, and he'd enjoy it. The doctor told him to get more exercise. As long as it'd be okay with you."

"Sure. We'd appreciate it." He needed to get moving. "Do you mind if I have a peach-colored rose?"

"Not at all. It's a real shame the yellow and pink roses are a bit wilted, but there's new blooms coming in. If you keep coming by, you can give your lady friend a different color rose every day of the week."

Reaching into the pocket of her housecoat, Lois held up a small pair of scissors. "Never hurts to have these handy." She pointed to one of the gently blooming roses. "How about this one?"

"Perfect, thanks. Her name is Anna. Your neighbor."

"I look forward to meeting her. I've seen her head down to the diner and, judging by her uniform, figured she's working there. She sure is a pretty girl. I can see why she's caught your fancy."

Lois snipped off the rose and handed it to him with a smile. "The peach rose is a good one if you don't know Anna all that well yet. It represents more platonic friendship or a way to say thank you and express gratitude although some say it represents modesty and the blush on a pure maiden's face."

Taking the flower from Lois, Weston felt sure *his* face might be a little flushed. "How about one more?"

"I'd suggest a white rose. Look how lovely this one is." She put her hand behind the rose, lifting it and bringing it forward. "It's not fully opened yet, but rather, it's awakening. The white stands for a new beginning."

"Sounds great." He figured the white color had to represent purity.

After snipping the stem, Lois handed the bloom to him. "The white rose can also symbolize chastity, purity, innocence. Also spirituality."

Of course. He almost chuckled. At least spirituality was thrown into the mix. "I had no idea the colors meant anything special."

"Oh, honey, I reckon most people don't know what the colors are supposed to mean. A woman always loves getting flowers from a man. They're a thing of beauty, and you're right, it's the thought behind giving them that counts most. Give it your own meaning and interpretation, Weston. I'm sure Anna will love them, and it's such a romantic gesture on your part."

"I walked her home the last two nights," he said, apparently feeling the need to chat. "I told Anna my grandparents used to court while sitting on a porch swing like the one over at her house. I'd like to try and revive that tradition. Darling seems the perfect place, and I'm hoping Anna will agree."

Lois's eyes filled with moisture. "If it blooms into love, then you'll be blessed. If it doesn't, then you'll be blessed for having known one another for however long. I don't believe in coincidence, Weston. You two met for a reason, but at this point, perhaps only the good Lord knows what that reason is."

"I agree, Lois. I'm a believer in God things."

She smiled. Lifting her arm, she showed him a small surface scratch on her left forearm. "See this? No matter how careful I am, I always seem to get scratched by thorns and branches whenever I work with my roses. In a lot of ways, I think that's what God does to us."

"What's that, ma'am?"

"The good Lord more or less *prunes* us in order to try to reach the untapped beauty He *knows* what is inside us, just like in these flowers. Along the way, we get beat up sometimes, but it's worth it in the long run."

Lois gave his hand a light tap. "You'd better take those flowers on over to Anna now before they start to wilt in this heat. I'll send Raymond down to the construction site this afternoon with several gallons of whatever you'd like."

"Water's best while we're working as much as I'd love a big tall glass of sweet tea."

"Then I'll have Raymond bring some sweet tea just for you."

"Thanks, Lois. I'm glad we met."

"Same here. Hope to see you again soon." With a parting smile, she waved and walked around the corner of the house. He'd need to think more about Lois's words. There was a lesson in there somewhere, but right now he had a mission.

The official courting of Anna Redmond had begun.

Chapter 17

Slowly, Weston climbed the steps of Anna's house to the front porch as thunder rumbled in the distance. Any moment, they might be deluged in rain. He doubted they'd be spared.

Sliding the backpack off his shoulder, he dropped his gear beside the front door. Should he put the flowers in front of the door and leave or knock on the door? What man his age did something like this? Heaven forbid if Neil or one of the other guys caught wind of it.

"Sweet and romantic," he repeated under his breath. He'd given girls corsages and flowers before, but that'd been when he'd landed on their doorstep to pick them up for a date. Admittedly, he'd done it as much to make a good impression on the parents as to please the girl.

High school stuff. He'd been around long enough to know women liked flowers, and he'd given his share to a few women in the past. Most recently, he'd had them delivered to Madison for her birthday. Even he'd known better than to send roses, especially not red ones. They hadn't been dating all that long. His mistake was sending a bouquet to her at the school where she taught. Word spread like wildfire and fired up the old gossip train among his mother's circle of friends.

Maybe he should rethink the two roses in his hands and send Anna a bouquet instead. Small and elegant might be the way to go. Let her know he was thinking of her in an appropriate way. Did Darling have a florist? No, Anna seemed the type of woman to appreciate the more simple gesture like the two roses.

He needed to trust his first instincts. Get on with it before he was late to work. Way not to overthink this. "You're twenty-eight. Suck it up, man. Let's do this already."

Shifting on the porch floor, Weston raised his hand to knock. Seeing a flash of something, he jumped when a face appeared in the window to the right of the front door.

Nick. Not the person he'd hoped to see this morning.

Seconds later, the front door flew open. Nick wore long black athletic shorts, a gray muscle shirt, and neon yellow running shoes that had to glow in the dark. His hair was a dark, wild mess, and he looked like he'd just rolled out of bed.

"Happy Friday. How are you, mate?" He eyed the flowers. "Ah, you shouldn't have." British Nick was obviously back. This man's weird personality quirks, obsessions, or proclivities were none of his business.

"Morning, Nick. Nice shoes."

"Thanks. Anna's upstairs in the loo grabbing her morning shower." He leaned against the door, almost losing his footing when it shifted. Nothing seemed to faze the guy.

"Here's an idea," Nick said. "Why don't you go upstairs and fetch her? I'm sure that'd be a nice surprise. She was knackered last night and again at breakfast. Seeing you will help start her day off on a high note."

"That won't be necessary." Weston hoped Nick wasn't implying Anna was the type of woman who'd be agreeable to that type of behavior. And he wasn't about to ask what *knackered* meant.

"Is Charley around this morning?"

Nick chuckled. "Hands off my woman, mate. Charlotte's already spoken for."

"I wondered if she'd put these flowers in water so they don't wilt before Awna—*Anna*—sees them." Weston chewed the inside of his cheek not to laugh. This whole scenario was absurd. He glanced at his watch. "Listen, I only have ten minutes to get to work."

"Oh, of course. Charlotte, love! We have company. Come and see who's here."

"I take it you and Charley have decided to stay in Darling a few more days?"

"We have a flight back to New York on Sunday. The missus and I kind of like it here, and it gives Charley and Anna time to catch up with one another. Female bonding and all that. In the end, we guys benefit, you know."

"I wouldn't know, but I'll take your word for it." Weston was thankful Nick hadn't winked. He didn't take kindly to guys winking at other guys under *any* circumstances.

He felt an inner nudge. *Ask him.*

He sighed. *Really, Lord?*

Ask him.

Weston grunted. "Are you flying out of Atlanta?"

"That's right. I tried to charter a jet, but none were available at such short notice."

Charter a jet? These people must live in a parallel universe. Was this the kind of world Anna lived in? Did she live in New York, too?

"Nick, I'd be happy to take you and Charley into Atlanta if you don't mind riding in my truck. There's plenty of space." The unfortunate thing was it only seated three so Anna wouldn't be able to accompany them.

Nick's eyes narrowed. "That's a very generous offer, mate."

A man cleared his throat from inside the house and Nick stepped aside. "Got her all tuned up?"

The other guy held a black case in one hand. "Sure enough. She should be good to go now."

"Do you need me to sign anything?" Nick said.

"Miss Redmond took care of it beforehand. Have a good day."

Weston stepped aside for the man to pass by him, giving him a nod. The mystery deepened even more. He'd try not to wonder what *that* scenario was all about. Hopefully it'd been a *thing*, and not a person, who'd needed tuning. Namely, Anna.

None of your business, mate.

Charley ducked beneath Nick's arm and gave him a warm smile. "Hey, Weston. We'll take you up on your offer to take us to the airport. That's very kind." The streak of color in her hair was now pale green. Sure enough, she sported matching fingernails. Based on Charley's long cotton sleep pants, tank top, and wild hair to match her husband's, they'd had themselves quite a night.

"Hi, Charley. I need to get to work now, but would you mind putting these flowers in a vase for Anna?"

"Oh, of course." Charley took them from him. "Such beautiful roses! Aren't you the most precious man? She will love them."

Nick spoke up. "Anna gets lots of flowers from her admirers, but I'm sure these will mean more coming from you."

"Her admirers?" What did *that* mean?

"Well, yeah. From her—"

"I've always said one or two flowers, especially roses, from someone *special* mean more than a dozen from anyone else." Charley elbowed her husband. "Take notes, hubby."

"Always, my love. I get it. At times, less is decidedly *more*." Planting a kiss on her temple, Nick moved his hand around Charley's waist and drew her close.

Say and think what he might about him, this man treasured his wife and openly showered her with affection. From all appearances, this couple's relationship was solid. Weston had to wonder why Charley had run away from home. Maybe for that female bonding Nick had mentioned. On the other hand, perhaps it was a game they played—she'd run away and he'd come after her. What a life, but he wouldn't speculate further.

"I've gotta run, but I'll plan on picking you up here on Sunday whatever time you say." Weston reached for his gear.

"Thanks," Nick said, sounding genuinely touched. "About three should be good. Say Weston, old man. I've heard something about a local fair in town. Care to go with us tomorrow night? I'm sure Anna will be agreeable. Charlotte and I will make ourselves scarce and go find a kissing booth or some such fun. You'll be free to ride the Tilt-A-Whirl, Scrambler, or whatever you'd like with my wife's sister and enjoy your private time together."

Charley snuggled closer into the crook of Nick's arm. "I hear there's a dance at sunset." She lifted her brows and gave Weston a sweet smile. "Anna hasn't…danced…in a long time."

That comment gave Weston pause. What was *with* everybody in this town? Did the soaring temperatures and high humidity bring out their raging libidos or the need to make suggestive comments? Or was it possible his mind was overactive when it came to Anna?

"Sounds like fun," he said. "I'll stop in the diner later today and ask Anna. We could meet you at the fair." The opportunity to hold Anna in his arms and dance with her? That sounded like the best idea of the decade. He'd be crazy not to say yes to that opportunity.

"Sure. Whatever you'd like, mate." Nick smiled and saluted like Charley had done the other night.

"I'll make sure Anna gets your flowers," Charley said. "That was a lovely thing to do."

"It was my honor." Nick had gone elsewhere, so he'd seize the moment. "Charley, I have to ask. Why was Anna"—what was that word?—"*knackered* last night? Then again this morning?" He hiked the backpack over his right shoulder.

Charley ran her finger over the peach rose petals. "I'd say it's because she stayed up late talking with a man she likes. Very much."

"Oh. So, *I'm* the cause for Anna's state of knackerment?"

She giggled. "It only means she was exhausted. You won't hear Anna complaining. She had a big smile on her face earlier in spite of being tired."

"One more question if you don't mind. Do you or Anna play the piano?"

Charley bit her lip and lowered her gaze. "You could say that." Then she glanced back up at him. "You're good for her, Weston. More than you know."

He nodded. "Thanks, Charley. See you soon."

"You bet."

Weston took off in the direction of the construction site at a sprint. Smiling the entire way.

Chapter 18

Let the weekend begin.

Weston appreciated how Brad Colson gave them weekends off for this particular project, especially since most of the crew came from the Atlanta area. The crew had worked extra hard to get off early. The rain had pelted them a few times during the day but hadn't lasted long enough to delay them for long. Lois was right in that it was humid as anything.

He'd run home, grab a quick shower, and then head over to The Darling Diner for dinner. Fried chicken, biscuits, and flirting with a beautiful girl on a Friday night sounded like a great way to start what he hoped would be an eventful weekend.

Weston was relieved to find the apartment empty. He'd heard Tom and Brandon mention going home for the weekend, and prayed he wouldn't have another run-in with Darcy. Once was enough. If Neil insisted on spending the night with the woman, maybe he could bunk at Darcy's place instead of bringing her into their apartment. He didn't want to waste energy thinking about all the *what ifs* until faced with the reality. Neil knew he hadn't been happy with the events of last night. As usual, he'd blown it off, in one ear and out the other.

After his shower, Weston tugged a nice light blue shirt over his head. Mom gave it to him for Christmas from one of those chain stores. What was that smell? He lifted the bottom of the shirt and sniffed. Reminded him of the mall. Nope. He'd need to wash it first. Off it went.

Planting himself in front of the small closet, Weston surveyed the scant selection. Other than work T-shirts and jeans, he'd brought a red polo and a short-sleeved white dress shirt for church. He hadn't planned on courting a woman while working in Darling. He spied two pairs of shorts—one khaki and one navy—and lightweight gray dress slacks.

With the high heat and humidity, he could only stretch the wardrobe so far before he'd need to pay a visit to the Darling Wash & Dry. After dropping Charley and Nick at the airport, he'd drive over to his house and pick up more clothes.

He grabbed the white shirt from the closet. He'd save the red polo for the 4-H Fair. He didn't want to wear the white shirt to the fair and then again on Sunday morning or people might talk. He didn't care what anyone said about *him*, but he didn't want busybodies speculating about why he was wearing the same thing, even in church, especially if he was seen with Anna both places. Sometimes church members could be the worst offenders when it came to gossip.

Neil was right. He was feeling protective of Anna. He'd started out that way, and he'd continue to watch out for that woman.

Weston pulled on his last pair of clean jeans. He buttoned and tucked in the shirt. Check. Zip the jeans. Check. Never hurt to make sure. He couldn't afford any embarrassing wardrobe malfunctions with Anna.

Opening the dresser drawer, he rifled through his socks and underwear. "Where is that belt?" He hoped he hadn't forgotten it back home, but thought he'd thrown it in to wear for church. Locating it, he quickly threaded the brown belt through the loops and fastened the buckle.

Next decision. Boat shoes, tennis shoes, Tony Lama cowboy boots? He wasn't sure why he'd brought the boots, but he liked wearing them. As long as he didn't wear his construction boots, he'd be okay. He grabbed a pair of socks from the drawer and within the minute, tugged on the boots.

"You are such a *girl*, Galloway. Don't overthink this."

Never in his life had he spent more than five minutes thinking about what to wear or getting dressed except for his senior prom. Next he'd be parading in front of the mirror and checking out his rear view. *Not.* He chuckled at his own idiocy.

Yeah, he was in trouble. The *best* kind of trouble.

All to impress a woman.

After a quick trip to the bathroom, Weston grabbed his keys from the top of the dresser. On the way out of the apartment, he spotted Neil's cream-colored Stetson hanging on a hook by the front door. It was like the hat called his name. *Wear me. Be a cowboy.*

Chewing his lower lip, Weston tugged his cell phone out of his pocket and clicked on Neil's number. "Hey, Neil. It's Wes. Listen, I'm headed out. Do you mind if I borrow your Stetson? I'll take good care of it. Okay, thanks, man. Appreciate it. Have a good evening."

Thankful Neil hadn't pressed for details of his weekend, and didn't share *his* plans, Weston tucked the phone back in his pocket.

Lifting the hat off the hook, he settled it on his head. Unbelievably enough, it was a perfect fit. Even if it wasn't, he figured it'd be close enough. What was it about a Stetson? He had one back home and wore it on rare occasions. A man walked a little taller, his shoulders looked a little broader, and it seemed to give a guy confidence. His chest puffed out a little more and his ego might have grown just a bit.

Women like a man in a Stetson. That was the bottom line. Anna wasn't like most women, but maybe she'd like seeing him in one. That alone was worth the risk.

"Let's go, Cowboy." Maybe he could pull off the image, anyway.

Weston climbed into his brand new truck, his red Ford F-150, his pride and joy. His baby. Leaning over the seat, he gave it a quick once-over. A few bags from fast food places and some old truck magazines. Not bad, but he should vacuum and clean out the back before transporting the Parkers to the airport on Sunday night.

Whoa. Back up a second.

With the Lord's favor, he'd be driving Anna to the fair tomorrow night. Yep, he'd need to clean out the truck and give it a shine tomorrow afternoon. The thought of riding the Ferris wheel with Anna made him smile. He'd buy cotton candy or fried dough and feed it to her. Share a footlong hot dog. He was a decent shot and could win one of those teddy bears or whatever animal she wanted at the shooting gallery. Do a little dancing under the stars.

He hadn't been to any kind of fair with a girl since he'd been sixteen and got his face slapped after he'd tried to kiss Sandie Myer behind the fun house.

"Thank you, Sandie. Hope you're enjoying life." His mom told him she'd married a guy from Texas and moved down among the oil wells and skyscrapers in the Houston area.

Technically, the fair could be considered his third outing with Anna. He'd been thinking about kissing her all day. They'd already shared a lot and somehow he didn't think she'd be adverse to a little peck. Maybe more. It was the *maybe more* he shouldn't dwell on.

He'd learned to be much more of a gentleman since the cocky kid he'd been with Sandie. To the point where Madison had finally demanded that he kiss her good night. That'd been the sixth date. She'd counted and let him know it was time.

Weston put the truck in gear and it took all of three minutes to get downtown and park on the east side street of The Darling Diner. He couldn't even get on the *highway* in three minutes in Atlanta.

Candee waved and gestured for him to take a seat anywhere when he strolled into the diner. He spied Anna standing by the front counter talking with an older woman. Twirling the peach rose between her fingers, she looked happy. *Wow.* No woman should look that good in that uniform, those shoes, and silly fake glasses halfway down her nose.

"You gonna sit down, Cowboy, or stand there and stare all moony-eyed at my waitress all afternoon?"

"That's a tough choice." Weston turned and smiled at Roz. "How are you this fine day?"

She harrumphed. "I'd fire her, but Anna's good for business. Customers like her. Keeps bringing you back, too, I've noticed."

"Ah, come on now. You're not fooling me. Look at her. She's keeping that lady at the counter happy. Anna's more relaxed, and she's not spilling, dropping, or breaking as much now. She's only been working here a few days. Considering she's never done anything like waitressing before, she's doing a great job. Think what a fantastic server she'll be by this time *next* week."

"Yeah, well, it's not like *you're* the most objective customer." Roz gave him a light swat with the towel in her hand. If Weston didn't know better, he'd think she was being playful.

"I'll keep her around," Roz said. "She's not so bad. Only 'cause I like seein' your handsome face. You're lookin' fine all spit-shined, mister. You clean up real nice."

"Roz, are you flirting with me?"

"In your dreams, youngster. Want a sweet tea?"

"Sounds great. Thanks. Which one is Table 9?"

"Why? That your lucky number?"

"No, but my Grandpa Galloway likes it. Seems as good a reason as any."

Roz led him to a table in the middle of the diner and pulled out a chair. "Have a seat, and I'll send Anna over to take your order if she can unstick her nose from that rose long enough to function. Thanks for that. Her head's been in the clouds ever since she got here earlier."

"You're welcome." Weston sat back in the chair and gave the diner's owner his most charming smile.

"Nose out of the rose. You're a poet and don't know it," said a young guy clearing tables nearby.

Roz shot him a look. "Lance, keep cleanin' those tables and keep your comments to yourself."

Across the diner, Weston's gaze locked with Anna's. She angled her head toward the rose in her hand and mouthed *thank you*. He was still trying to come up with something smooth and suave when the front door opened and Neil, Tom, and Brandon trudged inside. Great. He refused to let these guys dampen his mood. Late on a Friday afternoon, they shouldn't stick around long. Neil still wore his work clothes, but the other guys had changed into their weekend wear.

Neil headed straight for his table and slid into the adjacent chair. The other guys claimed the remaining seats.

"Figured I'd find you here." Neil smiled at the others. "I guarantee he's not here for the food though it's not half-bad either."

"It's Darling's favorite gathering place," Weston said.

Neil nodded to the Stetson. "Nice hat."

"Thanks. I think so."

"Hi, y'all." Anna appeared beside their table. "Want something to drink?"

Weston blinked and stared at her, slack jawed.

"What? Is something wrong?" Anna glanced down at her uniform. "I spilled mustard earlier, but—"

"Wes, shut your mouth, bud." Neil chuckled. "Your drool's about to drip on the table." He slung his arm around the back of Weston's chair. "Say, Anna, you're looking fine today."

Ignoring Neil, Weston met her gaze. "You said y'all."

Her brown eyes grew wide. "I did not."

"Oh, I beg to differ, darlin'." Weston exaggerated his drawl, knowing she liked it. "We're gonna make a southern girl out of you yet." Judging by the way Anna's cheeks pinked, she didn't mind.

Neil slapped the table. "Time to get this party started. How about a light beer? Whatever you've got on tap is good. I'm not particular."

"We don't serve alcohol here." Roz leaned between them and set Weston's glass of sweet tea on the table. "If that's what you're lookin' for, you can head down to Clancy's. Three blocks south."

"We're acquainted with Clancy's," Neil said. "Then I'll take sweet tea like my pal Weston here. Got any limes?"

"Of course," Anna said, taking over from Roz.

Tom raised his finger. "I'll have a Coke."

"Root beer," Brandon said. At least those two could speak for themselves. Weston had never worked with such quiet guys. Not that it was a bad thing, especially at the apartment. At the worksite, the rest of the crew picked up the slack in the conversational arena.

"I'll be right back with your drinks." Anna departed the table, and Weston swallowed the inclination to tell Neil to keep his eyes to himself.

"So, what's on the agenda for the weekend?" Weston said to divert Neil's attention.

Brandon brightened. "Me and Tom are goin' home. We're leavin' right after we have our drinks."

"Turns out Brandon has a girlfriend back home," Neil told him.

Weston nodded. "That's great." At least Brandon hadn't picked up another girl since he'd been in town. If he *had*, Weston figured his ignorance was bliss. He listened as Brandon told him about his childhood sweetheart, Kym.

"We're talkin' about gettin' engaged for Christmas and married early next summer."

"Congrats, man." Neil drummed a rhythm on the tabletop. "I'm hoping Wes has a good time tonight in that hat. I don't call it my lucky hat for nothing. I've scored more—"

"Neil, cut the act." Brandon slapped one hand on the table. "Stop actin' like you're God's gift to women. You've got nothin' to brag about, and we don't want to hear none of it."

They all stared at Brandon. Meek, quiet Brandon.

"Go back to your cute little girlfriend and leave me alone, Country Boy." Neil rose to his feet. "Is there a jukebox in this place? We need some country tunes on a Friday night."

Weston wouldn't have been surprised if Neil slammed out of the diner. That was one thing about the guy—to his credit, Neil didn't walk away from confrontations.

Anna brought their drinks and carefully placed them on the table. "The jukebox is in the corner. Still only a quarter a tune." She lowered a small dish with limes on the table.

"Thanks, babe. Order me a chicken fried steak sandwich and fries, would you?" Neil jumped up from his chair, scraping it against the floor. Digging into the pocket of his jeans, he pulled out a few coins.

"Weston, let me get you some more tea," Anna said. "Sweet, right?"

"The only way a self-respecting southern boy drinks it. Thanks." He handed Anna his glass, wondering how she'd react if *he* called her babe. With Neil, it seemed ingrained in his personality. Chances were he hadn't thought about it.

Anna leaned close for his ears only. "Neil doesn't bother me. Nice hat, by the way."

He caught her free hand. "Do you have a break coming up anytime soon? I'd like to talk with you."

"Not for a couple of hours. I can ask Roz. I haven't committed any grievous offense today, so she might be feeling charitable."

He removed the Stetson and set it on a nearby chair. "I can talk to her if you want."

Anna gave him another one of her *I can handle it on my own* glances. He was growing accustomed to, and *liked*, those glances.

"I'll ask Roz." She slowly withdrew her hand from his.

"Girl, jump in my truck and let's paint the town red tonight." Neil sang along with the country tune and moved to the front of the diner. With a small bow, he offered his hand to the older woman at the counter. "Dance with me, darlin'?"

Tom and Brandon snickered and looked the other way as Neil coaxed the woman to the small area in front of the jukebox. Weston was surprised she'd agreed.

"Would you look at that?" Roz stopped behind Weston's chair. "I haven't seen Della smile like that since her husband, Van, died." So, this was the widow Anna had mentioned.

Sitting back in his chair, Weston observed the pair as they danced together. Neil smiled and talked with Della, acting respectful, a gentleman. Seemed the guy had a decent heart, after all, waiting to rise to the occasion. He'd suspected it was inside him somewhere. His roommate was a classic case of looking for love in all the wrong places, like a lot of people, men *and* women, in those *love 'em and leave 'em* songs Neil seemed to like.

Weston rose to his feet. "How about it, Roz? Care to take a spin on the dance floor?"

The woman's face flushed deep red, and he felt sure he might be on the receiving end of a slap. "Well, I…" Reaching behind her, she quickly removed her apron and tossed it over a chair. "All right, young fella. Let's show 'em how it's done."

Like Neil, Roz seemed to know most of the lyrics to the next country tune Neil had selected. The woman was surprisingly agile, and Weston had to work to keep up with her.

"Let your hair down and move a little closer." She beckoned to him with her finger. He tried to hide his shock when she shimmied her shoulders. She wasn't flirting, but the woman sure could dance. Who knew?

"Trust me, this is all the hair I have to let down."

Roz's laughter was good to hear. From the corner of his eye, Weston caught Anna's smile as he spun his partner beneath his arm on the third song.

"Oh, my stars." As the song ended, after one final spin, Roz moved one hand over her chest, panting a bit. "I haven't had so much fun in a long time. Thank you, Weston."

"My pleasure, Roz. Thank *you*."

Next to them, Della kissed Neil's cheek. "Thank you for giving an old widow a sweet memory."

Neil's smile was as close to shy as Weston had ever seen. "The honor's all mine, ma'am."

Twenty minutes later, Neil sat with him at the table. He'd been unusually quiet as they ate, and Tom and Brandon had departed for the weekend.

"That was a nice thing you did for Della." Weston finished his fried chicken and wiped his hands.

"It was fun." Neil took a drink of his sweet tea and lowered the empty glass to the table. "You were right, Wes."

"About?" This should be interesting.

Neil frowned and sat back, crossing his arms over his chest. "Not sure you'll believe me."

"Try me."

"I told Darcy we should slow down. That girl's a little loco. She's talking marriage, man. I mean, who *does* that? I thought she understood we were just playing around and having fun. No emotions and nobody gets hurt. I never made any promises. I don't want her going all mental on me and boiling a rabbit or trying to stab me like the crazy chick in that *Fatal Attraction* movie."

Weston ate the last bite of his biscuit and then wiped his mouth. "Who does that? Maybe a woman who might equate sex with love. Or a woman who might crave the physical affirmation of your affection."

Neil laughed. "In English, Wes. What are you, like a psychologist now or something?"

"I'm saying it's possible Darcy interprets sleeping together as a promise."

Neil dropped his head in his hands before lifting it seconds later. "Why would she believe something like that? We've only seen each other a few times."

"Yes, but you're talking about more than going to dinner and dropping her off on her doorstep at the end of the evening. Ideally, sex should be an intimate expression of love in a marriage relationship where you're *emotionally* invested."

"No, dude." Leaning close, Neil lowered his voice. "Sex doesn't mean love. Having sex is the *easy* part."

Weston found it difficult to believe they were having this discussion in the middle of the diner, but everyone around them appeared to be involved in their own conversations. Good thing. He wouldn't want the teenage couple to their left or the young mother and her kids on the right to overhear. Didn't change the fact this conversation was another like the one he'd shared with Neil in the kitchen at the apartment—honest and real.

"It's all a matter of perspective. Why do you think it's the easy part?" Weston knew the answer but wanted to hear it directly from Neil.

"It's instinct. Primal. Fulfilling needs. You know how hard we work, so it's nice to unwind. I don't know how to talk to a chick, and

I have no idea what Darcy wants to hear. You must know the right thing to say."

Neil angled his head at Anna. "Look at her. She keeps looking at that rose and then over here at you. You make her smile, dude. Ten to one you gave her that rose, didn't you?"

"I gave it to her this morning." Weston resisted glancing over his shoulder. "Look, I know where you're coming from, Neil. I know what it's like to want a woman. I'm not immune to the images plastered all over social media. I confess my thoughts to God all the time and ask Him to forgive me."

"You?" Neil snorted. "Saint Weston?"

"I'm no saint. Far from it. When I was twenty, my conscience got the better of me and everything I'd learned from my folks and my pastor finally started to seep into my thick brain." Weston paused for effect. "I was disrespecting the girl I was with because I was consumed with selfishness. I only wanted physical gratification, but a woman deserves so much more. She deserves my best."

"If she wants it, too, I don't see the big deal." Neil's eyes met his. "Did you ever—?"

"No." Weston kept his voice firm and held Neil's gaze steady. "But in my mind, I was there, and that's the same thing in God's eyes. I finally woke up one day and realized I didn't want to be that kind of man. I saw my buddies go from woman to woman, from one shallow physical relationship to another."

"You think I'm shallow?"

"I think you've got more depth inside you than you want or allow others to see. *You're* not shallow, Neil, but your behavior is. One of my best friends was a firefighter. He had a beautiful wife and kids, the happiest guy I knew. But then he died in a fire trying to save someone else. But you know what? David died doing what he loved, he knew he was headed to heaven, and he knew he was loved by his family. In a lot of ways, he was my hero."

Neil stared at the table, not speaking. Weston longed to tell this man about the love of the Lord, but something held his tongue. He needed to dig a little more first, and make this guy think. Get *him* to start questioning his behavior and reckless actions.

"I don't believe you're as apathetic and indifferent about relationships as you come across."

Neil jerked his head up and stared at him. "What's that supposed to mean?"

Lord, give me your words.

"You act like you don't care if what you do is right or wrong, but I think you do," Weston said. "What you just said about Darcy, for one thing. About how you don't know how to talk to her. That shows that, deep down, you *do* care. Tell me something. Are you afraid to fall in love?"

The other man reared back and held up both hands. "Who said anything about love, man?"

"Relax. I'm only asking a question, friend to friend."

"You consider me a friend?" Neil swallowed, clearly surprised.

"I care about you, and we work together," Weston said. "I'd like it if we could be friends."

Neil's frown deepened. "I've only had one relationship that lasted more than a few months. It's not exactly like I'm qualified to be anybody's boyfriend."

"What happened?" Weston sipped his sweet tea as he waited.

Neil traced one finger through the thin film of sweat on his glass. "When I was eighteen. Our relationship was intense. I told her I loved her—only girl I've ever said that to—but then Lily dumped me not long after for my best buddy. She went from me to Jake in the span of an hour. Some love, huh? Tell me that doesn't do something to a guy's self-confidence. All because I wouldn't pick up her dog at the vet. That was just an excuse. I found out later she'd been two-timing me with Jake all along. Then she dumped him a few months later."

"I'm sorry, but not every girl's going to do that. Do you think subconsciously you might look for the same kind of woman to date?" *Date* was the gentle term but the best way Weston knew to ask.

Neil met his gaze. "I'm not following."

"Women like Lily and Darcy. There's no risk involved since you figure you'll get hurt somewhere down the line, anyway. That way, you're free to move on without any regret or guilt. In other words, it's a defense mechanism so you won't get hurt. Putting up walls around your heart."

"What do you mean *women like Lily and Darcy*?" Neil's defenses were up again.

Weston swallowed. He needed to speak the truth. Spit it out. "Think about it. Does Darcy remind you of someone? Maybe Lily, too?"

"What do you…?" Neil propped his elbows on the table and rubbed the heels of his hands over his eyes. Finally, he planted both hands flat on the table and pushed to his feet. "I need to get back to the apartment. Darcy's coming over in a half-hour. Don't judge me if she ends up spending the night."

"It's not my job to judge," Weston said. "If you ever want to talk, I'm here for you. Whenever. Wherever."

Neil started to pull his wallet from his pocket.

"Put your money away. I'll cover it."

The other man nodded. "See you around."

Weston watched as Neil headed out the front door. Again, the man could have stomped away at any point during that conversation. But he hadn't. He'd take it as another small victory.

Anna made her way over to his table. "Everything okay with Neil?"

"I'm not sure. In a way, I think a small miracle might have just taken place. Neil's starting to think about some things. Pray for him if you would."

Her brow creased. "Of course. I'm on a ten minute break and thought you might want to dance. If you'd rather not, I'll understand."

"Roz is okay with her employees dancing in the diner?" He'd catch up with Neil later on. For now, the prettiest girl he'd ever met was asking him to dance.

"Roz has already danced with the most handsome man in the diner. I demanded equal time."

He rose to his feet with a wide smile. "Getting a little bold with the boss, aren't you? Aren't you still in your probation period?"

Anna gave him a cheeky grin. "I'll take my chances. So, do you want to dance or not?"

"Definitely. Don't go anywhere. I'll pay the check and be right back."

"I'll pick out some tunes." She winked. "Wear the hat."

What a woman. And a wink? Yeah, this would be fun.

"I'll take that for you, Cowboy." Where had Roz come from?

When she held out one hand, he placed the check with a couple of bills across her palm. "Keep the change for the tip. Our server was excellent."

Roz's lips upturned. "I'll make a note of it." She handed him the small, damp towel she held in her other hand. "You had the chicken. Better wipe your hands. You don't want them slippin'."

He laughed and obliged her. "What would I do without you to take care of me?"

"I'm sure you'd think of somethin'. Go get your girl, Cowboy."

"I'll do my best." Grabbing the Stetson, Weston pulled it on and ran his fingers around the brim. Anna had moved over to the jukebox and the strains of the familiar Ray Charles standard "Georgia On My Mind" filled the diner. The first few notes made him smile as they always did as he strolled across the diner to join her.

"May I have the honor of this dance, Miss Redmond?" He held out one hand and bowed.

Anna's smile made his pulse pound in his ears. Lacing his fingers with hers, Weston lightly rested his other hand on her small waist. They began to slowly sway to the music. Leaning close, he enjoyed the fresh scent of her hair. Her softness. Her sweetness. Anna reminded him of all that was right in the world.

"This song became the official state song of Georgia in 1979," he whispered, keeping his cheek on hers. They moved well together. Anna was no stranger to dancing. He enjoyed dancing but hadn't had many opportunities. She made it easy. The best place to be on a Friday early evening. *Any* evening.

When he felt Anna's slight shiver, Weston drew her nearer without being *too* close considering they were in her place of employment. Aware others watched, he tuned them out, lost in the moment.

"Georgia, Georgia," he sang softly. "The whole day through, just an old sweet song keeps Georgia on my mind."

He twirled her beneath his arm and then brought Anna close, clasping her hand against his chest. Never hurt to let a woman know his heart was functioning properly and that it pumped faster when in her presence.

"You stopped singing." She pulled back. "You have a very nice voice."

"Thanks. I'll keep going if you take off those glasses."

"Deal." Removing the glasses, she dropped them in the pocket of her apron.

That was too easy. He smiled and moved his gaze to her feet.

Anna tapped his chin. "Eyes up, mister. I'm still on the clock so the shoes stay on."

Weston chuckled and continued to sing. "A song of you comes as sweet and clear as moonlight through the pines." He hummed when he could no longer remember the words. "Anna, I find my relationship with you something of a paradox."

"How's that?"

"I know no more about you now than when we first met." He touched his lips to her cheek and then whispered close to her ear. "Yet I know you *better* than any other woman."

As the song ended, Anna stepped back. "Thank you. That was fun."

"Yes, it was. Thank you." That's all she could say? That dance was *way* more than fun. Lowering his arms, Weston missed her already. Did this woman have any clue how much he wanted to find out everything there was to know about her? How much he wanted to *kiss* her?

He cleared his throat. "Do you need those glasses when you work? You haven't worn them anywhere except here at the diner."

Her brows furrowed. "Do they really bother you that much?"

"Not at all. I just wondered since you don't seem to actually *need* them here, either."

She took a deep breath. "The truth? I wear them so men like Neil will keep their distance but other people will take me seriously."

"*I* take you seriously."

Lifting her chin, her brown eyes searched his. "You're not just people, either, Weston."

Better. He'd take her words as encouragement. "I, um, came into the diner for a specific reason. Other than eating, of course. And seeing you. That goes without saying, and—"

"Just tell me." The corners of her lovely mouth tipped.

"When I stopped by your house this morning to leave the flowers from Lois and Raymond's rosebushes, I was leading up to something. I was hoping—"

"Who are Lois and Raymond?" When Anna moved behind the counter, he followed.

"Your neighbors. Lovely older couple. They said to tell you they've enjoyed your music. Then Lois snipped the roses, gave me some good advice, and wished us well."

She'd started to wipe down the counter but paused and glanced up at him. "What do you mean she *wished us well?*"

"In my pursuit of you. Or my courting of you. Take your pick." He whipped the Stetson from his head and held it between his fingers.

Anna's brows lifted. "Did you *tell* them you're pursuing or courting me?" She hesitated. "Take your pick."

What was that supposed to mean? Was she upset? Had he said something wrong?

"If I didn't, I'm sure my intentions were clear." He couldn't remember exactly what he'd said to Lois, but he'd definitely implied it. "Is that so wrong?"

"No, it's not wrong, but it's not very realistic." Lowering her gaze, Anna began the *check the salt and pepper shaker* routine again, same as she'd done on Wednesday night. Might as well ask her for that date now so she could shoot him down if she wanted. More than anything, he didn't want her to shut down and close him out of her life altogether. He was already invested.

"Is it also unrealistic to ask you for a date tomorrow night? Look, I know we've only known each other a few days, but the way I see it, the time we've spent together has been quality. So, in the mind of Weston, it's like we've passed that awkward first date stage. Matter of fact, I thought we'd moved way past that point."

In the mind of Weston? He wished he could take back those words.

"You're my friend, Weston, and I've enjoyed our time together more than you know. But I thought you understood we're both only in town temporarily, so why get in any deeper if nothing can come of it?"

"Lady, I beg to differ." Lowering his voice, he stepped closer. "You can stand there refilling those salt and pepper shakers and act like it's meant nothing all you want, but we're in this pretty deep already. Contrary to what you might believe, I don't walk a girl home when I'm so tired I can barely think or see straight. I don't pour out most of my life story and share things with a girl I've just met and might never see again. I don't give flowers to a girl I've known only a few days. And I don't dance with just *any* woman. In my book, that's got to *mean* something."

Man, he sounded desperate. Not his finest hour. On the other hand, he'd meant every word of that impassioned speech. Except the *lady* part. He'd never said anything like that to a woman in his life. Blame it on the Stetson effect.

Anna stopped her busy work and glanced up at him. Finally. "It depends on what you're asking me, exactly. I suppose we can go somewhere together as long as we both understand the rules."

He coughed. "The *rules*? You want to clue me in here so I'll know what they are?"

"Anna, say yes already and put the poor guy out of his misery." Roz pushed the swinging door on her way into the kitchen.

"Nick mentioned the 4-H Fair and said he and Charley are headed there tomorrow night," he said. "If it makes you feel any better, they can be our chaperones."

She laughed under her breath. "You've seen them in action. *They're* the ones who need a chaperone."

"If nothing else, go with me so you can tell me who you *really* are. I'll buy you cotton candy, a funnel cake, whatever you want. Take you on rides. Win a teddy bear at the arcade." He lowered his voice again. "Kiss you at the top of the Ferris wheel." That last one might have been a mistake, but he might as well shoot for the stars.

Anna didn't flinch but neither did she say anything. Indecision was written all over her expression.

Planting both hands on the counter, Weston waited until he had her eye contact to speak again. "That might violate your *rules*, but I know God's in this relationship. You can't tell me He's not."

She lowered her voice to match his. "Tell you who I really am?"

"You're a smart woman, Anna. You know *exactly* what I mean. I've glimpsed your heart, and it's beautiful. But I know very little about you other than your mother was your best friend and died when you were seventeen. You have a sister, Charlotte, also known as Charley, a brother-in-law named Nick Parker, and they live in New York. And can apparently afford a private chartered jet. I want to know where you've been and where you're going. I want to know *you*."

He moved one hand over hers, pleased when Anna allowed it without protest. "Whatever it is you're afraid to tell me, I promise you it's not going to scare me away."

Anna's frown deepened as she stared at their joined hands. "Scare you away? Are you implying you think I've done something *wrong?*"

"I'm not implying anything, but I guess it's up to you to set me straight, isn't it? Seems to me I'm the one doing all the talking here. Instead of repeating what I'm saying and asking questions, I'd like to hear some answers."

Those gorgeous brown eyes narrowed. "You're a sneaky one. Not to mention a little pushy."

"It's one of my best qualities. So, will you go tomorrow?" He'd never wanted to hear the word *yes* more in his life.

Anna appeared to be weighing her options. "I like caramel apples."

Weston's smile came from the deepest part of his heart. "I'll pick you up at your house at six tomorrow. Be ready." He replaced the Stetson and headed straight for the front door before she'd have a chance to back out. He wasn't about to give her the opportunity.

Halfway out the front door, he heard glass breaking.

What now?

When he heard Anna cry out, Weston turned. His heart pumping, he dashed back through the diner.

Chapter 19

"Anna, no! Don't touch that glass!"

Weston flew to her side and, with his shoulder, pushed her away from the table. Seconds later, she spied blood dripping from his right hand.

She gasped. "Weston! I'm so sorry. What happened?" Grabbing a napkin from the dispenser on the table, she pressed it on his bleeding middle finger. The cut looked fairly deep. "I'm afraid you're going to need stitches."

His blue-eyed gaze bore into her. "I was trying to stop you from picking up that broken glass. I heard you cry out. When I saw the shards on the table, I thought you were hurt."

Her heart melted a little bit more. "You really *are* my hero, aren't you?"

"Yeah, well, you seem to need one." Wincing, Weston removed the crimson-stained napkin partway and inspected his finger. "I think you're right about stitches. Great." He shook his hand. "Now the napkin is sticking to it."

"Oh, no. Obviously, I wasn't thinking. Hang on a second. Let me get you a towel, and then I'm going to drive you to the medical clinic."

"You're not leavin' until your shift is done, girl." Roz stood behind them, arms crossed. "I'll get Mike or Hector to drive him. You stay here and finish waitin' on your customers."

"Roz, it's my fault Weston's the walking wounded. I'm going to take him so I can take care of his bill. That's the least I can do."

"I have good medical insurance—" Weston said before she waved her hand to silence him.

Anna stared down the other woman. She shouldn't care if she lost her job although she'd come to enjoy it more than she could have imagined. Maybe she should have her head examined. "I'm sorry, Roz, but I have to go. I don't have time to argue."

Pushing through the swinging door, she grabbed one of the thin towels from the kitchen and then dashed back into the dining room. Anna stopped short when she spied Roz helping Weston rinse the affected finger in the sink under the front counter.

Taking the clean towel from her, Roz wrapped it around his injured finger. "We'll talk later," she said. "I'll clock you out, and Candee'll come back in and help. Get this man's finger sewn up before he bleeds all over my diner. That's not good for business."

"Yes, ma'am. I'll be back as soon as I can."

"Don't worry about it. Take the rest of the night off to play nursemaid. We can cover. Just be sure and show up on time for your shift tomorrow."

"Got it. Thanks you, Roz."

After grabbing her purse, Anna walked to the door with Weston beside her.

The older gentleman Weston had talked with previously was coming into the diner and eyed Weston's wrapped finger. "What happened, son? You have an accident?"

"Hey, Jerry. Sliced my finger on some glass."

Anna spoke up. "Weston was protecting me. I'm taking him for stitches."

"Sorry. I hope it's not too bad. Take care of yourself." Jerry disappeared into the diner.

"Why do people always state the obvious?" Weston mumbled as they reached the front sidewalk.

"Be glad they care. I think it's their way of expressing concern when they don't know what else to say."

"You're right. I think I asked Candee's son if he was okay after he wiped out on his bike in front of me. Listen, Anna, you don't have to do this. I drove my truck into town. I can drive myself to the clinic."

"It's not a matter of capability, Weston. I can't have it on my conscience if you bleed all over your truck. If that song Neil played is true, guys have a ridiculous obsession with their trucks."

"I'm not obsessed, but yeah, I love my truck." Weston glanced up and down the street. "Late Friday afternoon in midtown Darling. Where's your car?"

"Around the corner." Warmth crept into Anna's cheeks. Since she'd arrived in Darling, she'd housed her rental car in the garage. "It was raining, so I decided to drive to work. It's a rental."

"Might as well get your money's worth. Lead the way, Rental Girl."

"Please don't be sarcastic. I'm trying to help you out here."

"Sorry. I don't mean anything by it. I get grouchy when I'm wounded. Not that this is anything serious."

"Not a problem. The car's right over here." Pulling out the keys, Anna led him around the corner and stopped beside the light blue BMW parked by the curb.

"*This* is your rental?" Weston whistled under his breath. "Like I said, who *are* you, Anna Redmond?"

That's the question of the day. She'd tell him once he'd been seen by the doctor. And hopefully under the influence of anesthesia. No, they wouldn't give him anesthesia for a minor cut, stitches or not. Part of her wondered if he knew and that's why he'd made a dive for that broken glass.

On second thought, Weston couldn't know. If he did, he'd have told her in the midst of that speech. The man wasn't the least bit shy. He spoke his mind. Secretly, she'd adored those words he'd spoken. In his own way, Weston was fighting *for* her. He truly wanted to know her, like he'd said.

A hero all the way around.

"At the moment, I'm the woman trying to make amends," she said. "You've come to my rescue twice. Three times. Wait…I've lost track. Just look at this as a small way I can repay you."

"I never asked you to repay me."

"You're right about one thing. You *do* get grouchy when you're hurt." Anna made certain Weston was settled inside the car and then helped him fasten his seat belt. "I'm glad you're allowing me to help you now." After sliding behind the wheel, she turned the key and started the engine. As usual, it purred to life.

"A man's gotta do what a man's gotta do. Doesn't mean I'm happy about it." Resting his right elbow on his thigh, Weston kept his hand elevated.

"Let me guess." She angled her head at a red truck parked farther down the street. "That's your beloved?"

"Yep. Ford F-150. Built Tough. That's my baby. How'd you know? Lots of guys around here drive a truck."

"Not sure. Call it a hunch." She laughed. "Like it or not, I'm going to play nursemaid for you like Roz said. Although, technically, nursemaids are for children."

"Then you can look at me as an overgrown kid." Weston tossed her a grin. "It's only a cut. I'll live."

"Milk it, Weston. You can, you know. At least for now."

He unwound the towel and peeked at his finger. "I was never any good at playing the wounded warrior."

She turned left at the intersection. "Never? Even when you were a firefighter?"

"Nope. Especially not then. I don't like people making a fuss over me. Draws unwanted attention I don't need or want. I prefer coming to the rescue. I had a red Superman cape when I was a kid. That was pretty cool."

"Should we go to the hospital ER or the emergency clinic?"

"The clinic," he said. "It's only a few blocks from here."

"I get it," she said. "You're the martyr type."

"Right. Aren't you the same way?" He pointed out the front window. "The clinic's the next block down. You can go down the alley and park in back."

"Been there already, have you?" Why did he think *she* was a martyr?

Weston shot her a glance with lifted brows. "Seems my injury brings out someone's punchy side. No, I haven't been there before. I noticed it when I drove by the other day." He chuckled. "Cut me some slack and give me some more sympathy, will you? I like that much better."

"I'm sure you do." Anna turned the car into the alley beside the clinic.

"Do me another favor," he said as she parked the car. "Take the Stetson and put it on the back seat."

"I don't know, I think it adds to the whole hero image." When he gave her a look, Anna did as he asked, trying to ignore those blue eyes watching as she carefully lifted the hat from his head.

Within a minute, they stood at the front counter to check in with a nurse behind the glass partition. After she asked for Weston's health card, he angled his head to the back right pocket of his jeans.

"Anna, can you get my wallet out for me? My health insurance card's in there, and I need my right hand to do it."

"Of course," she assured him. Hmm. Those jeans weren't exactly baggy. Were *his* cheeks a little flushed? She could do without the smugness in his grin.

"And here I thought I'd seen every ploy in the book." The nurse laughed and shook her head. "Don't worry, honey," she said to her. "I think he'll still respect you in the morning."

Weston coughed into his hand. Anna tried not to laugh. This small-town nurse sure felt free to speak her mind. That seemed to be a common thread among most citizens in Darling.

Leaning close, Anna whispered to him. "Try not to get too much of a thrill out of this. You called me a martyr, and this duty definitely qualifies. Goes waaaay above and beyond." She tucked her fingers into Weston's back pocket. Not a whole lot of wiggle room back there. Now *her* cheeks had to be red. Finally, she gave the wallet a swift yank and tugged it out. "That tedious chore's finally done. What's next?"

Weston chuckled. He was enjoying this way too much. "I give you permission to open my wallet. My insurance card should be on top."

"How many cards do you have? A spendthrift, are you?" What was *wrong* with her? Some kind of weird latent flirting gene must be kicking in.

"One is my Red Cross frequent donation card. Another is the Goodwill card for…"

"You put me to shame," Anna said. "What's your blood type?"

He balked. "Why does *that* matter?"

The nurse spoke up. "For one thing, it's good to have in case you need a blood transfusion."

"Come on, ladies. For a minor cut? Fine. My blood type is A positive," Weston told the nurse before turning back to Anna. "What type are you?"

"I'm not really sure. Can I get back to you?"

"You never had a need to know, am I right?"

"Your point?" Anna frowned. "You should be glad to know I'm healthy and have never been in the hospital except when I was born."

"Oh, I am. This my glad face. That you're healthy. I was just curious."

"Okay, you two lovebirds. Take this and fill out these forms. Bring them back to me completed if you can stop flirting long enough." The nurse put a clipboard on the counter. "I suggest you do it soon if you want that digit seen by the doctor sometime today, young man."

"Got it. What's a digit?"

"Your finger."

"Whatever you say. Anna, a little more help here, please? You're going to have to fill out those forms for me since my right hand is currently incapacitated."

"I'm more than aware. I'll take care of it. Be back shortly," she told the nurse. Grabbing the clipboard, she followed Weston and settled in a chair beside him in the patient waiting area.

"Name? Weston *Obnoxious When He's Wounded* Galloway." Anna pretended to write. "What's your middle initial?"

"J for James. What's yours?"

"C for Cecile. My paternal grandmother's name."

After recording the names of his parents, Weston's home address, and other basic information as well as his family health history, Anna handed him the pen. "Now that I know everything I could ever want to know, please give me your autograph if your ego's not too swollen."

He burst out laughing. "You're going to kill me with your sarcasm. Yet another side of Anna Cecile Redmond, eh?"

"You never know. Don't dally. The nurse is waiting."

With the towel still wrapped around his finger, Weston did his best and then Anna returned the completed forms to the nurse. "I'd like to pay his bill." She opened her purse.

Weston was beside her in seconds. "I've got this." He all but pushed her out of the way as he handed the nurse a credit card.

"It's my fault you're hurt, Weston. Paying the bill is the least I can do."

"You drove me here and showed me sympathy. I appreciate it, but that's all I need. It's only a copay. I can handle it, Anna."

"Fine." She could take a hint. Men could be so weird about money. For once, she needed to sit down and shut up, so she plopped back into her chair. Above all, she wouldn't want to wound the stubborn man's pride.

"I notice you had no trouble pulling your credit card out of your wallet," she said when Weston reclaimed the chair next to hers.

He slumped back and crossed his arms. "This would be the moment when I'd cover my face with the Stetson."

Six stitches later, Weston climbed back into the car beside her.

Anna made sure he was buckled in again. "Feel like grabbing a bite to eat or should I take you back to your place?"

"Definitely not the apartment. I could eat, but…"

"As long as it's not The Darling Diner, I'm all for it," she said. "Here's an idea. You're not allergic to cashews, are you?"

Leaning his head back on the leather seat, he chuckled, a welcome sound. "No allergies." He glanced over at her. "And I'm kind of partial to nuts."

"Then, if you're okay with it, let's go back to my house. I'll make you cashew chicken."

"I'm more than okay with it, but don't go to any trouble on my account."

"No trouble. It's actually kind of a selfish reason," she said. "I make really good cashew chicken, and I want to prove to you that I'm not a complete klutz in the kitchen."

"You're not going to force me to eat with chopsticks are you? I don't do chopsticks."

"No, you're safe. I don't have any at the house."

"Good, especially since I'm right-handed, and my *digit's* not operating at full capacity. Will Nick and Charley be joining us?"

Anna turned out of the alley and headed back up Magnolia Avenue. "Sorry to disappoint you. They went into Atlanta, and I don't expect them back until late tonight."

"How'd they get there? Do they have a car here in Darling, too? A Mercedes or something?"

She shot him a look. "They called a taxi. Trust me, I'm trying to teach them how to use their money wisely. So far, they're not listening."

"What a life," he said, shaking his head. "I'm not disappointed. As entertaining as they are, I like the idea of spending time with you tonight, Anna. Alone." Reaching his left hand across the console, Weston wrapped his hand around hers. "Take me back to my truck first."

At least one of them was thinking straight.

Chapter 20

Anna sat beside Weston on a barstool in the kitchen. She preferred the intimacy of sitting beside him instead of eating across from one another in the small dining room.

As soon as they'd arrived at the house, she'd excused herself and run upstairs to change out of her uniform. She wished she'd had time for a quick shower, but instead brushed out her hair, spritzed on light cologne, and changed into a sleeveless black tunic and white capris. When she slid her feet into her flat sandals, she'd breathed a sigh of relief.

The look in Weston's eyes when she came around the corner into the kitchen was one she'd tuck away in a secret part of her heart and treasure no matter what did—or didn't—transpire with this man.

He was right, all those things he'd said in the diner. In response, her pitiful attempt to resist him had proven to be a short-lived, incredibly spectacular failure. Not that she minded the least little bit. It might actually be the best *failure* of her life.

"Kudos on the dinner." Raising his wine glass filled with his usual sweet tea, Weston lightly touched it to hers. "You were wrong, though. This cashew chicken is more than good. It's *fantastic*. And to think you made it in the microwave. My mom never trusted the microwave. She doesn't like it that I have one and to this day warns me to stand at least five feet away. Hates blue and black icing, too. I think she's convinced those things will give a person cancer."

"I assure you, I'm not trying to kill you." Anna took another bite. "How does your mother feel about cell phones?"

"She doesn't have one. Hates them with a purple passion, whatever that means."

"I'm not overly fond of mine, either, but I can admit they come in handy," she said. "As far as the meal, I'm glad you like it. I may not know how to cook many things, but I discovered this dish during one of my, um, business trips."

This was silly. Time to tell Weston more. How should she approach it? Announcing *I'm a concert pianist* between bites of cashew chicken somehow hadn't seemed appropriate. Besides, she'd been hungry. Starting a conversation like that on an empty stomach wouldn't have been good.

He stabbed a piece of chicken. "Now we're finally getting somewhere."

"I'll tell you after we eat. Promise."

"Sure, but why wait until after dinner?" Weston paused with his fork midway to his mouth. "Is it like some big secret? Just blurt it out already. It's easy. 'Weston, I'm a preschool teacher…on Mars.' Or 'Weston, I test drive BMWs…in Germany.' Or 'Weston, I'm a mail order bride passing through Georgia on my way to Florida to meet my *betrothed*.'"

When she swatted his arm, he laughed and swallowed his bite. "Come on. I'm not oblivious. Or stupid. You don't belong in that diner any more than I belong in a BMW."

"I thought you looked good in one today. It's just a car, Weston."

"Excuse me, *just* a car?" Sputtering, Weston put his napkin over his mouth. "Anna, a BMW is a German luxury vehicle manufactured by the same company as the Rolls-Royce."

"Well, huh. I didn't know that." Anna took another bite and chased it down with her water. "You were right about throwing the peas and carrots in with the rice. Adds that little something extra. Positively inspired."

"The BMW model you're driving is a 430i Coupe." The man really liked talking about her rental car. She'd humor him for now.

"Brand new, that car costs about forty-two grand, and that's just the *starting* price." After pushing aside his plate and downing more of his sweet tea, he spun around on the barstool and faced her with a grin. "So, I'm sure you can understand my fascination with my nursemaid. And you're welcome to ride in my truck anytime. You'd class it up real nice."

"Well, that's a compliment I've never heard before. Weston, I'm not even sure where to begin."

"Okay, then. Let's speed this along. Are you in the witness protection program?"

"No." Almost tempted to laugh, she shook her head. "Thank the Lord. Is my life a *game* to you?"

"Of course not, but you haven't exactly been forthcoming. Let's see. You're not on the run from an abusive ex-boyfriend, husband, boss?"

"Nothing like that." Finished with her meal, Anna wiped her mouth and then drained her water glass.

"Good. I've gotta say, I'm relieved." He slid off the seat and held out his hand. "Come with me, please."

"Where are you taking me?"

"To the living room."

"Do you have something against a big reveal in the kitchen?" Giving him her hand, Anna allowed him to pull her off her seat and into the living room.

Surprising her, Weston quickly circled her waist and pulled her close. Anna rested her hands on his arms. Those firm, muscular arms. She felt a little dizzy.

"Are you planning on dancing the information out of me? That's a method I've never heard of before."

Weston leaned his forehead on hers. "I'm going to kiss you in the next few seconds whether you tell me or not. I'd like it if I knew more about the woman I'm kissing." His lips hovered so close she could smell the cashew chicken on his breath. Not the most romantic thought, but a deliciously tempting one.

Anna inched her hands upward and felt the powerful muscles beneath her fingers as they reached his broad shoulders. Why she'd done that, she wasn't sure. Maybe instinctual, but it certainly wasn't helping matters. "We both know anything between us is only temporary."

"Are you starting with that again?" He kept his arms around her in a firm hold. "I vote we toss your rules. If you think those statements will stop me from wanting to kiss you, then you're sorely mistaken. Unless you don't *want* me to kiss you. I respect you, Anna. I never want to do anything you don't want. I trust you understand that."

She swallowed. "I understand, but it's kind of hard to think with you this close."

"Do you want me to let go?" Weston's expressive blue eyes revealed so much when she dared to look into them.

"No, not really."

His lips curved. "You can trust me with the truth. No matter what it is." He pressed his warm, gentle lips to her forehead. "Did you take an oath or something?"

"No," she whispered, leaning into his touch.

"Are you running away from a rich daddy who's trying to pressure you into marrying some jerk who works for him?" His voice had grown husky.

She shook her head slowly and lowered her gaze. "No. It's not anything like that, either."

"I know you believe in Jesus," he said. "Look me in the eye. Please."

Lifting her chin, she did as he asked. "Yes, I believe in Jesus. With all my heart. Since I was fifteen."

"Then surely you know He wouldn't want you to lie."

When she started to pull away, Weston tugged her back into the circle of his arms.

"Please don't use my faith as a bargaining tool, Weston. And don't patronize me. That's condescending. I'm not lying to you."

He skimmed his thumb across her cheek. "I didn't mean to do that, but it's really very simple. I'm falling for you, but I need to know who you really are. Tell me." He teased her lips with his. So very well. The man knew precisely what he was doing in wearing her down.

Lord, this can't be wrong.

Weston lightly sifted the fingers of his left hand through her hair. "Your hair's so soft. Your cheek. And then there's this. . ." He kissed one corner of her mouth and then the other.

"The things you say, Mr. Galloway." The last of her resistance drained from her. Anna could hardly think straight, and she no longer cared about anything other than this man's kiss.

His blue eyes lit. "Shall I continue?"

"Just be quiet and kiss me, Cowboy."

"The honor's all mine, darlin'." He lowered his lips to hers. Anna's knees went weak, a phenomenon she'd never experienced nor fully understood until this moment.

Weston's kiss—warm, firm, filled with tender emotion—sent shivers through her in the most glorious way, making her want to tell him anything he wanted. *Give* him anything he wanted, but Weston wasn't that kind of man. He wasn't selfish or demanding. Neither was she that type of woman though she'd been pressured and put in that situation before with a man she'd wanted to trust. Until she'd learned there were few people she *could* trust. And thanked God for His protection.

Weston truly, deeply cared for her. This unselfish, handsome, caring man wasn't seeking anything from her other than friendship and possibly her love. He certainly knew how to make a girl feel cherished. And, oh, this kiss. He could kiss extremely well. *My, oh my.*

Anna's eyes flew open. Fine time for her conscience to take control. As much as she might want to, she couldn't give or offer him anything more than friendship. That wouldn't be fair to either one of them.

With a low groan, Anna planted her hands on his firm chest and pushed him away. "I can't do this to you, Weston. I'm sorry."

Chapter 21

Dazed, Weston tried to catch his breath. What just happened?

Anna had invited his kiss. She'd wanted it as much as he had. God help him, if emotion wasn't clouding his judgment, he wasn't just falling…he was already *in love* with Anna. Telling her that *now* would be a mistake or she might run as fast and as far as she could. She might be independent and strong in some ways, but in others, he needed to approach this carefully and not overwhelm her with too much, too fast.

Wait. First, he needed to find out what she had to say.

Weston paced the floor and then stopped in front of her, crossing his arms over his chest. "You can't do this *to me?* I'm not sure what that's supposed to mean. Could you maybe share it with me and then we can make an informed decision *together* about whether or not to take the risk?"

That was a little abrupt. Slowing down and cutting back on the defensive attitude would be a better way to handle this situation. He lowered his arms to his sides. Not knowing what to do with his hands, he resorted to the old standby and shoved them in the front pockets of his jeans.

Stifling her cry, Anna put one hand over her mouth and looked up at him through those wide brown eyes that tugged on him every time. Clearly, she didn't know what to do or say any more than he did.

"Anna, I've wanted to kiss you from the first night I walked you back here to the house. You can't tell me you couldn't tell." Lowering his head, he puffed out his cheeks. "Look, I know I fumble my words when I'm around you, but I hope you can read between the lines to what I'm *trying* to say."

With her hand still covering her mouth, Anna bobbed her head. "I can." At least that's what he thought she'd said.

"Can you please move your hand away from your mouth so you don't sound muffled?"

She did as he asked. "Weston, the problem here is that I wanted to kiss you, too. More than I've ever wanted to kiss anyone. Not that I've done much kissing in my life."

That was gratifying to hear all the way around. He started to stroke his beard, but it wasn't the same with a bandaged finger. "That's a problem…how? I'm a guy, so talking about *not* kissing only makes me think about it more. I thought the kiss was pretty great. Was there a problem?" What a dumb question.

She shook her head. "No, it was fine, but kissing—or talking about it—only compounds the situation. I can't jump into something I can't finish. As tempting as it is, I don't *do* casual relationships."

"You think I do? And it was way *more* than fine." He was already steamed and his impatience was showing. Problem was, he was fresh out of ideas and couldn't offer any solutions. Didn't change the fact that he still wanted to kiss her. Given the opportunity, he'd try and kiss some *sense* into the woman. She seemed well on her way to making him lose his mind. After only one kiss.

His dad's words from a few years ago popped into his mind. "One kiss from the *right* woman makes all the difference." No kidding. Now more than ever he understood the meaning, and the wisdom, behind those words.

Weston forced himself to breathe. "Look, we're both adults here. Christians who've been around the block enough to recognize a good thing when we find it." He wanted to slap himself. A *good thing*? Could he sound any more like a cliché with legs?

"Well, maybe *you've* been around the block, but I've never been in a relationship before. If you want the truth, I've barely even kissed a man. Definitely not like *that*. I just hope I did it right."

"Oh, you did it right, Anna. So right I can barely think straight."

Tension and simmering heat hung in the air between them. Anna could deny it all she wanted but his words had to please her on some level.

"Well, that's. . .nice to know."

"Call it arrogance or male pride, but I like it that you haven't kissed many guys." As usual, that might have been the wrong thing to say, but it was honest. "I don't understand how it's *possible*, but I believe you."

"Weston, why did you call me a martyr?"

"Maybe martyr is too strong a word, but it's the idea that you think of serving others before doing something for yourself. That's a rare gift." When she said nothing, he searched his mind for a good example. "Take Charley. You share your love, your home, and the resources at your disposal. I'm pretty sure you'd share anything you own to help her out if she needed it. Tell me I'm wrong."

Anna lowered her gaze. "You're not wrong."

"Give me one reason we shouldn't pursue a relationship," he said. "Tell me why it's not realistic." He stepped closer. "Fair warning, though. It'd better be a real *good* reason, darlin'." Okay, maybe he shouldn't have thrown that name into the equation, but she seemed to like it.

Her expression was impossible to decipher as they stared at one another. "Okay, then. I'm a concert pianist who travels sixty percent of the year." She raised her hands in the air. "There you have it. Is that a good enough reason for you?"

What? After trying to pry it out of her, Weston couldn't believe she'd said it in such a conversational manner. Like the weather forecast for a mild day. No dramatics, no big deal. Of all the scenarios he could have imagined—and his overactive imagination had come up with some whoppers—he hadn't expected to hear anything like *that*.

Anna slid her hands down to rest on her slender hips. "Well? Aren't you going to say anything? No matter what you thought, it's not like I'm a call girl, or an ex-con, or a leper, or—"

"Don't be ridiculous. I'm glad you finally told me, but it has nothing to do with being good enough, especially for *me*. That does explain a few things, though. Like the baby grand piano over there in the corner. And why Lois and Raymond mentioned your music. Then there's your excellent posture."

"*They* mentioned my posture?"

"No, that's all me. Not to mention how graceful you are in spite of the adorable clumsiness. I didn't have any clue you were a *professional* musician."

"Would you expect a concert pianist to walk around moving her fingers in the air over an imaginary keyboard?" She demonstrated for good measure, and he stopped just short of laughing at her antics. The woman was nutty but even more beautiful when fired up.

"Well, maybe you do in private. How would I know?" He scratched his head. "Does Roz know? Candee?"

"Yes, but only because Nick more or less forced me into telling them," she said. "I'm shocked no one told *you* before I could."

"So, I'm the last to know?"

She frowned, obviously not pleased with that question. Admittedly, he could have phrased it a little better without the defensiveness.

"Don't take it personally," she said. "As far as I know, only the staff at the diner knows. I'm sure that's subject to change at any moment. I asked them not to tell anyone and was waiting for the right time to tell you. But honestly? I'm starting to not even care. So what if people know? It shouldn't be a big deal. It certainly isn't to *me*."

"Yes, but surely you understand having a world class musician serving food in a small-town diner isn't exactly the norm."

"Fine." She stalked across the living room to the piano. "Please have a seat, Mr. Galloway."

Moving to an armchair, feeling a bit stunned, Weston did as she asked. He'd be quiet if it was the last thing he did.

Closing her eyes, Anna began to play. Because he'd played the guitar for years, he could appreciate the time and effort it took to coax a pleasing sound from any instrument. But this? Anna was coaxing more than a pleasing sound from the piano. Her skill and love of playing was a thing of beauty, a work of art, and then became a form of worship as she transitioned from a classical piece into "The Old Rugged Cross."

He began to sing as she played. "So I'll cherish the old rugged Cross, till my trophies at last I lay down. I will cling to the old rugged Cross, and exchange it some day for a crown."

When she finished, Anna kept her eyes closed. "Your voice is *your* instrument."

"I try, but you are phenomenal. *Words fail me* phenomenal."

She blushed prettily and dipped her head. "That means more to me than the applause in a concert hall."

"Your skill is obvious, but I love your interpretation," he said. "You know when to add extra flourishes. When you played about the rugged cross, your playing was simple, but I could still feel the emotion and the love. You know exactly when to play softly and when to build to the crescendo, for lack of knowing how else to explain it. I've never heard it played like that before, but it was perfect and suited the *meaning* of the hymn."

Anna's eyes were bright. "I think you explained it very well. You also picked up on something a lot of people don't. I try not to *just play the piano*. I want to evoke emotions in the listener and make them think. Music is more important than people realize. It's important in our daily lives. It soothes, it relieves stress, and it makes us feel good, more optimistic."

Weston nodded. "I'm already learning a lot from you. Just for the record, I play the guitar. I'm proficient, but it's nothing like what you just did." Until he ever finished that song for her, he'd keep it to himself that he also composed.

Her eyes fluttered open. "You do? Did you bring your guitar to Darling?"

"I did. If you want to jam sometime, we could. If concert pianists even *do* that. It might be a little hard to play for a while with this." He raised his bandaged right hand.

Lifting out of the chair, Weston crossed the room. After nudging her to scoot over and share the piano bench, he began to pick out "Chopsticks." Anna joined him and they played the duet. It brought back her smile, and for that, he was immensely grateful.

"I should go." He slid off the bench as they finished the song. "If I don't, I'm going to kiss you again, and I might not be such a proper gentleman this time."

"Now you're teasing me. Weston, I'm confused. This has been a crazy few hours, so I have to ask. Where are we? I mean, where do we stand? Or am I not supposed to ask?" Running one hand over her hair, Anna gave him a helpless look. "Turns out I know *nothing* about the rules. Hopefully now you understand why I didn't want to tell you. I was enjoying getting to know you without my career creating a barrier between us."

"Why would you think that matters to me?"

"Because it *does* matter whether you realize it or not. My career has a way of pushing my personal life to the side. Even if it doesn't now, it will eventually."

Weston dropped down beside her once more, lost in thought, before he finally spoke. "I suggest we explore the possibilities while we're both here in Darling. I figure we'll either be madly in love or hate each other in another few weeks. Then we take it from there. We can't predict how this relationship will play out. Pun *intended* that time."

"Time is a precious commodity I don't normally have," she said. "But for a few short weeks, I do. That's got to count for something, right?"

"I think so. I hope you're planning on sticking around town. If you do, we could pack an awful lot into a few short weeks." He winked. "Try not to think about that great kiss and the obvious chemistry we share. That will only cloud your decision."

Chewing her lower lip, Anna didn't have a quick comeback as he'd expected. "Can you stay at least another thirty minutes?"

That was unexpected. "If you twist my arm, I could make the sacrifice." Curious as to what was on her mind, Weston reclaimed the armchair as Anna aimed the remote at the big screen television. "We're watching a movie?"

"A movie would take longer than thirty minutes. You'll see." The familiar theme song from *The Brady Bunch* began.

"Oh man, is this what I think it is?"

She grinned. Better. "You know it."

"This is going to be fun." The girl was spontaneous and kept him guessing, a very appealing quality. "I hate to break it to you, Anna, but your favorite Monkee died."

"I know. I cried a few tears for Davy when I heard, but that doesn't mean we can't enjoy the moment in his honor." She fast-forwarded through the program before gesturing for him to join her. "Here it is. Up we go."

"You, my dear Miss Redmond, are nuts."

"As I recall, you said you're kind of partial to nuts."

"So, I did. Nothing like throwing my words back in my face." Unfolding from the chair, Weston followed Anna's lead and they began to sing along with Davy Jones as he sang, "Girl, Look What You've Done to Me."

"Here, take this." Anna tossed a heavy looking brass candlestick holder at him and then grabbed the matching one. Her mouth formed an *O* after it fell to the floor with a thud at his feet. "Sorry. I should have thought that through."

"Not a problem. I'm just thankful it didn't land on my toe." Bending over, Weston snatched the holder in his right hand and lifted it up and down like a barbell. "For future reference, could you warn me if you plan on throwing things? I like to be prepared. I'm not entirely useless, but what am I supposed to do with this candlestick?"

"It's your microphone. Sing!" Anna began to sing off-key, and he tried not to cringe. At least the woman could play the piano well.

"So, this is what you girls do in your teenage fantasies? Hey, I have no sisters," he protested when she gave him a look. He jabbed his thumb into his chest. "Only child here. Remember?"

"Stop talking! Sing, Davy. *Sing!*"

"Gull, look what you've done to me." Weston faked a bad British accent and prayed Nick wouldn't walk in the door anytime soon. He'd never live this down. Nah, if he were here, Nick would join in.

Keeping one eye on the large screen television, he began to sway and imitate Davy. Weston licked his lower lip, moved his gaze to the ceiling, and enunciated the words. Acting like a fool never felt so good.

"Move your hands around and bounce up and down a little more," Anna coached. "Oh, and watch what he's doing. Curl your fists and move them back and forth. Watch me."

"You sure you're not a control freak? I'm trying my best here." He forced himself to stop laughing and concentrate. Then he exaggerated the way he sang *bet-tire* instead of *better* in the best imitation of Davy Jones he could muster. They took turns singing the surprisingly easy lyrics and then sang the chorus together. Cute little song. Innocent.

Dancing about the living room, Anna stopped and pretended to swoon. "I love you, Davy!" Then she moved her hand over her chest. "You've just gotta come to my school and sing."

"Calm down, Marcia. No worries. I'll perform at your dance since you already jumped the gun and promised everyone. I'll save you from yourself and even be your date. I can't wait to sit in your living room in my groovy, black-and-white striped jacket, and chat with Carol and Mike."

She laughed hysterically when he put one hand on his imaginary headset and rocked back and forth. He was really getting into it now. Scary fun.

"You were wrong," he said in the middle of it all. "Davy *does* pronounce the 'r' in girl."

"I guess you're right although sometimes it's more obvious than others." Anna laughed. "It's still a fun way to find out."

"You know it." Weston shook his head as he finished the song. "I haven't done anything so idiotic in a long time. Are all you concert pianists this wacky?"

"I wouldn't know," Anna said. "What I *do* know is that I wouldn't have missed seeing you act like a teen heartthrob for anything. Idiotic looks very appealing on you."

"No one's ever given me such a weird compliment. See what being around you has done to me?" Realizing what he'd said, Weston groaned. This woman was good for his *soul*. If he didn't know better, she was looking for another kiss.

She moved forward, closing the distance between them. "Thanks for humoring me. You did a great job. And I don't think it's idiotic at all. I think it's sweet and wonderful."

Reaching for him, Anna grabbed the front of his shirt, bunching it between her fingers. Oh yeah, the woman wanted to be kissed. No more than he wanted it.

"Girl, look what you've done to me." This time he wasn't singing.

"Are you complaining?" Those brown eyes would be his undoing.

"You're the one with your hands on my shirt." If he didn't make a move away from her, his lips would be on hers again in no time flat. He'd welcome that, but first he needed to hear more about Anna's life and career.

Capturing her hand in his, Weston led the way to the front door.

"Let's go sit on the swing. Time for some courting."

Chapter 22

Anna appreciated how Weston waited for her to be seated first before dropping onto the swing beside her. Once they were settled, he pushed off the porch floor to get them started.

"I'd like to hear more about your life and career." He laced his fingers through hers, resting their joined hands on the seat of the swing.

"My full first name is Annalise. I use it professionally, but off-stage, it's Anna. Well, except for Nick. He seems to prefer my given name."

"Annalise is a beautiful name. For a beautiful girl." He dropped a light kiss on her lips.

"Thank you." Weston couldn't know how much his compliment meant for her heart. "By any chance, did you try to find me on social media?"

He arched his brows. "No. Is there a reason I should have?"

"Doesn't matter, but I'm glad you didn't. I understand that's what most people do these days to find out about someone for dating, friendship, or a job. They go on Facebook, Twitter, or one of those other social media sites."

Weston sat back on the swing. "I don't make it a habit to search the Internet for *gorgeous female concert pianists*. I only look up singing primates." He chuckled. "I'm sure by now you realize we're not most people, you and me. On the other hand, do you mind if I look you up now? I could use a new screensaver."

"Go ahead. Let me know if you see photos or anything that shouldn't be there so I can report back to my manager, Felicia. She's the one who basically oversees my life."

"Let me guess. She's the one you were talking with on the phone when we met up in town? Before we went to Paulson's?"

"Yes. How'd you know?"

Weston chuckled. "A guess. I didn't hear any of the conversation, but you didn't seem too happy with the way she was managing your life right at *that* moment."

"She was warning me about the hazards of southern living. I'll tell you more about her in a minute. I owe a lot to Felicia, but you're right. I also have an accountant I trust implicitly who handles all the financial accounts. My publicist manages my website and social media. She posts things about concerts and special promotions, but I don't have an active presence online. That's another perk of being famous without actually being well-known."

"I never would have thought of that distinction," he said. "Kind of like you're the scriptwriter behind a very successful show. The guts without the glory, in some ways. That probably didn't make sense."

Anna nodded. "I know what you mean. The actors are well-known, but the scriptwriters don't have to worry about people coming up to them all the time, wanting or expecting things, and demanding their time and attention."

"There are *some* people who recognize you, aren't there?"

"Mostly patrons of the arts, people who work in concert halls or orchestra staff, and other musicians. For whatever reason, I'm recognized a lot more in Europe than I am here. They revere their history and sometimes hold to more traditional things, including classical music."

"I can see that," he said. "Besides, those countries are a lot older than our infant nation."

"About a year ago, I had a cyberstalker, so Felicia hired a security firm that scrubbed all my personal data. They made sure no one could find out anything about me if they searched under the first name *Anna* paired with my last name."

As soon as the word *cyberstalker* left her lips, a frown had creased Weston's face. "Please tell me that took care of the stalker?" Even if she *could* tell him, she'd stay mum about the maestro.

"Yes, but I wasn't all that worried. I'm thankful I have people looking out for my best interests. It's always possible a random person could start following me whether or not they know I'm a professional musician."

"Not helping." Weston's frown deepened.

Anna squeezed his hand. "I have no reason to live in fear. If it makes you feel any better, I never walk around the streets of *any* city alone. Especially when I'm on tour, I'm rarely by myself except in my hotel suite. We have security in every venue. But that's another reason why I love being in a small town like Darling where I can freely walk down the street."

She smiled and leaned her head on his shoulder. "I never know when I might catch a glimpse of a handsome guy on my way to work. If he happens to wave and smile, or call out to me to have a great day, then it's the most wonderful thing in the world."

Weston dropped a light kiss on her forehead. "I'm glad you have people to watch over you and take care of you. Not that you're not capable of taking care of yourself. So, when you're on tour, what is *Annalise's* responsibility?"

"To stay healthy, practice, travel, and perform. Like I said before, I tour about sixty percent of the year with single performance dates and tours, both domestic and abroad that can last a month or more. I've done some studio recordings, solo work as well as collaborations. I enjoy it, but I prefer the live performances."

An array of emotions crossed Weston's handsome face. "Let's backtrack and start from the beginning. Where were you born?"

"Philadelphia. I was an only child, and my parents divorced when I was three. My dad remarried a woman named Kaye not long after, and Charley is their only child. We're almost two years apart."

"I thought that might be the case," he said. "How old were you when you first started playing the piano?"

"I was six the first time I ever laid my hands on piano keys. I was visiting my friend, Lesley, at her house. Her mom told her to practice her lesson. So, she practiced while I played with dolls in the same room. I remember I asked Lesley a few questions, and then she invited me to sit on the bench beside her." She grinned and nudged Weston's arm. "Guess what we played?"

He chuckled. "Oh, I don't know. 'Chopsticks?'"

"Right. What happened next is one of those things I'll never forget, and I realize how impossible it might sound. I sat on the piano bench for a full minute, just staring at the keyboard. Then, without any hesitation, I started to play the same song Lesley had been practicing. I somehow knew the notes, knew the entire *song*, although I'd never heard it before. It's like when my fingers found the keys, I knew exactly what I was doing.

"I remember hearing Lesley's mom whispering in the other room. She'd called my mom and asked her how long I'd been taking lessons. Mom told her I'd never had a lesson. Not long after, I was tested and enrolled in advanced classes. The rest, as they say, is history."

"You were *born* to play the piano, Anna. It's obviously a God-given talent. Sounds like the world owes your friend, Lesley, a debt of gratitude. Do you still keep in contact?"

"We lost touch, unfortunately. Her family moved away not long after."

"Your light was meant to shine, that much is obvious." Resting one right arm on the swing, Weston shifted to face her while still keeping the swing in motion. "Where did you train?"

"The Juilliard School in the Upper West Side of Manhattan. It's part of the Lincoln Center for the Performing Arts. They train musicians, actors, and dancers. Once I moved to New York, I never left. It's been my home base ever since."

Weston whistled under his breath. "I've heard of Juilliard. How old were you?"

"I started training when I was ten and graduated when I was fourteen. Juilliard has no minimum or maximum age requirements," she added when his brows lifted. "My mom stayed in New York with me during the entire time I was there. She was the one who absorbed my tears, tantrums, and the occasional meltdown. Mom listened to my fears that I'd never measure up or be good enough to pursue a professional career as a concert pianist. One of the downsides of starting out that young was that I wasn't emotionally equipped to handle the stress, but Mom did everything she could to give me encouragement and instill confidence in me."

"So, you were a child prodigy?" Weston shook his head. "That blows my mind, but in a good way."

"Some called me a prodigy, but by my own personal definition, a prodigy starts earlier. Mozart started composing when he was three," she said. "Technically, the definition of a prodigy is a child under the age of ten who produces *meaningful work* on the level of an adult. To be honest, that label put a lot of pressure on me early on. In some ways, I never had much of a childhood."

"I'm sorry, Anna. How old were you when you first started touring?"

"Sixteen, but I did shorter tours when I was younger. Between the ages of fourteen and sixteen, I practiced and continued to study. I've been blessed to work with some of the greats. That was pretty much my life, not that I'm complaining. When you love something so much, when it's your passion, it's not work. It's a labor of love."

"What about parties, dating, things like that?"

"There wasn't time," she said. "Students at Juilliard live in their own world. They don't call it *Planet Juilliard* for nothing. It's a mindset and a way of life where you're solely focused on training to be the best. Like any other field, you'll find graduates of Juilliard fulfilling their dreams, but there are some who were disillusioned and left."

He nodded. "I hate to say this, but it seems like classical music is getting pushed aside." She could tell Weston was being careful with his words. "I've heard orchestras all over the country are struggling to stay afloat financially."

"They are, and it breaks my heart." She heaved a sigh. "Subscriptions for orchestras and chamber ensembles are under increasing financial pressure. Government arts financing has dried up, and professional musicians struggle with low pay and lack of benefits. They scramble to find work, and the recording industry has shrunk. The younger audience doesn't have the same appreciation of classical music, unfortunately."

Leaning her head on the back of the swing, Anna frowned. Weston shifted his position and stretched his arm behind her.

"Thanks. That's much better."

"Glad to oblige." Weston pressed a kiss to her hair.

"I understand tastes change," she said. "For example, authors in the past had to use very descriptive writing. People didn't have visuals like movies and television to help them 'see' everything. Today, books are written in a choppier style with shorter sentences, and the emphasis is on dialogue. Music, on the other hand, has stayed the same through the centuries. The classical pieces are every bit as beautiful and relevant today as when they were first composed. Not that writing isn't, but. . ."

"You're saying the *listener* has changed, but not the original composition."

"Yes, exactly!" She patted Weston's arm. "I'm glad you understand."

"Well, the good news is that it sounds like *your* career is thriving. I'm happy for you." Weston caressed his thumb over the top of her shoulder. The action seemed unconscious on his part, and she enjoyed it more than she should.

"I'm one of the blessed ones. Felicia took me under her wing and is responsible for developing my career. I owe her so much, especially since she took me in after my mom died."

"How about your father? Are you close with him?"

"Not really. I talk to Dad once a month on average, and I leave tickets for him at the WILL CALL counter in Philly whenever I'm in concert there. He's claimed the tickets twice out of a dozen or so times."

"I'm sure he's very proud of you, Anna. How could he not be?"

"I hope so. Mom told me he wanted to be a singer early on, and she thought he might be jealous of my career. I don't know if there's any truth to that or not, but he didn't get far in music and ended up in an insurance underwriting job he's always hated." She twisted her hands on her lap. "For a long time, I thought my parents divorced because of me."

"That's too bad, but it can't be true since you'd never played the piano until you were six."

"I didn't mean it that way." She breathed in deeply. "Dad wanted me to be his little princess. He expected me to wear pretty party dresses and be someone I wasn't. Instead, he got this shy little girl who only wanted to read books and live in a pretend world. I had girlfriends, but I didn't play sports, and I hated parties. Then he had Charley, and *she* became his world. I've never resented my sister, and I'm actually grateful she could fill that role for him. If nothing else, it alleviated the pressure."

Beside her, Weston shook his head. "Do you know how many people are messed up because they tried to fit the mold of someone else's expectations? Whether it's their parents, their spouse, or someone else. Sometimes I think my mom wonders why I gave up firefighting. She took pride in it, but she worried about me constantly. Not that I failed by switching to construction, but I've always felt there was something there. Maybe a sense of disappointment."

"I'm sure she understands you're saving lives in a different way," Anna said.

Weston's smile conveyed his appreciation. "I love your perspective. I'm sure your parents splitting up had more to do with something lacking in *their* relationship than anything to do with you. You were an innocent child. I also think we tend to put way too much pressure on *our*selves."

"On the positive side, I think my dad's lack of expectation—combined with my mother and grandmother's encouragement—helped shape me into the person, and the *musician*, I am today."

"You're a very strong person, Anna. I think you're stronger than you realize."

"I try." With tears in her eyes, she grabbed Weston's hand. "You're good for me. I'm thankful you seem to have such a great relationship with your parents now."

"Me, too," he agreed. "I admire the relationship you have with Charley and Nick. You seem to have a solid mutual support system in place. A lot of people never have that, especially with family."

"We do, and it's one of the biggest blessings in my life. Charley comes running to me whenever she has an issue with Nick, but there've been times when I've needed emotional support, too, and I've shown up on *their* doorstep."

"I hope that doesn't happen often," he said. "Do you still live with your manager?"

She grinned. "No, thank goodness. I moved out when I was eighteen. If I hadn't, I think we might have killed each other. We've never been especially close. Felicia has emotional barriers and doesn't allow anyone private access."

"That's too bad, but eighteen is young to be living on your own in New York."

"I live in the same building as Felicia. She's nearby but on a different floor."

"I'm sure your faith has a lot to do with the person you've become," Weston said. "You mentioned coming to know the Lord when you were fifteen?"

Anna nodded. "I visited a church in South Carolina that summer. At the time, I was struggling, worrying that I'd never be good enough. The pastor hit home when he gave a message based on Ephesians 2:10: 'For we are His workmanship, created in Christ Jesus for good works, which God prepared beforehand so that we would walk in them.'"

"That's a good one, especially for a professional musician."

"I think so, and it's also the theme verse for my life outside of performing," she said. "The pastor talked about how we're all sinners and deserve nothing, but how God poured out His mercy, love, and grace in sending His Son to die for us. He stressed how each one of us is God's masterpiece, and how He's teaching and training us, bringing us to where He wants us to be. And how if we *allow* Him to work in our lives, we can become a manifestation of His power, love, wisdom, peace, joy…all those wonderful qualities that make up who God *is*."

Anna glanced at their joined hands. "Those words gave me an entirely new perspective and an inner peace that I was following God's will for my life and bringing what talent He's given me to bless others. When the pastor gave the invitation to accept Christ, I knew it was a step I needed to take. I play a hymn at the end of my solo concerts. Then in closing, I say something like, 'Thank you for coming. May God's grace go with you now and always.'"

"I think it's exactly what that pastor said. We need to understand God has a plan for our lives, no matter what we do or where He's planted us," Weston said. "He's always working behind the scenes, but it's up to us to take that step of faith, embrace it, and walk *into* it. And then wait and see how His plan unfolds."

"The glorious unfolding." Anna kissed Weston's cheek, making him smile. "I never want to stop learning, and I love discovering something new about who God is and how He works in our lives. Sometimes when I least expect it. Your turn."

"In Sunday school when I was seven, Mrs. Kirkenbaum taught the story of Daniel in the lion's den. I'd heard that story before and it was a favorite. I liked the whole thing—how evil men made the decree about praying only to the Persian king for thirty days to entrap Daniel, but how Daniel was faithful and continued to pray to God. I loved how God sent the angel to shut the lions' mouths. So, I raised my hand and told the teacher I wanted to ask Jesus into my heart that day. I mean that *second*. Even back then, I was impatient."

Weston laughed under his breath. "Bless her heart, she didn't ask me to wait. Two other kids did the same thing, and we all became kids of the Kingdom right then."

"That's great! I love talking with you, Weston. You talk so openly about God and don't care what anyone else thinks. I can't tell you how much I admire that. I've never met anyone like you, and I mean that in the *best* way."

"Then I hope you agree it's not random that we met," he said.

"I agree, but with all the traveling I do, I still don't see how—"

"Shhhh." He placed two fingers over her lips. "We've started something special. We need to trust God to work out the details." Lifting his eyes to the porch ceiling, Weston sighed before returning his gaze to hers. "Have I given you enough reasons why we should follow this through and see where it leads? I've got lots more where that came from."

"I'm good. Your powers of persuasion are impressive."

"Then we should make good use of our time together."

Her mind was wonderfully muddled by his nearness. "I think—"

"Anna?" His voice was deeper, huskier as Weston moved his hands to either side of her face.

"Yes?" she squeaked.

Weston brushed his thumb over the corner of her mouth and lightly tugged on her bottom lip. How could a simple gesture like that drive her crazy with need?

"Don't think. You Anna. Me Weston. Basic biology. Kiss the boy already."

"Great idea." Her heart soared as his lips met hers.

In that moment, Anna understood why she'd waited so long for these special kisses.

She'd been waiting for *this* man.

Chapter 23

Lost in thought, Weston was stretched out on the bed in the dark, arms crossed behind his head. He started at the sight of Neil's frame silhouetted in the doorway.

"Hey," Neil said. "I didn't mean to scare you, man. Sorry."

"That's okay. It takes more than your ugly mug to do that." Weston shoved up in the bed and propped his knees. "Come in. Toss the clothes off the chair and take a seat." He squinted after Neil flicked on the light switch, illuminating the bedroom.

"What happened to your finger?"

"*Anna* happened, that's what. She broke a glass at the diner, and I tried to stop her before she hurt herself."

"Always her hero, huh? Can you work with it wrapped like that?"

"Not a problem. I'm glad they didn't splint it. I have to be careful, and I'm not supposed to get it wet. Might make it a challenge to take a shower. Stitches come out in ten days."

Neil put the clothes on the small desk and pulled the chair closer. Dropping onto it, he propped his feet on the end of the bed and folded his hands on his lap. "I found out something about Darcy tonight." He ran one hand over his rough jaw and rested an elbow on the arm of the chair. His expression was conflicted, his eyes more weary than usual.

"What's that?"

"She's got a problem with cocaine."

Weston shook his head. "I'm sorry to hear that, man."

"Me, too." Neil leaned his head on the back of the chair and slowly exhaled. "I had a bad experience with meth when I was fifteen, and I've stayed away from drugs ever since. Some of my friends got real messed up, a few killed themselves being stupid. I sure can pick 'em, huh?"

He laughed without humor and lifted his head to meet Weston's gaze. "Look, I know you were talking about my mom earlier in the diner when you asked if Darcy and Lily remind me of someone. They're both like my mom. They stick around as long as something's good for them. When it's not, off they go." He waved his hand in the air. "I guess I should have seen it, but a person's more blinded to his own faults, you know?"

"True, and that goes for me, too." Weston leaned back against the wall. "I shouldn't have said anything, Neil. I'm not a trained psychologist, and it wasn't my place. I call them as I see them, but I'm sorry. I shouldn't have come down so hard on you."

"You're okay. You seem to understand people and you're smart. Whether it's a pipeline to God or whatever, you were right. Again. I'm thinking I can probably learn a lot from you."

"I don't know that it's so much being smart as watching people and observing human nature," Weston said. "I like trying to figure out what motivates someone and why they do the things they do. Most people don't realize how much their background and family shape their values and how they react to things later in life."

Neil nodded. "You don't know my mom or Lily, but you met Darcy. What made you say what you did? What made you think they reminded me of my mother?"

"We often gravitate to people with the same type of personality we're familiar with. In your case, because of what happened with your stepfathers, you probably felt unloved or unwanted, especially by your mom."

Neil dropped his gaze. "Keep going."

"You might have wondered why your mom didn't step up to defend you to men who weren't your father. Why she seemed to prefer them over you when you're a blood relative and they're not."

Weston slowed his words and gentled his tone. "Why she allowed at least one of them to physically abuse you. Why she didn't protect you. The result now is that you keep the walls you've erected around your heart so high that *no* one can penetrate them."

A tear dropped down Neil's haggard face. "I'm not crying, man."

"It's okay if you do."

"No, it's not."

Weston waited while Neil took a moment to compose himself. After rubbing his eyes, he looked back up. "I'm listening, man. I'm not going anywhere."

"Subconsciously, you hope someone will find their way past those walls. *Fight* past them even. But, instead, you choose women similar in personality to your mother because you know they're not going to hurt you any more than you're already hurting."

"Yeah, that's what you said before. In the diner earlier."

"Sorry to repeat," Weston said.

"Sometimes we've gotta hear something a few times for it to sink in." Neil's jaws hardened. "I know Darcy came on to you the other night, Wes. I heard some of what she said before I came down the hall. I was tired, but I wasn't drunk. I heard enough to know you just wanted in the bathroom, but she wouldn't move out of the way and was pawing you."

Weston shook his head. "I'm sorry you had to see that. For what it's worth, I'm glad you know the truth. At first, I thought she was intoxicated. But I didn't smell alcohol on her breath, and her words weren't slurred."

"I confronted Darcy tonight and begged her to get help. I told her I'd stay beside her if she'd let me. I've never told a girl something like that, but I meant it. If she needed me, I'd be there. Then she cussed me out and said she never wanted to see me again. So, I guess that's it."

The poor guy looked lost. He *was* lost.

Now's the time.

"I'll pray Darcy gets the help she needs," Weston said. "Tell me about your dragon tattoo, Neil. I've wondered about it. Why you got it, what it means."

"I was drunk one night about four years ago, that's what it means. Some buddies took me along to a place in Atlanta. So, I figured why not? When in Rome, right?"

"Dragons have symbolism for some people." Weston waited, knowing Neil would probably elaborate. He figured there was more to the story.

"My grandma used to like dragons," Neil said. "They weren't scary or anything to her. She used to tell me stories. Told me how they'd protect me. Then she talked about the treasure in me."

"Inside of you?"

Neil met his gaze. Resting one elbow on his thigh, he moved his chin to his fisted hand. "I grew up thinking a dragon protected me. I thought they helped me figure out stuff since she always said they'd help me follow my dreams and all that. . .stuff. I'm not sure that's working out so well."

Weston's pulse was pumping. Unwittingly, Neil had led him into the perfect segue. He'd searched the word DRAGON on the Internet and, in a *God* moment, found a direct correlation with sharing about the Lord.

"Neil, I read up a little on dragons. There's a book that talks about how dragons represent treasure, like you said. About how the treasure refers to something that can be misplaced but never lost. Buried, but never destroyed. You can't earn it, can't spend it. It's real but intangible. Not a thing but the essence of *all* things. And how—if you don't know what you're looking for or where to look—you could pass over the treasure and miss it altogether."

Neil sat back in his chair and shook his head. "Man, there you go getting all psychological on me again."

"Maybe, but I *think* you know what I'm trying to say. That's what matters here."

Nodding slowly, Neil appeared deep in thought and chewed on his thumbnail. "I think so."

"May I make a suggestion?"

"Depends." Neil grunted. "Why do I get the feeling there's a Bible verse involved?"

"Because there is. Only one."

"Lay it on me, man. I've got nothing to lose."

The door had opened. *Thank you, Jesus.*

"It's from the New Testament, and it says, 'If we confess our sins, He is faithful and righteous to forgive us our sins and to cleanse us from all unrighteousness.' Neil, bear with me here, but I think a lot of your trouble stems from anger at your mother. In order to get past it, and to discover that treasure inside you, you need to try and forgive your mother."

Neil half-laughed and sat back, his knuckles white as he gripped both arms of the chair. "Oh, that's rich. Why does that psychology stuff have to be about the mother? You think sleeping with girls like my mom meant. . .?" He scrubbed a hand over his face. "I don't care what Freud or whatever his name said, that's just sick, man."

"What I'm trying to say here has nothing to do with that. In your case, I'm guessing you have anger built up inside you for both your parents, but more at your mother. You were dealt a bad hand, and

I'm sorry about that, but *God* knows. I believe that's one reason our paths have crossed, yours and mine. I can help you, Neil, if you'll let me. My parents set the example, and they taught me to find the best in people. And my dad told me something once that I've never forgotten."

The other man met his gaze. "What's that?"

"He told me to try and see others the way *God* sees them. As someone worthy of His love."

Neil wagged his head. "God couldn't love me, man. I'm not worthy of spit."

"He *does* love you," Weston said. "Why do you believe you're not worthy?"

"For starters, I've slept with women. I curse, I drink…shall I go on? I've broken most of the Ten Commandments—at least the ones I know—except murder. But the others? Yeah, I've been there." He raised his hand. "Guilty."

Weston raised his hand and appreciated how Neil's eyes widened at the gesture.

"We're all sinners, Neil. One of the best things about God is that He offers His love to you freely, but it's *your* choice whether or not to accept it. God expects our best, but we're human. God knows better than anyone how often we fail.

"Jumping into bed with a woman might satisfy a temporary physical need, but if the emotional connection's missing, in the end you'll be left empty. Alcohol fills a void and gives you a temporary high. Cursing is something you use to give you a sense of empowerment, but you can consciously control it. The bottom line is this: unless a change takes place in your life, you'll probably continue in the same cycle."

"A change? Like what?"

"A *decision* you make to accept God's free gift. *That's* the hidden treasure inside you. A dragon's not the key to happiness or inner contentment and fulfillment. *Jesus* is. If you confess to Him those sins hidden in your heart and can acknowledge that Jesus died for you and *your* sins, and ask Him to cleanse you of those sins, He'll fill you with an unbelievable peace. Then those sins, every single one of them—past, present, and *future*—will be washed clean. God will leave you with the gift of the Holy Spirit to help you make decisions and guide you."

"You really believe all that, don't you?" Neil sounded more curious than doubtful.

Weston nodded. "I do. Like I said, *that's* the treasure inside you. It's just waiting to be claimed."

"No one's ever explained any of that to me. Never been around anybody who's gone to church or talks like you do." Neil scratched his chin. "I take it Anna believes like you, too?"

"Yes, she's a Christian. Having that bond of faith gives us a solid basis for friendship and any other kind of relationship."

Neil hunched forward, resting his arms on his thighs. "I've watched you at the site, Wes. You're different than the rest. You treat everybody the same. You're fair, and you work harder than any of us."

"I don't know about that. You're a—"

"Hear me out, man. "You *do* work harder, okay? I've seen you pray here at the apartment, and I can tell you care about the guys on the crew. You care about *me*. No one's cared about me for a long time. Really cared about whether I live or die. Not since my grandma died. Why? Why do you care about me?"

Lord, give me your words.

"Because Jesus changed me from the inside out. You said you see something different in me. That difference is *hope*. If I died in my sleep tonight, I'll have died knowing my future in heaven is secure because I took that step of faith. Jesus promised He'd return one day, and we can't know what tomorrow will bring. He could come any day, and I honestly believe we're living in what's called the end times. Part of what I'm called to do as a believer in Christ is to share God's love with others. I fail a lot, but I try."

"What happens if I don't believe?" Neil's eyes bore into his. "Give it to me straight."

Weston held the other man's gaze. "Then you'll face an eternity in hell and separated from God. I'd hate to see that happen. But *with* God, you're promised an eternity in heaven. Neil, I'd love nothing more than to call you my brother in Christ."

Rising from the chair, Neil appeared lost in thought as he moved it back to its original position and draped Weston's jeans and shirt over the back. "You've given me a lot to think about."

"I know. Just remember I'm here if you want to talk. I don't have all the answers, but I'll try my best to do what I can. To listen or whatever you need."

"Yeah." Neil turned off the light and closed the door behind him.

Weston settled in his bed. He might not be a firefighter anymore, but he felt like he'd been putting out fires lately. On the other hand, he hoped he'd stirred the embers in Neil's heart.

"And now, you're just being corny again," he mumbled.

Thanks, Lord.

He'd kissed Anna. A few times. It'd been great. They'd shared their hearts and their faith. They'd agreed to see where the relationship might go.

He was tired. Another day was done. All in all, a *great* day.

"I'm in love with that girl, Lord. I guess you already know that, huh?" He chuckled. "Help us figure this out when we leave town, but for now? I'm really looking forward to learning everything there is to know about her."

Weston bunched his pillow beneath his head and closed his eyes.

"Good night, Darling."

Chapter 24

Anna pulled the wet clothes from the washer and piled them into a laundry basket.

If only Felicia could see me now.

Who knew the simple act of washing clothes would make her feel more like a woman, more empowered, and self-sufficient? Maybe she was going a little overboard, but like that Davy Jones song, the world seemed a little brighter this morning. What a great feeling.

"What's happening?" Charley bounced into the small room at the back of the house, munching on a granola bar. "What are you doing up this early on a Saturday morning?"

"I should ask you the same thing. This, dear sister, is called doing laundry." Anna continued sorting through more clothes. "Observe and be amazed. How was Atlanta?"

"Busy. Crowded. Hot. Traffic was horrible. But good otherwise. Nicky met with a potential buyer, and he's interested in commissioning three sculptures for his new office, so it turned out to be a worthwhile trip."

Charley watched as Anna continued her work. "You don't do laundry at home, do you?"

"A lot of my clothes are dry clean only, so I send them out. But certain things I do myself. Believe it or not, I did my own laundry on the island."

Her sister waggled her brows. "I'm surprised you needed much clothing on St. John."

"I'm not *you*." Anna winked.

Charley took another bite of her granola bar. "I'm sure even Darling has a laundromat where you could drop off your clothes."

"They do, and it's not far from the diner. As difficult as it is for you to believe, I *want* to do this myself. I like doing laundry, and there's a wonderful sense of accomplishment in being self-sufficient." Anna continued separating the clothes.

"I'll take your word for it, but your job is to take care of *you*," Charley said. "Look at it this way: you brush your teeth, but you still go to a dentist for checkups. You eat right to stay healthy, but you go to the doctor to make sure you stay that way. You should let others take care of your laundry, cooking, cleaning, and everything else. You have more important things to do in life like fulfilling your destiny as one of the great classical pianists of this century."

Anna laughed. "Are you *trying* to swell my head? On the other hand, this helps keep me humble. Working in the diner does the same thing."

"Yes, but it's only temporary," Charley said. "You're allowed a few momentary lapses of madness. Seeing how the other half lives for a few weeks should be enough to show you how good you've got it on an ongoing basis. But when you get back to the 'real world,' it'll be time to focus again on that whole destiny thing."

Anna shook her head. "That's the thing, Charley. In some ways, *this* is the real world much more than my life in New York. But it's the only life I've known until now. Did you ever see the movie *Roman Holiday* with Gregory Peck and Audrey Hepburn?"

Charley scrunched her brows. "I've heard of it, but I haven't seen it."

"Audrey's a young princess who goes from one press conference or royal event to another. She's become tired of it all and longs for adventure to see what's beyond the palace walls. When she visits Rome, she escapes one night. Gregory Peck plays a newspaper reporter who befriends her, and he begins to squire her all around the city. His photographer friend goes along to record everything on film after he and the reporter realize she's the runaway princess. A romance develops between Gregory and Audrey, but then her sense of duty returns. There's this poignant moment at the end when it's the reporter's turn to meet the princess at her press conference in Rome. He hands over an envelope, and she sees that it contains photos of their adventures together. She knows her runaway secret is safe and holds in her hand the precious memories of that time in her life where—just once—she was allowed to be *normal*."

"So, it's like the reverse fairy tale where the royal becomes a commoner for a few days," Charley observed. "Did that movie inspire you to run away from your life and come to Darling?"

"Maybe subconsciously but on a much smaller scale. It's the whole idea of doing things I've never done before and experiencing life outside of what I've always known. It's also shown me how *spoiled* I've become."

Charley stopped chewing. "Wait. Was that a crack? You think *I'm* spoiled?" She smirked and dodged the pillowcase Anna tossed at her.

"Just a little," Anna said. "I think you'd be less inclined to run away from home if you had a hobby or a pet project. Tell you what, *you* do the laundry for me now, and I'll go play the piano. How's that?"

"Anna, did you ever consider I might have come to Darling to make sure *you're* okay?"

She stopped sorting through the clothes. "*Is* that why you're here?"

"That's a big part of it. Okay, it's true I was ticked at Nicky, but I was also really worried about you, especially after I heard those rumors." Charley lowered her gaze. "Not that I believed them for a second. And…well, to be honest, Felicia called and asked me to come here."

"I should have known." Anna growled under her breath and tried to keep her aggravation in check. "Felicia apparently doesn't believe I can function on my own in the 'real world' without her."

"Well, you showed her! Now that I'm here, I can see this break has already been good for you," Charley said. "From my perspective, you *do* seem happier than you've been in a long time."

"That's because I *am* happier," Anna snapped.

"If you don't mind my saying, you don't seem happy right this second."

"Sorry," Anna said. "Not your problem."

"Not to be crass, but maybe it's time to sever the umbilical cord with Felicia."

Anna stared at her sister. "How can I do that? That'd be like firing you as my sister."

"Keep in mind that Felicia's a hired employee. *I'm* family. I mean, sure she took you in after your mom died, but that's not the same thing as a blood relative. It's in her best interest to take care of you. You're her star client. I know you've never been especially close with her, but that's not such a shock considering she's not exactly warm and cuddly. To be blunt about it, she's made a very good living from her relationship with you the past decade."

"Honey, I didn't mean it that way," Anna said. "*Nothing* will ever change my relationship with you, but Felicia does a very good job handling my career. I'd be crazy to let that relationship go. You might be interested to know I've already decided that once I return home, I need to sit down and have a heart-to-heart talk with my manager. It's time to establish new boundaries and discuss plans for my future. Starting with cutting back on the tour schedule."

"There you go!" Charley slapped her hand on top of the dryer. "That's the spirit!"

Anna finished sorting. "I'm glad you're here, Charley. It's good to catch up."

"I agree." With the half-eaten granola bar clenched between her teeth, Charley easily hoisted herself on top of the dryer. "I knew those gymnastics skills would come in handy again one day." Sitting cross-legged, she gave Anna an impish grin.

"Where's Nick? Still sleeping?"

"I'm not sure." A frown creased Charley's face. "He wasn't in bed when I woke up. You haven't seen him either?"

"There was an empty bowl in the kitchen sink but no sign of Nick."

Charley slowly chewed another bite. "I'm sure he'll turn up soon. Maybe he jogged to that park downtown."

Anna almost laughed but caught herself in time. "Nick jogs?"

"He tries. That's why he bought all those athletic clothes."

"Maybe you should go with him sometime. You're obviously very limber. You know, the whole idea of the couple who jogs together. . ."

Charley shook her head. "Nope. Jogging's way too hard on the knees. I prefer other forms of exercise. By the way, I saw a couple of really cute guys from the upstairs window. And, oh yes, they're half-naked, tan, and buff."

"Excuse me?" Anna measured liquid detergent into the washer.

"Your hunky boyfriend's one of them. They're helping that sweet older couple next door. Cutting the lawn, trimming hedges, all that fun stuff."

"That's nice of them, but I wish you'd stop saying provocative things. I think these steamy summer temperatures are giving people ideas." After adding fabric softener, Anna closed the washer lid.

"Okay, if it's more palatable for you, they're *shirtless*. I'm not purposely trying to be provocative. I'm only telling the truth as I see it. Like it or not, thinking about the opposite sex is basic human nature no matter what season it is." Charley broke off a section of the granola bar and plopped it in her mouth.

"Weston's not my boyfriend. I mean, I don't think he is. Not really. Maybe. Last night. . . Oh, I don't know. How can I call someone I haven't known a full week my boyfriend? How is that possible? I've never had a boyfriend to know what being a girlfriend *feels* like."

Charley burst out laughing. "You are so cute! That was quite a mouthful. The length of time you spend with someone doesn't matter as much as the quality. You might not have dated much, or ever been a girlfriend, but you and Weston have *chemistry*. That intoxicating curl-your-hair, fog-up-your-glasses, hormonal kind of thing. You can't fight it, so you might as well give into the attraction."

"How can you possibly know that about us? And having chemistry doesn't necessarily mean two people belong together." She wouldn't tell Charley *everything* that happened with Weston last night. It was still too new, too precious. If she told her sister, she'd be plied with questions she wasn't prepared to answer.

"I know that, but most relationships between a man and a woman start with some kind of attraction, and usually it's physical. If you deny that, then you're out-of-touch," Charley said. "I could see something happening between you two at the diner. Weston's great. He's funny, he's *normal*, and you seemed to have a fun banter thing happening between you. So, I guess you could say he's intellectually stimulating for you. A girl needs that."

Anna smiled. "Yes, you could say that. Last night, I told Weston what I do for a living, where I live, basically my life story."

"Good. I'm proud of you, sis." After shoving what was left of the granola bar into her mouth, Charley wiped her hands down the front of her shorts.

Anna added more clothes to the washer, adjusted the settings, and closed the lid. "See? Doing laundry is easy as pie. Come outside now and keep me company. There's a clothesline in the backyard, and I'm going to hang the clothes to dry."

Charley swallowed. "Again, Miss Domestic, I have to ask *why* since you have a perfectly good dryer right here. Beneath me." She patted her hand on the top of the appliance again.

"I've always heard how great clothes smell when they're dried in the fresh air, especially sheets. It's not like I can do that in New York."

"You're right. Since you're so nice to put Nicky and me up while we're in town, it's the least I can do. It'll be a nice perk if you get a glimpse of Weston."

Charley uncrossed her legs and dropped to the floor. "If he were still putting out fires, he'd be perfect for one of those firefighter calendars. The guy's got awesome abs and some serious muscle."

"Do I need to remind you of your marital status? Again?" Anna led the way and Charley followed close behind as they traipsed down the short flight of stairs into the backyard. Yes, she'd like to see Weston, but she couldn't dwell on it. The morning was already warm enough.

"I can still look, Anna. There's no crime in that. Don't you worry about me. The home fire's still burning bright."

Anna tried not to groan at her sister's pun as she lowered the basket. The wet clothes weighed down the load, making it heavier than she'd expected. Hopefully, she wouldn't pay the price later for wanting to play domestic. If only Nick had arrived before she'd moved that furniture around to make room for the baby grand piano. Her brother-in-law might be skinny, but the man *was* freakishly strong.

Charley squinted up at the clothesline. "I'm going to need a step stool or a ladder."

"No, you won't. I'll hang the clothes. All you have to do is hand the wet things to me."

"That's easy enough. Where are those wooden doohickey things?"

"The clothespins are in the blue paisley bag hanging on a hook by the back door," Anna said. "Let me run back inside and get it."

"I know where it is. You stay, and I'll go. Be right back."

A minute later, Charley still hadn't returned. Where was that girl? Anna moved one hand over her eyes to shield them from the blinding sun. Charley appeared at the back door, pointing to her cell phone. Wonderful. Probably giving her daily report to Felicia.

Don't be smug. She should be thankful she had people in her life who cared about her well-being.

Marching across the yard and up the stairs, Anna grabbed the clothespin bag and headed back outside. She hung the bag on the line and then pulled the queen-sized flat sheet from the basket. A breeze caught it and blew it across her face. After struggling with it for a full minute, laughing, she finally got one corner hung on the line. "I am woman, hear me roar!"

Feeling proud of herself, Anna wiped the sweat from her brow and finished hanging the sheet on the clothesline. Next, she tugged out the fitted sheet and repeated the process.

After leaning down to pull a pillowcase from the basket, she jumped when a man's hand appeared in front of her face, dangling a clothespin, swinging it back and forth.

"Doohickey?"

Chapter 25

Anna moved one hand over her chest as she caught her breath, keeping her back to Weston. Did people get a thrill out of scaring her half to death? Behind her, she heard his soft chuckle.

"Are you half-naked? I've heard unconfirmed reports of partial nudity next door."

His chuckle became a full-blown laugh. "I prefer to call it half-*clothed*. Only way to find out is to turn around."

She rotated a half-turn. Weston, hair wet, sweat beaded on his forehead, stood before her in his Purity Promise T-shirt, navy shorts, and athletic shoes. The man looked terrific, as always. In the morning sun, his eyes were cerulean-blue. Breathtaking. Unforgettable.

"Let it be known I'm not the kind of guy who seizes a cheap, easy opportunity." He offered her a sweaty glass filled with light brown liquid. "Iced coffee?"

"Sounds great. Thank you." After pressing it briefly to one cheek and then the other, Anna took a quick sip. "Ah, that's refreshing. Perfect for a hot morning. Where'd you get this?"

"Lois made it and insisted I bring a glass to you. She wants to meet you, by the way."

Anna lowered the glass along with her gaze. "Did you...?"

"Tell her there's a world-class concert pianist living next door?" Weston waited until she looked up at him again. "No. I don't make a habit of spilling secrets, either."

"Thank you for that. So, how's the digit this morning?" She took a long, slow drink of the iced coffee, relishing the rich, smooth liquid as it slid down her throat.

"Better. I didn't need over-the-counter painkillers. I am man, hear me roar!" Weston winked. "Thanks again for nursemaiding me last night. It proved very enlightening."

"You're welcome, and yes, it did." Anna licked her lips. "Were you spying on me just now?"

"Not at all. Well, not unless you count hearing Charley use the word *doohickey*. That was too good to pass up."

Anna tilted her head. "I see your curls have gone missing." She tried not to let her disappointment show.

"Lois gave me a trim." Weston rubbed one hand over the back of his neck and grinned. "Don't worry. I'll grow them again to keep me warm for the winter."

"I see." Either she was too obvious or the man was too perceptive. "Did you bring one of your roommates to help out next door?"

"Neil came with me." Weston's smile sobered. "We had a good talk last night, and I shared about the Lord. He didn't run away screaming, and I'll try to build on that foundation here and when we get back home to Atlanta."

Anna smiled. "That's an appropriate comment coming from a man who works in construction. Neil's blessed to have a friend like you, Weston."

"The Lord's challenged me to help him. I deal with a lot of people in the ministry, and what kind of Christian would I be if I ignored the one in the next room?"

"I hope he'll take what you said to heart." Anna handed the glass back to him and wiped her mouth. "You can finish it for me. I'll introduce myself to Lois and Raymond in the next few days. I'm not in the habit of doing that, but I might as well take advantage of this new empowerment."

"Aren't people in New York friendly?" Weston took a drink from the glass.

"They can be. After our conversation last night, I'm sure you understand I've led a sheltered life. Other than church, I don't really get out much."

"That's easy enough to remedy. What do you do with your downtime?"

"If I'm not reading or relaxing, I attend art gallery openings or soirées." She shrugged. "Things like that."

He chuckled. "Sounds…"

"Boring?"

"I wasn't going to say that," he protested. "Don't put words in my mouth. Tell me about these soirées. I have no idea what that means, only that it sounds French."

"It's a party, usually at a private home, and music is involved."

"Doesn't sound like downtime to me. That's why you need me."

She laughed. "Good Time Weston. That's what I'll call you."

"I've been called worse."

"Before I came to Darling, I was on the island of St. John," she told him. "It was at the end of a tour, and I needed a few days to myself."

"Good for you," he said. "I noticed the tan lines on your wrist from your watch. Caribbean island hopper, are you?"

"You know it. When I get back to New York, I'm thinking of expanding my horizons with my downtime, now that you mention it. Charley already put me through the inquisition the morning as to why I'm doing my own laundry."

"What'd you tell her?" Tipping the glass, Weston drained the last of the iced coffee.

"That I'm enjoying being self-sufficient for once in my life."

He grinned. "Maybe you should tell her your next adventure is to work in a laundromat in Manhattan. That'd be a kick."

She shook her head but laughed with him. "You're talking to a girl who didn't even get her first driver's license until she was twenty-two."

"That's not so surprising for someone who lives in the city, is it?"

"I guess not, but Felicia always takes care of the details and arranges transportation. My manager would be horrified to learn I've been on the subway a few times."

Weston mock gasped. "You rebel! I'm glad you survived. Let me help you with the rest of your laundry." He set the empty glass on the ground.

"Are you finished next door?"

"For today, anyway. We might come back later in the week. There's a lot to be done. Neil already took off, so I'm all yours. By the way, you look as lovely as the sunshine and a breath of fresh air combined this morning." Weston kissed her cheek, bringing with him the scent of freshly mown grass and the outdoors. Mingled with iced coffee.

"You're very poetic today."

"The Lord knows I try." After grabbing a handful of clothespins, he pulled a pillowcase from the laundry basket. "What time do you work at the diner today?"

"I have to go in at noon, and I'm off at four. My shortest shift of the week."

"Anna, how come you're still working there?"

"You mean now that my secret's out?" She pulled out a cotton skirt, grateful none of her unmentionables were in that basket. Considering she wasn't exactly sure where they stood in terms of a relationship, she certainly didn't want the man seeing her underwear. Her cheeks warmed and not only from the morning sun.

"Right." Weston hung one of her uniforms on the line. "I have a vested interest in you sticking around town." He gave her an irresistible grin over one shoulder.

"I told Roz if someone comes into the diner who needs the job more than me, I'd step aside. She keeps threatening to fire me, so anything's possible." She watched as he finished hanging the uniform. Somehow that seemed almost. . .intimate.

"She won't fire you."

"You sound pretty sure about that. Thanks for the vote of confidence."

"You're doing great, and as long as you're willing to stay, Roz would be a fool to send you on your way. It's going to be hard enough when you *do* leave town."

"We have a few more weeks before that happens." She handed him a pillowcase.

"Right," he said. "Tell me how often you practice. Did you have to learn all new songs for this upcoming tour?"

They worked together as she answered his questions.

"When I'm home, I play four days a week and vary the days off. I practice anywhere from an hour to five or six hours, depending on my mood and energy level. For the new tour, I learned several new compositions, and I mix them with old favorites. I also have a short session in every concert where I play abbreviated favorites that audience members have requested ahead of time."

"So, when you go home to New York, it's sort of like maintenance? You need to practice but not overdo it?" Weston pulled out a white cotton nightgown.

"Here, let me take that." Anna practically snatched it from his hands. "You've been very helpful, but I can handle it. Just keep me company while I hang the rest of these things."

"Why? Are you embarrassed for me to hang your nightie. . .thing?"

"Sort of. Let's not dwell on it, please."

"You're adorable." Weston dropped a quick kiss on her lips. "I guess I thought you had to practice hours on end, especially before a tour." He stood aside and watched as she finished the task. "Like cramming for a test."

"Overdoing it would only make it worse. I still need days off, and they're every bit as important as the days I practice. If it helps, think of it like a bodybuilder who's told to rest the day after a workout," she said. "The workout tears down the muscle tissue. The day off is when it's rejuvenated and built up again and becomes stronger than before. Our brains are like that, and we need rest periods. If I thought I had to practice every day, I'd get stressed out and feel guilty about missing a session. Then I'd want to cram in an extra-long session the next day. That method doesn't work. I'd end up making more mistakes and getting frustrated."

"Well, we can't have that." He sniffed one of the sheets.

She laughed. "Are you being weird again?"

"Maybe. My mom and grandma used to hang sheets on the line to dry. Nothing like sleeping on them. I'm guessing you haven't?"

"Nope, but ask me tomorrow." After hanging the last of her clothing on the line, Anna nodded with satisfaction. "I've missed out on a lot of things in my life. There's no doubt in my mind that's one reason God led me here."

"*I'm* glad you're here." Grabbing the glass off the ground, Weston gave her a smile that made her weak in the knees and her pulse go haywire.

"Weston, do you want to know why I said yes to going to the fair with you tonight? Well, besides the obvious."

A slow grin crossed over his face. "What's that?"

"The way you took off the Stetson and held it in your hands while we talked in the diner. While you were making that. . .persuasive speech."

"Okay." He tilted his head, obviously not comprehending.

"You're a gentleman, mannerly, polite. Thank you for that."

He tipped an imaginary hat. "It's my honor. I'll pick you up at six. Save room for a caramel apple."

As Anna headed back into the house, smiling, her cell phone rang. Pulling it from her pocket, she was surprised to see the phone number for The Darling Diner.

"Hello?"

"Anna, honey, it's Candee." She spoke in a hushed whisper. "Listen, we've had a little situation here at the diner. I wanted to give you fair warnin' that Roz is on the warpath today."

Wonderful. "What have I done now?"

"It's nothin' *you* did, sweetie. I guess you could say it's more of an indirect thing."

"I have no idea what that means. What happened?"

"It seems that brother-in-law of yours decided to paint somethin' here at the diner. He said he was doin' it *gratis* so we assumed she'd approved it. Well, you know what they say about that. Anyway, I thought Roz was gonna blow a gasket! She was already grumpy about somethin' when she got here, so that didn't help matters. To tell the truth, Anna, we're all gettin' a kick out of the whole thing. If she weren't so mad, I think Roz would, too."

Anna hoped Nick had a good attorney. Small town or not, defacement of private property was an act of vandalism. A *crime*.

"Is this painting on the outside of the diner or inside?"

"Outside. On the window, so it's not as bad as it might sound. It didn't interfere with business since the paint fumes were only outside. Roz ordered Mike to clean it off, but I guess Nick used some kind of paint that's hard to get off without scrapin' or whatever. Then Francie convinced Roz to leave it there until the insurance guy could come and snap pictures as evidence. Hector and Lance tried to tell her it was good for business. Get this—old Harry Barnes and Kenton Dunwoody nearly collided on the street while they were lookin' at it!"

Candee giggled. "For now, it's still there on the window, and it's drawin' a small crowd."

Anna hated to ask. "May I ask *what* Nick painted?"

"That's what's so funny and creatin' all the excitement. Nobody knows exactly *what* it is. Mike asked Nick, but he was tight-lipped and said it's *in the eye of the beholder*. Looks like a bunch of color splotches to me. Some say it's a cow, some are sayin' it's a portrait of Roz. I think that's what's makin' her the maddest, especially after hearin' people say it looks like a cow. Jerry says it looks like a Double Darling with ketchup oozin' over the side. Those two old coots who almost had an accident over it think it looks like a naked woman. Can you imagine? Men! Della thinks—"

"Candee, is Nick at the diner now?"

"No. He packed up his stuff and left about twenty minutes ago, mumblin' in British like I hear he's done before. Oh, and that reminds me of somethin' else. Might as well tell you now that people are startin' to come in here askin' for the famous piano player. They're requestin' that you wait on 'em. Might as well bring a piano in and set a jar on top. Class the place up."

That last part *almost* made Anna smile but not quite. "I'm sorry about what Nick did."

"Oh, don't be, sweetie. That's not why I told you. Doesn't bother me none. I'm the one who's sorry that people seem to know about you. I guess there's loose lips so now tongues are waggin'. Bound to happen, I suppose, but I know you wanted to keep it quiet and not have people gawkin' at you."

Anna felt a headache coming on. So much for the beautiful day. "That's okay. I appreciate the call. I'll see you in a few hours."

"You bet, sugar. I'll try to talk down Roz a little before your shift starts."

"Thanks, Candee. I'll be there."

Anna chewed her lip, uncertain whether to laugh or cry. If she dropped, spilled, or broke one thing during her shift, that would probably be it for her so-called career at The Darling Diner. The end of the line.

This might be the day to turn in her apron once and for all. She'd tried her best, and she'd enjoyed her short stint as a waitress. Perhaps she should book a seat on that flight back to New York tomorrow with Charley and the Public Property Defacer.

Leaving the empty basket in the laundry room, Anna headed into the main part of the house. Maybe she should calm down first so she didn't approach Nick with righteous indignation, but at this point, anything was fair game and she'd had it. Zany was one thing, but this time he'd stepped over the line.

"Nick!"

Chapter 26

Sitting on a pew in Darling Community Church on Sunday morning, Weston prayed for Anna. Who could have predicted she'd be attacked by fire ants at the 4-H Fair? He felt responsible for her affliction. Aside from claiming her skin was on fire and wanting to scratch the itch all the way down to her *bones,* Anna mercifully hadn't blamed him.

She was a charitable woman.

"Do you have room for me?"

At the sound of Anna's voice, Weston broke into a smile and rose to greet her. In her pretty flowered dress and sandals, her hair in a braid, little makeup, she was a vision. *Beautiful.* Even with several welts dotting her arms and legs.

The guilt started in on him again.

"I always have room for you. Good morning." Taking her hand, Weston kissed her cheek and tugged her down beside him. "How are the spots this morning?"

"Better." After pulling out a thinline Bible and dropping her purse on the floor, she held out her arms and stretched out her legs for him to see. The welts—a dozen or so, mostly on her arms but a few on her legs—had blistered overnight. From personal experience, he knew they'd fill with a lovely pus-like substance soon enough. He'd pray they wouldn't leave scars on Anna's skin. He wouldn't mention any of that to her and pray for the best. Not what he'd anticipated praying for in church this morning.

"Thanks for manning the sick bay last night," she said. "I'm thankful you had presence of mind to ask Lois for the tea tree oil. It did the trick and took away that awful itching. Although it makes me itch again just thinking about it."

Anna wiggled a bit on the pew. Man, she was cute in spite of her discomfort.

"How's Nick feeling this morning?"

Anna shook her head with a small smile. "Dramatic as usual. Claiming he feels *snockered*, and griping that the aftereffects of junk food at the fair are worse than any hangover he's ever had. When I left the house a few minutes ago, he was stretched out on the living room sofa, hugging a bottle of antacid and groaning. Charley's nursemaiding him. I'm just thankful she didn't get bit by the fire ants, too, or I'd probably never hear the end of it."

Weston chuckled. "Forgive me if I don't have much sympathy for Nick. He was eating everything in sight. I warned him to slow down after the third corn dog. Or maybe the fourth."

"I know," Anna said. "I lost track after his second round of fried dough. I think he learned his lesson, but to be honest, I'm thankful to get out of the house this morning. Don't worry, though. I'm sure he'll be fully recovered by the time you drive them to the airport later. One good thing about Nick is that he bounces back quickly. I appreciate your offer to take them into Atlanta since I know it'll take up a big chunk of your day."

"Glad to do it. My biggest regret is that you can't come along."

Anna grinned. "Strap me on as a hood ornament, and I'm good to go."

Weston chuckled and pressed one hand to her forehead. "You must be delirious. I'll have your likeness carved as a figurehead for my truck. While I'm there, I'm going to stop by my house and pick up some clothes. Then I'm having a late supper with the folks."

"That'll be fun. By the way, Roz decided to leave Nick's painting on the front window of the diner, at least for now."

Settling back on the pew, Weston crossed his arms. "I still haven't seen it. Did Nick ever say what it's supposed to be?"

"No, and I'm beginning to think he painted it that way on purpose."

"What do you mean?"

"His paintings are modern and open to individual interpretation," she said. "What better way to draw attention to the diner but a conversation piece? Only Nick knows if he did it on purpose, but whatever the reason, it doesn't seem like such a bad thing now. He signed it, and some of the townspeople are saying it might be worth money. They might be right since his paintings sometimes bring an obscene amount of money. I was furious with him at first, but as it turns out, that crazy man's painting has already boosted the diner's business. Even since yesterday, it's stirred interest and promoted conversation and interaction among the townspeople."

He chuckled. "I find it more intriguing that you'd be *furious* with anyone."

From the corner of his eye, Weston caught a flash of pink. Candee hurried up the aisle with her four children in tow, all dressed in their Sunday best.

"Well, good mornin'! I was hopin' y'all could join us today. Great to see you both here, and I hope you'll enjoy our service."

The kids filed into the pew directly across the aisle. Candee gave Anna a quick hug but then her smile faded when she pulled back. "Oh, honey, did you get bit by those pesky fire ants? They've been just *horrible* this summer."

"Yes, I'm afraid they're my lasting reminder of the 4-H Fair," Anna said. "I'll be fine. Nothing time won't heal. Weston took good care of me."

"We take care of each other." Weston lightly nudged Anna's leg with his.

"Well, now, isn't that special? You are adorable together. Did you get to meet Pastor Anderson yet? I've been tellin' him about you two."

"He introduced himself to me a few minutes ago, right before Anna arrived," Weston told her. "So did Jesse."

Candee beamed. "I'm glad about that, on both counts. Weston, honey, do you mind if Connor comes to sit with you for a bit? You're his hero these days." She winked at Anna. "I didn't think you'd mind sharin' him."

Anna ducked her head and smiled.

"Send him over," Weston said.

"I need to scoot, but can you join us for Sunday lunch today? We're doin' it picnic style on our deck out back. Fried chicken with all the fixin's and peach cobbler for dessert. And my mama's special fried cornbread. You haven't lived until you've tasted it."

Weston's mouth watered. "Sounds great, and I'm game if Anna is."

"I wouldn't miss it," Anna said. "I have a refrigerator stocked with food at the house, so Charley and Nick can fend for themselves. Can we bring anything?"

"Just yourselves and big appetites," Candee said. "I'd better get over to our pew and make sure those kiddos of mine are behavin' themselves. You never know. Last week Peyton took a blue magic marker and decided to draw baby Jesus on the back of the pew. Jesse and I are singin' a duet this mornin', and I don't mind sayin' I'm a little nervous. Feel free to say a little prayer for us. We're not the best singers in the world, and we're not trained by any means, but we like makin' a joyful noise."

"I love that woman," Anna said after Candee moved back across the aisle. "It's nice to know people still invite others over for Sunday lunch."

"That's southern hospitality for you." Weston grinned and stretched his arm along the pew behind her. Her smile found its way into his heart. Life was especially sweet on this Sunday morning in Darling.

A minute later, as the pianist began to play the prelude, Connor slid onto the pew beside him. "Hi, Mr. Weston."

"Morning, Connor. Meet my friend, Anna."

The boy inclined his head toward her. "Mornin', ma'am."

She smiled. "Hi, Connor. I work at the diner with your mother."

You're also a world class pianist. How could she be so humble and unassuming? Sometimes he found it hard to believe this wasn't some crazy dream. Having Anna next to him felt *right*.

"Mama said I could sit by you if I behave myself." Connor's features scrunched into a frown. "I said Peyton's the one she has to watch, but she told me to quit bein' ugly."

Weston grinned. "Southern mamas say that a lot. You're okay. How's the knee?"

"Healin' up. It don't—*doesn't*—sting anymore."

"Glad to hear it."

The service began and Weston opened the hymnal. Anna motioned for him to share with Connor and pulled another from the pew rack.

Weston's mind wandered as they sang "To God Be the Glory." One day, would he stand in a church service, sharing a hymnal with *his* son? Bounce a baby girl on his knee? He darted a glance at Candee, Jesse, and their kids. Children were among God's greatest blessings, their innocent and trusting nature one of the most precious gifts a man could ever be given next to a godly, loving wife.

Wife. The hymnal almost slipped from his hands. Anna reacted quickly, steadying the book. He thanked her, mad at himself for losing his concentration. In the many times Madison sat beside him in a church service, he'd never felt the same contentment he felt with Anna beside him now.

Why did Anna have to live in New York? Why couldn't Madison be more like Anna? He'd sent that email to Maddie, but she hadn't answered, not that he was surprised. No doubt she didn't like it that he'd sent her an email instead of a text or a phone call. In that girl's mind, a *smoke signal* would have been more intimate than an impersonal email.

The woman beside him now was wife material. Did he dare believe that way? Think of a future with her? Was he worthy of Anna?

Connor elbowed him. "Are you okay?"

"Fine." Weston gave him a reassuring smile. "I had a revelation."

"You mean like the last book in the Bible?"

The question made Weston smile. "More or less. Related, anyway."

"You're talkin' funny again. Are you a daddy?"

"Not yet, Connor, but I hope to be a dad someday."

Connor grinned up at him. "You'd be okay at it."

"Thanks for the vote of confidence, kid." Weston ruffled his blond curls and then rested his hand on Connor's shoulder. He wondered if Anna heard any or all of that conversation, but he avoided glancing her way.

The service continued with the week's announcements. When the youth pastor called for the children to come to the front, Connor made no move to join them.

Weston nudged Connor's arm. "You going up there?"

"Nah. I'm ten." Connor sounded appropriately offended. "It's only for the little kids."

Candee appeared beside their pew with Peyton. "Connor, I need you to take your sister up there and stay with her. When it's over, sit with your brother and sisters."

"But Mama—"

"Just do it, son," Candee whispered. "Daddy and I are singin' our song next. Besides, I've invited Mr. Weston and Miss Anna to lunch today at the house. You can talk to 'em again later."

"Yes, Mama." Connor gave them a wave and slid off the pew. Good kid.

The rather sizable group of boys and girls were cute, their responses to the youth pastor's questions funny and sometimes embarrassingly honest. What was a children's sermon without humbling a parent or two?

Sitting on a step at the front, Connor leaned his elbows on his propped knees, swinging them back and forth. He stared at the ceiling with a bored expression, making Weston chuckle at the reflection of what he'd been like at the same age. His hair had been blond like Connor's but the only curls he ever had were on his neck when he wore his hair long enough.

After the offering, Jesse wheeled his chair onto the platform with Candee walking beside him. She retrieved a microphone from the stand and handed it to Jesse before taking one for herself. Weston felt empathy pains when he noticed how her hand shook. When he first started singing in public, he used to shake. But when he'd begin to sing, the Holy Spirit took over and calmed his nerves.

The music began to play and the couple began their song, a rousing, southern gospel tune that soon had most of the congregation tapping their feet and clapping along. A few shouted out encouragement or a hearty *Amen!*

Anna seemed to know most of the lyrics. Singing quietly, she swayed on the pew. Watching her, Weston was entranced by the effervescence that bubbled up from inside her and the clear *joy* she felt in her relationship with the Lord. He'd only known her a few days. How was he going to let this woman go after spending several *weeks* with her?

You enjoy the time you're given, that's how. Rest in Me.

"Go, Mama! Shake your boot-ay!" The sound of a sweet child's voice carried across the pews. That must have come from cute little Peyton.

Candee stopped singing as the color drained from her face. She stared straight ahead, eyes wide, as though frozen.

"What? That's what Daddy said—"

Too late, Connor slapped his hand over his little sister's mouth and pulled her onto his lap. He buried his head on her shoulder while Taylor and Alex giggled and scooted down farther into their pew.

Jesse's mouth gaped as twitters of laughter reverberated throughout the sanctuary. The person running the sound system stopped the music, leaving the congregation in stunned silence.

Weston felt for the couple and wanted to help. Although familiar with the tune, he didn't know the lyrics. Should he go forward?

Be still. All will be well.

"Now *this* is my kind of church!" an older gentleman seated on the opposite side of the congregation bellowed. He rapped his cane hard on the wooden floor several times. "It's real. It's honest!"

An older lady seated on the pew behind them grunted. "Well, I never!" The man seated next to her, presumably her husband, hissed at her to shush.

Candee looked at Jesse, clearly torn over what to do. She replaced her microphone on the stand. When she started to leave the platform, Jesse called to her.

"Candee." He held out his hand, waiting. "Come here, baby. Come sing with me."

Anna slipped her hand in Weston's as everyone in the congregation waited to see what would happen next. Hesitating only a second, Candee walked back across the platform to her husband and took his hand as the music started up again.

Jesse began to sing in his pleasant tenor. It was a beautiful thing to witness Candee gaining more confidence as their song progressed. Her soprano voice blended well with Jesse's, and when they finished, many in the congregation cheered and rose to their feet, clapping enthusiastically.

Pastor Anderson strolled across the platform and gave Candee a hug before shaking Jesse's hand. He turned to face the congregation. "Ladies and gentlemen, I believe what happened here this morning was no accident. Jesse, if you're willing, why don't you share a few words?"

Jesse reclaimed the microphone from his lap without relinquishing his hold on his wife's hand with the other. "I'm not a public speaker, but fifteen years ago this week, I married my childhood sweetheart right here in this church. And yes, I'm talkin' about my Candee girl."

Weston chuckled. Beside him, Anna wiped away a tear.

"When we stood before God and pledged our lives to each other, we had no idea what would happen. It's been hard at times, but we've stuck it out through sickness and in health, just like we vowed we'd do. There've been plenty of days I didn't like myself, but my wife"—Jesse's eyes filled and he swallowed hard—"she's showed me what God's grace and mercy is all about. She's given me four great kids, and shown me the kind of love most people can only hope of havin' in their lifetime. I want to publicly thank my beautiful wife for always bein' there for me. I love you, Candee, and I look forward to seein' what the Lord's got in store for us. Thanks for takin' the journey with me."

Wiping away her tears, Candee leaned to speak into the microphone. "Most of you know we don't have many secrets in our family. As our little girl's outburst this mornin' proves, we sometimes say things around the house that, well, they might not exactly be appropriate for a three-year-old child to holler out in the middle of a church service."

She paused as some in the congregation laughed quietly. "We love hard, and we love good. God's blessed us with each other to take care of, and by God's great mercy, that's what we're tryin' our best to do. May y'all be so blessed. Amen!"

The congregation clapped again as Candee and Jesse made their way down from the front and settled on their pew. Weston smiled when Candee tugged Peyton onto her lap and peppered her cheek with sweet kisses. In his wheelchair next to the pew, Jesse put one hand on Candee's knee, a wide smile on his face.

After opening his Bible, Weston retrieved his bulletin to find the Scripture verse. When he saw it was 2 Corinthians 5:17, he said a quick prayer for Neil, wishing his roommate could hear the message. Maybe one day he would.

Weston rose to his feet with Anna for the reading of the Word. In unison, they read the passage along with the pastor. "Therefore if anyone is in Christ, he is a new creature; the old things passed away; behold, new things have come."

A man dropped down at the end of the pew as the reading ended. Returning to his seat, Weston darted a quick glance down the row.

Neil.

Weston nearly gasped and his pulse pounded. Opening a pew Bible to the passage of Scripture, he handed the book to Neil. With a small nod, Neil took it from him.

As Pastor Anderson began his sermon, Weston struggled to maintain his composure. He felt shaken in the best of ways.

Lord, I love how you always know.

He'd been praying hard for this man all morning. Been praying hard all *week* since that first conversation in the kitchen, then at the diner, and especially since their conversation Friday night. He hated how Neil felt no one loved him. How God *couldn't* love him. Just like many of the people he ministered to with Purity Promise, Neil had been in his proverbial backyard for a few years. Yet it took coming here to Darling to bring him to Weston's attention.

Lois and Raymond had embraced Neil. The older couple had invited his roommate for dinner one night during the upcoming week. Ray told him their only son had been killed in a car accident years ago when he was only sixteen. Apparently, Neil reminded them of their boy.

Lord, help Neil to feel your love. I pray for your peace to flow over and through him.

"A young couple, knowing a tornado was headed their way, had no time to take cover," Pastor Anderson began. "They laid their baby on their living room floor and covered him with the only thing they could—their bodies. The tornado swept through their tiny town with a vengeance and left destruction in its wake. The storm leveled a row of homes, including the one where the young couple lived.

"Hours later, when rescue workers rummaged through the homes, they heard muffled crying. Soon after, they came upon the lifeless bodies of the young couple, but there was joy in the midst of sorrow for the baby was found safe beneath their bodies. You see, folks, they'd given the ultimate sacrifice in giving their own lives to save their beloved child. Just as Jesus gave up His life for us on a cross at Calvary."

Neil shifted on the bench. Weston almost reached out one hand in case the other man started to bolt. If he *did* leave, he'd need to let him go. He'd come to the church. Sat on a pew. Had the Bible on his lap. Seemed to listen. That was a start.

Lord, keep him here. Allow Neil to hear the message with his heart and not just his ears.

Leaning close, Anna whispered. "He's here. Let that be enough for now."

She was right. Sensing Neil's eyes on him, Weston gave him a nod as the pastor continued.

"Through the years, there have been many stories where people perform heroic feats of supernatural strength to save a loved one— lifting cars, pushing a train off a track, things of that nature. Things scientists can never logically explain because they're impossible to explain with theory and logic. But as Matthew 19:26 reminds us, '...With people this is impossible, but with *God* all things are possible.'"

Neil shifted again, but he remained on the pew.

"Our life is not our own," Pastor Anderson said. "We've been bought with the price of Jesus's death. Because of His sacrifice for our sins, we're called not to serve ourselves but to serve Christ. Freedom is an illusion, folks. We like to believe we control our own lives, but that's not the case at all, is it?

"I've learned through the years, and I'm sure you have, too, that we're not the master of our own fate nor the captain of our soul. We can delude ourselves all we want. Those who don't know Christ indulge in sinful behavior because they live in ignorance, but many also live moral, honest and upright lives. My friends, being good in and of itself doesn't assure an eternity in heaven. Neither do good works guarantee us a ticket to the gates of heaven."

As the pastor continued his message, Neil stared straight ahead.

"Should I show him the Scriptures?" Weston whispered to Anna.

She squeezed his hand. "Let this be enough for now. He seems to be listening."

"Thanks. I'm glad *you're* here."

"Me, too."

As the service ended, Weston smiled when he noted the closing hymn was "Take My Life and Let It Be." He heartily sang each word of every verse.

Take my life and let it be
Consecrated, Lord, to Thee.
Take my moments and my days,
Let them flow in endless praise.

Take my hands and let them move
At the impulse of Thy love.
Take my feet and let them be,
Swift and beautiful for Thee.

Take my voice and let me sing,
Always, only for my King.
Take my lips and let them be,
Filled with messages from Thee.

Take my silver and my gold,
Not a mite would I withhold.
Take my intellect and use,
Every pow'r as Thou shalt choose.

Take my will and make it Thine,
It shall be no longer mine.
Take my heart, it is Thine own,
It shall be Thy royal throne.

Take my love, my Lord, I pour
At Thy feet its treasure store.
Take myself and I will be,
Ever, only, all for Thee.

Weston checked the end of the pew. *Empty.*
But you led Neil here today, Lord. Thank you.
For now, he would be content in the small victories.

Chapter 27

Weston sat at the picnic table on the back deck of Jesse and Candee's home, enjoying the view. A slight breeze blew through the trees, giving them blessed relief from the stifling humidity of the last week. Anna chased Peyton around the yard, and the child's squeals of laughter made him smile.

He liked this family. They were solid, good, hardworking people. Jesse was a big man, a teddy bear with bushy dark hair and a thick beard. As demonstrated by what happened in the church service, he could handle a pressurized situation with grace and humor. Their kids seemed to be a combination of both their parents in both looks and personality. Candee reminded him of a younger version of his mother—heartfelt, a great mother, wife, and a woman who didn't hesitate to speak her mind.

"You love her, don't you, sweetie?"

Yep, a *lot* like his mother. Minus the sweetie part.

Candee scrambled onto the picnic bench beside him. Leaning an elbow on the table, she tucked blonde curls behind one ear.

Weston smiled. "You filled me so full of food, I can't move. How do you get love out of that?"

"You can't fool me, mister. I know love when I see it. I see it in the way you're watchin' Anna now. Love is in the little gestures, the quiet times, the stolen glances," she mused. "I might not be the smartest person in the world, but I like to believe I've got a way of seein' through to a person's heart. You two share somethin' rare. I hope you can hang onto it. Fight for it if you have to, Weston, but find a way to meet Anna halfway between Atlanta and New York."

He sipped his root beer. "You're not only a great cook, you're also perceptive."

"The gift of discernment is what Jesse calls it. I just wish I could predict when things are gonna happen, like Peytie Jo callin' out what she did." Candee's cheeks flushed and she laughed. "That one's gonna go down in the record books."

"As one of the great moments in the history of Darling Community Church. Here's to your and Jesse's fifteenth anniversary. Wishing you many more together." Weston lifted his can and clinked it against hers.

They sat quietly together for a few minutes, enjoying the sunshine and the sound of the kids' laughter. Jesse pulled Peyton onto his lap and took her for a ride in his wheelchair.

"Candee, I hope you don't mind my asking, but has Jesse ever considered getting a prosthesis?"

She lowered her gaze and sipped her drink. "He's prideful about it. We all have our issues and stumblin' blocks, I suppose. I finally stopped askin' him. Before you say anythin', it's not about money. Insurance will cover most of the cost. Neither is it therapy, rehabilitation, or whatever else he'd need."

"He seems content and comfortable without it," Weston said. "I was just curious."

"I think the answer is that he's *man* enough *without* it. It's not a big deal to him."

Weston nodded. "He's got a great wife, and that makes all the difference."

"You're sweet for sayin' that, Weston. Thank you."

They both watched as Anna and Alex began tossing a ball with the younger children.

"I met Jesse on my first day of fifth grade," Candee said at length. "I hated most boys at that age, but lookin' back, I think I knew even then there was somethin' mighty special about that tall, gangly, dark-haired boy. He wasn't particularly charmin', and the Lord knows he couldn't talk to a girl to save his life. But there was somethin' I liked, a good strong character inside him. We started datin' our freshman year in high school and never looked back."

Candee's voice had grown softer. "He's the only boy I ever dated. The only boy I ever *wanted* to date. Married him when I was eighteen. I've known Jesse when he was what most people consider *whole*. I loved him then, and I love him even more now. He's not broken like some people think. In some ways, he's more whole now than he ever was before. You wanna know what I've learned in all our years together?"

"What's that?"

"God's shown me the power of love even more since Jesse's accident in Afghanistan. He served his country bravely, and he could have died from his injuries. But he didn't, and I honestly think it's because God's not done with my husband yet. He has a higher purpose and callin' in mind for Jesse."

"Anna said something similar when I walked her home that first night we met. Thanks for encouraging that, by the way."

Candee took a quick sip of her drink. "Glad I could help. I felt one of those little God nudges just like you did in givin' me that big tip. Thanks for *that*, by the way."

They shared a smile.

"I used to be a firefighter in Atlanta, and Anna told me her uncle had been a firefighter, too," he told her. "We were discussing life and death issues. On a smaller scale, maybe, what I experienced on the job was like what Jesse must have seen during his stint in the war. I saw people live, but I also saw people die. Anna's theory is that—given a situation where one person is spared and another dies—it means God still has more to do in the one who survives. I think she's right, but I also know it's only by God's grace that *any* of us are here."

"Love's about sacrifice as much as anything else," Candee said. "Startin' with our great God who gave us the ultimate example in sendin' His Son to die in our place. Doesn't that blow your mind sometimes?"

Weston nodded. "Yes, it does. I've been trying to share with my roommate, Neil, since we've been here in Darling. His showing up in church this morning was the last thing I expected. On the other hand, I don't know why I'm surprised. It was an answer to prayer. I get impatient, but I've learned that you can't beat people over the head. You try to live your life as honestly as you can and lead by example. Guide them when they come for counsel. But, like anything else, it's on their terms, but ultimately in *God's* timing, not ours."

Candee sat up straighter on the bench and startled him by slapping her hand on the table. "Amen, brother! When that man first came into the diner, I don't mind sayin' I thought he was a sleaze the way he eyed Anna up and down. You made yourself known as a gentleman right from the start, but that one…" She shook her head.

"Neil had it rough growing up," Weston said. "Not to excuse or defend his behavior, but in spite of the way he acts and what he says,

I can see the good inside him, Candee. He's lost, and he needs the Lord, just as we all do. He's starting to ask questions, and he's seeking answers. I pray the Lord will continue to use me to reach him."

"Well, I'll be prayin' that prayer for Neil right alongside you. Don't give up. Jesse didn't know the Lord until high school, but I kept prayin' for him. He wasn't resistant so much as he didn't grow up in the church and didn't have the best examples at home. I tried all kinds of things, and I'm embarrassed to admit bribery was one of 'em, to get that man to come around."

Weston turned to her. "What happened? Not the bribery," he stipulated, chuckling.

"In Jesse's case, it started at his grandfather's funeral. They were close, and his Pap was a strong believer. That boy heard the gospel message at least five times durin' the service." Candee sipped her drink and laughed. "It lasted two hours, but those good seeds were planted.

"Then we were sittin' on my front step later that night, not talkin' but just bein' together, you know? I knew he was hurtin' bad, and I just wanted him to know I cared. Then, all of a sudden, Jesse turns to me and announces, 'I want what Pap had. Everybody's talkin' about him ditchin' his cane and dancin' up in heaven now. He's not hurtin' no more, and they say he must be happy. I see how happy *you* are, and I want that, Candee.'"

Candee's eyes filled. "With all he's been through, Jesse doesn't cry much. But he had these big ole tears streamin' down his handsome face that day. He said, 'Tell me what to do. I want to know Jesus.' So, I told him, and Jesse prayed with me right there on that step."

Weston smiled and lightly squeezed her hand. "I think the testimony of someone we love, like Jesse with his grandfather, makes a huge impact on us. The finality of death is something a lot of people don't think about until they're staring it in the face."

"I'm sure you're right." Candee nodded. "Don't get me wrong. Through the years, there've been plenty of times I've been ready to throw in the towel 'cause Jesse's stubborn as all get out, but then I stop and think about all that man's sacrificed for me and the kids. And that's when I thank God for all He's given me and how He's blessed us."

"Like you said, we all have our issues, our prideful ways, and our hang-ups," Weston said. "Jesse seems like a terrific guy. There's great wisdom there, and it's plain to see he's obviously learned from his trials. Some people *never* learn."

"Thanks for sayin' that," Candee said. "They don't come any better. He's here for our kids when they get home from school. He cooks supper for them if I'm still workin' at the diner, and he does a better job than I do of delegatin' and gettin' the kids to help with the dishes and clean up. The kids admire their daddy, and Jesse's more patient with them than I am. He can be a disciplinarian at home, but Jesse prefers to back off and be more low key in public."

"He handled what happened this morning very well."

Candee blew out a sigh. "Yes, he did. There's people in this town who judge my husband and make jokes behind our backs about Jesse bein' only half a man because of what happened to him. But the joke's on them. First of all, those people don't know nothin' about somethin' that personal. My Jesse's more of a man than people who hide behind their big jobs, fancy houses, and expensive cars. Just because a man is prideful and boasts to the outside world of his worth and how important *he* thinks he is doesn't make him a hero. Fightin' through the anger, the loss, the pain, and the ignorance of others has made Jesse stronger."

Weston nodded. "He's been through the refining fires and emerged triumphant."

"You know it. Now, let me tell you somethin' not many people know. Jesse makes wood carvings of eagles. He's got a heap of talent, and that's not only a proud wife talkin'. Remember how I said God has a higher callin' for my Jesse? I think this could be it. He puts a Bible verse on the bottom of each one and prays for the person who'll buy it before he ships them off."

Weston was momentarily distracted by the way she added the *ing* to the word *carvings*. Anna would find that interesting since Candee was a classic case of a person who dropped the *ing*.

"Candee, you have every right to brag on Jesse."

"They're not just a hobby where he does an okay job, either, and people buy 'em just 'cause they feel sorry for the damaged war veteran. At first, Jesse stayed exclusive to museum gift shops and upscale stores in Georgia. But now his pieces are in demand, and people all over the country are collectin' 'em. We've even had orders comin' in from Germany and England."

Candee tapped her hand on the top of the table. "How about that? Isn't that somethin'?"

"Sure is. Candee, do you think I could buy one of Jesse's eagle carvings? I need a birthday gift for a very special woman." Weston's gaze strayed to Anna. Catching his eye, she waved.

Beside him, Candee nudged his arm. "I'm sure we can work out somethin'. You any good at softball?"

"I've played on a few Little League baseball teams, so I can swing a bat. Why do you ask?"

"The Darling Diner Drivers are out a hitter this season since Billy King is workin' down in Mobile. Think you could help us out while you're here in town? If you're not too tired? They play weeknights out at Brown Field." Her gaze moved to his bandaged finger. "Can you play with your stitches?"

"Not a problem. Candee, you've got yourself a deal."

Weston checked the time. He was running twenty minutes behind after unloading Charley and Nick's luggage at the airport curbside check-in. Those two must pay a fortune in bag fees. Nothing with them was simple, but in a weird way, that was another part of their charm.

Nick had given him a hearty handshake and a man hug before telling Weston he hoped to see him in New York soon. Charley gave him a sweet kiss on the cheek and whispered, "Thank you for making my sister so happy. I think she's right about God bringing you both to that little town at the same time." Words that thrilled him to his core in several ways.

Weston's cell phone rang. The display read *Dad*. He'd hoped it might be Anna, but she must be back at the house enjoying the peace and quiet. He couldn't blame her.

"Hey Dad," he said through the headset. "I'm running a little late, but I expect to be there in about ten minutes."

"Not a problem. Change of plans, though. Instead of coming to the house, meet us at The Market instead."

That was a surprise. "Uh, sure. Whatever's easiest." He'd been looking forward to one of his mom's home-cooked meals and tried not to reveal his disappointment.

"Is Mom okay?" Weston switched lanes. He needed to take the next exit for another highway closest to The Market, about ten minutes from the house on the outskirts of the city where he'd grown up and his parents still lived. Thankfully, the Sunday evening traffic was light.

His dad chuckled. "She's fine, but I thought it might be nice to take your mother out for a change. That way, we can get caught up without your mother fussing over the meal. I tried to call you earlier. I left a message, but you didn't pick up."

"Sorry. I had lunch with friends after church. But get caught up? I've only been gone a week." As soon as the words left his lips, Weston realized how much can happen in a week's time. *His* week had been the most eventful ever.

"Everything's fine here at home, but we want to hear how you like Darling and how the bank building's coming along. I've only passed through there once that I can recall. Quaint little town. Old-fashioned in some ways."

"That it is." Weston grinned. "You didn't happen to stop in at The Darling Diner, did you?"

"No, but everything seemed to be on a few main streets."

Weston signaled and headed onto the exit ramp. "You're right. Mom deserves a break. And I insist on picking up the check."

"You don't have to do that, son."

"Humor me. Are you at the restaurant now?"

"We're getting ready to walk out of the house now. We'll see you soon. We have a reservation, so ask for our table. If you get there first, go ahead and be seated."

"Will do. I'm looking forward to it. Hey, I'm only wearing shorts and a polo. Won't that violate their dress code or whatever?"

"No worries. Pretty much everything goes at these places anymore."

"Okay. See you soon."

After he disconnected with his dad, another call came in. Weston smiled when he saw it was Anna. "Galloway Transportation. No load is too heavy."

She laughed, making his smile grow. "Are you talking about emotional baggage or otherwise?"

"Depends. What have you got for me?" Weston groaned. "I really should think before I speak. Do your sister and bro-in-law always travel with so much stuff?"

"Afraid so. Hope your back's okay. I still feel responsible for the finger incident."

"No worries. I still feel bad about the fire ants. Let's call it even."

"I called to say thank you again for taking Charley and Nick to the airport. I hope you have a great time with your parents tonight."

"Thanks. Anna, I'm not sure what to tell my folks about you. Is it okay if I tell them about us? Everything?"

"That's up to you. I'm okay with whatever you want to tell them."

"Great. Thanks." After turning a corner, he stopped for a red light two blocks from the restaurant. "What I mean by *everything* is how I've met a beautiful, talented, compassionate woman."

A woman I'm in love with after a week.

Although he had a great relationship with his parents, that announcement might be premature and push their limits. His parents had known each other five years before they'd started dating. Then they were engaged for two years before getting married. He clearly hadn't inherited the patience gene. He reminded himself that his parents were also younger than he was now when they'd been married.

After exiting the highway, Weston parked his truck a few minutes later and entered the upscale restaurant. He figured his parents picked The Market since its location would save him serious time when he headed back to Darling later.

"Reservation for Galloway," he said after the hostess greeted him.

"Certainly. Right this way, sir." Weston followed as she led the way to where his parents sat studying the menu at a table in the middle of the restaurant.

Weston's steps faltered as the third person at the table glanced up and smiled.

Madison.

This should be fun.

Chapter 28

Weston had been on the receiving end of Madison's smile many times in the past. His pulse skipped a few beats, but not from eagerness. His parents had invited his ex-girlfriend to dinner? He couldn't begin to figure that one out, so he wouldn't try. Most likely, she'd wrangled an invite at church that morning. Still, he felt somewhat blindsided. A little warning might have been nice.

"Hi, Weston." Madison waved and patted the seat next to hers as he approached the table. "I saved you a chair."

No kidding. He forced a smile. This was certainly an unexpected turn of events. He couldn't fault his parents. How could they have known he'd fallen in love with a runaway Manhattan concert pianist in a week's time?

"How are you, Madd—Madison?" He gave her a polite nod and took the seat next to her, across the table from his parents. How cozy. To keep it more impersonal, he probably shouldn't call her Maddie. No need to give her encouragement.

His mom and dad greeted him with wide smiles. They'd always liked this girl. She was pretty and personable. With her last name being Adams, Dad thought it was clever how her parents named her after two U.S. presidents. Mom liked that she was a preschool teacher. Because that obviously meant she must love children enough to birth a few. Which, in turn, translated to a pretty strong guarantee of future grandchildren.

Plus, he was almost thirty and their only child…yeah, no pressure there.

"Oh, you poor baby." Madison touched his bandaged finger and stuck out her lower lip. "What happened?"

"Cut glass got me. No big deal."

"Did you need stitches?" Mom asked, her expression worried. Ironic considering all the broken bones he'd had through the years. It *had* been a while, though.

"A few. They'll come out soon enough."

"As long as you can work at the construction site with it," Dad observed.

As they ate, between conversations about church news and world events, the trio took turns asking him questions about the construction project, how he liked Darling, and how his truck was holding up. That last one made him smile, but a southern boy's truck was like a member of the family, especially since he didn't have a dog. Give him time and he'd definitely remedy that.

Halfway through the meal, as the questions from his parents and hints from Madison became more blatant, Weston knew he needed to broach the subject of Anna. His parents could claim ignorance. They were probably only trying to help him reconcile with the woman beside him and thought they were doing him a favor. Maybe he should have told them *why* his relationship with this girl had died. Madison, on the other hand, knew better, and he hoped she hadn't coerced his folks into this dinner under false pretenses.

No matter. Time to get on with it. Weston swallowed down a bite of steak and downed a long swig of his sweet tea. He'd already downed two glasses of the tea.

Time to finally get on with it. *Showtime.*

"I, um, have something I should tell you." His glance encompassed Madison.

"What's that, son?" Dad forked a bite of spinach. He'd never liked vegetables but humored Mom by eating more after suffering a minor heart attack two years ago.

Weston avoided glancing at Madison. She'd batted her big blue eyes at him throughout the entire meal. There was no easy way to do this, so he might as well get on with it.

He drew in a deep breath. "I've met someone."

He heard Madison's quick intake of breath.

"Weston, honey, do you mean here in Atlanta?"

"No, Mom. I've met a girl in Darling."

"That tiny town?" Madison sipped her lemonade, obviously dismissing the idea. "What kind of girl lives there? I'd do anything I could to escape." She winked at his mom and smiled at his father.

What kind of girl lives there? A humble woman *who* chooses *to live there.* No matter that it was temporary. She had chosen Darling, but he also figured God led her there.

For their part, his folks appeared stunned and quietly continued eating although he'd caught the uncertain look exchanged between them.

"Not everyone likes the city," Weston said. "Anna's from New York, as a matter of fact. She's only in Darling temporarily, same as me."

Madison lowered her glass to the table. "Then that makes even less sense." Her eyes widened. "Does she have something to do with your construction project?"

"Her name is Anna, and she works in The Darling Diner. For now. She has her reasons." He stuffed a big bite of loaded baked potato in his mouth and chewed slowly. He hoped she wouldn't push it further. But this was Madison. Of course, she would.

"A waitress? Not that there's anything wrong with that." Dad stabbed a bite of his broiled chicken. Poor guy. Weston felt for him as he cut another bite of his own steak. He'd offer his father half his slab of meat in a red-hot minute if he knew his mother wouldn't shoot him down faster than a kamikaze pilot.

"I think they prefer being called *servers* now," Mom said in a lowered tone. "Speaking of which…Jason, could you help me flag down our server and ask her about my broccoli? It tastes like it's been microwaved."

"Paula, how can you possibly tell something like that? You know microwave ovens are more sophisticated and safer than ever these days. Your aunt dying of brain cancer has nothing to do with them no matter what her crazy family claims."

Great. His dad who normally kept his cool was irritated now. Weston hoped the tension he'd caused wouldn't give Dad chest pains.

Madison ignored both the *server vs. waitress* interchange and the microwave debate between his parents and twisted in her chair to face him. A quick glance at her plate confirmed she'd eaten very little of her salmon and had only picked at her steamed vegetables.

Weston's eyes widened when she placed her hand over his and stroked her thumb back and forth over the top. That was a bold move in the presence of his parents, especially after that announcement he'd just made.

He slowly withdrew his hand and leaned close. "Madison, that's inappropriate considering we're not dating. Anymore."

Hurt flashed in her eyes. "Didn't you get my message?"

"I did. I responded in an email. I'm not sure about the mission trip yet."

"That's not what I meant."

"I know," he said under his breath. "But I don't think we have anything else to discuss."

"I'd really like to try again, Weston."

His dad wiped his mouth and cleared his throat. "Weston, it's a nice evening. If you're both done with your meals, why don't you take Madison outside for a walk on the back terrace?"

Weston obediently rose from his chair. "Shall we?" Being alone with Madison was the last thing he wanted, but Dad was right. Better to talk this out privately.

In her pretty black dress, pearl necklace, and heels, Madison must have planned to join them all along. He knew from experience it normally took her forty minutes to primp for a date. He'd waited in her living room enough times to know.

The terrace was busy, so they found a stone walkway behind the restaurant leading down to a small gazebo. The setting sun was lovely, the atmosphere romantic given the right circumstances, making him wish Anna walked beside him.

"I didn't mean to make that awkward, but I had no idea you'd be here tonight, as evidenced by what I'm wearing," Weston told her as they walked.

"You look great, as always. Hang on a second. I can't walk on these stones in these heels or I'll turn my ankle." Grabbing onto his arm, Madison removed one of her sandals and then the other. "That's better. Thanks."

With her shoes dangling from one hand, she made her way beside him in her bare feet. "Oh, my," she said, hopping around a bit. "I wouldn't have thought these stones could be so hot this late in the evening."

Was she hinting for him to pick her up? Perhaps he needed to stop being suspicious of her motives. Weston steered her to the side of the walkway. "Let's walk in the grass instead."

"Great idea." When she linked her arm with his, he ignored the way she leaned into him. He listened as Madison chatted for a few minutes about her recent vacation to Florida. Uppermost in his mind was getting this conversation over and done.

"Weston, your parents mentioned at church this morning that they were meeting you for supper. If you're thinking I imposed myself on y'all tonight, that's not true. Your sweet mother invited me to come along. So, tell me more about Anna. More specifically, what about her do you find so attractive?"

"I'm not sure this is the best conversation to have," he said. "Let's agree to move on." She'd found Tate *before* breaking up with him, after all. Madison had a lot to offer the right man, but especially after meeting Anna, he definitely wasn't that guy.

"Anna's from New York. *I'm* here," she pouted. "Long distance relationships never work, even if she stays in Georgia."

"I've never been in a long distance relationship, so I can't say. Have you?"

Madison pushed her long blonde hair behind one shoulder, a familiar gesture. "Just one, and it was a long time ago. That's how I know they're not a good idea. You can't tell me she won't get tired of that little town and eventually move on, especially if she's from New York." She squeezed his arm. "I'd hate to see you get hurt."

"It's still a new relationship, but I don't expect to get burned." Once Anna left Georgia and returned to New York, he wasn't sure *what* would happen, but he wasn't worried. During the church service this morning, and the time spent with Anna at Candee and Jesse's house, he'd been filled with a peace he couldn't explain if he tried.

"Why a waitress?" Her question brought Weston out of his musing.

"Why *not* a waitress?" he shot back. *Too defensive, old man.* The muscles in his jaws clenched. "I never would have pegged you as pretentious, especially about someone you know nothing about. That's presumptuous and unfair."

"Oh, someone's a little defensive. What is it you're *not* telling me?"

Weston stared at her for a long moment. "What do you mean?"

"Remember, I've known you for a few years," she said. "I can tell when you're holding something back from me."

He ran a hand over his forehead. This was a mistake. "Madison, don't push it. Let's agree we're better off as friends and leave it at that."

Madison pulled a cell phone from the purse slung over her shoulder. "What's Anna's last name? Is she on Facebook?"

"No." Was she serious?

Her brows arched, her expression incredulous. "You've got to be kidding, Weston. Everybody who's *anyone* is on Facebook."

"That's not true. I'm rarely on it. Maybe she has better things to do with her time."

Madison waved her phone in the air. "Or maybe that's an excuse and she doesn't really exist."

"This conversation is over." He'd had it with social networking. His grandparents had the right idea with courting on the porch swing. *That* was romance and getting to know someone, not social media where people communicated through computers and cell phones instead of one-on-one face time.

She lowered her phone. "I'm sorry. I just wanted to look her up since you seem so interested in this Anna person."

"Why?" *So you can cyberstalk her?* No, saying such a thing wouldn't be good. Madison might be a little misguided, but she wasn't crazy. At least he hoped not.

"I'm heading back inside now," he said. "I'm sorry you came with my parents tonight if you thought we could pick up where we left off. I hope we can at least be civil to each other, if not friends, at church."

"Of course. You really care about her, don't you?" Madison's shoulders fell.

"Yes. I do. Very much."

"Then I wish you the best. I know I didn't handle the whole thing with Tate well, and for what it's worth, I really *am* sorry."

"So you've said. It wasn't in God's plan for us, Madison, but I'm sure there's a great guy out there for you." The corners of his mouth twitched. "I'm glad it wasn't Tate."

Madison smiled. "Me, too." She twirled a long strand of hair around her finger. "Say, are you still working with that cute blond guy? Neil something?"

If it were possible, Weston thought his eyes might jump out of his head. Madison was interested in Neil? Wow. He couldn't have seen that one coming by any stretch of the imagination.

"Neil? Uh, yeah. He's working on the bank project in Darling with me now, as a matter of fact. He's one of my roommates." He wasn't sure how best to approach this subject. While he could think of a hundred reasons for her *not* to pursue Neil, he held his tongue. Call it another nudge.

Give Madison a reason to pray for Neil.

"He's not a Christian, and he's had it rough. I've shared with him, and I think—in time, Neil might come to Christ. He came to church this morning. That was surprising but terrific to see."

"So, he doesn't have a girlfriend?"

Weston shook his head. "Not currently, no. I'd encourage you to tread carefully if you go that route. Pray for him. That's the best thing you can do for him."

"I will." She offered her hand. "Friends?"

"Friends." Weston pulled her into a brief hug before releasing her. She'd given him more to think about than she could have known.

Madison and Neil? Well, Neil *did* have a presidential last name— *Carter.* He stopped short of laughing out loud.

Lord, I give this one to you.

"Just give me her last name," Madison said as they walked back into the restaurant. His parents looked up at them with plastered-on smiles as they approached the table.

"Redmond," he said, against his better judgment. Anna said everything had been scrubbed or whatever. All good.

"Wait a second." Sitting down beside him, she worked her fingers furiously over her phone.

"You're not going to find anything," he said in clipped tones, seething inside. Weston stared at the plate of carrot cake that had mysteriously appeared at his place. Mom must have ordered it, knowing how much he liked it.

"You said she's from New York, right?"

A sense of dread settled in his stomach. "Yes. Thanks for the cake, Mom."

"You're welcome." Mom took a drink of water, her eyes big over the rim of her glass.

He ate a bite of the cake but tasted nothing. Hard to do considering Madison was now staring at him, her mouth agape. "Does Anna play the piano?"

He dug into his carrot cake. "Maybe," he said around a mouthful. His mom could tell him later that he'd eaten like a pig.

"What's going on, Madison?" That from Dad.

She looked up at his parents. "It seems your son has found himself a classical concert pianist from Manhattan. Very successful." Her brow creased when she looked at her phone. "I have to admit, she's gorgeous."

"How do you know all this?" His dad appeared incredulous while his mother moved her hand over her heart. Hopefully, *she* wasn't having chest pains now. Good grief.

"My mom listens to classical music all the time," Madison said. "The last name sounded familiar. It's called putting two and two together."

Weston wanted to groan. How was he supposed to know that? He couldn't believe she'd figured it out, but that's what he got for loose lips. He'd met Madison's mother a few times, but the topic of musical tastes had never come up. He shoved another bite of carrot cake in his mouth.

Madison's fingers still flew over her phone. He wanted to grab the dumb thing from her hands and toss it in the goldfish pond off the back terrace. But, no. That would serve no purpose other than to make him feel better for two seconds. Then he'd be guilted into buying her another one.

She held up her cell phone. "Is *this* your Anna?"

Weston coughed into his fist and glanced at the screen. "Yes, that would be Anna. But I'd appreciate it if you didn't blab to anyone. She wants to be low-key for now."

"Well, I guess so." Madison slumped in her chair. "I can't believe it. I suppose the good news is that at least you dumped me for someone like Annalise Redmond."

Weston almost choked on his bite. Ah, so Madison told everyone that he'd dumped *her*? That was as rich as the sour cream frosting on his carrot cake.

"May I see?" His mother reached for Madison's phone across the table. "Weston, she's lovely."

Dad nodded. "Pretty girl, but I think we need a little more explanation."

Was it any wonder he couldn't wait to get back to Darling?

Weston forced another smile. "Bring it on." Then he took another bite. This might take a while.

~~❤~~

Anna stopped playing when she heard her cell phone buzzing. She'd ignored it too long. Charley had already called. She and Nick had landed safely in New York and were on their way back to the penthouse. Weston was enjoying dinner with his parents. The only other person who'd call her would be Felicia, and she wasn't up to a chat with her manager tonight.

She lifted rather gingerly from the piano bench. "And it *didn't* creak, Felicia." She had indulged a bit recently, but had only gained a pound. She'd work off any excess weight before she returned home. No problem.

Retrieving her phone from the sofa, Anna glanced at the display. Weston had called three times? How had she missed that?

Please, Lord, let everything be okay. She prayed he wasn't stuck by the side of the highway in that big red truck. Even if he were, he wouldn't call *her* to come to his rescue.

He picked up on the second ring. "Hi, Anna." She could tell he was using his hands-free headset, a good thing so he could keep both hands on the wheel.

"Is everything okay? I see you called a few times. Sorry I missed you, but I've been playing."

"Everything's fine, but I ended up meeting my parents at a restaurant instead. They brought an unexpected guest, so it took a little longer than I'd thought. I'm headed back now."

"Oh? Who was the unexpected guest?" Maybe it was none of her business, but he'd brought it up.

"My ex-girlfriend, but that's not why I called. Not directly, anyway. Listen, I know it's late, but will you be up a while longer? I'd like to stop by the house and talk."

Her heart rate picked up speed. "Should I be worried?"

"Nope. I should be there in twenty-five minutes tops. Meet me outside on the porch?"

"Sure. I'll see you then. Drive carefully."

Anna disconnected the call. "I wonder what *that's* all about?"

After splashing water on her face and combing her hair, Anna went out to the porch and sat on the swing to wait. A hundred possibilities of what Weston might want to tell her ran through her mind. She could barely sit still. He'd assured her it wasn't anything to worry about, but why would seeing his ex-girlfriend have anything to do with her?

Almost exactly twenty-five minutes later, his truck pulled up in front of the house. The man was punctual, a very good quality.

"Built tough," she whispered, sinking into the swing. Seeing Weston's broad smile as he climbed out and bounded up the front steps did her heart a world of good. He hadn't seen her on the swing and started to knock on the front door.

"Hi, Weston."

Swinging around, he broke into a wide smile when he spied her. "Hey, Anna."

She patted the empty spot beside her. "Come sit with me?" She hated the nervousness in her voice. Wasn't sure *why* she was apprehensive.

Taking a seat beside her, Weston moved his hands to either side of her face, being careful with the bandaged finger. Not speaking, his gaze roamed over her face in a leisurely manner, as though drinking her in, not wanting to miss anything.

"What is it? Has something happened?"

"No," he said, shaking his head slowly. "Everything's very *right*. Anna, I had an epiphany, a revelation or whatever, on the drive back here from Atlanta."

She gulped. "And that is…?"

He pressed his lips to hers and then pulled back. "I love you." Then he said it several more times between kisses.

Anna's breath caught and tears sprang into her eyes as he pulled her into his arms and hugged her as though he never wanted to let her go.

"You *love* me?"

"Yes!" Releasing her and jumping up from the swing, Weston went to stand on the edge of the porch. Planting his feet apart, he lifted his arms. "Do you hear me, Darling, Georgia? Weston James Galloway loves Annalise Cecile Redmond!"

They both turned as they heard a side window being raised at the house next door. "Weston, is that you over there shoutin'?"

Weston laughed and moved beside the swing, resting one hand on the chain. "Yes, Ray, it's me. I love Annalise!"

"Yeah, yeah. We heard you the first time. So did the rest of the town. As if we didn't already know. Help yourself to whatever color roses the lady wants. Pick her an entire bouquet."

Lois came into view beside Raymond. "Weston, honey, are you just now figuring this out? Is Anna over there, too, or are you just standing on her porch and shouting to God and the wind?"

"I'm here!" Anna rose from the swing, smiled, and waved to her neighbors. She'd met the lovely couple earlier in the afternoon and they'd enjoyed tall glasses of sweet tea together.

"I hope you give that boy the answer he wants to hear," Ray called. "We'll leave you two young people to your shenanigans. God love ya."

"Thanks! Talk to you again soon." With a goofy grin, Weston turned back to her. "Nothing like making a public spectacle, huh?"

"Weston, please sit down with me again." She'd never seen him so animated and energized.

This wonderful man loves me. Anna felt like doing a little jumping up and down herself. As it was, she couldn't stop smiling and felt she might *never* stop. She didn't know how they'd work out the details, but God did. He'd brought them together, so as Weston said, they'd figure it out.

Weston did as she asked and then took both her hands in his. "Anna, I don't expect you to say anything right now, but I wanted to make my intentions known. In time, I hope you can—"

"Weston?" She placed two fingers over his lips, her heart full.

"Yes, Anna?" The corners of his mouth twitched and his eyes lit.

"Me Anna. You Weston." She wrapped her hands around his neck and lifted her chin. "Basic biology. I love you, too." He lowered his head, bringing his lips closer.

"Kiss the girl already," she murmured.

"The honor's all mine, darlin.'" She loved the endearment, loved *him*.

His lips met hers. And then, he kissed her. Oh, how he kissed her.

Of all the places she'd been in the world, Anna's new favorite—hands down—was a porch swing in Darling, Georgia.

Chapter 29

Four Weeks Later

"Happy birthday to you, happy birthday to you…"

Anna clapped in delight as Weston—with his parents, Candee, and Roz on one side and Charley and Nick on the other—made a slow path from the kitchen into the living room, singing as they moved forward as a group. In his hands, he carried a large sheet cake with twenty-seven burning candles.

"Happy birthday, dear Anna, happy birthday to you!" Weston ended with a flourish as he carefully set the cake on the coffee table. She smiled when she saw *Happy Birthday, Darlin' Anna* written on the cake. Peach and white icing roses lined the outer edges of the cake that looked rich as anything.

"Make a wish, Miss Anna!" Peyton jumped up and down. Her party hat was askew, and she'd discovered the joys of blowing a party horn, in and out, in and out. In and out.

"Let me see. What shall I wish for?" Anna tapped her chin and gazed at her friends and family gathered in her living room to help her celebrate. "Can I cheat and have two wishes?"

"Of course, you may. It's your birthday," Nick said. The others nodded in agreement.

"If you need some help in the wish department, I'm your go-to girl." Charley winked from where she sat on the piano bench, her hair striped with bright fuchsia, her nails a paler pink.

"I'm good, thanks." Closing her eyes, Anna made her first wish. *Lord, I hope Charley and Nick will be expecting a baby soon. Thank you for the negative test results that put their minds at ease.*

"Any day now!" one of Candee's kids called. Sounded like Connor. He was the impatient one.

Anna held up a finger. "One more to go. Hang on. Won't take me long."

"We'll just start cutting the cake while you're making your wishes," Lois teased.

"No, wait! She's gotta blow out a hundred candles first!" Sounded like that protest came from Alex.

Lord, help Weston and me to find ways to see one another during my upcoming tour.

Little hands planted themselves on her knees. Anna's eyes fluttered open.

"Are you prayin' or wishin', Miss Anna?"

"Both." Anna hugged the child and gave her a quick kiss on the cheek. "Peytie Jo, want to help me blow out all these candles?"

"Yay!" The little girl bobbed her head with enthusiasm, sending her blonde curls—so like her mother's—brushing across her round cheeks.

"Yep. Before they burn down the house!" Connor called, making them all laugh.

"I'm starting to feel old here," Anna said, laughing.

"Don't spit on the cake!" That had to be Mike. Sure enough, it was, with Hector standing beside him and ribbing him with an elbow.

Anna shook her head. What was a birthday party without being teased? She didn't care. This was the best birthday party she'd ever had. One of the few she'd ever had. With her belly full from dinner, she doubted she could eat the cake, but she'd give it her best effort since her friends at the diner had made it special.

As he'd promised, Weston had taken her to dinner at a five-star restaurant in a nearby town—complete with silver, fine china, crystal, linen tablecloths, and soft music. All evening, she hadn't been able to stop staring at how handsome he looked in his navy suit with a white-and-navy pinstriped shirt opened at the collar. She'd learned he detested fastening the top button on shirts. He'd danced with her while they'd waited for their dinners, holding her in his arms like he'd never let her go. Again. He'd gotten in the habit of doing that.

"You can't begin to know how much I'm going to miss you," he'd told her as they climbed back into his truck after dinner. The man was romantic and corny as anything, and made her melt all over again. They'd talked quietly and stolen kisses. Until he knew his next job, Weston couldn't make plans to fly to New York or to join her tour. But he'd promised to come and see her as soon as he could.

In retrospect, she figured he'd been stalling so this marvelous group of people could prepare for her party, and what a surprise it was. They'd hung a banner above the front porch and colorful paper streamers dangled from the light fixtures and above the doorways. The bittersweet truth was that, even though the party was for her birthday, it was also her *going away* party. She'd been trying to push that thought out of her mind, a rather challenging proposition.

After Lois cut the ceremonial first piece of cake, Weston's mom, Paula, handed her it to her with a fork. "Here you go, Anna. Enjoy." Such a sweet woman. Other than her opposition to microwaves and refusal to eat anything cooked in one, she was lovely. Anna was thankful her birthday cake didn't have any blue or black icing.

In the past few weeks, she'd bonded with his parents, especially over their mutual love for Weston. His mother doted on him. His father, Jason, was a well-mannered, quiet man, who'd worked as a supervisor at a plastics engineering plant all his working life. Weston was a couple of inches taller than his father, and he'd inherited Jason's dimples and smile along with his mother's striking light blue eyes. Good people, solid people, and they'd raised their only child well.

"Oh, wait! I almost forgot. Be right back." Weston darted into the kitchen. Within a minute, he came back into the living room with a large container of Paulson's ice cream and a scoop.

Anna laughed. "Is that what I think it is?"

Weston winked. "If you guessed butter rum, you would be correct. We have vanilla and chocolate for everyone else." After digging into the container, he plopped a large scoop of the butter rum on Anna's party plate. Peyton squealed when the ice cream almost missed the plate.

As the group enjoyed the delicious dessert, Lois asked Weston to tell them where he'd taken Anna on the weekends.

"Of course, the first thing was a command performance at my folks' house so they could meet Anna." Weston straddled the arm of the sofa next to her. "Once she played the piano for them, they didn't want her to ever leave. I know the feeling." He kissed the top of her head. "Of course, I've discovered a few other equally lovable things about her."

"I hope you'll play something for us tonight, Anna."

Anna nodded to Roz. "Of course. I'd love to. That's one thing I can do even with a tummy full of cake and ice cream." *And a heart full of memories.*

She told them the highlights of visiting Stone Mountain and how Weston explained the finer points of baseball as she'd cheered alongside him at an Atlanta Braves game.

"And then Galloway took her to Callaway," Weston said in reference to the beautiful resort near Pine Mountain. He told them he'd also taken her to the World of Coca-Cola Museum, the Georgia Aquarium, and Centennial Olympic Park.

Jason patted his shoulder. "Sounds like you're a worthy ambassador for Georgia, son."

"Anna, sweetie, we have some presents for you." Candee wheeled the kitchen cart, with brightly wrapped gifts stacked on top, into the living room. "Ta-da!" She parked it in front of the sofa.

Smiling as she finished her bite of cake, Anna wagged her finger at Weston. "Is this your doing? You dear, kind people. You really shouldn't have."

Weston caught her hand and pressed a kiss to her palm. "What can I say? I was outvoted. People are going to do what they want, and they all love you. Especially me." He kissed her amidst the *oohs* and *ahhs* and an *oh, gross!* from one or two of Candee and Jesse's children.

"Kids, why don't you help me open the gifts?" Anna suggested. "It'll go faster that way."

"You don't need to ask them twice." Jesse chuckled. "Kids, behave and do what Miss Anna tells you. No pushin' ahead. Listen and let *her* tell you when she's ready."

"I'm ready. Come on, kids."

First, Anna opened a framed menu from The Darling Diner courtesy of Roz, Candee, Mike, and Hector. Francie couldn't be there—most likely off at a knife convention somewhere—but she gave Anna a special cutting knife. As soon as she opened that gift, Candee spirited it off into the kitchen where little hands couldn't touch it. Good thinking.

Charley and Nick presented her with a bottle of her favorite perfume. A second package from them held a small, all-weather bag with an opening in the center. Fanciest clothespin bag money could buy, to be sure.

"That's for all your doohickey things in the city," Charley told her with a wink. "In case you get the urge to do laundry."

"Oh my, is that something X-rated?" Lois moved her hands over Peyton's eyes.

Weston laughed so hard Anna thought he'd fall off his perch on the sofa. She had a difficult time restraining her own laughter as she explained the gift to everyone.

Next, Weston's parents gave her a lovely silk scarf and an album of pictures of Weston as well as photos they'd snapped of the two of them together. Anna thanked them with tears in her eyes, overcome with emotion at their thoughtfulness. "Thank you. I'll treasure these."

"Here you go. Open this one next." Weston handed her pretty gift bag with a large bow.

"What's this?" Anna tossed the tissue paper aside and pulled out a box. Connor promptly started to dig at the tape securing the top flaps of the box.

"Here. Let me take care of that for you." Taking out his pocket knife, Weston quickly slit the seam on the box.

"More stuff!" Anna dug through a mound of Styrofoam noodles and packing paper inside the box to unearth something encased in bubble wrap.

"You are such a kid," Weston teased before winking at Peyton. The little girl tossed and batted the Styrofoam noodles in the air.

"Is this from you, Weston?" Anna said.

He nodded. "Yes, but with the help of someone else in this room. You'll see in a minute."

Anna continued to unwrap the gift and finally uncovered a wood carving of an eagle, its wings spread as if in flight. "Oh, Jesse. This is one of *your* carvings, isn't it?"

"It sure is." Candee beamed from where she stood behind her husband's chair.

In awe, Anna ran one finger along the lines of one of the eagle's wings, then over his head, and finally down his beak. It had no color, but it needed none. The piece was perfect as it was.

"This is exquisite. I've heard about your work, but this is the first one I've seen." She clasped it to her chest. "I will treasure it. Thank you. And thank you, Weston." She touched her lips to his.

"Welcome," he whispered. "I'm glad you like it."

"I need to give this special eagle a name," she said, loud enough for all to hear. "What do y'all suggest?" Placing the eagle on the coffee table, she sat back on the sofa.

Weston leaned close and whispered, "You said *y'all* again. Told you we'd make a southern girl out of you before you leave town."

Anna grabbed hold of his hand. "I've been called worse," she whispered back. "It's addictive, and I kind of like the sound of it."

"How about Jesse?" Raymond suggested from where he sat in a nearby armchair. "Makes sense seein' as how he's the one who made it."

"Ray, you are brilliant!" Anna nodded. "That's the *perfect* name." She'd need to find the perfect place for this lovely eagle in her New York apartment.

Retrieving the carving, Weston showed her the bottom. "Jesse always inscribes a verse of Scripture on the bottom."

"Isaiah 40:31," she read. "That's the verse about mounting up on eagle's wings, right?"

Jesse cleared his throat. "Yet those who wait for the Lord will gain new strength; they will mount up with wings like eagles, they will run and not get tired, they will walk and not become weary."

"That's a perfect verse for how I feel sometimes when I'm on tour. And then I remember why I'm touring and Who sustains me. It's beautiful. Thanks again."

"One more." Lois presented her with a small box which Taylor helped Anna open. She pulled out an exquisite porcelain bouquet of multicolored roses—including peach and white, the colors of the roses Weston brought to her most often. Her home had been continually scented with the heady blooms. Anna's gaze moved to the fresh bouquet on the baby grand piano that Weston brought to her when he'd first arrived to pick her up for dinner.

"This piece came from Italy," Lois told her. "My father picked it up in Rome during a visit years ago. It's dated on the bottom."

Candee stepped closer. "Peyton, honey, don't touch that."

"Yes, Mama." The little girl obeyed but stood close to Anna, admiring the lovely gift.

With wide eyes, Anna carefully turned it over. "It says 1940. Oh, Lois, this is an heirloom. Are you sure I should have this?"

"Ray and I want you to have it. We thought it might remind you of being here in Darling."

"I don't know what to say except thank you." She stood and hugged the older woman.

"You're more than welcome, sweet girl. I hope you can find some good people to rent this house, but none of them will be as special as you. We're going to miss our afternoon chats and sharing sweet tea or iced coffee with you."

"I have an announcement in that regard." Anna inhaled a quick breath. "I've signed a purchase contract to buy this house, but I don't know any more than that yet. I might rent the house, or I might keep it for when I can come back and visit. Stay tuned. I'll let you know as soon as *I* do."

The unspoken part of the equation was how her relationship with Weston developed. So many things dangled in the air with no easy answers. She'd take it one step at a time.

"Oh, will you come back? We'd love that so much." Candee's eyes lit and the kids cheered. "You know you always have a free meal on the house at the diner."

Roz cleared her throat. "Speak for yourself, Candee. I'm not in the habit—"

"Of givin' out freebies," Anna finished for her. "So I've heard. You run a tight ship, Roz."

"That's *gratis* to you!" Nick hollered from where he played a game of checkers in the corner with Connor and Taylor. "By the way, that's the name of the painting on the diner window."

"What *is* that thing, anyway?" Raymond asked. "I've heard all kinds of speculation."

"I'll never tell." Nick winked at Anna. "Part of the beauty of modern art is that it creates discussion and promotes a fun sense of community."

"Well, it sure does get people going, and it's brought in business," Mike said. Hector nodded his agreement.

"You come visit us again, too, Mr. Weston." Connor looked at him expectantly.

"I hope so, Connor." Weston's smile was in place, but Anna could read the uncertainty in his eyes.

"Just don't come crawlin' back expectin' a job at my diner," Roz said to her. "Some girl from New York kinda spoiled it for the rest of my new hires."

Anna enveloped her in a hug. "I'm going to miss you, too, Roz."

"Here, I got you somethin' else. This one's from me." The woman thrust another gift bag in her hand.

Anna wiped away a tear and pulled out a white apron with GIRL embroidered on it and the name of the diner embroidered along the bottom edge.

"I hope you don't take offense," Roz said. "Where you're concerned, that's just another way of sayin' we love you. You can wear that in your fancy Manhattan kitchen and think about us whenever you cook. Or spill, break, or tip over something."

"I sure will." Anna smiled through her own tears. "I'll treasure this, too."

Anna looked out over the room, her eyes blurring from a heart overflowing. "I'm going to miss all of you so much. You've become my extended family. If you'd told me when I first arrived here in town that I'd grow to love Darling, Georgia, and the people here. . .well, I might not have believed you, to be honest. But you've welcomed me and made me feel—for the first time in my life, really—that I truly belong somewhere. Thank you for opening your arms, and your hearts, to me."

"That goes double for me, too." Weston stood beside her and wrapped his arm around her shoulders. "We'd appreciate your prayers as Anna begins her tour next week. As you might know, the heavy rains in the last few weeks have delayed work on the bank. We have an extension for a couple more weeks, so you'll need to put up with me and the crew a little longer."

"No way!" Jesse laughed. "Get out of town already."

Roz waved her hand. "You're plenty hard to put up with, mister."

"Don't listen to them," Candee called.

Weston whispered in her ear. "Ready?"

Anna deep breathed. "I'm ready."

Seated on the piano bench a minute later, Anna closed her eyes and said a quick prayer. This concert was every bit as important as the one she was scheduled to give in Carnegie Hall in a few short weeks. In many ways, this performance was much *more* important.

Weston loved to hear Anna play. Loved *her*. How he'd miss her. The carefree Anna who'd opened her birthday gifts was the woman he'd known had been waiting to emerge from beneath the burden of expectation and responsibility, the relaxed version of the world-famous classical concert pianist.

The woman who'd stolen his heart and freely given hers.

His parents adored her. Ditto everyone who'd grown to know and love her. He assured them all that he had every intention of making it work with Anna. He wanted so much more, but it wasn't possible—yet. Above all others, the *Lord* knew Weston Galloway wasn't a patient man.

If she'd have him, he'd marry Anna tomorrow.

Now *that* was an idea. Unfortunately, it wasn't feasible.

So, for now, he'd bide his time. Anna would return to New York and then tour points domestic and abroad while he'd finish the project here in Darling and then resume his life in Atlanta as best he could. As if it were possible after being around the shining light that was Annalise Redmond these past five weeks.

Some glittering points of light were meant to shine forever and be shared with the world. Others were meant to shine bright for a short time and then fade into quiet oblivion. Anna was the former, and he couldn't stand in her way. Was it possible to have the best of both worlds? No, not without sacrifice on her part, or his, or both. But wasn't what love was all about?

Could they make it? He'd hope so. More importantly, he'd *pray* so.

As she played, Anna held her guests spellbound. No one stirred, no one spoke, not even the kids. Another small miracle. It's as though they realized they were in the presence of greatness, not only of magnificent talent, but also of a person with uncommon character.

During the last few weeks, she'd played for him many times, and her talent humbled him. Anna took nothing for granted, and her heart attitude was in the right place. She didn't play for money or status. She played for the love of the piano and the love of the Lord.

"Please sing along as I play 'Amazing Grace,'" Anna invited as she began her finale.

Amazing grace! How sweet the sound
That saved a wretch like me!
I once was lost, but now am found
Was blind, but now I see.

'Twas grace that taught my heart to fear
And grace my fears relieved,
How precious did that grace appear
The hour I first believed.

Through many dangers, toils and snares
I have already come,
'Tis grace hath brought me safe thus far
And grace will lead me home.

When they reached the final verse, Peyton crawled onto Weston's lap and snuggled against him. His heart jumped. Kissing the top of her head, he wrapped his arms around her.

When we've been there ten thousand years
Bright shining as the sun,
We've no less days to sing God's praise
Than when we'd first begun.

Chapter 30

An hour later, all the guests departed Anna's house with final hugs and well wishes.

Watching them, Weston maintained a brave front, but his heart was suddenly weighted with a heaviness he held deeply, all the way down to his *soul*, knowing she'd be leaving at the crack of dawn tomorrow morning with Charley and Nick.

He'd known all along this day would come. Dreaded the truth, pushed it aside, tried to ignore it. Tonight he wanted to *fight* it. Now that Anna's departure was imminent, Weston warred with the fluctuating emotions of overwhelming sadness and anger. How was it possible in such a short time that he'd grown so accustomed to the *everything* of Annalise Redmond? He wasn't ready to let her go. *Ever.*

After helping Anna with the kitchen clean up, Charley gave him a hug and kissed his cheek. "I hope I'll see you in New York soon," she whispered. "Thank you for loving my sister. Hope everything goes well tonight. We'll be making ourselves scarce now."

"Always, and thanks."

"Weston, it's been a pleasure." When Nick extended his hand, Weston gave it a firm shake before pulling him into a man hug.

"Same here, Nick. Promise me something, will you?"

"Anything, man. What's that?" Nick released his hand. He'd dropped the British accent, at least for tonight, and wore normal jeans and a Genesis T-Shirt—the rock band, not the first book of the Bible. Maybe one day.

"Keep painting for the generations and keep Charley happy. Make babies with her and never lose your sense of adventure and fun. But I hope you'll also keep an open mind. Don't close it to the things of God. See the possibilities in what the Master has created. He's the true Creator who gives you talent, and He loves you. All I ask is that you consider the magnificent work He can do in *your* heart."

Nick nodded slowly. "I've never been one to make such promises, but being around you and Anna has made me see there might be something to this faith you share. It's hard to explain, but it's something that's always seemed unattainable."

Weston tilted his head. "How so?"

"I guess because it involves letting go of preconceived beliefs and prejudices, and acknowledging *I'm* not the one in control."

He hadn't expected such honesty, but Weston was grateful.

"We all like to believe we control our own destiny," Weston said. "It's when we realize the fallacy of that and can admit to a greater power outside ourselves—the power that is God Almighty—that we can truly *live*, and experience the greatest personal freedom ever."

Nick smiled. "You're deep, Weston. I like that." He slapped his arm. Hard. "We'll talk."

"Yes, we will. I look forward to it." Weston returned his smile. "Good night."

As he watched Nick climb the steps, Weston wondered where that speech had come from. He knew very well. From the Spirit of the living God inside him, giving him the words. The words that might touch this man to see his life differently, to think beyond himself.

He'd continue to pray for Charley and Nick the same as he prayed for Neil. And thank the Lord for bringing him into contact with all of them.

Anna came up behind him. Slipping her hand in his, she leaned her head against him. Weston moved his arm around her easily, loving the way she fit into the circle of his arm, how well-suited they were in every way.

"I had the best time tonight," she said. "Thank you for helping to arrange the surprise party in my own home. That was an amazing accomplishment. In case I haven't told you lately, you're a wonderful man, and I'm so blessed by you."

Weston wrapped her in his arms. In that moment, he wished it could be *their* home. If that were the case, he'd sweep her in his arms and carry her up the stairs and spend the rest of the evening loving her. Instead, he shook his head, needing to keep his focus on the reality and not allow his thought life to carry him away to places best left alone. Again, perhaps in time. . .

"Happy birthday, beautiful Annalise." He lowered his lips to hers and lost himself. He poured his emotion and how much he loved her into the kiss, understanding these precious few remaining moments with her tonight would have to last him until he could see her again. Hating that he didn't know when that would be.

"That's definitely the best birthday kiss I've ever received." That shy smile he'd come to love seared Weston to his soul. He was feeling poetic, romantic, and *lost* all at the same time.

"I should hope so. I love you."

"I love you, too." Once more, she touched her lips to his in a kiss sweet as morning and ripe with promise. "I had another unexpected surprise while I was in the kitchen. My father called. Charley might have reminded him that it's my birthday, but that doesn't matter. What matters is that he called."

Weston touched her long hair. "Was it a good conversation?" He kissed the tip of her nose and then moved his lips to her cheek. "Such soft skin. Lovely."

"The best I've had in a long time. My conversation, I mean. With my *father*." Closing her eyes, Anna leaned into him, clearly distracted by *his* distraction and the way he gently sifted his fingers through her hair. He knew she liked it, and perhaps he was taking unfair advantage.

"He's, um, agreed to pick up his tickets in Philadelphia when I'm there again in a few weeks. And you know what?" Opening her eyes, Anna looked up at him through a dreamlike haze.

"What's that?" His voice had gone husky again.

"I think this time he will."

"He'll what?" Oh, he had it bad. Weston kissed her again, his lips lingering. He didn't want to stop kissing her. He held her against him.

"You're trying to drive me mad, aren't you?" she whispered.

"I'm storing up for the fall. I can't help myself. You do things to me, Anna. Very *good* things, but it's making it very difficult to concentrate." But glimpsing the hopefulness in her eyes after speaking with her father, and hearing it in her voice, made him glad for her. "I'm thankful he called. I love how happy it's made you."

"*You* make me happy, Weston."

"Then come with me. I have a final birthday surprise for you tonight." He tucked her hair behind one ear and kissed her temple. "Let's go outside to our swing."

He opened the front door, and Anna ducked beneath his arm, reminding him of the night they'd gone to Paulson's. "I'll be right there," he told her. "Save my spot. I'll get my guitar and be right out."

Although he'd played for her before, and he'd played a couple of times in the church services in Darling, he'd been saving this special composition for their final night together. Well, he could only pray it'd be special for *her*.

How thankful he was that Anna decided to buy the house. If he allowed his thoughts to wander, he could see himself in a few years on a porch swing—holding Anna as his wife, rocking their baby, a dog resting on the porch floor at their feet. Where that porch swing would *be* was the burning question. Here in Darling or elsewhere?

Unlatching his guitar case, Weston took it out and slipped the strap over his head. Then he headed out to the porch to join her.

Anna waited, her feet propped beneath her, her pretty pink toes winking at him. She'd worn his favorite dress tonight, the same flowered one she'd worn to church that first Sunday. She'd pushed most of her hair to one side, cascading over her shoulder.

Swallowing his sigh of longing, Weston sat down beside her and began to softly strum his guitar. He angled his head over one shoulder at Ray and Lois's house. "Think I'll keep the neighbors up with my song?"

"I don't think they'll complain." Her smile was gentle. "Not tonight."

"Anna, this is a song I wrote for you called 'Whisper to My Heart.' I got the idea that day I met Nick in the diner." He shook his head, chuckling. "I hope you understand I didn't write it *for* Nick."

She laughed quietly, her eyes sparkling. "I'm not worried."

"Remember when Charley came into the diner? She realized Nick had come to claim her. They made their way to each other in the middle of the diner, oblivious to everyone else around them. They held each other and said nothing, yet something unforgettable passed between them. Unforgettable for those of us who witnessed it, too. Something almost tangible and palpable. The kind of deeply felt look shared between a husband and wife, between lovers, between two people who intimately know the heart of the other."

"It's rather difficult to forget that day," Anna said. "In its own way, it was a beautiful moment." In the dim lighting of the front porch, Weston made out a faint blush coloring her cheeks.

"Nick and Charley whispered to one another." He continued to quietly strum his guitar. "Have you ever noticed how whispering is associated with a time of tenderness, quiet, and reflection or meditation on God's Word?"

Anna nodded slowly, her eyes never leaving his. "Yes."

"A whisper can be part of the romance between a man and a woman, but it's also an element of our relationship with the Father. I believe God whispers in our hearts. It follows along with the idea in your theme verse of Ephesians 2:10 of how we are to be His workmanship and to walk in faith. A big part of that is taking the time to stop and *listen* to what the Lord whispers in our heart."

"In other words, paying attention and following through with those little nudges from the Holy Spirit," she mused. "Then carrying on His work and hopefully blessing others with our efforts."

Weston's smile emerged, pleased that she understood. "You pay attention."

"I try." Anna untucked her legs and shifted her position to make more room for him on the swing. "I want to hear your song. Sing for me, Weston."

"You asked for it." With a small smile, he began.

She came to me in a dream
Fine and delicate as gossamer
As sweet as the rose of summer
As precious as the morning rain.
She moves in strength, in light, in love
The beauty of the One within her
Shining bright for all the world to see.
She makes me ponder my heart, my life, my all
Whisper to my heart.

Anna's eyes filled as she listened. He wasn't the best songwriter, he couldn't rhyme the lyrics to save his life, but this song came straight from his heart. For her. And she could tell. That's all he asked, all he needed, all he longed to know.

My love must bid me sad farewell
But the promise of sweet reunion lingers still
For as sure as dew coats the morning lawn
Her heart fills me with hope and promise.
And the One who gave us life and love
Will wrap my love in all His glory
She's waiting, longing, to seek His face
Looking to eternity to complete the race
Whisper to my heart.

Her soft touch lingers on my skin
Her kiss wraps me in clouds of glory
Transporting me to heights of grandeur
The blessing of which I've never known.
I shall long for her now and always
For she is my forever love.
My forever love is she
Forever thine, forever mine.
Whisper to my heart.

Anna stared at him, wide-eyed, as he strummed the final notes. She moved one hand over her heart and breathed out a deep sigh.

"Weston, you composed the song *and* wrote the lyrics?"

"I did." Weston carefully lowered his guitar to the ground. "You inspire me. What can I say?"

"That was truly beautiful," she breathed. "Words fail me, they really do."

"Then let me do the talking for a minute." Moving closer on the swing, he captured her hands in his. "I need to ask you something very important."

Her eyes widened. "Ask me. . .what?" She swallowed hard and looked at him with eyes so innocent, so pure, his breath was gone, his heart unsteady.

"Maybe it's not fair to say anything, and maybe it's not the right time or the—"

"Weston, just say it. Please."

"Anna, I love you with all my heart, and you are the woman I want beside me through this journey of life. I want to be your hero, your husband, and the father of your children if you'll have me. No matter where I go, or what I do, I'll always carry you in my heart."

"Weston, are you asking me to marry you?"

"I believe I am, yes. As usual, I'm not the best at words."

"You're doing just fine. *More* than fine." A tear slipped down her cheek, and she let it go.

He reached for the maroon velvet box he'd put on the windowsill earlier, surprised she hadn't spotted it. Sliding down on one knee beside the swing, Weston opened the lid. He held up the box for her to see the Marquise-cut diamond nestled inside.

"Annalise Cecile Redmond, will you give me the honor of becoming my wife?"

Anna's countenance was radiant, her love for him shining in her bright brown eyes. "I love you with all that I am, and I'll be honored to call you my husband, Weston James Galloway."

His heart full, he sat beside her again. "Let me try to get the ring out of the box and slide it on your finger without dropping it."

"It's gorgeous. I'm guessing Charley helped you?"

"Yes." With a triumphant smile, he removed the ring from the box and slipped it on her finger, blowing out a sigh of relief.

"It's a perfect fit!" Anna held up her hand as though in wonder. "I had no idea you were going to ask me. Tonight. Here. In Darling. On the porch."

"I wasn't sure when or if we'd be here together again. And I couldn't allow you to leave Darling without asking you. It's my promise to you that we *will* be together."

"Weston, no matter how many years the Lord gives us together, *this* will always be my favorite birthday." Drawing him close, Anna pressed her lips to his.

Music to his ears.

Chapter 31

Three Weeks Later—New York City

Standing beside Anna, Felicia stirred her drink slowly and then took a sip. As always, her manager was impeccably dressed in a deep maroon cocktail dress. Her jet black hair was now cut stylishly short, highlighted by sterling silver chandelier earrings that swung like pendulums with her every movement.

"There's a terribly attractive man standing at six o'clock," Felicia said. "I've never seen him before at these parties. Looks a little uncomfortable."

"Go talk to him." Anna only half-listened. Felicia normally dated a man a few times and then grew bored. She'd discover some obtuse aspect of his character she didn't like and that would be the end of it. After a short-term marriage in her early twenties, she'd never remarried. Although she'd been discreet, Felicia had brought a handful of men back to the Manhattan apartment she'd shared with Anna through the early years. She'd never lacked for male companionship on *her* terms.

"I think I'll go make him feel welcome." With a smile, Felicia departed.

"I'm sure you will." Anna sipped her cranberry juice as her manager made her way through the crowd. Others moved into her line of vision, filling the empty spaces, and Anna lost sight of her.

She caught a flash of a man with a beard, and her heart sputtered. Then heard a voice that reminded her of Weston. Longing for him filled her heart. She'd call him as soon as she could following the concert. The sound of his voice would help soothe the ache until she could see him.

You have it bad. Weston was a distraction that would need to wait a few more hours.

She'd spent enough time at the cocktail reception. She'd done her duty and put in her expected appearance. Setting her glass on the tray of a passing waiter, Anna exchanged pleasantries with a few patrons and then headed for the exit.

Time to go to her dressing room and change into her gown. Her afternoon rehearsal had gone well, much better than she could have hoped. Now it was time to mentally prepare and pray she could keep her concentration on her performance. The audience paid good money to attend her concerts, and she owed it to them to give her very best.

"Annalise!"

She turned at Felicia's call. Where was she? Then she spotted her. Her manager headed toward her, arm in arm with…*Weston?*

"Weston," she murmured. Her gaze drank in the dark suit and white dress shirt, opened at the collar. She'd expect nothing less, and it made her smile. Handsome yet casually elegant. A *very* good look for him. The man cleaned up exceedingly well.

"Surprise." Although the corners of his lips upturned, he acted nervous, out of his element. He extracted his arm from Felicia's and stepped forward to kiss her cheek.

Closing her eyes, Anna breathed in the scent of his familiar aftershave. She clutched the sleeve of his jacket, holding on, cherishing his presence, this man she loved.

"In this moment, all I can think of is how much I want to kiss you," she whispered close to his ear. "I can't believe you're here. I love you. I've missed you."

"I love you, too." Weston's warm lips brushed her cheek.

"That's my cue to take my leave." Felicia turned to him with a smile. "Weston, if I'd known your presence would bring this response from Annalise, I would have brought you to New York a couple of weeks ago. I'll see you after the concert. Enjoy."

Had Felicia *paid* for Weston to come? No way. Weston hadn't allowed her to take care of his copayment when he'd needed stitches. Who cared? He was here *now*, and that's all that mattered.

"Come with me." Weston led her into the closest alcove in the historic theater. "Is this private enough? I don't want you to get in any trouble."

"I won't get in trouble, but I have a better idea. Come with me, please." Tugging him by the hand, Anna quickly walked with Weston down the long hallway.

He whistled under his breath as she stopped outside her dressing room. "A star with Miss Redmond's name," he said as she opened the door. "This must be an honest-to-goodness dressing room?"

"Yes." She gave him a flirty smile. "Honest to goodness." He followed her inside and closed the door. Before she could say another word, his arms moved around her, and his lips were on hers. Warm, welcoming, and oh so wonderful. The taste of Weston, the scent of him, filled her senses.

"I've missed you," she murmured between kisses.

"Now *that's* the kind of hello I could get used to." He cupped her face with gentle hands and his adoring gaze roamed over her face. "You look beautiful tonight. I'm afraid I'll mess you up."

She smiled and smoothed one hand over his shirt. "You were turning heads out there in your suit, although I'm kind of partial to the tool belt and safety helmet."

"Don't forget the safety glasses."

"Right. Can't forget those. And the Stetson," she said as Weston's lips gloriously found hers once more. His hold on her tightened as she leaned more fully into his kiss. Finally, she placed her hand flat against his chest. "I hope I can play tonight. You have a way of getting a girl all worked up in the *best* way."

Weston chuckled and wiped his mouth with the back of one hand. "If you're looking for an apology, you're not getting one."

"You're the most distracting man in the world, Mr. Galloway. Please tell me you're staying for the concert."

"Nope. I drove all this way in a fancy suit just to kiss you passionately. Then I planned on climbing in my truck and driving straight back to Georgia."

His smile surfaced. Such a handsome man.

He chuckled. "Somewhere in there is a country song waiting to happen. Of course, I'm staying for your performance. I wouldn't miss my first Annalise Redmond concert for anything in the world. It's the second best reason to be here tonight." Dropping another kiss on her lips, Weston kept it soft and sweet but made her want more.

Charley was right. She'd been seriously man-deprived. Now she wanted to play catch up with the only man on the planet she ached to kiss.

"Weston, having you in the audience tonight will make it more special than any other performance."

"Ever?" He cocked his head and grinned. "Say it again."

"Don't let it swell your ego."

He laughed. "Fair enough. I'll say good-bye for now."

"Did Felicia arrange a seat for you in the concert hall?"

"No." Reaching into an inner pocket of his jacket, he pulled out his ticket and held it up for her to see. "I didn't tell her I was coming and bought my own ticket. I'm sitting on the third row."

"That doesn't make sense. I mean, of course I'm thrilled, but Felicia told me this concert's been sold out for weeks."

"I can be resourceful when I want. I called and pled my sorry case to the ticket agent in the theater box office. My new good friend, Allison, felt sorry for me and gave me her Aunt Edna's seat. Edna claims you're her favorite pianist, by the way."

"Let me guess." A smile parted Anna's lips. "You promised Allison that I'd meet Aunt Edna after the concert?"

When Weston chuckled, she felt its familiar timbre all the way down to her toes.

"You know me well," he said. "That can only be a good thing. I didn't think you'd mind since I know a little something about your generous spirit."

"I'll be happy to meet her, but you need to go now since I have a performance to give. I hope you enjoy it."

"I've enjoyed the private performances more." He ran a hand over the back of his neck. "That sounded more provocative than I meant. Sorry. I'll never learn."

She gave him a final quick kiss. "You're tempting me. Go. *Now.*"

"Yes, Miss Redmond." With a smile, he bowed and backed toward the door. "I'll see you after the performance." He moved a hand over his heart. "Whisper to my heart."

"Have you ever met Annalise before?"

Weston half-turned to see if the man had addressed him. Of course, he hadn't. Why would he?

Two young men around his same age stood not far from where he waited for Anna in the theater lobby post-performance. Dressed in tuxedos, impeccably groomed, snooty corporate types. He knew their kind well and stayed as far away as possible. It wasn't so much their appearance—although Weston detested hair gel and polished fingernails on men—as their attitude and arrogant posturing that put him off.

"I'm hoping tonight I'll have the pleasure. She's a great-looking woman, isn't she? I've had my eye on her for a while now, and I'm going to ask her to dinner."

"I thought you were engaged?"

"Right," the man scoffed. "Hillary's history. Good riddance."

Try as he might to tune out the conversation, those remarks caught Weston's attention, especially the part about Anna. These guys were all talk. As long as they didn't disrespect Anna, he'd hold his tongue. He'd be better off to walk away, but something kept him rooted in place.

"What makes you think she'll go out with you?"

"My company's the biggest sponsor of her tour. Obligation alone, not to mention gratitude, should score serious points in my favor."

"I heard she doesn't date."

"You're not getting my point, Ross. I'm not asking to *date* Annalise. I just want dinner and, if I'm in luck, a roll in the sheets."

That did it. So much for trying to give these jerks the benefit of the doubt. Weston turned around to face them, staring them down with a withering look. He moved toward them and handed off his glass to a passing waiter.

"What did you say?" *Lord, help me not to haul off and deck these guys. Even if they deserve it.*

The taller man laughed. Weston's gut instinct told him this was the one who'd made the derogatory comments.

"I'd say you must have heard me since you're spitting nails at me now, bud."

"Anna—Annalise—is a lady and deserves your respect."

"And do *you* know her?" Crossing his arms, he returned Weston's glare. "Intimately?"

Weston seethed and struggled to maintain his composure. "Not in the way you're implying, but yes, I know her. Very well. Above all, she's my good friend."

She's the woman who's agreed to marry me. This man didn't deserve to know that truth. Narrowing his eyes, Weston met his gaze head-on. "I guarantee she won't be going anywhere with you tonight. Or ever." He sounded hokey, like he was in a bad movie, but he didn't care. When it came to defending Anna's honor, he'd be corny as anything and go down fighting.

"Is that right?" The man dropped his arms and advanced toward him. "I'm sure the *lady* can make her own decision, pal. She doesn't need a man"—he raked his gaze over Weston in a disparaging manner—"in a second-rate suit hanging around hoping to grab leftover crumbs of affection from Annalise Redmond. Go back to whatever rock you crawled out from."

Yeah, a really *bad* film with even worse dialogue.

"Is that right?" Weston took another small step toward the lowlife scum masquerading in an expensive suit.

"Stephen, you've said enough. Come on, man. Let it go." At least Ross what's-his-name had more common sense and decency, and he laid a hand on the instigator's arm.

Stephen shrugged him off. "Not until I finish this guy off first."

"Finish me off? Really." Weston's brows lifted as his mind searched for a Scripture.

Lord, empower me with your words.

"Stephen, are you familiar with Isaiah 45:2?"

As expected, the guy backed off. Calling him by his first name had knocked him off guard, giving him the early advantage.

"What's that? Some kind of religious mumbo jumbo?" Stephen cursed under his breath.

"It's a verse of Scripture. From the Bible."

"I know what the Bible is, idiot."

"It says, 'I will go before you and make the rough places smooth; I will shatter the doors of bronze and cut through their iron bars.'"

Stephen shook his head in disgust. "You're crazy, man. Who goes around spouting Bible verses? Are you like a priest or something?"

"I'm a construction worker."

Stephen laughed. "That explains a lot. Of course you are. No wonder you're talking about bronze and iron. And bars. Spent some time behind them have you?"

"Stephen." Ross shot Weston a helpless look. Pity he had such poor taste in friends.

"That verse reminds me that, as a believer in Christ, God will fight my battles. The actions of those who do wrong to others will eventually come to light."

In seconds, before Weston could react, Stephen's fist connected with his jaw, knocking him backwards. Reeling, Weston fought to keep his balance. By the grace of God, he remained on his feet.

Stephen shot him a contemptuous glance. Cursing under his breath, he wrung his hand. "You wearing an iron vest under that shirt? I guess working construction is good for something." He laughed derisively. "Wait. *God's* protecting you, right?"

Keep your cool. Don't fight back. Weston rubbed one hand over his cheek. At least no teeth were dislodged. Stephen's blow hadn't had as much force behind it as he'd initially thought. He wiped his hand over his mouth. No blood.

When he turned to go, Stephen roughly grabbed him by the arm and moved up close and personal. In his *face* close. "You always let God fight your battles, Construction Boy? What's wrong? Too weak in your own strength? You—"

As soon as the vile word left Stephen's lips, Weston pummeled his fist into the other man's stomach. Hard. That filthy word was on his short list of those he couldn't tolerate.

Two burly men with headsets, presumably security for the theater, came running from nowhere. One of the guys grabbed him while the other corralled Stephen, and then they hauled them both toward the theater entrance doors.

Disgusted with himself for losing his temper, Weston didn't protest although Stephen yelled out things like *don't you know who I am?* Tuning out the increasingly profanity-laced tirade, all Weston could think about was how he'd need to call Anna and apologize. He'd let himself down, and Anna would be disappointed by his actions. He'd been in enough scrapes and fights as a kid. Apparently he hadn't learned much.

Now he was only fighting guys in fancier clothes.

"Wait!" Felicia wore an angry frown and stomped in his direction. Leaning close, Anna's manager kept her voice low and controlled. "I hope this isn't your usual behavior, Mr. Galloway."

She addressed the security officer. "I need a word alone with this man first." Then she tossed a withering glare at Weston. "*Then* you can toss him out the door."

Weston squared his shoulders. Fine. He could handle the protective lioness. He'd handled worse. She was only protecting her client, after all, and doing her job. For all she'd done for Anna through the years, Felicia deserved his respect.

"I'm sorry." He hoped this woman understood his repentance was sincere.

"Considering you claim to care for Anna, I'm going to give you the benefit of the doubt. Unfortunate as this incident was—and I hope we can keep it out of the press—I realize you wouldn't have come all this way only to be thrown out of the theater."

"Of course not. In fact, I was trying to defend her honor."

Felicia stared at him as if he'd said something in a foreign tongue. "Why do you think Anna needs a hero? In her world, men don't spar with fists. They fight with words or other means at their disposal."

The fight drained from Weston. "Think what you want about me, but I couldn't stand there and listen to some scum spewing derogatory, slanderous things about the woman I love."

Felicia sucked in a breath and moved one hand over her chest. "You *love* her?"

"I do. In case you didn't know, I'm her fiancé." The engagement ring had been on Anna's finger when he'd seen her before the concert. "Haven't you noticed a diamond ring on her hand?"

"Anna removes her jewelry for her concerts. So, to answer your question, no, I haven't noticed a diamond ring. Perhaps the thing you need to be concerned with is why she hasn't bothered to mention it to me."

That surprised him, and disappointed him, but he'd let it go for now. It wouldn't do him any good to be puffed up with male ego and allow pride to stand in his way. Anna must have her reasons, professional or not, why she hadn't always worn her ring or even mentioned their engagement to her manager. He couldn't allow negative thoughts to seep into his subconscious. Thinking that way was deceitful, destructive. If he allowed them access, those thoughts could tear down and rip apart his relationship with Anna and everything they'd built together.

On the other hand, this woman might be a convincing actress. He wasn't dumb enough to believe she'd wax poetic about him. That'd be contrary to her best interests. The more likely truth was that she considered him a threat for Anna's affections. If that was the case, she'd have a fight on her hands. Was he going to have to fight everyone in her world with either his words or his fists?

"If I didn't love her, why else would I start out on a 13-hour trip to drive here in record time? Only to basically turn around and go straight back home? Anna's performance tonight was spectacular," he told Felicia. "I'd appreciate it if you'd pass that on to your client." Phrasing it that way kept it somewhat professional. Never mind the *reasons* for this conversation were way less than professional. He'd acted like a huge fool. Still, he didn't regret decking Stephen.

"I will, and I agree. I was proud of her. She's back."

"Yes, I suppose she is." Weston's heart plummeted with every word. As though he knew he was already losing Anna and there was nothing he could do about it.

"I hope you understand she'll be on the road with constant traveling the next few months." Felicia's brown-eyed gaze bore into him. "There will be no time for flying back and forth to Georgia except on rare weekends. In November, her tour takes us to Europe for six weeks. Anna needs her full concentration on her work. As her manager, I can't have her gallivanting around like a lovesick bird."

A lovesick bird? Stunned speechless, all Weston could do was nod. Swallowing hard, he sought the right words. No question in his mind, he'd wait for Anna. As long as it took. His prayer was that this woman wouldn't somehow manage to poison Anna's mind against him in the meantime.

Once again, he needed to get a serious grip on his emotions. They were all over the place, and his stewing about it wasn't doing either of them any good.

Lord, please keep Anna's focus on you. Keep my patience and focus in check.

"Contrary to my behavior tonight, I can be a very patient man. Anna and I belong together, but she'll need to figure that out for herself. She already has people making every other decision for her," he muttered. "Good night. Kudos on an otherwise successful evening."

Felicia's nod was curt. "Good-bye, Mr. Galloway."

He'd said more than enough. Giving Felicia a polite nod, Weston turned and left the building.

Chapter 32

"Where's Weston?" Anna dashed into the mostly emptied lobby, out of breath, partially from hurrying down the hallway but also in anticipation of spending time with Weston. Her post-performance interviews had taken longer than expected. Too long.

Where was he? Her pulse raced. Surely Weston hadn't tired of waiting and left the theater?

Felicia walked past her. "Not here. Let's do this in your dressing room."

"Do *what*?" When Felicia kept walking, Anna stood her ground. "Felicia, tell me now. What happened?" A sense of dread settled in her stomach. The only others in the lobby were a cleaning crew vacuuming the carpet and a few theater employees who tried their best to act like they heard nothing.

The other woman turned. After glancing around the lobby, Felicia walked back toward her and spoke in low tones. "Your *friend* was in a physical altercation here in the lobby. It was an embarrassment, and he and the other man were escorted from the premises. No charges were filed, so if you're worried about that, you can rest easy."

"That makes no sense. Weston wouldn't fight unless he was provoked."

Felicia gave her a patronizing look. "No matter the circumstances, this isn't the kind of man you need in your life. He's impatient and obviously has a short-fuse temper. You can't afford to have anyone upset you."

"I am not a child. I've gotten to know Weston well the past few weeks. He's a good man, a solid man of faith. The best man I've ever known in many ways. I need to go now." She darted back down the hallway.

"Anna! Where are you going?"

"To get my purse, and then I'm leaving. Don't worry. I'll be here for the sound check tomorrow. Until then, please don't call me or text me. I need time alone."

"Fine, but heed my warning," Felicia said. "Don't make a mistake with that man. Have fun with him then cut him loose."

Anna whirled around from halfway down the hallway. "That's *your* way, not mine."

"Is it true you've agreed to marry him? He's given you an engagement ring?"

"Yes, it's true. I intend to marry Weston as soon as possible."

Felicia stared her down. "At least your flighty sister married well."

Tamping down her anger, Anna squared her shoulders and resisted the urge to clench her fists. "After all these years, I'm not sure you even know who *I* really am. My biggest mistake will be if I *don't* go after Weston now."

"Running after a man won't solve anything. It only proves you're weak."

"He came all the way from Georgia to see me for a few precious hours. The least I can do is find him and talk with him. I'll see you tomorrow."

How dare Felicia say such things? What a pretentious snob. She'd always known it, but the other woman's snide remarks incensed her. She needed to calm down before she dealt with her manager again.

After grabbing her purse and lightweight shawl from the dressing room, Anna hurried back down the hallway. Thank the Lord for favors, Felicia was nowhere in sight.

One of the security guards was stationed beside the front entrance doors. He gave her a polite head tilt. "Evening, Miss Redmond. Will you be needing a taxi?"

"Yes, please." She glanced outside the double glass doors. "I imagine they're all gone?"

"I'm sure another one will come by shortly. You wait here, and I'll flag one down."

"Thank you." She wanted to ask the man what had happened with Weston, but Felicia had schooled her in what was proper—and not—to say to anyone when it could affect her professional *or* personal reputation. So, it was better left alone although the burning questions were on the tip of her tongue.

"Miss Redmond?" A young man in an usher's uniform strolled into the lobby, removing his bow tie as he walked. "I hope you don't mind me saying, but I saw what happened earlier, and I heard what that lady told you. That wasn't the whole story."

"I see."

"The taller guy was egging on the other one. Sounded a little drunk to me."

Weston wouldn't egg anyone on, especially someone he didn't know. "Go on." She had to know.

"The other guy was defending your honor. He didn't throw a punch until the other guy hit him first. I don't blame him. I was glad he slugged that slime in the stomach."

"He did? He slugged him?"

"Yes, he sure did. I'd say he's your hero."

Emotion choked her throat. "Yes, he is. Thank you for telling me."

"You going after him?"

"If he's not already halfway out of the city, I'll certainly try my best."

Ten minutes later, Anna sat in the back of a taxi outside the darkened theater. She'd dialed Weston's cell phone number continuously, but he hadn't picked up.

"Please answer, Weston." She closed her eyes and dropped her head to her chest. *Lord, please let him be okay. Please let him pick up.*

Her phone vibrated in her lap, making her jump. Fumbling with it, she blew out a sigh of relief when she spied his cell phone number on the display.

"Weston! Where are you?"

His silence made her wonder what he was thinking. Weston was rarely at a loss for words. She bunched the folds of her voluminous skirt with one hand. In her haste, she hadn't bothered to change out of her performance gown.

"I'm headed out of the city now." Weston's voice was low key. Subdued. Was he hurt, physically or emotionally?

"No! You can't leave. Tell me where you are. Wait, you didn't get a hotel room for the night?"

"I did, but I…well, I figured I might as well go ahead and leave town."

Anna bit back her cry. "Well, that's a little selfish, isn't it? You drove all this way for my performance and now you're leaving without saying a proper good-bye?"

"What do you consider a *proper* good-bye?" Tears misted her eyes when she detected the slightest tinge of humor in his voice.

"I'm sure we'll think of something. Where's your hotel? I'll meet you there."

"I don't think you're thinking straight to ask me that."

"Don't let your imagination run amuck. Notice I didn't invite you back to my place."

"True enough. I'm guessing you heard what happened at the theater?"

"Felicia filled me in."

"Great. I hope she could be halfway objective."

"Don't worry about her. Felicia doesn't know your heart. But I do."

He gave her the name of the hotel. "I'm turning around now and headed back into the city."

"Hang on a second, Weston." Leaning forward, Anna tapped the driver on the shoulder and asked if he knew of a coffee shop near the hotel that might be open late. The city was full of them on nearly every street corner.

A few seconds later, she told Weston, "Here's what you do. Meet me at The Broadway Café. It's two blocks west of your hotel. Take your time and be careful. I'll wait however long it takes." She didn't care how desperate she sounded.

"I'll see you soon," he said. "I'm sorry for my behavior. Your performance tonight was awe inspiring. Sometimes I can't believe I know someone so talented. Not to mention incredibly beautiful."

Her voice caught in her throat. Digging in her small handbag, Anna searched for a tissue. "Now why'd you have to go and say that? You've got me all choked up."

"God's blessed you with a magnificent talent. I'm glad you're following His path for your life."

"Same as you are, Weston."

"Did you meet Edna?"

Anna wiped her eyes. "I did, as well as Allison from the ticket office. They both send you their regards. I think they were disappointed you weren't there to meet them."

He chuckled, a terrific sound. "I doubt that, but thanks for the strokes. I'm glad it worked out and thanks for meeting with them. Oh, and Anna?"

"Yes?"

"I'll…" Anna heard his deep sigh. "I'll see you soon."

A knock sounded on Anna's dressing room door the following night as the makeup artist hovered over her. For a second, Anna's heart leapt with hope it might be Weston. But no, that was impossible. He'd already returned to Georgia. Not only that, but he'd taken two days off from work to drive the equivalent of a full day to come to her performance, grab a few hours of sleep, and then go home.

Another knock.

"Come in." Anna tried not to frown when she spied Felicia's mirrored reflection as she entered the room.

"Good evening." Closing the door behind her, Felicia dropped her small handbag on the settee. She crossed her arms over her middle and came to stand behind Anna's chair.

Felicia greeted Mary and the two women exchanged pleasantries.

"The tour sponsors are extremely pleased with your sold-out performances, Anna. Apparently, your little hiatus might have been a wise move for your career in terms of making you more in-demand."

"That's good to hear, but it's not why I took time off. I didn't consider it a career move."

"I realize that, but it's clearly turned out that way." Felicia waited as Mary applied the final touch of lipstick and checked Anna's hair.

"You've worked a miracle with my hair tonight, Mary." Anna turned her head from side to side. "Looks great from all angles. Thank you." She'd tried a different style, simple as always, but sleek and elegant in the manner of a 1940s movie star, parted on the side, and added waves.

"You're welcome, Anna. I'll see you in three days in Toronto." Mary returned her makeup supplies to her case and, after giving Felicia a polite nod, quietly departed.

"I hope you had a good time with Weston last night." Felicia settled on the settee.

"I did." Anna rotated in the chair to face the other woman. "Tell me what's on your mind."

"Anna, you've had many men interested in you through the years. You're a beautiful woman. You've turned down most of them—men of social standing, talented musicians such as yourself, men of means and social influence. The world, as Shakespeare said, is your oyster, or at least it could be. But instead of taking advantage of the opportunities you've been given, you've chosen instead to live like a cloistered nun. I'm wondering why this man? Why now?"

"Weston is the first man who wanted to know me without knowing anything *about* me." Anna stopped. That sounded like a classic Weston line. "For all he knew, I was a waitress who aimlessly moved from town to town."

First Charley accused her of living like a nun, and now Felicia? She wouldn't begin to address the snide insinuation about Weston's lack of money or social influence.

Her manager shook her head with a small smile. "You couldn't pull off that charade if you tried, dear heart."

Anna tamped down her irritation. She didn't like being called *dear heart* and Felicia knew it. Coming from her, the nickname sounded patronizing, as though Anna were a child incapable of making competent decisions on her own. No matter what she'd done for her in the past, in no way did this woman *own* her, especially now that she was an adult.

Felicia felt strongly about this subject, however, or she would never risk having this discussion *before* a performance. They'd never needed to have a discussion like this in the past.

"After the fiasco with the Maestro with Many Hands, I was humiliated, embarrassed, and didn't want anything to do with any other man on the concert circuit." Anna bit her lower lip then stopped. That would ruin her lipstick.

"That doesn't make him the *right* man for you."

"Of course not. That's not why Weston is so special."

"Then why don't you explain it so that I *can* understand." Felicia crossed one long, slender leg over the other and clasped her hands together over her knees. "Other than the fact that he's a very attractive, virile man."

"Weston has a genuine need to help others. He's a hard worker, he listens to others, and he always tries to draw out the best in people. Weston makes me laugh, something I haven't done near enough of in the past decade. He wants the best for me, and he's a man of strong faith. That's most important to me, Felicia. For my *heart.* I've prayed to meet a man who loves the Lord and has a sincere desire to serve Him. That's rare in our world, as you well know. Now that I've found Weston, I don't want to ever let him go. He wants to marry me, and I have every intention of doing that very thing."

"Nice speech, but I doubt Mr. Galloway will want to follow you around the world. I agree he's a strong man, and he's also demonstrated a great deal of pride and self-respect. As much as it pains me to admit this, I doubt any amount of love would allow him to live in your shadow and be content."

Anna bristled. "That's not how it will be at all. In essence, are you telling me no man will ever love me enough to actually *marry* me?"

"No. I'm suggesting you should find someone in the industry to marry. Someone in one of the orchestras in any number of cities you visit fairly often."

The idea that had been forming in Anna's mind took root. Time to speak her mind. "Perhaps it's time you begin to mentor Kyndall Symes."

Felicia's jaw all but gaped. "Kyndall? What does she have to do with this discussion?"

"I'd say quite a bit. I'm suggesting you groom her as your next protégé." Inhaling a deep breath, Anna knew she had to keep going and say what needed to be said. "You know how much I've appreciated everything you've done for me, especially after Mom died. But you had to know the time would come when I would begin to tire of the lifestyle and need to make a life change."

"Your performances have been stellar. I've never seen you play as well as you have since your little break."

"That *little break* was exactly what I needed to show me there's a wonderful world out there waiting to be explored with so many *normal*, everyday things I've never experienced before, Felicia. Weston helped me see and taste those things. He gave me a glimpse of what my life could be like if I settle in one place."

"With all due respect, you *are* in one place. Manhattan."

"I'm not sure that's where I belong. Once upon a time, yes. But the fairy tale is over. It's high time I learn to live in the real world for a change."

Felicia slapped her hands on her knees and rose to her feet. "A few weeks in a tiny town in Georgia that's barely on a road map and now *you* think you know what you need? Open your eyes, Anna. Don't be blinded by a handsome man and people you believe are your friends. You were destined for greatness, and you're achieving it. Leaving your career now would be the worst decision you've ever made."

"I've achieved everything I've ever wanted from my career and more. Who said a break has to be forever? Actresses get married and have families all the time."

Crossing her arms over her middle, Felicia approached the chair and stood in front of her. "You know as well as I do that if you leave, you'll never be able to regain the career you have now. You might be able to play a few concerts here and there based on your reputation alone, but in time that will fade. It could never be the same again. Comebacks are rare among concert pianists."

"That's not always true. Tausig made a brilliant comeback."

Felicia's lips twisted in a smirk. "You're talking about a man who lived in the mid-1800s and died at twenty-nine of smallpox or some such disease."

"I want a husband and children, Felicia." She wanted to surround herself with others who loved her and wanted only the best for her.

Her manager fidgeted with her hands, a telltale sign she craved a cigarette. After years of trying to quit, a slow and painstaking seesaw of success and failure, Felicia had finally kicked her three-pack-a-day habit in the past year. Anna hoped she wasn't suffering a setback. She didn't want *that* burden on her conscience. She had enough to contend with as it was.

Taking a deep breath, Anna said what she'd been debating the past few weeks. "I'll finish out this tour, but then I'm taking an indefinite hiatus."

Felicia made a sound of disgust. "Don't make sudden decisions you'll regret."

"I won't regret it." Anna slid out of the chair. "It's time for me to step aside and find my future. Time to let Kyndall have her time to shine. She's got a lot of talent."

"Yes, she does, but don't play the martyr card with me. It won't work. It will take *years* to fully develop Kyndall into the professional you've become."

"I remember you said the same thing about me. A year later, I was ready for the concert stage and haven't looked back. Now it's time to step into my future with Weston Galloway."

Felicia closed her mouth. Point taken.

"Just promise me something," Anna said.

"What's that?" She waited until Felicia's brown eyes met hers.

"Whatever you do, keep that girl away from the maestro."

Felicia stared at her for a long moment before speaking again. "She won't need to worry about him, Anna. Trust me."

"Why is that?"

"He's currently in prison."

Anna gasped. "Why didn't I know about this?" Come to think of it, she hadn't heard anything about the man in the past eight months or thereabouts.

Her manager's gaze bore into her. "Why do you think? It was suppressed in the press. Again. I only know because I'm currently seeing an international law attorney. So, you see, I'm violating confidentiality laws by telling you now." Felicia stepped closer. "You've heard nothing."

Anna nodded. "Agreed. You have my word. But, I have to say, I'm thankful that justice is finally served. Thank you for telling me. I've had nightmares about that man doing to some other unsuspecting girl what he tried to do to me."

Tears stung her eyes and she wiped away a tear.

Felicia's gaze softened slightly. "I'm truly sorry for that mess, Anna. It never should have happened, but at the time, I did what I thought was in your best interest by having you sign that contract."

Taking a deep breath, Anna squared her shoulders. "Protect Kyndall. That's all I ask. Show her the same kindnesses you've shown to me all these years. Give her your best as you've done for me."

"You're leaving me, aren't you?" Felicia's eyes were moist. As long as Anna had known her, her manager rarely revealed much emotion.

"Not right away," Anna said. "I'm still working out some things in my mind, trying to figure things out with Weston. But we will. Rest assured, I'll keep you informed what's happening."

Felicia nodded. "Very well." She headed for the door and then turned. "No matter how many musicians I'll ever manage, *you* Annalise Redmond, are the best client—the best *person*—I've ever known. For what it's worth, I thought you should know that."

Felicia closed the door behind her.

Chapter 33

Six Weeks Later

"Tell me again." Anna snuggled in Weston's arms as they sat on the sofa. She gazed through wistful eyes at the panoramic view of Chicago from her twentieth floor suite.

"You're the most magnificent concert pianist who ever walked the face of the planet."

She lightly swatted his arm then twisted around so she could better reach his lips. "Not that, silly man. The other thing."

"You're the most beautiful woman in the world, and I love you madly."

"Not that one, but I'll take it." She giggled as he leaned in for a long, deep kiss. With a contented sigh, Weston sat back. "This sofa has too many cushions."

Anna laughed. "That's not what I wanted to hear, either."

"Okay, then. How about you're going to make the best aunt a child could ever want?"

"That's the one. I'm thrilled beyond words for them. Charley was so worried, but I've been praying with her and she told me she knows those prayers worked. I wonder what they'll name their child. I have the feeling it'll be one of those gender neutral names."

Weston chuckled and ran his fingertips lightly up and down her arm, springing every one of her senses to life. "I'm afraid to ask."

"I know the feeling. Do you want more to drink?" She motioned to the fresh pitcher of sweet tea she'd had delivered by room service.

"As much as it pains me, Anna, I need to go."

She struggled to sit up. "Why so soon?"

"My flight leaves in less than two hours." Something about the way Weston said the words, or perhaps something in his expression, tipped her off words remained unspoken. Serious words, and ones she might not want to hear.

"Weston, what is it? Tell me."

He blew out a sigh. Dropping his head on his chest, he clasped his hands together, between his knees. "I'm trying to think of how best to say something without mangling it." He glanced over at her, making her feel a bit more encouraged. "How to say it so that you'll understand."

Anna felt as though her heart stopped at the same time as a sudden pounding attacked her head. "Are you breaking up with me?" Tears pricked her eyes, and her breathing slowed.

"No, baby, I'm not breaking up with you."

"Then why are you sitting there with those sad eyes and looking at me like you've lost your best friend?"

"Because in a way, I feel like I have."

Anna forced slow breaths in and out. "Me? You feel like you've lost *me*?"

He blew out a sigh. "Yes and no. I know the woman I love is in there somewhere, but this"—he gestured around the suite—"is foreign to me, a fantasy in some ways. It's not me, not part of my world. I'm not used to drinking out of fancy glasses, going to cocktail hours, and making small talk with pretentious people."

"I thought you did that for me. I don't enjoy them any more than you do," she groused. "Talk about reverse snobbery."

"You're right. I go to those things for you, and I love being with you. You know that." The look Weston gave her was one of helplessness. "There are a lot of people clamoring for your attention. Rightly so. But I can't be selfish, and I also can't ignore the fact that I have *zilch* in common with more than ninety-five percent of those concert patrons."

"You knew it was going to be like this," she said, trying not to sound petulant. "We discussed it. Besides, you love music. You're a musician yourself," she said. "I'd say the percentage is much higher than you estimate. You just need to give them a chance. If you want, skip the cocktail parties." Anna frowned. "Do you think I only want you beside me for window dressing?"

She heard him suck in his breath and those broad shoulders drew back. "I *didn't* think that, but I guess I do now."

"I'm sorry," she said. "I'm only trying to say that when I see you walk into my dressing room, or into the theatre, my heart is full. It's complete."

"I feel the same way, but I also miss the girl who dropped those dishes at The Darling Diner and charmed me with a simple offer of pie and ice cream. It was so much more than dessert. You offered light and love in my life."

"It was pie and ice cream, Weston."

"Call it what you want, but I miss that girl. I miss my Anna."

"She's right here." Anna moved one hand over her heart. "The surroundings and the circumstances may change, but I'm still the same otherwise. I have the same thoughts, the same feelings, the same insecurities. Which right now you're not helping, by the way."

"Sorry."

"If you're not breaking up with me, then exactly what *are* you trying to say?"

"I can't be alone with you like this. In hotel suites across the country."

"Felicia's good enough to bring you here…"

Weston's head snapped around so fast, his blue eyes wide and angry, that Anna almost gasped.

"What did you just say?"

"Which part…?"

Weston unfolded from the sofa and began to pace. "Let me get this straight. You think Felicia's been *paying* my way to the concerts I've attended?"

"Well, yes. I thought that's what—"

"Lady, you are sorely mistaken." He paced some more, pounding her increasing sense of dread into the carpet with each step. When he used the word *lady*, the man was definitely riled. As if she couldn't tell. She might have made some assumptions, but it seemed Weston had some of his own.

"What kind of man do you think I am, anyway? That'd be like I'm a…*kept* man." He spit out the word as if it were venom and moved his hands to his hips. "You should know me well enough by now to understand I'd never agree to an arrangement like that. *Never.*"

"Okay." Her mind swirled. "Did Felicia *offer* to fly you to the concerts?"

The muscles in his jaw flexed. "Yes, but I soundly refused. *Soundly.*"

"I understood it the first time. You don't have to keep repeating the words." If it were possible, she'd be able to see steam coming from the man's ears. Maybe even his nose. She'd gladly give up her money in exchange for taking back the last five minutes.

"I can't believe you thought I've been taking charity to come and see you," he said. "For the record, I've saved a lot of money the past few years. I've bought my own home, paid cash for my truck, socked funds away in a retirement account, even taken a couple of nice vacations. I've paid my own plane flights to come to your concerts. They might not be first class seats, but they're good enough for me. And yes, you've left a ticket for me in each venue. Thank you for that."

He paused to collect his breath. "I bought the best engagement ring I could find within my means, and even then, I stretched it some."

"I love the ring, but I wouldn't have expected you to overextend yourself. I also don't need a rundown of how you spend your money, and it's a joy for me to give you tickets to my concerts."

He stopped pacing. "Here's the thing. I spend my money where my heart is. Where it counts. Where it *means* something. At least that's what I thought I was doing." He reached for his jacket and draped it over his arm.

"Don't storm out of here without at least telling me why you started this discussion in the first place. I can't believe we're having a conversation like this. If you have something else to say"—Anna bit back a small cry and forced herself to continue in spite of the tears threatening to surface—"please just say it."

Weston stared at her for a long moment that seemed like forever. She never wanted the man she loved to believe he wasn't good enough, or didn't make enough money, or wouldn't be able to provide for her.

"Anna, I helped start a ministry that promotes purity. Purity of mind, spirit, and physical purity."

"I know all that."

"I need to reiterate it so that *I* remember it, if you don't mind."

She gestured with one arm. "Go on, please. Don't let me stop you. Whatever you need." She swallowed the irrational urge to laugh.

He advanced one step toward her and stopped, maintaining a respectable distance between them. "I'm finding a conflict of interest when I'm around you. Frankly, I'm having trouble being with you without wanting more. I've confessed my impure thoughts to the Lord, but it doesn't seem to lessen the desire I feel for you. Part of loving you is wanting you. In every sense of the word."

"You *want* me? That's what this is all about?" She bit her lower lip. Call her sinful, or a heathen, but that sentiment was precious. Not so much for its literal translation as what it meant for her heart. Other men had wanted her, but only for what she could offer physically, not for her mind and her spirit. Certainly not for her faith in Jesus Christ. Didn't make it any easier for Weston, but they'd figure it out together if he wasn't so mad that he actually *did* break up with her.

The Lord knew she didn't want that to happen. Not now. Not ever.

Lord, help Weston keep his focus on you. Help me focus on your plan for us.

"Well, yes. That's a natural progression in a relationship, but I can't be alone with you in your suite like this anymore, Anna. It's not working. My thoughts are going to places they shouldn't. Especially since you're wearing my ring on your finger—that is, when you're not performing—and I know that eventually I'll be able to make you completely mine, I'm kind of having a hard time keeping my thought life straight."

"So, like I said about me being...well, me"—Anna resisted the urge to roll her eyes—"I'm still the same no matter where I am in the world. What's that famous line from a movie? 'It's just geography.'"

"I thought you didn't see movies."

"I don't see *many* movies, you exasperating man! And I prefer the classics." She shook her head and blew out a sigh. "In essence, what you're saying is that you can't be alone with me anywhere. Because you can't. . .control yourself?"

He made a sound she couldn't define. A snort? A sigh? The man was confounded, that much was clear. That made two of them.

"Give me some credit. I can be alone with you, but not in a hotel suite on a sofa—holding you, kissing you. You smell great, you look beautiful, and you're way too tempting. Like I told you that night in Darling, if I didn't have Christ in my life, I'd probably act the same as the rest of the world. But I hope you can see it's a problem when I work with a ministry that promotes purity, and all I want to do is carry you off somewhere and . . .love you."

His eyes met hers. "I'm sure you can fill in the rest. Not that I'm encouraging you to."

"Should I be offended or apologize? Because I refuse to be offended. It's a wonderful thing for a girl to know she's desired, Christian or not. And I'm human, so I'm not about to apologize."

He shook his head. "I don't expect an apology, but I know you appreciate the truth."

"I do," she said. "I guess the only safe place for us is a porch swing."

The tiniest hint of a smile twitched the corners of Weston's mouth but he said nothing. Then he ran his fingers over his beard. She'd miss that familiar action if she didn't have him in her life.

No! She needed to stop these thoughts *now.* This *second.* This was their first big fight—if it could even be called that—and only a momentary bump in the road. It had to be. That's all it *could* be. Anna couldn't fathom anything else. Neither could she panic. Love didn't work that way.

Anna rose from the sofa and crossed the suite to the black grand piano positioned near the floor-to-ceiling windows. She ran her hand over the smooth, shiny surface of the closed lid. "Weston, did you know that when the grand piano isn't being played, the pianist generally keeps the lid down?"

Turning, she locked gazes with him. "They do that to prevent the dust from collecting and clogging the interior of the instrument."

"I'm sure you're trying to tell me something important here, but I'm not always good at reading between the lines," he said. "I do see you have Jesse perched on the piano." He angled his head to the carved eagle.

"Jesse travels with me wherever I go."

Leaving the piano, Anna moved across the carpet in her bare feet, her high heels forgotten on the floor beside the sofa. She stopped inches away from Weston, aching for his smile to reassure her, his arms to protect her, his soothing words to tell her that everything was fine. She wanted him to pull her close and whisper to her heart.

Tell her he'd see her in a few weeks.

Tell her nothing had changed.

But it had.

"When the piano lid is *open*, the one playing it can bring about a sound that is beautiful and melodious," she told him.

"Provided it's well-tuned."

She managed a small smile. "Yes, that's true. As long as our hearts are willing to seek God's will, then our lives will remain open to those whispers in our heart, as we've said before. But, don't you see? If we shut down and give into our doubts, insecurities, and human frailties, then the dust will collect in our *hearts*. And that would be a tragedy for with it comes the potential to destroy all the beauty He's created in *us*. In our relationship and in the love we share."

"That's a wonderful analogy, but I need to go now so I don't miss my flight. I need time to wrestle through some things in my mind, that's all."

"Weston, know *this*. You are the most wonderful man I've ever met. You're unselfish, a man of strong faith, and you see through a person's exterior straight to the heart. That's rare, valuable, and *precious*. I don't ever want to lose you in my life."

Tossing his jacket on the sofa, Weston gathered her close, holding her tight. "I don't want to lose you, either, Anna. I'll do everything in my power to keep that from happening. Know *that*."

The top of her head felt damp. She pulled back. Weston's beautiful eyes blinked at her, damp with moisture. "Are you *crying*?"

"No." He sniffled. "I don't cry." Emotion clogged his voice.

"Weston, you're crying. Even Jesus wept. You're in the very *best* company." Using her thumb, she lightly brushed it over the top of his cheek. "Oh, you precious, precious man."

She moved her gaze across his handsome face—the intense blue of his eyes, the planes of his face, the beard that hid those charming dimples until his laughter revealed them, his lips that kissed her with such heated passion and the perfect match for hers. . .

When he offered his hand, she walked quietly beside him to the door. He rested his hand on the side of her face. She leaned into it, closing her eyes, savoring the moment.

"This isn't good-bye," he said quietly. "Never think that, but I might not see you for a few weeks."

She opened her eyes and swallowed her misgivings. "Why do I feel this is the *it's not you, it's me* speech?"

"Like I said, I need to figure out some things. That's all. It'll be okay." He pressed his lips to her forehead.

"That doesn't help." Was he trying to convince himself or her? Anna chewed on her lower lip but then forced herself to stop. "You told me once you like to solve puzzles. I wish you well in whatever you need to figure out."

Weston moved his arms around her and brought her tight against him. "Trust in *us*, Anna. But more than ever, trust in *His* love. I love you more because *He* first loved you. With His help, we'll figure this out."

With a final kiss, he grabbed his jacket, opened the door and was gone.

Chapter 34

The Following Sunday

"Scoot over, Galloway."

Weston grinned at the familiar joke as Jesse parked his wheelchair in the middle aisle next to Weston's pew in Darling Community Church.

"Hey, Jesse. How are you?"

"Better than you judgin' by that scowl on your face. Didn't you know scowlin's not permitted in the house of the Lord?"

That made him laugh. "No, I hadn't heard that one. I thought the Almighty accepted us as we are."

"He does. I'm just teasin' you. I didn't know you were back in town. How long you stayin' this time?"

"Two or three days. The boss sent us back to finish up a few last details. Neil's here, too, and we're stayin' with Lois and Ray."

"That's good. The bank looks real good. Your crew did a bang-up job. Connor can't stop talkin' about it."

Weston smiled. "Thanks. I appreciate that."

"Some of the guys in town are mighty grateful to you. The diner's softball team won their division this year. First time in ten years. You're a regular hero. Don't let it swell your head."

"That's great, but I'm no hero. I wasn't even here."

"No, but you started 'em on the road to victory, and that means a lot in this town." Jesse fixed him with a probing glance. "The service is about to start. Why don't you share your burden so I can pray for you? The Kleinerts are singin' this mornin', and the good Lord knows I'm gonna need somethin' else to distract me."

Weston laughed but then piped down when the same older lady who'd frowned at Peyton's outburst shushed him then stared him down. He'd never seen a person with such perpetually puckered lips. He'd need to pray for her. What was wrong with people? Life was a lot harder without humor to lighten up the everyday irritations.

Maybe it's you, Grouch. He needed to get a serious grip on his crazy emotions.

"I saw Anna this week in Chicago," he told Jesse, lowering his voice. "For one thing, she mistakenly assumed her manager's flown me to her concerts."

"You're a man, and your pride's hurt. Let it go, man. That's ego."

"I can admit that's true," Weston said. "I've flown coast-to-coast, and it hasn't been cheap, especially for a few days at a time. Basically we steal time together between Anna's rehearsals and concerts. I've seen how hard she works, but she feels guilty because she can't spend much time with me."

"Is it worth it? That's a big investment of time and money for a few hours of her company."

That question disgruntled him. "Of course, it is. A minute with Anna is worth more than a thousand hours spent with any other woman."

"Don't growl at me, man. Just checkin'. You passed the test. I'm sure you set her straight. What else is botherin' you?"

"To be honest, I'm having trouble being with Anna and keeping my thoughts straight, especially when we're alone in her hotel suites. Maybe it's better for now that we're *not* in the same town. Jesse, you remember that evening we all went out to the lake for a swim—your family, me, and Anna? I had a hard time keeping my eyes off her."

Jesse nodded. "I remember. I've been there, buddy. Anticipation can be a good thing. As long as you keep your hands to yourself and confess those thoughts, you'll be okay."

"Not helping, man. I know that, but without a wedding date, I'm frustrated in more ways than one. I don't want to do anything to compromise her faith *or* mine. I can't believe I'm talking about this in church."

Weston lowered his head to his hands with a low groan. "I'm weak, Jesse. So very weak."

The other man's hand landed on his back. "So, you're human, too. Hate to break it to you, Wes, but we're all weak. Not one of us is immune to temptation and an impure thought every now and then. She's a pretty lady, and you're wantin' to be married. Nothin' wrong with that. I'd say you'd be more suspect if you *didn't* have those feelin's. And, if you ask me, the church is the best place to be makin' your confession."

"I know." Weston lifted his head. "You sound like your wife. So, *Candee*, tell me why I'm so miserable."

"Candee's got a lot of wisdom, so I won't take offense." Jesse laughed under his breath. "I can see why those things might pose a temporary problem, but they're not insurmountable. Not by a long shot."

Frowning, Weston sat back on the pew and crossed his arms. "What do you mean? I'm pouring my heart out here. Where's the sympathy?"

"Think about it. You love this girl, and she loves you. The solution as I see it is to figure out a way to marry her. What's stopping you from that?"

"For the moment, careers and distance."

"Either one of those things insurmountable?"

"No, but—"

"I said, are either of those insurmountable?" Jesse's dark eyes pierced through him.

Weston stared at the other man. "You're kinda partial to the word *insurmountable* this morning, aren't you?"

"Sometimes you've gotta say somethin' a few times before it finally seeps into someone's thick as molasses *brain*." Using his fist, Jesse lightly tapped Weston's head.

Chuckling, Weston ducked and shrugged him off.

"Candee told me you asked a while back about a prosthesis for my missing leg."

"I hope that doesn't offend you, man."

"I'm not offended. It's not like I haven't been asked before by my own family members. Think about it, Wes. I spend most of my time carvin' my birds. Don't need to stand up to do that. I want my kids to know that a man's leg—or any other part of him—isn't more important than his soul. The part of me that's missin' isn't who I am inside. It doesn't define me, doesn't make me a better man."

"Of course not, but you could take walks with your kids."

Jesse blew out a sigh and fingered his dark beard. "I do that now. I'm just sittin' down to do it."

"I admire you, Jesse. You're a good man."

"The one thing that might change my mind is wantin' to walk one of my daughters down the aisle one day to meet her groom. So I can look that boy in the eye instead of from the chair. Tell him to take care of my baby girl and make her happy or he'll be answerin' to me."

Weston's eyes misted. "Yeah," he rasped. "Although I'd suggest having that chat *before* a guy's standing at the altar."

Jesse chuckled. "I reckon you're right. I'm sure Candee will make sure of that."

"No doubt." Weston looked up at the wooden cross mounted on the wall behind the podium. The old rugged cross. "It was for freedom that Christ set us free," he quoted, "therefore keep standing firm and do not be subject again to a yoke of slavery."

"Walk by the Spirit," Jesse said, his voice equally reverent. "Don't be subject to the doubts of man. Be set free from the chains of worry and stand strong, believin' He will take care of things in *His* way and *His* time, not yours."

Weston glanced at Jesse. "Is that a verse of Scripture? I don't recognize it."

"Nope. That one's all me. Just seemed to apply to the situation."

"It's great advice, Jesse. Thanks for the reminder."

"Anytime. One of the verses I claim is First John 5:14, 'This is the confidence which we have before Him, that, if we ask anything according to His will, He hears us.'" Jesse moved his large hand to Weston's shoulder, squeezed, and left it there. "Let's pray."

Weston bowed his head, thankful for the other man's friendship and wise counsel.

"Father, I pray for my friend, Weston, today. Help him to know you're always in control. Help him to let go of the worry, and give him peace to know you always have his best interests in mind. Be with Anna as she continues her tour, keep her safe, and help her to seek your will and direction for her career. I pray these two of your children might be able to see one another again soon so they can talk through these things and seek your will for their future together. All these things I ask in the name of your Son, Jesus. Amen."

"Amen," Weston echoed, grabbing hold of Jesse's hand. "Thank you, brother."

"Always. I'd better get back over to the kids and make sure they don't blurt out somethin' they heard at the house lately. You never know with our crew."

"Where's Candee? I haven't seen her this morning." Weston waved to Peyton across the aisle.

"She's home with Taylor. Poor kid was up half the night. I'll spare you the details."

"I'm sorry to hear that. Give her my best, and I hope Taylor gets better quick. Send Connor over to sit with me if he wants. I could use the company."

"Will do," Jesse said. "I hope you know my prayers don't stop at the church doors. I'm sure it'll all work out with you and Anna. The Lord's got this. Remember that."

"Appreciate it, Jesse. You're a good friend."

Weston watched as Roz and Jerry took seats in another pew across the aisle. He nodded when they both waved, and the organist began the morning prelude. First time he'd seen either one of them in church. Anna would be glad to hear this news. Had they come together?

"Hi, Mr. Weston."

He moved down the pew and smiled. "Hey, Connor."

"You back in town to stay?"

"For a couple of days. We have a few more things to finish up on the bank, and then I'm headed back home again."

"What about Miss Anna?"

Weston focused on the cross again. "What about her?"

"You love her, right? I mean, she's gonna be your wife?"

"I sure hope so, Connor."

"That's cool. Hey, is it okay if I come see you tomorrow at the site? Can you show me around like you said before?"

"Sure. Come by around noon, and then I'll take you to lunch at the diner. Wait a second. Aren't you in school now?"

"I'm homeschooled this year by a lady here in the church. She'll let me come. It'll be like a field trip or somethin'. A real learnin' experience and all that good stuff."

That brought a smile to Weston's face. "Okay, but be sure and ask your Mama and Daddy for their permission first. And make sure your mom knows we'll be coming to the diner for lunch, okay?"

Connor grinned. "Sure thing."

As the service began, Weston recalled Jesse's words.

Be set free from the chains of worry and stand strong, believing He will take care of things in His way and in His time, not ours.

"Amen," he murmured. Connor had the hymnal opened and offered it to him. Taking it, Weston joined in singing the first hymn, "How Great Thou Art."

Chapter 35

Weston stood beside Neil at the site late morning on Monday. "Thanks for coming back to help with these last details, Neil. You do good work."

Neil nodded. "I appreciate the vote of confidence. It means a lot coming from you. I know I didn't make it easy for you while we were here in town."

"Things going okay for you now?" Neil had kept a much lower profile and seemed quieter after the talk at the apartment on that Friday night. To Weston's knowledge, from that point on, no female guests had spent the night, and Neil had returned to the apartment early most evenings. But that was the extent of their talks. Weston had hoped the other man might have come to him with more questions.

Patience, Galloway. He needed to give the Lord time to work in Neil's heart.

"Things are getting better, I guess." Neil started to pack up his tools. "I've been thinking about those things you said."

"Did you come to any decisions?"

"Maybe. I don't know. Things going okay with you and Anna?" He scratched his head. "That one blows my mind, man. That she's famous."

Weston nodded. "I know. Sometimes I can't wrap *my* head around it, either. The long distance thing is challenging, but we're making it work." No matter that the last conversation he'd shared with Anna in her Chicago hotel suite hadn't exactly gone well. Since then, other than a few texts, their cell phones had communicated more than they had.

He'd need to call Anna later. He missed her voice. Missed *her*. So much for old-fashioned courting. If he were like his grandfather, he'd travel to wherever in the world his woman was and haul her off to the preacher. No, if he were truly like his grandfather, he'd throw Anna over his shoulder first and *then* plant her in front of the preacher. Modern women didn't appreciate everything about old time tradition. He'd settle for the Stetson every now and then and calling her darlin' since it brought that pretty sparkle to Anna's eyes.

"Congratulations, man. I'm real happy for you," Neil said, breaking into Weston's thoughts. "You deserve the best, and Anna's a fine woman. I mean that in the most proper sense of the word."

"I know." Weston offered his hand, and Neil shook it.

The other man narrowed his gaze. "Wes, you know that girl you used to date?"

Weston twisted his lips. "Can you be more specific? We've worked a few projects together the past few years." A few girls he hadn't actually dated from his singles class had stopped by the construction sites on occasion to bring him lunch or to visit.

"The gorgeous blonde. Big blue eyes. You were seeing her sometime in the last year."

Understanding dawned. "That would be Madison Adams." He'd forgotten Madison had stopped by a few times when he was at work. So, she'd caught Neil's attention.

What he *hadn't* forgotten was that Madison had expressed interest in Neil.

"School teacher, right?"

Weston nodded. "That's her."

"Do you think she might take a chance on a guy like me? Would that be weird for you? You still talk to her?"

"She's in my class at church, so I see her."

"Do you think you could put in a good word for me sometime?"

"Neil, I don't know." Weston rubbed his hand over his forehead, not sure how to respond. The guy was trying, but he didn't know the Lord. He made a split-second decision he hoped he wouldn't live to regret. "You know what, I will. I can tell you're trying. But you need to know she's a Christian."

"I got it, man. I'm not good enough for her."

"No, that's not it, Neil. It's just—"

They both turned after they heard a noise downstairs.

"Mr. Weston? You here?"

Connor. He'd all but forgotten. His mind was too distracted lately, not a good thing. "Yeah, kiddo. We're up here. Hang on a second, and I'll be right down."

Twenty minutes later, Weston walked outside with Connor beside him. Neil had stayed behind with them and helped answer some of the boy's questions that he couldn't. That'd been gratifying.

Connor spied one of the heavy pieces of equipment still parked to the side of the bank. It should be moved soon since the bank was scheduled to open in a few weeks.

"Can I go climb on that?"

"No. Sorry, bud," Weston said. There were safety regulations and company liabilities to consider. He didn't want to put either Connor or his employer at risk. "My stomach is rumbling. How about that lunch I promised you at the diner?"

"Sure." That seemed to brighten Connor a bit.

Weston turned to Neil. "How about it? Can you join us at the diner for some food?"

He shrugged. "Sure."

Neil fell into step beside Weston as they followed behind Connor. A flash of lightning sparked across the sky.

Hearing the rumble of rolling thunder seconds later, Neil glanced up at the darkening afternoon sky. "Better hurry. Looks like it's brewing up a doozy of a storm any minute now."

Weston hastened his steps, a few paces behind Connor. He heard a burst from the sky followed by a cracking sound. "Tree's been hit!" His eyes widened and he cried out. "Connor! Get out of the way!"

The boy seemed oblivious and had stopped and turned back toward them on the sidewalk. Putting his hands on either side of his mouth, Connor hollered something, the sound lost in the sickening, splintering sound of that massive falling tree.

Weston and Neil both dashed to Connor. His pulse pounding, Weston managed to shove the kid out of the way just as the tree fell across the sidewalk. They hit the pavement at the same time, all three of them sprawled less than an inch from where the tree landed.

Panting, Weston sat up. He rested his hands on his propped knees to catch his breath. Neil had already moved over to Connor. "Kid, are you all right?"

"Connor." Scrambling to his feet, Weston made his way back to the boy and stooped beside him. He wasn't moving. "Connor, speak to me."

With a groan, Connor put one hand on his forehead and stared up at him. "I'm okay. Just got the wind knocked out of me. What happened?"

"Careful now," Weston said while Neil watched. "Don't make any sudden moves. Did you hit your head?"

"Nah. My arm was beneath my head."

Weston glanced up at the sky. "We need to get out of here. We might get another lightning strike."

Neil scoffed. "I thought lightning never struck the same place twice."

"It can, and it does," Weston said. "That's a myth."

Connor propped himself up and leaned back on his hands. He appeared to be trying to regain his bearings. He eyed the fallen tree, then looked from Neil to Weston and back again. "You pushed me out of the way so I wouldn't get hurt?"

"Yeah, kid." Neil avoided Weston's probing gaze. "I did what I could. Glad you're okay."

By this time, a few passersby had gathered around them. Weston sat back on his haunches, trying to absorb what just happened. They'd both been there. He'd been the one to push Connor out of the way, but he'd only been seconds before Neil. To his credit, Neil had been equally intent on helping Connor reach safety.

Shaking his head, Weston slowly rose to his feet. Connor was okay. That's all that mattered.

Connor appeared a bit stunned, but he rose to his feet. Weston watched as Neil moved his arm around the boy and answered questions from some of the townspeople as they headed for the diner.

Images of his friend David in that burning house on that awful night scorched Weston's brain. He stumbled on the sidewalk, dizzy and unsteady. Anyone seeing him now might suspect he was drunk. He *felt* like he was drunk. Weston stopped and leaned over at the waist, moving one hand over his stomach, trying to will the world to stop spinning. He prayed he wouldn't be sick.

Make it stop, Lord! Make the spinning stop!

No one else was around. They'd all walked with Connor and Neil or else scurried out of the storm. Once the rain passed through Darling, then they'd chop up that fallen tree and move it off the street and sidewalk.

The rain began, but Weston was helpless to move. Rain pelted him, beating down hard on him. Still, he waited. Gasping, he couldn't seem to catch his breath. He deep breathed in and out. What was happening? Then fell to his knees on the pavement, splaying his hands on the wet sidewalk.

"David, I'm sorry. I'm so sorry!" he wailed. Words lost to the wind and the rain. No one there to hear him but God. "God knows I tried to save you. You were my friend, and I loved you, buddy. If I could have died in your place, I would have. Sometimes I wish I had."

The driving rain pounded his jeans, his T-shirt, soaking him through clean to his skin in no time flat. Another flash of lightning streaked across the sky followed by the roar of deep thunder, giving sound to his angst and pain.

"God forgive me. I couldn't save him." Weston's tears mingled with the rain, streaming down his cheeks. He was as broken as he'd ever been, prostrate before the Father.

He'd told Neil to forgive his mother, but he'd never forgiven himself for David's death. Like he'd told Anna, he thought he'd resolved the pain, but he hadn't. Not completely. After several years, he still blamed himself.

You are forgiven. You are loved. You are a child of the living God. Rise and walk in peace.

He heard the words in his heart, felt them in his soul.

David died because of the foolish actions of another. Weston hadn't caused the fire that killed his friend. And David had done what Weston and every other firefighter had done. Their job. What they were trained to do. They'd rushed in that home one after the other. Weston got to the old man first and pulled him out. Then started back in that house when it collapsed with David and the man's wife still inside. A terrible tragedy.

But it wasn't your fault.

More tears fell on Weston's cheeks. "I miss you, friend. But I know you're in a better place, and for that, I thank the Lord. In some ways, in death, you were spared. You never knew what happened in that burst of flame."

Rolling over, flat on his back, he stared as more lightning raced through the dark sky. It was a miracle no townspeople stood above him, poking him, asking him questions. That made him chuckle. A chuckle! Yeah, he wasn't crazy. He wasn't out-of-his-mind nuts. Well, maybe a little.

You are redeemed. You are my child. Rise up, go and make disciples of men.

With a groan, Weston hauled himself to his feet.

Then he took off for the diner.

Feeling freer than he had in a very long time.

Chapter 36

Weston dashed inside the diner. Dripping wet, he ran a hand through his hair. He stopped when he saw Connor standing near the register. A very *angry* Connor from the looks of it.

How long had he been out in the rain?

"Why are you lying?" Fists clenched, Connor glared at Neil, who sat at a nearby table. "You're tellin' everybody you're a hero and how you saved me. That's not the truth."

Neil stared at the boy with an impassive expression.

"Connor, back off. That's enough." Jesse wheeled over to his son and put one hand on his shoulder.

Connor shrugged off his father and planted himself in front of Neil. "Admit it! Weston's the one who pushed me out of the way. *He's* the one who saved me. Not you!"

"What do you know, kid? Everything happened fast. We all wear the same work clothes." Neil glanced his way but again wouldn't meet his eyes. "Weston and I look enough alike that we could pass for brothers. You're just confused."

"I am *not* confused!" Connor's hands slid down to his hips. "Dad, I'm telling the truth."

"Son, I wasn't there." Jesse looked at Neil and then moved his gaze to Weston. "My son tells the truth as he knows it. I'm sorry we've made a scene. Whichever one of you pushed my son out of the way to safety, we're thankful for what you did. God bless you both."

Connor crossed his arms and huffed. "Mama will figure it out."

"I'm out of here." Neil abruptly pushed his chair back from the table. Grabbing the check, and a carryout bag, he headed to the register.

"On the house," Roz called out to Neil.

"Thanks." Neil elevated his voice. "Seems there are perks to saving a kid's life in this town." He pushed open the door and exited the diner.

Weston stooped down beside Connor. "Connor, let Neil be your hero. We were both there. We both wanted to save you. That's all that matters."

"But, Mr. Weston—"

"Connor, please look me in the eye."

After shuffling his feet and crossing his arms, Connor returned his gaze to Weston's. "I'm listenin'."

"Let. Neil. Be. Your. Hero." He leaned close and whispered. "God knows. Neil has a good heart and he's never felt like a hero before."

Connor raised a skeptical brow. "He could use an attitude adjustment."

"Yeah, well, sometimes we all need that. Take care, kid." Weston patted the boy's shoulder and rose to his feet, weary to his bones. He hadn't felt *this* tired since his firefighting days, and he'd been bone-tired most days working construction.

Weston lumbered across the diner and slumped into a chair at a back table. A puddle started to form on the floor beneath his chair. He'd been felled by memories of David's death as much as that falling tree.

But he was redeemed and forgiven. The Lord had filled his soul and made him whole again. He just needed the blessing of sleep. Everything would seem clearer after a good night's rest and the sunshine of a new morning. Hopefully.

"Honey, you come with me before you flood the place." Candee stood beside him. "Weston, you all right?" She moved one hand to his face and pressed her hand across his forehead. "You look a bit peaked and like you've seen a ghost or somethin'. Not that either one of us believe in all that hooey. Just a manner of speech."

"Candee, stop. Please." He shooed her hand away. "I'm okay," he mumbled. "I just need. . .to regroup."

"Well, while you're regroupin', you're comin' in the back with me, mister. We're goin' to get you in some clean, dry clothes. Mike keeps extras in his locker. You're about the same size, more or less."

He waved his hand. "I'm fine. Really."

"That might be so, sugar, but you let Candee take care of you. We're goin' to get you clean and dry and then get some solid food in you."

"Is Connor all right? That's all I care about."

"He's a bit shook up, but he'll be fine. Doesn't seem to have a concussion or nothin'. I'm not sure what happened out there, but I'm just thankful to the good Lord above you're all okay. Now, up we go." Candee tugged him by the hand. "Come on. You've gotta give me a little help here, Weston."

He allowed her to pull him up from the chair and then trudged through the diner behind her, leaving a puddle in his wake. His clothing must weigh twenty pounds or so heavier wet than dry. That was nothing. His firefighter gear had weighed a whole lot more.

Another twenty minutes later, Weston sat at a table and pushed his food around on his plate. It'd lost its appeal after a few bites. He noticed that someone had mopped up the wet puddle beneath the other table. Roz kept shooting him concerned glances but she was busy. Since Anna's departure, they were short a waitress.

"Stewin' while you're chewin'?"

Weston gave Candee his best attempt at a grin. "That'd be an apt description."

"May I?" She gestured to the empty chair beside him.

"Of course. As long as you won't get in trouble. I know you're shorthanded these days."

"Roz and I have an understandin'. If I sit down at a table with a customer, she knows I have good reason. Besides that, I'm on my ten-minute break. In case you haven't noticed, the boss has a soft spot for you. Don't you worry about her none. She'll leave me be."

"In that case, can I buy you a cup of coffee?"

Candee smiled and settled in the chair. "I'll grab somethin' in a minute. Look, I know it's none of my beeswax, but I was watchin' that whole scene just now and tryin' to figure out why you're lettin' Neil get away with takin' credit for what you did."

When she seemed to be waiting for a response, Weston grunted. "Because you're sitting here with me, I'm guessing you came up with a reason." Why wouldn't she let it go?

"I did." Leaning close, Candee lowered her voice. "You're tryin' to protect Anna."

He rubbed his chin and pushed his plate away. "Anna's a big girl. She can take care of herself. How do you figure that?" When Candee didn't answer right away, Weston glanced back at her. "What?"

"Okay, then, I think this situation has more to do with you wantin' to help Neil and make him feel like a hero. Pushin' yourself aside for the good of that man."

She laid a gentle hand on his shoulder and gave him a quick squeeze. "Humility is an admirable thing, but I want you to think about somethin' else."

"What's that?"

She touched a hand to his cheek. "You seem a little out of it. Are you listenin'?"

"Oh, believe me, I'm listening," Weston said. "I'm soaking it all in."

Candee laughed. "You're okay if you can make your jokes. I want you to think about what kind of lesson that shows Connor when his hero lets someone else take the credit. My boy respected you from the moment you helped him after that tumble off his bike."

"I don't know, Candee." Weston rested both elbows on the table and rubbed his fingers over his eyes. "Seriously, it's not a big deal. I don't want anyone to *make* a big deal out of it, either. Let Neil have his time to shine. That way everybody's happy."

"I guess there's two ways of lookin' at it. You ask me, that's the easy way out. It's coverin' up the truth, and that's a form of lyin'." Candee's forehead creased. "I never would have expected you to be the type to lie."

"I'm not. Look, Candee, there's part of me that hopes Neil will wise up, man up, and admit it wasn't him. But sometimes people need to figure things out for themselves in order to learn the lesson." Weston slumped back in the chair.

Candee held up one finger after Roz called to her. "One more minute, boss." Then she turned back to him. "You know why Connor was at the worksite in the first place, don't you?"

"I told him to ask your permission," Weston said. "You knew he was going to be there, didn't you?"

"Yes, I was aware. That's not what I'm talkin' about. Connor is in awe of what you do," Candee said. "He thinks workin' on a buildin' is the greatest thing ever. I have a Bible verse framed and it's hangin' on our kitchen wall. It's from First Samuel 16:7. I put it up for Jesse's sake, but I think it applies to your situation too. It's where the Lord says to Samuel, 'Do not look at his appearance or at the height of his stature, because I have rejected him; for God sees not as man sees, for man looks at the outward appearance, but the Lord looks at the heart.'"

Candee gave his shoulder another quick squeeze. "I'd say your heart is mighty healthy, my friend. Promise to think about it, okay?"

Weston reached for her hand. "Thank you. The Lord knows I'm trying my best."

"That's all any of us can do. Keep on. You'll be just fine. I also think you're missin' Anna so bad you're in what my mama called a blue funk."

"I take it Jesse told you about our conversation in church yesterday?"

Candee lowered her gaze and shifted in the chair.

"It's okay. You're a good friend. The more people praying for us the better."

"You know you've got my prayers. I best scoot on back to work now." She rose to her feet and pushed in the chair. "The Lord always has a way of workin' these things out, Weston. You know that as well as I do. You and Anna are meant to be together, no question in my mind."

"I sure hope you're right."

She patted his shoulder and winked. "I usually am, sugar."

Weston sat in the swing at Anna's house, a lightweight blanket covering him. The rain had long stopped, and he was enjoying the quiet of the late evening. As tired as he was, he hadn't been able to sleep. He'd quietly left Ray and Lois's house and come next door.

Some of his favorite memories in Darling were all about this swing, mostly memories of Anna. He pushed off the porch floor. A faint creak alerted him that he'd need to oil the chain.

"Why'd you do it?"

His thoughts interrupted, Weston glanced up. Neil stood on the top step of the porch in his sleep pants and a T-shirt, a mirror reflection of his own current attire.

"I couldn't sleep," Weston said.

Neil ran a hand through his messy hair. "Me neither, but that's not what I meant."

"I know what you meant, man. Just stating a fact."

Neil leaned against the front post and hugged his arms over his torso. "Night's are getting a little chilly now."

"Yeah." He could probably stand to be a little more sociable, but he wasn't in the mood.

"Look, Wes. I went over to Candee and Jesse's house and talked to Connor."

Weston nodded slowly. "I can't lie, Neil. I'm surprised."

"Scoot over." Weston did, and Neil dropped down beside him. "Don't get any ideas or anything."

That made Weston laugh. The release felt good. "I'll share my blanket if you don't think it's too weird."

Taking it, Neil pulled a section over him. "That kid's okay. I told him *you* were the one who pushed him out of the way. I don't even know why I said what I did. I'm just glad Connor's okay. I'm sorry, man."

"Don't worry about it," Weston said. "You're forgiven. I'm proud of you. You did the right thing."

"Connor's smart, too. He told me how God sees what we do, the good and the bad. He told me Jesus was proud of me. I told him I didn't know Jesus. And you know what that kid said to me?" Neil hesitated, and Weston heard the catch in his throat. "He said, 'But Jesus knows *you*, and He loves you. He's waitin' on you.'"

"Sometimes I think kids understand God and faith more than adults do," Weston said. "We tend to complicate things, but they keep it on a more simple, straightforward level."

"I also went to see my mom a couple of weeks ago."

"Oh? How'd that go?" This was quite a night of revelations.

"It was kinda weird, but good in the end. We talked through some things. She apologized for stuff and said she wished she could go back in time and redo her life. That was sad to hear from my own mom. She told me my dad took off all those years ago because he had cancer and didn't want us to see him die. He's been dead a long time and buried in a cemetery in Atlanta."

"Wow. I'm sorry, Neil."

"Me, too. Would have been nice to know so I didn't have to wonder all these years. I got one of those arrangements of fake flowers, and we took it out to his grave. At least I know where to find him now. Not that he's really there."

"I hope that gives you some closure. Might not make it any easier, but now you know." Weston said.

Neil nodded and leaned his head back on the swing. "Yeah, it does. I'm tired, man. I'm twenty-five and feel like I'm twice that sometimes. I don't like the man I see in the mirror."

"I'm sure I look pretty ragged myself right now."

"I'm not necessarily talking about what I see on the outside." Neil cleared his throat. "My mom's a Christian now."

That caught his attention. Weston pushed himself up straighter on the swing. "That's great, Neil. Praise God! I'm glad to hear it."

"She found a little church, and she's been going there regular. She shared her testimony or whatever it's called and told me she'd been praying for me. I don't think I'd have believed her if you hadn't told me all those things before. I told her what you said about the dragon, and she agreed. I've been going over all that stuff in my head. I see the change in my mom. It's like you said. She's a different person now." Neil looked over at him. "Changed from the inside out."

"That's the power of Christ. Once you claim His free gift, He goes to work inside you."

Neil nodded. "You think you could pray with me, Wes? Now? I'm ready."

Weston swallowed hard. "Of course." His voice came out raspy, but inside, he rejoiced. "Unless you'd rather your mom pray with you."

"You've laid the foundation, and I wasn't ready until now. It's like you said about how Jesus could come back at any time. Mom said the same thing. If He happens to come tonight, I don't want to be left out in the. . .chilly air."

Weston broke into a smile at Neil's words.

Lord, I do love how you work.

And so, another miracle took place while Weston sat beside Neil on the swing. Neil Carter confessed he was a sinner and asked Jesus into his heart. His soul was cleansed, the holes in his heart were filled. He became a changed man from the inside out. A man redeemed.

After Neil said good night and headed back across the yard a short time later, Weston closed his eyes and curled up beneath the blanket. For whatever reason, he wanted to stay on the swing a few more minutes.

Closing his eyes, he prayed for Neil, his family, friends, and then. . .Anna.

"I love you, sweet Anna," he whispered. He was sleepy. So very sleepy.

Chapter 37

"What?" Weston started and flailed his arms. Where was he? He opened his eyes, blinked hard a few times, and tried to focus. He was still sitting on the swing on Anna's porch. Movement by the front steps caught his eye.

"Anna?" He stared at her as though she were a mirage, a figment of his overactive imagination. But, no, it *was* her. She stood in front of him. Beautiful as ever in jeans and a lightweight jacket. Looking at him as though he'd lost his ever-lovin' mind. Maybe he had. Was he dreaming?

"What are you doing here?" he sputtered.

"I'm sorry, Weston. I tried not to scare you."

"You didn't scare me," he muttered. "I must have fallen asleep on your swing. Don't sue me for trespassing, please."

"I wouldn't think of it. I heard there was a bit of an incident earlier today."

He frowned. "It really wasn't much."

"That's not what I heard." She gestured to the swing. "May I?"

"Of course. You own it. Just keeping it warm." He lifted the blanket.

Anna sat down beside him and watched as he settled the blanket around her. Taking his hand in hers, she brought it to her lips. Then she waited until his eyes met hers.

"I own nothing, Weston. That's why I'm here. Without God, I am nothing. With *you*, I'm everything He wants me to be. I want to walk into the future with you. As soon as possible."

He stared at her for a long moment. "Sorry, it's been quite a night." With two fingers, he lightly pinched his arm. "I guess this is real."

She smiled. "Do you want me to repeat what I just said? It's kind of important."

"No, I heard you. I feel the same way. Give me a minute to catch up. That's all."

"I was miserable when you left my hotel suite last week," she said. "I don't want to be miserable. Judging by your behavior tonight, you've been a little cranky, too."

He chuckled. "Candee told you, didn't she?"

"Yes," she said. "When she told me about—"

"The incident."

Anna laughed softly. "You see, in order to get over my misery, I needed to come back to the place where I fell in love and found my future. Here in Darling. I needed to be with the man who'll be my husband, if he'll still have me. We'll figure out the rest later. Together."

"I'll always want you." Reaching for her, Weston pulled Anna into his arms. "Welcome home."

"I'm glad to hear you say that," she said after giving him a very memorable kiss. And one more for good measure. "I've taken the liberty of handling the details."

"Explain." His mind was spinning in the best of all possible ways.

"I have a dress. I've reserved Darling Community Church tomorrow at sunset. Charley and Nick are here. Even my dad."

"Your father's here?"

Anna nodded. "Dad told me you'd called him on my birthday to ask his permission to marry me." She rested one hand along the side of his face. "I'm glad you called him. We had a long talk the other night, and he can't wait to meet you. He's very impressed by my southern gentleman."

Weston put one hand on his head. "Seriously? Am I dreaming? Is this for real?"

She giggled. "It's for real. You don't mind that I made plans for us, do you?"

"Anna, I'm ecstatic. I think I'm still half asleep. Neil was here earlier tonight and accepted the Lord." He thumped his fist on the arm of the swing. "Right here on this swing."

"Oh, Weston, that's awesome! You'll have to fill me in on the details."

"Later," he said, unable to stifle his yawn. "I think I'm going to call this the miracle swing from now on. If your family's here, where are they now?"

"They're staying at a hotel a few miles up the road. All we need is our marriage license," she said. Leaning close, she whispered in his ear. "There's no waiting period. And I don't have another concert for a week."

Weston's eyes lit with understanding. "I'll need my birth certificate and a tux," he murmured, kissing her again. "And I'd better call Brad. You didn't call *my* boss, did you?"

"No, but I hope he'll be understanding."

"I'll use my powers of persuasion. If not, there are other jobs." When she gave him a look, he smiled. "It'll be fine. Promise."

"My European tour starts in November. If you can get a week off, how do you feel about extending our honeymoon to the beautiful Amalfi Coast?"

"I'm fine with it as long as I can look up where that is."

"The coast of Italy. We could sun ourselves on the Island of Capri, ride a Vespa through the streets of the charming towns, buy fruit at an open air market, laze about and feed one another strawberries…"

"I get the idea," he murmured, kissing her again. "You've sold me. Rings! What about rings? I already have the matching band for your engagement ring. I bought them at the same time, but it's back at the house in Atlanta."

"Your mother knows, and she's bringing it. And I have a wedding band for you. Your mother knows your size and said you'd like platinum. I had it engraved with Psalm 51:10. I hope that's okay. If not, we'll get another one."

"I'm sure it's perfect. You amaze me, Anna. You're even more resourceful than I thought. You told me once that you couldn't multitask before you came to Darling. I'm not sure I believe that. You seem to be doing it quite well right now."

"I have great motivation," she said, smiling. "Your parents are meeting us at the courthouse in the morning at ten. They're bringing your gorgeous, new, tan-colored suit. The one you wore in Chicago. Your mom thought you should have a traditional black tuxedo, but I told her it doesn't matter. My dress and veil are very simple. *Elegant* but simple."

"Just like my bride. Wait. I mean—" He moaned. "I'll never learn."

"Weston?"

"Yes," he said.

"Me Anna. You Weston. Basic biology. Just kiss the girl."

"I guess the tradition of not seeing each other on the wedding day doesn't matter to you?"

"No." She shook her head. "Who needs tradition? It's overrated. I say let's get on with it."

"My kind of woman."

Chapter 38

The Wedding
Darling Community Church

Anna walked down the aisle toward Weston on the arm of her father. Outside the church, the sun lowered on the horizon of the beautiful mid-October day. She wished her mother could be with her but liked to believe she knew. Mom would love Weston, and that thought made her smile.

Her groom waited at the front with Pastor Anderson. Never had a man looked more handsome. He wore a gorgeous peach silk tie and matching boutonniere. She smiled at his buttoned-up collar. That collar would be unfastened as soon as the photos were taken. Catching her eye, he winked and gave her a smile she'd always remember. A smile of joy, a smile of hope, a smile of promise.

Standing beside Weston, Nick winked and gave her his goofy smile. How she loved that smile. She'd never seen him in a suit, but he looked handsome as Anna had ever seen him in pale gray with a white rose boutonniere.

On the opposite side, Charley beamed. Her dear sister definitely had the glow of impending motherhood, another reason to rejoice. She'd streaked her hair with peach for the occasion and painted her nails to match. In her hands, she held an arrangement of peach roses, a smaller version of the bouquet Anna carried with the addition of lilies, her mother's favorite flower.

Candles on the end of each pew bathed the church in a soft glow, and arrangements of white and peach roses adorned the altar. Another miracle accomplished, courtesy of Candee and the ladies of the church.

As she made her way down the aisle, Anna spied Candee, Jesse and their kids near the front. Lois and Ray, with Neil between them, sat on the pew behind them. Many of the other pews were filled with customers from the diner, including Della as well as Jill and her family. Jerry sat with Roz.

A surprising number of Weston's friends and coworkers had made the drive down from Atlanta on short notice. He was a great guy, a loyal friend, and they'd caravanned to Darling for their wedding.

Anna's steps faltered slightly when she spied Felicia sitting near the front. That was a surprise, but a good one. She'd been such a big part of her life, it was only fitting she was here to share in this moment. Sitting beside Felicia was a pretty, dark-haired teenager, a former child prodigy named Kyndall Symes.

Pastor Anderson greeted them and the service began. As he delivered the opening words, prayed with them, and gave the charge, her groom's eyes never left hers. *You're beautiful*, he mouthed to her. When Weston slipped the wedding ring on her finger, she glimpsed the tears in his eyes, the same as when they said their vows. They matched the tears in *her* eyes. Happy tears which came from the joy in the deepest part of the soul.

Peyton didn't holler out anything in the middle of the ceremony and everyone behaved themselves. Well, until Pastor Anderson told Weston he could kiss his bride. He kept it sweet but lingered a few moments as everyone in the pews erupted in cheers and applause.

"Before I announce this beautiful, godly couple as husband and wife, we have a very special musical presentation," the pastor announced.

Nick handed Weston's guitar to him. Then a couple of the men from the church carried a large chair—decorated with roses and lilies like those in her wedding bouquet—and placed it on the platform.

"Please be seated," Pastor Anderson invited her, gesturing to the chair. "And now, your groom has a song to sing to his bride."

"Anna, you changed my life the moment you dropped those plates in The Darling Diner." Weston paused as those seated in the pews laughed quietly, and a few of the guys whistled.

"I never thought coming to this small town would change my life in such a profound way. Some people we meet are there for a short time. They make an impact, but then they move on. When I walked you home that first night, deep in my heart, I sensed meeting you was one of those moments that would change me forever. I knew somehow that you'd make a difference, that you'd change my life for the better, enrich it, and make it better. Make me a better *man*. Your kindness, your sweetness, your encouragement and love for me, and the purity of your spirit and soul—both inward and outward—shines in everything you do.

"You might have come to Darling to find a *normal* life, but in doing so, you made *my* life extraordinary. Thank you for showing me every day, in countless ways, the true meaning of love. I'll praise the Lord every morning for the blessing of you."

Anna mouthed *I love you* and smiled when Weston began to sing his beautiful song, "Whisper to My Heart."

> *She came to me in a dream*
> *Fine and delicate as gossamer*
> *As sweet as the rose of summer*
> *As precious as the morning rain.*
> *She moves in strength, in light, in love*
> *The beauty of the One within her*
> *Shining bright for all the world to see.*
> *She makes me ponder my heart, my life, my all*
> *Whisper to my heart.*

Anna closed her eyes as she listened, swaying slightly as she sat on the chair, loving the sound of Weston's voice, loving *him*, as he finished the song.

> *For she is my forever love.*
> *My forever love is she*
> *Forever thine, forever mine.*
> *Whisper to my heart.*

Weston handed off the guitar to Nick and pulled Anna from her chair and into his arms. "And now, I'm going to kiss my bride again."

"Go right ahead, son." Pastor Anderson laughed heartily.

And so her groom kissed her as the pastor officially pronounced them husband and wife.

Epilogue

Early Fall, Two Years Later
Darling, Georgia

"Good morning, my love," Anna whispered to her sleeping husband. She kissed Weston's cheek and slipped out of their bed. Wrapping her lightweight robe around her, she made her way down the stairs.

Stepping onto the front porch, she tugged the robe closer about her in the morning chill and loosely tied the belt around her waist.

She walked across the porch to stand at the top of the stairs. Leaning against the post, Anna relished the sounds of the soft, gentle rain. This was the time of day she loved most, the early hours before the rest of the world awakened. The quiet times, the times of reflection. It was when she talked with the Lord and thanked Him for the many blessings He'd bestowed upon them, especially in the past two years.

Delight yourself in the Lord, and He will give you the desires of your heart.

Soon enough, the leaves would begin to turn and they'd enjoy a morning frost and a warm fire in the hearth. The Darling Diner would change its menu from summer fare and begin to serve hot apple cider and pumpkin-themed foods. The annual Fall Festival would draw a small crowd from neighboring towns, and vendors would set up craft and food booths. They'd stroll the streets and greet one another, laugh, talk, and catch up on the latest news in the lives of their friends.

Such a great town for young families. A town to raise children, and a town where people could *love hard and love good*, as Candee said in church that first summer. Her dear friend's words made her smile.

God's blessed us with each other to take care of, and by God's mercy, that's what we're all tryin' our best to do.

"May y'all be so blessed," Anna murmured.

Yes, so *many* blessings.

Hearing the front door close quietly behind her, Anna turned.

Weston walked toward her in his long cotton sleep pants and a T-shirt, even more handsome than the day she'd married him. His hair was disheveled in the way she loved, the curls longer on his neck, the beard trimmed so she could still glimpse the dimples.

In his hand, he held a mug. "I brought you some of the red raspberry leaf tea."

"Thank you. I hadn't made my way into the kitchen yet."

"I'll put it on the table over here by the swing. I think it's still a little too hot." After setting it carefully on the small table, Weston moved behind her and wrapped her in his arms. His hands rested on her belly, and Anna leaned into him.

"How are my little Maura and her beautiful mama this morning?" He nuzzled Anna's cheek and then moved his warm lips to her neck, dropping a light kiss there.

"Wait a few seconds and see. She's been quiet the past half-hour which means she'll probably move around again very soon to greet her daddy."

They were both quiet for a few moments as the steady rain continued to fall. "I was just thinking how these are my favorite moments of the day," she said. "Before the rest of the world awakens, it's so peaceful and calm."

"Were you talking to yourself or God just now?"

"Both, but more to God. I was remembering what Candee said in church that morning she and Jesse sang."

"Which part?" Weston lightly rested his chin on her shoulder.

"About how God's blessed us with each other. She was talking about her family, but I know in the back of her mind, she also meant the wonderful people here in Darling."

He chuckled when Maura moved. "There she is. Good morning, baby. Your mama's taking great care of you, and we can't wait to meet you in a few months."

Anna moved her hand over his and sighed with contentment. "We'll need to make decisions about whether to raise her in New York or here. I want to give Maura the benefit of the best the city has to offer, but there are so many considerations. Darling has things to offer no city can match."

Turning her toward him, Weston kissed her tenderly, the lingering passion from the night before still obviously in his mind. He tugged on her hand and slowly led her to the swing. "Come sit, my love."

Once she'd done as he asked, he handed her the mug of tea. "We have time to make all the decisions. There's also the possibility we could hire a private tutor for her. She could go with you on tour dates, and then you could homeschool or have one of the ladies from the church teach her here in Darling."

Anna sipped her tea. "Hmm. This is so good. And you're right, we have time. But I want Maura to have solid roots in a community. The other part of the equation is. . ."

"Charley and Nick," Weston finished for her. "We're only a plane flight away. We can go there, or they can come here. I'm sure the cousins will see one another more often than not."

After blowing on the steaming tea, Anna smiled. "I still can't believe they named their son Noah Christopher. Who could have guessed? I thought it'd be something either unpronounceable or weird."

Weston chuckled. "Who—other than God, of course—could have known those two would come to church with us last year and *find Jesus*, as Nick puts it?"

"Hallelujah," Anna murmured, taking another sip. "At least he's finally given up the British thing. They don't want to confuse the poor child."

Anna shared a smile with her husband and nestled into the crook of his arm. "Speaking of answered prayer, have I told you lately how thankful I am that Brad Colson decided to open a branch office nearer to Darling so you can work on projects close to home? Not to mention how proud I am of your new title, Boss Galloway."

Weston stroked his fingers through her hair and kissed her forehead. "You've told me a few times. Neil's become an excellent foreman for our crew. Becoming an excellent *man*. Another testament of the power of the Lord working in someone's life. If he'd ever get up the courage to ask Madison out, I understand she's still single. I told him to sign up for a mission trip through the church in Atlanta, and that'd be a good way to get to know her."

"All in God's timing, as we both know." Anna yawned. "I'm so comfortable right now, I never want to leave this swing."

"Then you'd better let me take that mug from you."

She took another drink of her tea and handed it to him. "Thank you. You take such good care of your wife."

"It's my honor."

When Weston wrapped his arms around her, Anna snuggled into him, her favorite place to be. "You've been doing a great job of it ever since you carried me over the threshold after the wedding. That was such a beautiful evening, wasn't it?"

"Hmm," he agreed, continuing to stroke her hair. "The Darling Diner put on quite a spread."

"You know what I loved?"

"What's that?" His voice sounded dreamy, and she knew he was thinking of their first night together as husband and wife.

"How we came back here to the house, but you took the time to sit here on the swing with me. You knew I was nervous, but you took the time to court me, even then. You're a giving man, Mr. Galloway."

"You make it incredibly easy, Mrs. Galloway."

She laced her fingers through his. "Wake me when you need to get up."

"I don't have anywhere else I need to be until later. This is the only place I *want* to be, basking in the blessings God's showering on us."

With her head resting on his chest, Anna smiled. "You're starting to sound a little poetic."

She felt the rumble of his soft laughter. "Are you complaining?"

"Never. I have no complaints. Not a single one."

"Neither have I. Well, maybe one."

"What's that?"

"We need to talk about the dog."

"After Maura comes. Then we'll discuss getting the dog. Promise."

"Okay, but once we have one, you'll wonder how you ever got along without one. He'll be a great companion for Maura and. . .when the other kiddos come along."

"One new addition at a time, please."

Anna's eyes closed as her husband pressed his lips to her hair. In her mind, she could see Weston romping with their daughter across the front lawn and holding her hand as they walked to Darling Community Church together. He was going to be such a great father.

"I love you, Weston."

"Love you always, Anna." Once more, his hand moved to her belly in what was becoming an everyday occurrence, several times over. Family. Faith. Love.

She wanted to grow old in this wonderful place—a town forever imprinted on her heart—with the man she loved beside her.

Nothing could be better this side of heaven.

Sleepy in her contentment and satisfied in her *soul*, Anna smiled as Weston started the swing.

The End
~~♥~~

About the Author
~~♥~~

In addition to **Whisper to My Heart**, JoAnn Durgin is the author of the beloved Lewis Legacy Series as well as **Prelude**, the prequel to the series. Her other works include the Amazon bestselling **Catching Serenity**, **Heart's Design** and its sequel, **Gentle Like the Rain**, The Wondrous Love Series, **Echoes of Edinburgh**, **Perchance to Dream**, and the popular Starlight Christmas Series. A former estate administration paralegal, JoAnn now writes contemporary Christian romance full-time and lives with her family in her native southern Indiana.

JoAnn loves to hear from her readers! Please feel free to contact her:

WEBSITE: www.joanndurgin.com

FACEBOOK: www.facebook.com/authorjoanndurgin

www.ingramcontent.com/pod-product-compliance
Lightning Source LLC
Chambersburg PA
CBHW020232180626
46810CB00006B/2160